Celebrating the American Woman

ANNABELLE

D1023035

Annabelle

MEREDITH BEAN MCMATH

Servant Publications
Ann Arbor, Michigan

© 1995 For Old Times' Sake, Inc., Meredith Bean McMath
All rights reserved.

Vine Books is an imprint of Servant Publications especially designed to serve
evangelical Christians.

Published by Servant Publications
P.O. Box 8617
Ann Arbor, Michigan 48107

Cover illustration: David Hile Illustration & Design
Cover design: Diane Bareis

95 96 97 98 99 10 9 8 7 6 5 4 3 2 1

Printed in the United States of America
ISBN 0-89283-895-7

Library of Congress Cataloging-in-Publication Data

McMath, Meredith Bean
   Annabelle / Meredith Bean McMath.
      p.   cm.   — (Celebrating the American woman : bk 2)
   ISBN 0-89283-895-7
   1. United States—History—Civil War, 1861-1865—Women—
Fiction.   2. Fathers and daughters—United States—Fiction.
3. Physicians—United States—Fiction. I. Title. II. Series.
PS3563.C3863A56 1995
813'.54—dc20   95-14189
                                         CIP

Dedication

In memory of my father, L. Lee Bean, Jr.
a rare storyteller and a rare man.

Acknowledgments

Special thanks to my brother, Lorenzo Lee Bean III, whose love of Civil War history provided inspiration as well as a host of interesting facts, and to Wendy Webb, Wanda Munsey Juraschek, and Joyce Carrier for their excellent advice. To Cathy Deddo, Ginny Rhodes, and Karen Mazza for their well-timed encouragement, and to Ruth Smale and Deborah Starliper for their linguistic expertise. To Mr. William C. Whitmore for permission to use quotations from *The Diary of Miss Mary E. Lack, November 24, 1861 to November 11, 1862,* and to Jane Sullivan of the Thomas Balch Library of Leesburg, Virginia, for her excellent research assistance. To Robert M. Daly, owner of the Powder Horn Gun Shop of Middleburg, Virginia, for taking me seriously when I asked for information on guns of the Napoleonic War. To Steve and Jennifer Heyl for their kind encouragement and permission to use the Payne family letters. To Emily Barbee, the Hillsboro Bicentennial History Committee, and the Hillsboro Community Association whose *Hillsboro: Memories of a Mill Town* provided the heart of my research. To Aunt Elizabeth Savels for her love of books, and Aunt Virginia Hylton for preserving family history, especially the words of my great-grandfather, David Thomas Dortch. To my editors Beth Feia and Gloria Kempton for excellent advice and encouragement. And special thanks to my immediate family, charter members of the *We're Having Way Too Much Fun* Club.

ONE

"It is marked by the most ancient of poets
that in peace children bury their parents;
in war parents bury their children,
nor is the difference small."

David Thomas Dortch, ca. 1885
Confederate Veteran

After a full week of torrential rains the sun finally broke through, and Annabelle MacBain came out of her clapboard house with broom in hand to breathe the air, look around her and enjoy the out-of-doors before sweeping the puddles from the porch. The young woman took pleasure in the warmth of the rays for a moment, and then her eyes swept the main road of Hillsborough, Virginia—west, then east. Fallen branches lay scattered across the muddy road, but the rows of businesses and homes seemed in order, and so she lowered her head and began her sweeping. It was the morning of the eighth of July, 1863, and with the rhythm of Annabelle's sweeping came a childhood memory...

"Father, how'd the houses here come to be so close together?"

"Oh, now that's simple, Annie. You've seen a row of over-ripe peas grow square in the shell, haven't you? Well, just so, the houses were little and round at first, but when they had to grow up—as all things do—they squared off the way you see 'em now."

"Papa, does it hurt very much to grow up?"

His moustache twitched as he replied, "You know, I once put that very question to a pea, and he told me I could keep my Growing Up. That there was nothing so wonderful as staying little, and round and green, and if he never grew a speck larger he'd be ever so happy in this

*life, thank you very much. Says I, 'I can see you're quite content just as
you are, and contentment is a rare and admirable quality.' He
puffed up rather nicely at the compliment, I must say."*

"Then what, Father? Then what?!"

"Well, then I ate him, of course."

She smiled now and shook her head, but her daydream was
interrupted by a woman's voice calling out, "Annie, dear!" from
the porch of the home next door.

She pulled her arm up across her brow to see through the hazy
brightness. "Good morning, Mrs. Casey."

"And good morning to you, dear, but the Widow Brighton has
sent over a young man who knew her good husband and he wishes
to pay respects up at the grave. I told him one of your servants
could show him the way." Otelia Casey's eternally pink cheeks
could easily be seen in the short distance, her frilly lace cap
bunched around her face like tissues around a fresh peach. A spry
woman, she could have run up the hill to the cemetery herself, but
she took constant care of Mr. Casey, who suffered terribly with
gout.

Annabelle turned to call out for Shilla Flannery only to realize
she was down at the creek with the washing. And Thomas was a
mile away working a neighbor's field. "Drat," she mumbled, even
while turning back to nod in affirmation to Mrs. Casey.

Then a fellow Annabelle judged to be in about his mid-twenties
came limping from around the corner of the Casey home, hat in
hand. He halted as he looked up the hill to his guide. Annabelle
nodded to him and he to her.

She frowned.

His clothes gave the immediate impression of poverty, but his
stance revealed a complete detachment from the effect, a thing
which made her look twice at him as she put aside her broom and
began to roll her sleeves back down. While a sheet of black
unwashed hair hung over his eyes, the rest clung together past his
neckline at the back. More skeleton than man, his shirt hung from
his frame like a scarecrow on a cross of broomsticks. He wore

ragged overalls and his boots were chunked with mud.

Lastly she noticed his palmetto hat, held lightly in one hand, looking as though the straw had barely escaped a hungry goat.

Despite his appearance, he held his back perfectly straight and his chin sat forward on his jaw, and so the word that came foremost to Annabelle's mind was *arrogant.*

She walked down the steps and upon closer look observed a relatively clean but pale face, a straight nose and rather thin lips in a pleasant combination, and if she hadn't seen the look in his eyes, she would have gone on thinking this was some young, snobbish aristocrat made poor by the misfortunes of war. But in his eyes she saw something she couldn't or hadn't seen in his walk, a different story entirely. Now he looked very much like a young man wishing to pay respects at the grave of a poor fellow who had lost his life in a hunting accident as had Samuel Brighton. A Quaker, too, perhaps? His eyes were red and it was obvious he hadn't slept in quite a while.

Annabelle suddenly felt sorry for both he and Friend Brighton.

Brighton had gone into the woods with his rifle about ten days before to forage for a bit of meat, hoping, Annabelle was sure, that the recent lack of troops in the area would have brought the animals back to the woods, but his gun had fallen somehow and shot him through with a mortal wound. Annabelle's father, Dr. Ludwell MacBain, was a good friend to Brighton, and she knew her father would be sad to hear of his death, but he had gone on to Pennsylvania with General Lee and most of the Confederate Army, and the bad news would have to wait for his return.

Samuel Brighton was a sad case, indeed, she thought, as she walked with head bowed toward the stranger. One son had fought and died for the Union, and the other had become a Confederate missing in action—certain to be dead, as well. It was after hearing news of his second son that Brighton began to take Mr. Marsden's slave boy, Pella, under his wing. *Their friendship had an odd sort of grace,* she thought, *not unlike Pella's gentle carvings.*

Pella's angel! she thought with a start. *Oh, my.*

She was not three feet from the stranger when she looked up

and said briskly, "Pardon me, sir, and I'll be right with you." His chin dropped slightly, and she turned and walked swiftly back up the yard and front stairs and into her house. Gathering her skirts, she ran up the stairs to her room.

There on her desk lay the angel, hand-carved and so homely it made her smile. *Resourceful boy. However did he find mahogany?* she wondered, and then she turned, but at the door she caught a glimpse of herself in the mirror on the wall. Tucking the angel under one arm, she quickly smoothed her wavy red hair and ran her fingers back around and under her neck to catch the stray hairs up in to her snood. Yes, she had her father's looks—from his pale green eyes to his strong jaw line—but she had her mother's smooth skin to grace the high cheekbones and there was a natural pinkness to her lips. And when Annabelle spoke, it was with a slight Scottish accent, a lesser version of her mother's. Her petite figure came from her mother as well, and Dr. MacBain rather expected her to be as delicate and fragile as his wife. But she was not.

She stared at the angel as she proceeded down the steps. Pella had carved it for Samuel Brighton, and today she would place it for him on Brighton's grave.

Mr. Marsden's slave boy, Pella, wasn't allowed to go hunting with Brighton the day of the accident, and Pella told Annabelle he cursed himself for not being there to carry Brighton's gun for him, but Pella's master, Marsden, an owner of one of the town's busier taverns, didn't allow him to go that day. Then, in his young grief, Pella had fashioned this pegged wooden angel for the grave, and he'd asked Annabelle to take it for him because he couldn't bear to go himself.

When Annabelle returned to the stranger, he stared at the statue, but she felt she couldn't or shouldn't explain. She simply walked past him and turned left up the road, walking along the edge of the muddy path and assuming he would follow her. Despite his limp, he soon caught up, and they walked up the edge of the road in silence—he on one side and she on the other.

It was two hours before noon, but the heat and humidity were already near intolerable. *A hot and humid Virginia summer day,* thought Annabelle as they plodded upward, *"these are a redundancy of thought,"* as *my father would say.* A stream of water flowed down the center of the road, creating a watery pit for hapless men and their carriages, and so she carefully walked to the far left up the incline. But they hadn't taken many steps before she was wet with perspiration from the effort.

Now wiping her brow with her sleeve, it seemed impossible to her the trees were not melting before her eyes. The forest to either side smelled sweetly wet, with the rotting wood and mulch and moss drenching the senses like a heavy perfume. Annabelle thought how like heavenly elixir a cool cup of water would taste; how she wished she'd fought for a trade with Shilla over laundry that morning. Annabelle could be the one down at the stream right now, taking a cool sip from the North Fork of the Catoctin Creek.

Annabelle glanced at the fellow to see how he fared and then watched his limping gait from the corner of her eye. She decided he must have been discharged from duty with a wound to the leg but was determined not to ask, for it was likely a humiliation to him. And so she turned her eyes back to the road. *At least, it would have embarrassed Michael to be so asked,* she thought further. Whatever she learned from Michael Delaney, the suitor her father had sent away, was as much as Annabelle knew about young men and their peculiarities.

She wondered if the stranger were a relative of the Brightons. *Perhaps he's a Quaker, too. But, no, he wouldn't have a wounded leg, for a true Quaker won't fight for either army. He must be a soldier. A soldier, or a renegade.*

A thrill of sudden panic struck her. They were already a third the way up the hill, but she had no business being up the hill at all. Mrs. Casey certainly never intended for Annabelle to escort the fellow. Whatever was she thinking? She could carry Pella's angel up there another day.

With that, she glanced over at him again and found he was peering at her. This made her cheeks burn, but he quickly looked down at her feet and then back to the stream in the road, sweeping the perspiration from his brow with a dirty handkerchief as he walked.

His glance made her all the more self-conscious as she weighed the situation in her mind. Mrs. Casey said Hannah Brighton sent him, but she wondered if Hannah Brighton actually *knew* this fellow, knew *of* this fellow, or if she'd only just met him herself. Annabelle was afraid to ask him. Then she wondered if she could ask him to set the statue at the grave for her, but she was afraid to speak to him at all.

Suddenly, he began to whistle—an odd little melody which sounded like something of a march as well as a lullaby. Whistling was rude, she knew, and yet she liked the sound. If it were possible, Annabelle Shannon MacBain would listen to music all day long, for she loved a song almost more than she loved to draw. She wondered why there ever was such a silly rule about whistling to one's self. She watched him again from the corner of her eye and thought surely he was once a soldier, for this tune was a camp song if ever she heard one, and so she chided herself for worrying about him. *He's a soldier, for goodness' sake! And Southern soldiers have a code of ethics. No need to fear, and besides, how can I fear a fellow who can whistle a tune like this? Sweet and playful, but with the barest bit of sorrow.* She wondered what the words might be.

She didn't know if it was the mist in the woods, or the scent of the wild mint and honeysuckle, but soon she felt that his whistling was the most achingly beautiful thing she'd ever heard. But it wasn't just the tune. It was the way he brought it to the air.

Halfway up the hill, she mused on the thought of attempting to whistle this tune for her father the next time he came home. Perhaps he would know the words. Yes, the next time he came home, she decided happily, she would ask him about the song, but then she wondered what he would think of how she'd learned the tune.

She stopped in her tracks and bowed her head.

Abruptly the whistling ceased and he stopped as well.

Without looking at the fellow, she pointed up the road. "The third spruce on the left a way up there. The path is just past it to its left, sir, 'n there's a log cabin stands over it. Good day to you, then." And, too shy to say more, she turned to walk down the road.

But the fellow spoke up. "Pardon the intrusion, ma'am, but may I presume you knew Samuel Brighton?" His voice was as quiet and deferential as a Quaker's, but his speech gave him away, for there was no "thee" in his address.

"Yes, sir; I did, sir." But at that moment one foot began to slide in the mud and with a blush and a stumble she stepped quickly to the edge of the road. "My goodness!" she called out as she slid and then straightened up. When she finally found a rock to stand on, she looked up, afraid he would be laughing. But he held a straight face, and she gave him half a smile in thanks.

He pressed on, "You believe the grave will be easy for me to find?"

His accent, the soft slowness of his words and particularly his avoidance of a direct question indicated he was at least a southerner, quite likely a Virginian, and thus over all quite likely a Confederate. The thought calmed her considerably. *And renegades don't pay respects at gravesides,* she told herself.

"No trouble, not now; we haven't buried anyone save poor Samuel Brighton in quite a while, thank the Lord."

"I couldn't make it for the funeral because of this leg." He gave a half-laugh, a bitter one. "If he'd been buried back where I come from, I would have made it for the funeral. We don't try to bury a man in this muck. We wait. Dangerous work, this stuff." He threw out his arms, pointing to the road with disgust.

Annabelle smiled uncomfortably. He obviously wanted to carry on an entire conversation about it, and she wondered if the poor man had suffered an injury to his head. "Yes," Annabelle said politely. "Dangerous, as you say."

"Yes, a grave is dangerous to dig out in all this." He gestured toward the muddy road again. Then he said more quietly, "But of course he deserved a proper burial. Still, seems poor planning to risk more accidents. It must have been raining?" He looked at Annabelle with a raised brow of expectation, but for the life of her she couldn't imagine what he wanted her to say. When she nodded uneasily and turned to go, he said, "Yes, it must have been awful."

She turned back to him.

This was one of the oddest conversations she'd ever had. He simply was not going to leave off the gruesome subject, and she rued her decision to come up here with the poor creature. She thought about Samuel Brighton's funeral held only three days before: his widow throwing herself down in the mud by the grave as the minister droned on; her servants trying to gather her up from the ground to calm her as the rain beat down; Hannah Brighton wailing so loudly the minister could no longer be heard above the din; and the rain kept pouring down in a torrent from a black sky. Everything was covered with mud by the time the mourners left the hill that day—the carriage wheels, the garments, and poor, poor Hannah Brighton. *No*, she thought, *a proper burial it was not.* Suddenly it occurred to her why he might be asking her such strange things. He might wish to know the details of the funeral to comfort himself.

So, although she was still uncertain, she asked, "Would you like me to tell you about it?"

He took a deep breath and nodded.

She stared at Pella's angel in her hands. Then she described his widow's grief, how she had waited a week to bury him hoping there'd been a mistake about their sons, that one of her boys would come back, and so they finally had to bury him in the week of the rain. She told him how Samuel Brighton knew everyone in town—*had* known, that is—how he was so well loved and how there must have been a hundred people up there that day in the mud and rain. Then she surprised herself by saying quite out of the blue, "Yes, and I suppose that's probably why they buried him shallow. I hadn't quite realized why before, but..." She blushed and looked up and saw him hanging on her words. "They dug his grave half-deep because of the mud so... I suppose so it wouldn't cave in on them."

He put his hat back on his head and nodded. It seemed the conversation had ended.

My, but he's strange, she thought. She looked down at Pella's angel and once more hesitated to ask him to take it.

"Thank you, ma'am. You've been a comfort. I know it wasn't easy for you, but you've helped me considerably." And he smiled, the first one she'd seen, but as she smiled back he turned and doggedly took himself up the mountain road.

So purposeful was his walk he'd almost lost his limp, and that made Annabelle sad. *Look how he makes his way,* she thought. It gave her sudden courage. "Sir!"

He turned about quickly on his good leg.

Holding out Pella's angel, she hurried up the hill. "Would it be asking too much if you would, sir.... This little statue. Could you set it at Mr. Brighton's head?"

"Yes, ma'am, I will." He smiled pleasantly as he came back down to meet her and to take the angel from her hands. "That's a fair carving, ma'am."

"Oh, no," she said blushing, "it's Pella's angel. He... he... Pella is one of Marsden's... a neighbor." With eyebrows raised, the fellow waited for a further explanation, but her tongue seemed tied in knots, and now she was afraid she'd said too much, afraid she'd have to take it to the grave herself if this man would not do a favor for a slave boy.

Yet he would not quit looking at her.

Then it came to her. "Pella was a good friend of Samuel Brighton's... one among many." And that seemed to satisfy him.

He nodded. "No trouble at all, ma'am. I'll set it up there for you... for this Pella Marsden... if it won't sink." And he smiled.

She turned beet red as she rushed to tell him, "No, not Pella Marsden. He is not... He is..." The fellow raised his brows again. She gulped. "A friend of Samuel Brighton's."

"As you say," he answered.

She had a burning curiosity to know how he knew Samuel Brighton and why he was here, but she was sure she'd already broken several rules of propriety and so her face reddened once more and she remained silent. Besides which there was work to do back at the house. And so she nodded to him and mumbled, "Thank you." Then she turned and walked quickly back down the road.

Although she wanted to, she did not turn her head to see if he had found his way. Instead, picking her way along the stones, she walked quickly down the road.

Now and then she glanced at the muddy stream, but when she saw the rivulet divide itself around a large rock she slowed her steps. A memory had come to her so sharply she felt as though her father was there beside her.

She and her father riding in a caravan of carriages and wagons following one Confederate soldier on horseback along the mountain's edge. The road hugged that mountain like a snake coming down a wide tree. Her eyes had slid from the gray uniform of the scout to the notch of green trees below them and all the way to the Potomac River which ran along the valley until it turned up around a bend a thousand feet ahead. Just beyond her view the twin rivers of Shenandoah and Potomac met at the town of Harper's Ferry and made the one river that lay below them now. "Shenandoah.... Daughter of the Stars," she had whispered softly to herself, watching the river's flow and enjoying the sound. She turned to her father on the seat beside her. "Isn't it beautiful, Weem?" But, to her disappointment, his thoughts were far away, and he stared straight ahead as he led their horse along.

Then her father suddenly said to the mare, "That's a girl, Birdie, get along, almost there now, get along," And he clicked the reins. Then he turned to Annabelle. "Hmm?"

She gave a little laugh. "I said, isn't it beautiful?" And when he nodded and smiled, she pointed along the shallows. "Look there, Father, have you ever noticed how the rocks sit like fish scales under the water? You can follow their pattern all the way across the riverbed. I wish the river would chart a different course for a little while so I could see the rocks entirely."

Her flash of enthusiasm had apparently shaken her father's mind awake, and now he looked at her carefully and gave her a broad smile. Then he shook his head and laughed. "Annabelle, you've an eye for beauty like your mother but a head for gory detail like your father." He chuckled and snapped the leather ribbons.

"Just so, Father. Now you've said it yourself. I've a head for detail, so wouldn't I be of good service to you as a nurse?"

But he just smiled and shook his head. "Yes and no, Annie, yes and no."

Well, he'd finally allowed her to come with him to the encampment, but only to bring food for the soldiers. She knew her father's outward reasons for saying no: she was only seventeen, a lady should not perform nursing, and regular camp life was no place for a woman, but what he would never say directly was that he'd already lost his wife and he didn't want to lose her. But Annabelle thought she would fairly burst from wanting to help her father.

Oh, but it's hard when life seems just to be starting and you want to be doing things but no one will allow for your youth.

She kicked at a stone now and continued down the road. Not long after that conversation her father was called as an assistant surgeon to the 43rd Virginia, and with reluctance Annabelle took over the task of managing the household. "And I can no more do what I really wish than I can… can stop this stream from running down the mountain!" she whispered in exasperation, and in her present state of mind she was quite lucky she reached the bottom of the hill without breaking her neck.

Back home once more she thought on the stranger as she did her chores.

He had called her "ma'am." He must have thought she was married and that made her feel responsible and matronly. As she laid out the table for supper that evening, she looked down at her mother's wedding ring on her finger, raised her hand to look at it more closely, and then began to twirl it, a thin ring of fine beveled gold. Of course the stranger had thought she was married. And she could have been, too.

"Yes," she said to herself gloomily, "I could be Private Michael Delaney's own right now." She finished laying out the silver and then laughed at herself as she realized she was whistling the stranger's unearthly tune. She looked at the ring once more, and it came to her that she'd rather be wearing her mother's golden band than any ring Michael would have given her. The thought made her smile ever so slightly.

Hard as it had been to accept at the time, she knew now her father had made a good decision to send Michael away.

By nightfall, these same thoughts took on a different, more ominous tone. Michael was gone and she didn't even know if he were still alive. She was trying to run a household without benefit of regular income, for her father's army, when they could pay him at all, did not pay him well, and then there was the war itself making life miserable. It had seemed so romantic in the beginning as her sewing circle happily made uniforms and banners, and chatted about the service of their fathers, beaus, and brothers who had gone off to fight. But it wasn't long before the truth of things came clear.

As she lay in bed that night she thought of all the boys and men who'd died in the last two years. She thought about Samuel Brighton and the many lives a person will touch and help but whose efforts go unrealized until that person passes away, and then she could not help but think about her mother. All of her mother's charm and humor could not keep death away, and in the darkness of Annabelle's room the thought frightened her terribly. When Annabelle was ten years old and her mother had become so seriously ill, she remembered thinking God couldn't possibly take her mother from her. She'd just lost her grandmother the month before and she knew the Scripture that promised God wouldn't tempt His people beyond what they could bear, and she was sure she could not stand her mother dying, too.

But she did die, and somehow Annabelle did stand it. And now with the senseless, accidental death of Samuel Brighton fresh in her mind, her mother's death became a symbol of all the pointless death around her caused by this bloody war.

Fear for her father possessed her, sorrow for the loss of her mother overwhelmed her, and she could not sleep.

When the mantel clock downstairs chimed twelve, she decided to sit up, light her candle and try to read her Bible. But when the clock chimed one, she decided there was nothing more to do but walk up the hill to her mother's grave to pray and try to give her troubled thoughts up to the Lord. The Quaker cemetery she'd sent the strange visitor to this morning was the very one in which her mother was buried. A family of Quakers, or "Friends of the Meeting," as they called themselves, had once lived on the hill, and the cemetery had slowly become their cemetery, but they tended the place so well the MacBains were grateful for the arrangement.

Annabelle rose from her bed and saw through the curtains that the moon was full, and she was glad she would not need a lamp. She seldom left the house unescorted except for these outings. She had made this walk many times before when her loneliness became unbearable. It gave her comfort to be near her mother if only in this strange way.

She opened her wardrobe, took her calico work dress from the hook and quickly changed. Then, plodding down the stairs in her over-large mucking boots, she muttered, "That road'll only make a fool of me once today." She walked through the kitchen and out the back door, came around the back of the Casey's fence and made her way up the edge of the roadbed just as she had that afternoon.

The air was warm and humid still and soon the back of her neck was wet with a cool perspiration, but as she made her way up the muddy incline, she began to whistle softly. The tune the fellow had whistled that afternoon had not left her, refused to leave her in fact, and now the memory of the earlier walk came freshly to mind as she hummed the melody to herself and to the empty woods. She quickened the melody to quicken her pace, lightly stepping over the rocks and branches illuminated by the moon.

It was dark in the woods to either side of her, and she was utterly alone, but she wasn't afraid. There had been no bushwhackers in the woods for several months, as John Singleton Mosby's Confederate Rangers had quickly and quietly dispatched the last group found, so she told herself she had nothing to worry over. Mosby's Rangers were a godsend to the area, filling the void left when county lawmakers quit their posts to join the ranks. And so the walk was invigorating and comforting for Annabelle. A sense of total freedom came to her whenever she was out on her own like this. She stopped whistling and began to pray, thanking God for her health and her father's protection, asking Him to watch over Friend Brighton's family. Then she picked up the melody again, and by the time she reached the cemetery spruce, she was singing the tune aloud in a *fa-la-la* and imagining a grand accompaniment of bagpipes. She smiled to herself at this, even as she turned and walked for a while more until the headstones came into view.

Straightway she came to her mother's grave and knelt down in the grass beside it, resting an arm against the cold granite and then pulling her hand up and around it, as one might hug the shoulder of a friend. Since she was alone, she prayed aloud and then sang a little and prayed some more, and after a while, she knew she could go back home and sleep.

She stood up, stretched, and thought ruefully of how this midnight romp would visit her muscles in the morning. She stretched again and yawned, and she glanced over to Samuel Brighton's grave.

And her breath burst from her in a gasp as her hands flew to her mouth.

It was not to be believed! Samuel Brighton's grave was about forty feet from her, but in the clear light of the moon the mound of earth could be clearly seen. It lay to the side... *to the side*... of the open wound in the earth that was his grave.

TWO

It matters little now, Lorena,
The past is in th'eternal past,
Our heads will soon lie low, Lorena,
Life's tide is ebbing out so fast....

From the Southern song, *Lorena*

A fine sweat sprang to her upper lip as the fear tore through her. Robbery. Grave robbery!

She'd heard of the robbing of graves. But it hadn't quite occurred to her such stories could be real. To imagine it one would have to imagine the sort of person who could do such a thing, and that was clearly an impossible task. But the robbing was done. And now she let herself feel the anger.

She took an unsteady breath and walked with little steps to the edge of the hole in the earth, where she let the air from her lungs and then took a breath again. With a prayer and a hope, she finally found the strength to peer down into the shallow grave. She could see by the moonlight that the coffin lid was shut. *Well, thank you for that, anyway,* she thought with some relief even as her eyes filled with tears.

And then she remembered Pella's angel.

She pulled her sleeve across her eyes with an angry sniff and began to search to the right and left and then around the mound of earth. She stomped her feet in frustration as she looked, wishing for all the world she'd brought a lamp. The flowers someone had left at the foot of the grave were still lying there, limp and scattered, but the sad little angel was nowhere to be seen. Again she walked around the mud but more carefully this time, feeling for it with the toe of her boot in the wet thickness.

Nothing.

To take an ornament like that of no value to anyone but a slave child, that was truly despicable. Unless the fellow she'd seen earlier in the day had never placed it there. Unless he had taken it himself.

Oh, but never mind about the angel, she finally told herself. *Mr. Brighton's grave has been opened, for Heaven's sake!* She wrung her hands together, but her mind became a jumble to think what to do.

Well, she had to tell someone, and she had to do it now, even in the middle of the night, she thought in fierce irritation. There was no help for it. Someone would have to go looking for the thief or thieves, and when they found them... well, Annabelle supposed she would be considered a hero. That could be a pleasant turn of events, and yet what a thing to be remembered for.

She began walking quickly back down the road, but as she hobbled along the edge avoiding the mud, a creeping sensation came over her—what if the robbers were still in these woods, were there right now watching her? Their job may have been unfinished. Perhaps she had interrupted them. And if they were watching her now, well, they would want to stop her.

At that horrible thought, she threw herself down the road in a run as fast as she dared, her skirts pulled up in front and flying out behind her. She slipped and slid and hurt her feet and ankles badly on the stones and rocks along the steep road, but she didn't look back, nor did she slow down, and as she ran she tried to decide what to do, where to go and whom to tell.

Finally she came to the main road, entirely out of breath with hurting bones and wheezing lungs, but at least she was in one piece.

As she stood there trying to catch her breath, she thought of Mr. Henry. Mr. Henry! He would know what to do. He knew everyone and everyone knew him. He could gather men to search for the thieves. Surely he was the man to tell.

Now she ran west down the road, slowing down a bit as she neared his home to try and catch her breath again and finally leaning up against the cold stone of his home and breathing heavily. She took one more deep breath then and walked to the door. She knocked softly at first, and the tears welled up as she waited, but then, when she received no reply, her anger surged and she gave the door three great whacks. Finally, she was greatly relieved to look through the transom window and see a pale light come on in the hall.

Mr. Henry's manservant, Dan, opened the door, scratching his tired head, and Annabelle wasted no time telling him he must wake his master. He nodded but then shut the door in her face, and Annabelle wondered if he would just go back to sleep and forget all about her, he looked so ragged and worn. But then she saw the light upstairs and knew he'd awakened Mr. Henry.

A few minutes later, Mr. Henry himself creaked open the door three inches and gruffly said, "Who's there?"

"Annabelle MacBain, Mr. Henry. Please come with me." she gulped. "Please come with me to the cemetery. Someone's dug up Samuel Bright... Brighton's grave. Please come." She wrung her hands as she spoke.

He opened the door wide and there he stood plainly in his nightshirt, eye to eye with Annabelle, but his eyes were wide and bloodshot. "You saying a grave robbery, Annabelle?"

"Yes, sir. Please come quickly, sir."

"What are you doin' up the hill in the middle of the night... alone?"

All in a rush she answered, "I couldn't sleep. I visited my mother's grave." But then she lowered her head, adding "I... I sometimes do." She fiercely hated to have to tell it, for telling it to Mr. Henry was telling it to the world, she well knew.

"Well, hurum... hmm... let me get my coat, then, and..." He had hardly turned his face away when he boomed out, "Dan!" the sound of which made Annabelle jump.

In a moment Dan showed himself at the door again, still scratching his head but already dressed.

Soon the three were headed back up the street and then plodding up the hill. Dan led the procession holding a lamp high in his hand, Mr. Henry behind him, and lastly Annabelle. As they trudged upward, Annabelle forgot the pain in her feet as she stared at Mr. Henry's old revolver shoved into the belt of his coat like a buccaneer. The weapon threatened to be swallowed at any moment by the girth of his belly, and Annabelle wondered how easily the thing could be retrieved if they were set upon.

Halfway up her heart began to pound again. It was horrible to think she was resting in her bed just an hour before while someone was at the cemetery doing... the unthinkable. She'd seen how desperate people had become to get goods or money these days, but she never thought someone could be quite that desperate. Wasn't it easier to rob a home? Why would someone do this for a bit of gold he could probably find more of in another place? But then, that really wasn't true anymore. People were burying and hiding their gold from the soldiers. Still, a man was worse than a coward to do this. He would have to be less than human, she decided, and the thought caused her to shiver.

Finally they came to the cemetery spruce and turned, all in silence. More pacing and there was the cemetery, with Brighton's grave ahead of them at the far side nearer the woods. Even at fifty feet away, a terrible gut-wrenching feeling struck Annabelle.

They walked straight through the rows of pale headstones to reach it.

And there was the grave—perfectly well kept and looking exactly as it did the day Brighton was placed there, the earth neatly piled and smoothed on top. There were the flowers at the feet of the grave. And as they drew nearer she could see it—Pella's angel standing at the head. Annabelle was soaked with perspiration from the running and the walking, and as all three stood there looking, her head began to throb. She couldn't believe this was happening.

Mr. Henry looked at Annabelle with narrowing eyes. "Annabelle, what does this mean?" he asked, testily.

"I... I don't know, Mr. Henry. But the grave was open, it was. The angel wasn't there... and... there was a pile of dirt, and..." She stared at him with widening eyes. "It was open, I tell you. The grave has been tampered with, sir. If you dig him up, you'll... you'll..."

"... irritate another poor fella trying to get some rest." Placing one hand on his hip and flashing his revolver toward the grave, Mr.

Henry added with obvious disgust, "I don't know what you saw, young lady, but this grave ain't been touched." His slave shook his head miserably and they both just stared at her.

Then Mr. Henry took the lamp from Dan's hand and held it toward Annabelle's face to examine her, and she looked back at him blankly. In a more gentle tone, he said, "Annabelle, obviously you've had a lot of strain caring for things while your father's away, haven't you? You want I should send for him?"

"No. No. It has been opened, Mr. Henry. The dirt was piled here." She pointed to the side where she'd seen the mound. "See, you can still see some mud there."

"Just like it was, Annabelle, the day he was interred." He shook his head.

"Well, he... or they... must have heard me and piled the earth back when I left." She nervously touched her hands to her head and looked about her. Her glance darted out into the woods, and a little shiver went up her back to realize someone had been watching her while she'd been up here. He... or they... had waited for her to leave and then... She blushed ferociously to realize they had heard her singing and praying aloud—the brutes!

When Annabelle finally turned back to Mr. Henry, he was piercing her with a hard look, such that the ridiculousness of what she had said was shot back at her full force. Grave robbers don't put earth back on a grave. They don't put little angels back in place... or place flowers neatly down when they're done. Grave robbers take what they want and run.

The strangeness of the thing frustrated Annabelle beyond words, and her face reddened to think she'd just given Mr. Henry every good reason to believe her slightly mad.

But she had seen the grave open! Someone wanted to make it look as though it was never touched, but she couldn't convince Mr. Henry or anyone with the little information she had. When the finality of it came to her, she stomped her foot and bowed her head to think a moment, to get her mind in order.

Mr. Henry said once more, "I think I should send for your father."

"That's all right, Mr. Henry, thank you," Annabelle said quietly. "I'll write to him myself."

"Good girl. Yes. Can we go now? Yes. I think so." He stuck his revolver into the deep pocket of his coat, took her by the arm and led her back down the hill with careful steps and solicitous glances as if she were a dotty old grandmother.

When she was in bed again later that night, she thought of the look on Mr. Henry's face and groaned. *He'll tell everyone. Everyone,* she thought miserably. *And when the ladies in the sewing circle hear of this, I'll never live it down.* She was too angry to cry.

She went over the details of what she'd seen again and again in her mind and in a short time knew she would never fall asleep, and so, hoping she could make some sense of it all, she decided to get up once more and write it all down. She lit a candle, walked to her father's room and sat at his broad desk. A peace settled over her as she removed some of his fine writing paper from a drawer, uncapped the fat inkwell and found the ebony pen that fit her hand the way she liked. But then she stared at the empty page before her and sighed. *Up in the middle of the night to visit a cemetery, I think I see an open grave... no, I see an open grave, but it is cleaned up before I can return to the place, and now I am at home and completely at peace with a pen in hand and the stale smell of ink before me. I am growing more odd by the hour. Lord, help me,* she thought, half to herself and half in earnest to heaven.

And where to begin?

It came to her that all she knew was what she had seen, and so she shouldn't write it out—she should draw it out. With determination and a quick prayer, she dipped the pen and let her hand do as it wished.

From the pen came a sketch of the open grave. Then came the grave neatly back the way it was, and she thought about Pella's angel and the fellow this afternoon. She drew Pella's angel, and then she drew the fellow's face as she recalled him. His eyes were the most difficult to reproduce but finally she came to a close approximation and sat back pleased. She spread the drawings out before her, crossed her arms, and studied them.

That fellow. This afternoon he had placed the angel there for her after all, kind man. He couldn't have been the one. Then again, he was a stranger and directed to the grave that very afternoon. Peculiar, wasn't it?

"Could he?" she wondered aloud, and she stared forlornly at the drawings. The flowers were there. Pella's angel was gone. Then the angel was put back. By heaven, it was he. The shock of it caused her to sit up straight. She'd asked the stranger to put the angel at Samuel Brighton's *head*, but his grave had yet to have a headstone set upon it! In fact, the flowers were placed at the feet as if it were the head, but she knew better because she'd seen him buried. There were only two ways to know which end was which. You had either attended the funeral to see how the coffin was placed, as she had, or you had dug up the grave and saw for yourself how the coffin lay.

He could have placed Pella's angel with the flowers, but he hadn't. The grave robber could have left the grave open and run, but everything was put back exactly where it was supposed to be. It was as if he had done it all for her, and the thought made her absolutely miserable.

And then she remembered something about their conversation, their very odd conversation. He had asked... no, he had *wheedled* the information from her that Brighton's grave was dug shallow. She shivered. Oh, he was good, slick as oil, to be able to bring that from her lips.

The image of the fellow's dark, sad eyes stared back at her from the drawing pad. Could this man do such a thing? She tried to think what sort of person he could be to be digging up graves. She'd never met a person capable of such a heinous crime. But soldiers turned bushwhacker often enough.

So the scoundrel had used her to find the grave and had carried that angel for her, placed it for her. She had walked up the hill with... Oh, it was awful to think. Thank heaven he hadn't hurt her. She should never, *never* have gone up the hill.

And—oh, the horror of it—he'd listened as she rested on her mother's grave, had heard all her private thoughts and prayers.

An anger and a hate welled up in her such as she'd never felt before. If she saw him again, she'd... she'd have him arrested. She'd make them dig up the grave, and she'd explain about the angel and he'd be hanged. That's what would happen. He'd be hanged and good riddance!

But then she struck the wall of reason. The fellow had certainly cleared off by now, and she hadn't a clue as to who he was.

She thought for a long while and formed a plan. Perhaps she could find out from Mrs. Casey where he was from and what he called himself. If Mrs. Casey didn't know, perhaps Hannah Brighton knew. If not she, then perhaps someone in town had seen him. *He must pay for what he's done. People like him must come to terms with their deeds,* she thought angrily.

But—why did he put it all back? For my benefit? He doesn't even know me. Grave robbers aren't sentimental. So—perhaps there was something buried with Samuel Brighton the stranger doesn't want anyone to know he's taken? Something only Hannah Brighton and her servants know about?

She decided right then she would visit Brighton House tomorrow—that is, today.

Morning light found Annabelle with no more answers in her soul than she'd held the night before. And the questions were burning her alive. As soon as was reasonable, she walked next door to the Caseys to ask after the man.

The Caseys lived east of the MacBains in a three-story stone home with black shutters and a large white railed porch across its front. From the center of the second-story porch came two stairwells set against the home, one facing west, one east, as they descended. In all it was a grand affair that sat itself widely on the street as if it had something to say.

Annabelle made the short walk to her neighbors' steps and climbed them carefully. She knocked lightly, and Mrs. Casey appeared quickly, whooshing the door open and smiling at Annabelle, as cheerful as a little bird. "Annabelle, dear, do step in and have a cup of chicory! I was just preparing Mr. Casey's breakfast."

"No, thank you, Mrs. Casey. I've just had breakfast myself. Mr. Casey's condition is improving, I trust?" she asked politely as she stepped across the threshold.

"Oh, Mr. Casey has no complaints, no complaints," she replied merrily, while Annabelle smiled back at her, knowing full well she couldn't possibly be referring to her husband.

"Well," Annabelle said carefully, "I came to tell you Shilla's been baking all week and she tells me we have more cornmeal than she can make use of. Might I trouble you to take some off our hands?"

"Oh, no, we do well enough, thank you, dear." But then she flicked her head toward the stairs and came back to smiling at Annabelle as she added, "But now Mr. Casey does love a smattering of cornbread with honey now and then, truth be told. He might be unhappy with me if I passed up his dessert. All right, dear, you just bring us whatever you see fit."

This conversation had gone as so many little conversations did with Annabelle and her neighbor—a tactful presentation of charity, a first refusal, and the eventual acceptance of the goods—because Annabelle had established a cache of goods in the bottom of their smokehouse which she drew from now and then for the neighbors. Cornmeal, wheat flour, turnips, potatoes ("praties," Shilla called them), and some of the jarred goods she would take out of the hidden compartment and give quietly to people in need but in portions small enough so as to look as though they had little more than anyone else in town. Annabelle knew it seemed vile to horde goods when people wanted for so much all around her, but she also knew if she didn't mete it out this way, the soldiers would take it all and there would be none for anyone.

Annabelle smiled again at Mrs. Casey and turned to go, but then turned back as if she'd forgotten something. "Mrs. Casey, that fellow... the one who needed to pay respects yesterday up the hill... uh, Mr.... Mr....?" Annabelle hoped to have the name filled in for her, but Mrs. Casey just kept looking at her inquisitively. "Well," Annabelle finally said, downheartedly, "he had no trouble finding it, I presume?"

"No, Annie, dear, I'm sure he did not." An awkward moment fell between them, but Mrs. Casey must have sensed Annabelle's curiosity. "I didn't know the fellow. Young man said he was a good friend of Samuel Brighton's. Said Hannah Brighton sent him, but I don't believe he ever gave his name. A veteran, don't you think? And a handsome boy."

At the word "handsome," Annabelle shuddered a little. "Yes, a veteran, ma'am. I thought that too, but of course I didn't ask."

"Of course. Well, he can walk well enough. I'm surprised he isn't reenlisted as a volunteer. If Mr. Casey were only a little better, he said he would join up, and only last week Mr. Myers joined the volunteers with his bad arm, Mrs. Myers was saying, even though there's crops to put in, and now she'll be doing them herself, of course, but we all do what we can."

"Yes, yes, we do what we can." Annabelle said with distraction, realizing Mrs. Casey knew not one iota more than she knew herself about the stranger. She would simply have to visit Widow Brighton. She sighed as she said good-bye to Mrs. Casey.

As she closed the door, she heard Mr. Casey's rough voice from the stairwell. "Who be that, Otelia? You've made me come to the stair, now. What do you mean keeping my breakfast?"

Annabelle smiled as she thought of Mrs. Casey's bright little face telling her, *"No complaints, no complaints."*

As she walked back to her porch, she glanced at their home resting between the Casey's and the stately Humboldt House. Mrs. Humboldt's residence to the west was three stories of plastered stone standing widely on the hill like a grand hotel, with a magnificent double staircase descending from the second-story porch. The whole of it was large and quite tremendous. It was the sort of home ladies saw and said, "How marvelous!" But poor Mistress Hattie Humboldt was too old to enjoy it, now. She hadn't been able to walk the grand stair in many years, and in recent years she could only hobble from her kitchen door on the arm of their last slave, an inveterate runaway that now seemed gone for good. She never left the house anymore, and if it weren't for Annabelle, she would be near to starving.

The MacBain Home was squeezed between Mrs. Humboldt's and the Caseys', tall and thin and white. It was made of clapboard over log with five tall, thin windows flanked by blue-gray shutters and a front door surrounded by a bannistered federal porch. A double porch sat back and to the right of the main porch and served as doctor's office below and doctor's study above. The office was a mere three feet from the Caseys' stone wall. How she wished now she could walk up those steps, look through the windows and see her father hunched over his books.

"Miz MacBain?" came a little voice.

She turned on the stairs to see Pella, half her height and light in frame, looking at her from his small face and coming across the road to speak to her.

Before he could ask, she answered, "Yes, Pella. The angel was placed at his... head."

"Aw, thank you, miss." And for the first time in days, Pella smiled. Then he turned and walked slowly and stiffly down the street.

The tavern keeper, Mr. Marsden, kept Pella well-dressed for a slave, but Annabelle had decided it simply served to hide the cruelty with which he regularly treated the boy. *And he should have let him go hunting with Samuel Brighton that day. If he had, perhaps poor Friend Brighton would still be alive.* And then she thought again how the stranger wished to rob the dead body and make it seem as though it hadn't happened, and it came to her rather eerily that Samuel Brighton's death might not have been an accident. Perhaps it was good for Pella that he hadn't gone along. For a brief instant she wondered if the tavern keeper knew something, but first things first and next things next. She would go see Hannah Brighton.

She could not explain anything to Shilla yet, she realized, and so she would have to wait for Shilla to take food to Mrs. Humboldt next door. Mistress Hattie would keep Shilla occupied for at least an hour.

Shilla's visit gave Annabelle the idea of making a gift of cornmeal to the Widow Brighton as an excuse for conversation. It would be entirely appropriate to bring her an offering of sympathy since Annabelle's father had served as their doctor now and then.

Yes, that would work, and although she could never ask Widow Brighton what jewelry or gold her husband was buried with, she might be able to discreetly ask a servant. Their indentured servant, Jane, might answer her. And, until she had better proof, she certainly couldn't intimate to Widow Brighton that her husband's grave had been disturbed. That thought made her realize she needed to hurry, because soon Mr. Henry's information might make its way to the Brightons, if it hadn't already, and Hannah Brighton would certainly think Annabelle had lost her mind and would likely turn her away at the door.

It would not do to have the entire town thinking she was touched, but she wasn't about to let this hideous crime go unpunished.

Now as she changed into her riding clothes, hoping beyond hope she'd find an answer to who the stranger was, she couldn't help but think about how the town had suffered since the war's beginning. Today it was grave robbery. Just a short time ago, the soldiers had emptied everyone's pantry shelves. Hillsborough grew poorer each and every day, and there wasn't anything anyone could do.

Shilla finally left for Mrs. Humboldt's around ten o'clock that morning, and Annabelle made her way to Brandenburg's stable where both the MacBain mares were kept. Riding Lucy, Annabelle's own, was another pleasure the girl took without escort. Shilla always scolded her to mind her father's warnings about riding alone, that the danger was to both body and reputation, even as she watched Annabelle smile innocently and leave the house anyway. There were some things in life Annabelle MacBain had refused to learn.

Lucy nodded and snorted gently when Annabelle came round for her, and Annabelle stroked her velvet nose for a moment. Lucy was a pale yellow tan with a white nose, fourteen hands high, and she was Annabelle's first horse. Although the mare was eight years old, she was still a high stepper. Her father had given her the horse right after her mother's death, his gentle means of telling her she had become head of the house, a grown-up little woman-child, and so Lucy had become a companion for Annabelle.

She rode Lucy every other day unless some large movement of troops and equipment barred the roads. She found the only real relief from summer's heat when she could go east of town a mile and race with Lucy on the straight stretch of road there. She'd ride sidesaddle like a lady should all the way along the road until the houses disappeared and the straight stretch came into view. Then she would look way up and down the road to make sure they were alone, swing her long riding skirt around and send her right leg over the saddle to straddle the horse like a man. It was uncomfortable using a sidesaddle this way, but stubbornness kept her from admitting it.

And then they would run.

Sometimes she would turn Lucy toward a field, and they would jump the stone fences for a while before coming back to the road. Four-foot high walls of stone. Five-foot. Pure joy was that feeling of flight while jumping. When they were lifted into the air on a high fence, Annabelle sometimes felt as though time stood still and she only wished the feeling could last. Sometimes she hoped Lucy would turn into Pegasus, and that one day they would jump the last fence and simply never touch earth again, but then Lucy would always land solidly on the other side, bringing a different sort of exhilaration to Annabelle—earthly and real and heart-stopping—if never quite as broadening as flight.

She was always sorry to go back home, but she would return from their jaunts cool and refreshed and ever looking forward to the next ride.

Things weighed heavily on her mind that morning as she rode to Brighton House, and so Annabelle decided to run the road first and then ride back to the house, just to clear her mind. It wouldn't take long. The stretch she liked to run with Lucy lay just beyond the Brighton's home, in fact, and soon they were slowly plodding past its fine stone exterior.

Brighton House lay east of the town, but it was turned to face the sunrise on the edge of a fine hill overlooking a wide creek.

Annabelle eyed the house up and down, window to window, wishing the secrets behind Samuel Brighton's grave would somehow reveal themselves to her. She passed the great home and then the two barns that lay along the edge of the road and was about to cross the creek bridge, just realizing she'd forgotten the gift of a pound of cornmeal, when she saw movement up the tree-lined waterway. A man, his back to her, was stepping along the side of the creek bed, evidently looking for a place to cross the stream.

Her blood ran cold. It was the stranger... *the grave robber.*

THREE

Hear the "Battle Cry of Freedom,"
How it swells upon the air,
Oh, yes we'll rally round the standard,
or we'll perish nobly there.

From the Union song,
Just Before the Battle, Mother

Although the man was better dressed than yesterday, there was no mistaking the hair, the stature and the limp. She pulled up hard on the reins to halt Lucy and tried to think what to do.

She could almost hear the thumping of her heart. Don't grave robbers turn tail and run when they're done? Why in the world was he still here? She watched him as he began carefully stepping across the boulders far away and below her toward the Brighton House.

He held a gun.

Although he was less than two hundred feet away, he was looking down at his footing and moving slowly, and so he hadn't yet seen her. The sound of the water obviously kept him from hearing anything. But he would see her if she didn't turn around right then, she realized, and so she pulled Lucy's rein tight left, tapped her in the side with her left heel and drew Lucy back to where a barn blocked sight of him.

Now think! she told herself, *think! He did it. He has a gun and he's coming back to the Brightons for some strange reason.*

What should she do? Get Mr. Henry again? But this fellow would be at the Brighton home soon, and who knew what he had in his mind to do now. She had to warn Hannah Brighton.

Annabelle spurred Lucy back up the road, the crest of the hill protecting her from the stranger's sight, and then up the drive to the Brightons' front door. A servant took her horse, and Annabelle ran onto the porch and pounded fervently on the door until Jane opened it.

Breathlessly she said, "Would you please announce me to Widow Brighton, and quickly, Jane? Ever so quickly!"

"Yes, miss." Jane moved immediately up the stairs to find her mistress, all the while staring back at Annabelle in the foyer.

Annabelle bunched her long riding skirt indelicately in one hand and paced the hall as she waited. *Come down. Come down,* she thought frantically. *He'll be here any moment!* But Widow Brighton did not come down. Annabelle grabbed hold of the column at the base of the stair and began nervously tapping her riding crop on the bannister only to realize with horror she was tapping out the melody the grave robber had taught her the day before.

Just then the front door opened and the crop flew from her hand and clattered to the floor as she turned to look.

He stood at the door, his hand still holding the knob as he looked at Annabelle. He wore a fresh shirt properly buttoned to the collar, and his hair was washed and combed back behind his ears. His blue eyes were clearly visible now, but his face held no expression, while Annabelle knew she was pale and her eyes bright and large as she looked down at the rifle he held upright in his hand. Her body swayed a moment in her fright. *What will he do? What should I do?*

And then Hannah Brighton descended the stair.

Annabelle turned to look up at her. "I didn't come in with this gentleman," she said in a shaking, angry voice. "Could you know him?" And she pointed her finger most rudely at the fellow.

Annabelle watched the fellow turn his face up to the Widow Brighton and smile a relaxed and charming smile, the very smile he'd given Annabelle when taking Pella's angel from her the day before. His hand fell from the knob comfortably, and he set the rifle in the corner of the hall behind him. Then he stepped forward to the bottom of the stair.

"Well, of course I know him, Annabelle." Hannah Brighton laughed uncomfortably. "I hope my nephew has done nothing untoward?"

Nephew? Annabelle's mind rushed to understand what was happening. Samuel Brighton's nephew dug up his uncle's grave? Perhaps the Widow Brighton had authorized him to do so? She'd never thought of that. Perhaps something was buried with Samuel Brighton by accident and Hannah had asked the nephew to... help? Then they would want the whole thing kept quiet.

Oh, no.

How rude she was being—and in their time of grief! Now they would hear from town how she had accused someone of digging up Samuel's grave, and she would have needlessly embarrassed this house as well as her own father's good name. Oh, what had she done?

While Annabelle came full circle in this thinking, Hannah Brighton was making excuses for her nephew's presumed improprieties. She finished, and was now staring at Annabelle, a little smile coming and going from her thin lips as she watched the girl's face.

Utterly undone by the present circumstance, Annabelle hadn't a clue as to what to say next, and so she lowered her eyes and began to stare pitifully at the riding crop lying in the hall. The nephew calmly passed her and picked it up, turned and smiling graciously, asked, "I would hope this bit of gentlemanly behavior will make up for anything I've said or done? I would sooner harm an angel as insult you, miss."

Annabelle blushed. There it was: Pella's angel—a clear reference to their walk up the hill, and he was being so discreet about it all. Oh, how wrong she had been. She brought her hand to her mouth even as tears of shame stung her eyes.

How awful it must have been for him to have had to do this unspeakable thing for his aunt! And here Annabelle had stood ready to accuse him of the most horrible of crimes before the widow herself, no less! Mr. Henry would have told everyone in town by now and soon enough it would reach Brighton House as well.

Her pride was brought to its lowest, darkest depths—depths that only a seventeen-year-old suddenly faced with a blot on her young reputation could feel. The humiliation! The gossip! The horrible rumors she will have brought upon herself! And there was nothing to do but apologize and apologize again and then swallow it all. There was no explaining the situation to anyone.

"Yes, yes. I'm sorry. It must have been... You're forgiven, of course. Thank you, but I'm so very sorry." She looked up at Widow Brighton and back to him and searched his eyes, hoping he would sense how earnestly she spoke the words. "Please forgive me... my own rudeness. I hardly know what to say, I..."

"No more need be said," the fellow condescended, but it wasn't true. All three were marooned there in the hall, looking back and forth at one another in discomfort. Finally he added, "Aunt Hannah, the young lady permitting, would you be so kind as to favor me with an introduction?"

"Yes, oh, yes, of course. Annabelle, my dear, will thee permit me to introduce thee to my nephew..."

The fellow said helpfully, *"Malachi."*

"Oh, yes, Malachi. Malachi Norris?" Annabelle blanched and nodded. Hannah Brighton added quickly, "Pardon my forgetfulness, Malachi."

"Not at all, Aunt."

Now the widow and her nephew each visibly relaxed as they stepped onto the firm ground of polite formalities, but Annabelle wished only to push off from this shore and float far, far away.

But Hannah Brighton continued, "Miss Annabelle MacBain, Mr. Malachi Norris, only son of my late brother, Alfred." She became more and more cheerful as she went along, "... late come to us from the 33rd Battalion on a leave of absence to pay his respects... so good of him. My Samuel would be so glad, and all the way from the eastern shore. His last visit here was as a babe in cradle." Her nephew smiled at that. Then she turned her bright eyes once more to her nephew, saying, "Now, Malachi, this is Dr. Ludwell MacBain's daughter, our doctor, upon occasion. Dr. MacBain is now with the... the... oh, dear..."

"The 43rd Virginia," said Annabelle quickly.

"Oh, yes. My, but I wish they wouldn't number them so. It makes it very difficult to remember."

Malachi Norris looked at Annabelle and said under his breath,

"Miss Annabelle MacBain. Extraordinary." This, of course, made her wonder just what he meant. "M-a-c-B-a-i-n?" he spelled carefully.

"Why, yes, just so," she gulped, aware of his look and thinking he was surprised to find her unmarried.

Hannah Brighton looked back and forth at the two and, with a trill in her voice, enjoined them both to come and have a nice tea with her in the parlor, but she followed the invitation by prattling on for a moment about the fact it wasn't actual "tea," of course, but a fair substitute bought from a sutler that had followed General What's-it, oh, she couldn't remember his name just then, a foreign thing, but it was an herb tea, at least she was glad for that, but she wasn't quite ready, yet, to join them but she would be downstairs again momentarily.

She finally took a breath and began to make her way back up the stairs. Halfway up, however, she turned and addressed Annabelle, "Oh, my dear, thee must forgive me if I haven't lost my senses entirely." She looked around Annabelle in slight confusion, smiling uncertainly. "Please do have... Miss Flannel, is it? By all means have her come round back for tea with Jane as well. Wherever she may be?"

Annabelle gulped and nodded and gave curtsy, wishing for all the world she could see some humor in the moment, and then she watched the widow continue up the stairs. When the hem of the gown disappeared, she found herself still staring into the empty stairwell. Of course, there was no Miss *Flannery* attending Annabelle as there should have been. Against all sense of propriety, Annabelle had come alone, worst of all on horseback. Unthinkable. It was hard for her to imagine how many rules of conduct she had broken that morning and all because of a midnight walk up a hill, a thing she should not have done in the first place.

No, it began with a walk up a hill in the afternoon which she should not have done in the first place.

And to make matters truly excruciating at that moment, she sensed that *he* was still staring at her, and she would rather face a firing squad than meet that gaze.

"The parlor is this way," he said gently, and she blushed with anger and embarrassment.

"I really must go. Please give your aunt my regrets." With that they finally caught each other's eye. He was looking at her rather strangely, his mouth parted as if ready to speak again, but he didn't. She wanted to pull her eyes away, but she looked at him another moment, and then looked down. "Of course, I want to thank you for placing Pella's angel... *at his head.*"

"At his... *head*..." he repeated, turning the words over thoughtfully while still staring at her. Then, as the meaning came to him he simply said, "Well..." And he raised his brows before he sighed. "Aren't I the silly fellow?"

Annabelle rushed headlong into her apologies then. "Yes, well, yes. And, of course, and I won't say a word." She hesitated and drew a hand to one bright cheek. "Only I must tell you. I brought someone up there to the grave last night, although perhaps you saw it all. Not to worry. They didn't believe me, due to your putting things right, so nothing more'll be done." She looked away and dropped her hand. "I didn't tell them about you. I'm sorry to have caused you such trouble. I'm sure your aunt will hear of my interference, and I'm... I'm mortified, really." Tears welled up in her eyes. "I can't tell you how sorry I am, and I, I... I must go."

Annabelle rushed out the door then, spinning past Jane as she went and only very nearly avoiding an upset of the large tea tray. As she fled she heard Malachi Norris behind her saying, "Nothing more will be...? Wait. What do you mean?" But she didn't stop to give reply, even when she heard the clatter of poor Jane's tray as it collided with the fellow.

Annabelle rushed across the front yard to beg a passing field hand to please fetch her horse right away, and the servant, seeing her distress, ran toward the stable. As she walked quickly to the stile and stepped upon it to wait, she wrung her hands around her crop, knowing full well Malachi Norris was right behind her.

Lucy was brought up and she gained the seat, sidesaddle, but Norris was behind her then—right there, in fact, and he grabbed her arm and held it so that she couldn't start Lucy up without sliding from the horse.

Taking a deep breath she turned to him. "I am so sorry, please... I'll never speak of it again." And once more Mr. Norris took on a strange look but released his grasp. Annabelle nodded to him and tapped Lucy's flanks. She rode down the drive, turned east to the straight run, flung one leg over the saddle and began to canter. All the while she remembered that odd expression on his face. Malachi Norris's look made no sense to her, no sense at all.

She dug her heels hard into Lucy's sides and ran as fast as she would go, trying to lose her thoughts to the wind.

When the run was over and the last fence jumped, she reluctantly turned Lucy toward town and let her plod back. Taking a seat sidesaddle once more, Annabelle's head fell forward in deep thought, for during the run she had realized she couldn't tell anyone what she knew: not Mr. Henry, not Shilla, not even Sarah and Sally, and, if it were possible, this thought gave her an even more melancholy air.

As they passed Brighton House, she straightened up and determined to keep her eyes on the road. She'd simply been in the wrong place at the wrong time, that was all, and now she would have to suffer her wounds silently and alone. It would be the grown-up thing to do, the right thing, the thing her father would expect. She set her jaw. As long as no one in town wrote her father about this, she'd do all right. But she must do absolutely everything quite normally and properly from here on out, she decided.

And then the Ladies' Sewing Circle came to mind. Tongues would wag, and there wasn't a thing she could do about it. Oh, how she'd grown to hate that little circle.

An artificial sense of order and peace had always presided within that band of stalwart, industrious ladies, but they spent a great deal of time gossiping long and hard about their neighbors as they pieced together banners, uniforms and sashes. No one wished to think of it, let alone bring up the fact their handiwork might be consigned to a bloody field and a shallow grave.

If war did happen to become a topic, they would carefully chain the ensuing conversation to certain subjects that were in turn chained to certain modes of thought.

Many a conversation included states' rights, a concept the ladies had no trouble discussing to its limits, the limits being provided by the degree of a lady's education. But states' rights were certainly a cause to die for, they could all agree.

When the Emancipation Proclamation was discussed, it was said Lincoln was the one making an issue over slavery, besides which his Proclamation was considered a farce, a Northern lie. Annabelle remembered last fall when the shocking rumor came around of the first Proclamation. Mrs. McLean had said angrily, "Such a deception. See how he only frees our Negroes, and not the North's!"

And everyone in the circle agreed. Slavery was considered a necessity of life, if a painful one, like the sweat it took to farm a piece of land or the pain required for a woman to give birth. "Besides which," the ladies tittered worriedly, "everybody knows if you let the slaves go, they'll rise up to loot and kill. Only remember John Brown's raid." And Annabelle would readily nod.

John Brown's raid had taken place in Harper's Ferry four years before, not twenty miles from Hillsborough, and all Annabelle remembered was that she had stayed awake all night terrified, curled up in a knot under her sheets and blankets.

But now that she was a bit older, she looked at slavery differently.

In that sewing circle, one of the girls was saved from drowning by her mammy. Yet that girl had seen the same dear slave sold off just last year. Another was brought through a killing fever by their male domestic from Jamaica who had a knowledge of herbs, but she spoke of him as if he had no sense.

In every one of these conversations, something would rise up within and whisper to her conscience, "Is it right, Annabelle? But is it right? But is it right?"

Only once did she let the feelings strike her as hard as they possibly could. An older woman was telling the circle how slaves simply didn't feel things as deeply as they. She gave the example of how she had had to sell the children of a particular slave just this week, and that she was shocked at the lack of emotion the mother had shown. Nary a word of good-bye for them, she said; she just packed a bundle with their things and turned away from them on the porch step. It was two days since then, and yet this woman was doing her usual labor with no display of emotion whatsoever.

Two days? Two days ago Annabelle had seen that slave woman down by the creek, eyes closed and arms tight about herself, moaning as if her heart were shattered. She had swayed and cried where she stood, and no one had seen it but Annabelle. Annabelle had stared in fascination, naively wondering if the woman had put herself under some sort of spell. Now the truth of it was clear.

Annabelle felt her face grow bright red with her knowledge, and she opened her mouth to protest the old woman's words, but her friends had begun to nod and give hearty agreement. Soon several more examples were provided and still Annabelle made no sound.

A twinge of guilt rose up in her, but then she looked carefully at the friends and neighbors she had known her whole life long—and she simply let the twinge subside. She couldn't change this fact of slavery, after all, and perhaps the mournful woman by the waterside was an aberration. Yet, she had mourned. This one *had* mourned.

And so she finally opened her mouth to speak, but the words came from nowhere near her heart. "The South will bring slavery to a close slowly and carefully on its own, and no Northerner has a right to tell us when and how." All of them had smiled and nodded, and she felt the circle of friendship close around her, but as to feelings, she felt more numbness than peace—more order in her pronouncement than truth—for she had given hope of change without having to lift a finger toward it. And her mind said, *It is most important to do things properly, in good order, and quietly. Then and only then will everything be all right and we will be able to forget and forgive. The ladies in the sewing circle, my friends, everyone. We will forget and forgive.*

And in time, too, they would all forget the night Annabelle MacBain begged Mr. Henry to travel up the hill to the cemetery to see an unopened grave. And in time, she was sure, they would forgive her this impropriety.

She pulled up her chin, clicked her heels into Lucy's side and trotted into town.

As she came up to Brandenburg's Livery, Sarah and Sally Drum happened to come out of the store next door. They saw Annabelle dismount and came tripping over, giggling and laughing as they came. They could hardly be expected to notice Annabelle's quiet mood because they had delightful news: there would be a ball tomorrow evening, to be held right up at their old school, the now empty female academy. A nearby Confederate company whose commanding officer was fond of dancing had organized the affair. "Won't you go? And what shall we wear? Aren't you excited? The officers will be there and how wonderful it will be," they said in a rush to win their friend's enthusiasm.

Annabelle slowly began to smile... *Perhaps this dance is just the place to begin to show everyone I am all right, a means of presenting myself to everyone.*

Sarah and Sally had been good friends with Annabelle ever since their Ladies' Seminary days. Seminary ended when the war began, but the three girls were as close as ever, and Annabelle counted friendship with Sarah and Sally one of the most constant charms in her life. All their friends were of Southern persuasion, of course, the young people in town having long since divided themselves along the lines, as had their families, choosing schools and churches according to each family's persuasion.

Before the war, Hillsborough was a bustling mill town of over 250. There was a wagon maker, a blacksmith's shop, four taverns, a cooper, a joiner, a general store, a post office, a doctor's office, a tannery, two tailors and a shoemaker. The town limits were marked by grist mills on either end, and there was a lumber mill and a textile mill within a mile of town. But when war broke out, the town's abundance was immediately to its advantage and to its disadvantage: the advantage was that it took longer for the residents to become poor, and the disadvantage was that everyone came to take from them, and the town was tossed back and forth between troops. Finally, the churches and the businesses began to shut their doors. As goods became scarce, the bake sales and afternoon teas died off, and county fairs and dances (save military balls) became sweet memories.

In Annabelle's opinion, although the Confederate soldiers were more polite to the Southern ladies than were the Union boys, the actions of all soldiers seemed sadly similar: they were rude to the help, stole from farmers, shopkeepers, and the occasional home, and generally made a ruckus in the taverns. She supported the Confederate cause in honor of her father's choice, but she knew she had no real choice in the matter, and she wished it would just all go away. Oh, how she wished and prayed it would go.

Finally, in the month before this, General Robert E. Lee took himself and his men to Pennsylvania to harass the Union forces on their own ground. In the last two weeks she had slept more easily than she had in two years. People milled about the town and spoke with each other as they hadn't in many months, and the farmers thought of replanting and beginning again before the troops returned. Prayer meetings started up again. People were invited to each other's homes for tea once more (although the tea was more likely to be made of herbs). The hope was General Lee would win the war up there and it would all be over soon. And so, happy rumors flew around their heads like sparrows, full of energy and charm but spinning tantalizingly out of reach.

But no peace came.

And the very worst days were those when the names of friends and neighbors she had known since childhood showed up on the lists of dead or missing. On those days time seemed to stand still, and no amount of work could shake from her mind the images such news brought.

Yet even against this backdrop of war, Annabelle decided to join her good friends as they attended the military ball in the meeting room of their old female academy.

The hall on the main floor of the stone building was a large square room with towering windows, and it was draped with regimental flags from the nearby encampment and filled with the music of a military band. Since the surrounding countryside was not a secured area by any means, the officers brought their weapons in with them, although they politely left their pistols in the hallway and leaned their sabres against the walls when taking up the dance.

The weather had changed for the better. It had rained in Hillsborough that day, and now a cool breeze blew in from across the fields through the large open windows. The light winds kept the dancers comfortable while the servants were kept busy relighting the table candles and the old chandeliers.

Annabelle, Sarah and Sally all wore traditional summer white, but each dress was uniquely suited to the wearer.

Sarah and Sally were fraternal twins and their features were quite different. Sarah was taller than Sally, black-haired and black-eyed, with a strong chin and a stately neck. Her lips were beautifully formed, and Annabelle had noticed more than once how fellows could not take their eyes from her face as she spoke. Sarah loved society and was most happy when dancing on the arm of a dashing officer. Delightfully energetic at balls and parties, the young lady had already broken many a heart. That night she had chosen to wear a bright white gown whose sweeping neckline was as low as decorum permitted, and she wore a cluster of velvet red roses at her waist. She was the sort of young lady to whom fellows made a gallant bow and then lined up to fill her dance card.

Sally, on the other hand, had chosen a cream satin gown demurely buttoned to the neck. A petite young woman, her hair was the color of wheat and her eyes a cloudy gray. She, too, was pretty but in a quite different, less dramatic way. Sally's chin was petite, while Sarah's was strong. Sarah's neck was long and stately, but Sally held hers with more grace. Her face was heart-shaped, and her little lips trembled when she spoke to strangers for she was painfully shy and, thus, all too willing to let her sister sweep all the men from her path. Annabelle had brought peach rosebuds to wear at her own waist that night, but she gave them to Sally for a spot of color. Sally was the girl fellows fell for at a distance, but like the butterfly whose wings perish at the touch, if the gentlemen came too close she could hardly bring herself to speak and the men would always go away disappointed.

Annabelle wore a dress of lace her father had purchased for her on a rare trip to Richmond. It was only cotton, but it was made into a gathering of layers of the most delicate handwork cotton could command. And the shape of the dress was most becoming to her figure. Her father had gotten it for her the year before, and she found when trying it on that night she had filled out a bit, for it fit her far more snugly than her father ever intended, she was sure. Annabelle had the pale peach complexion of a redhead, and her shoulders, budding ever so slightly from the gathered sleeves, were dappled with light freckles. When people described Annabelle, the word they used most often was "striking." "If only she didn't have that red hair," they would say, or "If only Annabelle could cover those birthmarks, she would be quite handsome. But her looks are rather striking, don't you think?"

The three girls arrived at the dance arm in arm, but Sarah was soon asked to join the Virginia reel.

After that, Annabelle turned down one gentleman and then another, not wishing to leave Sally alone. To Annabelle's dismay, Sally turned down all her callers, too, until one fellow in particular began to approach them. This was a man Annabelle knew for certain Sally liked. He had just been made a lieutenant, and Sally's father had introduced the two at a military function several months before. Sally had talked about him ever since but didn't think he'd even taken notice of her.

He approached them slowly, looking to his right and left as if expecting something to pull him away at any moment, but Annabelle watched his progress with glee. Sally's father had given his stamp of approval on Lieutenant James Alton months before, and so she knew Sally could say yes to him if he would only ask her to dance. *But will he gather the courage to ask her?* Annabelle wondered as he slowly made his way.

Finally, he stood in front of Sally.

But Sally put her head down. For one painful moment, Annabelle thought he would turn and leave. But he took a great breath, and to Annabelle's delight, burst forth with a request to dance. Sally agreed but she was so quiet about it, Annabelle had to nod her own head and smile to let the fellow know it.

Sally looked up.

James Alton smiled and clicked his heels lightly and bowed a little, and Annabelle couldn't help but notice the fringe on his sash was shaking slightly as he took Sally's arm.

Annabelle gladly watched them walk across the room. *But, oh, Sally,* thought Annabelle with a grimace, *please hold your head up and smile back at the fellow.* And then, as if Sally heard her friend's thought from across the room, she suddenly looked up at James Alton and gave him a tremulous, beautiful smile, and Annabelle thought the fellow would actually swoon.

As they danced, Annabelle looked about and remembered how they had used this room as schoolgirls, how they loved to torment their professors at assemblies, knowing full well daughters of the well-to-do could never be dismissed from the place. What little urchins they had been.

She wished now she'd appreciated school more—taken advantage of it more. Although her father was always willing to pay the extra fees if she had wished to study Latin or Greek or French, she'd always told him no. She was supposed to be Mrs. Delaney by now, and Michael thought a girl had no need of books.

Then the war began, and the schools had all closed. First to close were the two in-town schools whose teachers signed up for duty as soon as they could. Her own school had only lasted two months longer, and now that she felt a desire to do more, to learn more, she was too old to go back and finish. Much too old. She would never go to school again.

"Pardon me?" Annabelle said absentmindedly, still thinking of her missed opportunities and watching Sally and James as another dance began.

A familiar voice answered, "I believe I said, 'Miss MacBain, may I have the honor of this dance?'"

Annabelle turned and her heart gave a pounding thud.

Malachi Norris looked charming and smooth, though he was smiling at her uncertainly. *By George, he is handsomely fixed up,* was all she could think, but then she felt herself blush with irritation. Why in the world was he here? She'd entertained a passing thought of his coming to the dance, but she assumed he would stay with his aunt in deference to the Quaker ways. If she had believed for a moment he would attend she would never have come. Her first inclination was to refuse him, but she knew this was the very thing people expected, and she felt the crowd watching them already.

Pulling her fan to her chin, her eyes swept the room. In the last day and a half, no one had said anything to her directly about the cemetery incident, but on the street she had received as many concerned looks and dark questions such as, "You are *well* this morning, Annabelle?" as she could possibly stand.

Everyone knew.

Sally and Sarah and Mary Huntington had told her everyone was talking about it. "Annabelle thought someone dug up Samuel Brighton's grave." "Dear Annabelle must be pining for Michael Delaney." "Annabelle is simply overwrought with her father gone, you know." It was horrid. She was only glad to hear no news of someone planning to write her father about the incident, and she was certainly glad they didn't know the whole of it—that this well-groomed fellow standing before her had done the very deed himself. In truth, it was gallant of him to ask her to dance, for it told everyone the Brightons had no quarrel with her.

She looked into his clear blue eyes and gave him a faint smile. "Of course, Mr. Norris."

He grasped her arm much more gently than he had at the stile the day before and, still walking with a slight limp, led her to the dance.

It was a waltz, and as they began to twirl around the room, Annabelle put on her loveliest smile to show everyone what an excellent time she was having. She felt wretched. They passed Sarah being twirled by a dashing colonel, and then they passed Sally and James whose eyes were now locked in a smiling embrace. They passed Annabelle's friends and neighbors dancing with each other and with soldiers she had seen but never knew, and then they passed them all again.

She tipped and crossed her head from side to side and tried not to waltz too close to him, and yet she smelled spice and starched linen and found it very pleasant, all in all. And he danced... well, he danced so expertly that she knew his bringing up was at the least equal to her own.

In fact, if her pride was not so hurt by the knowledge of what people were whispering as they waltzed, she might truly have enjoyed herself, for the music was lovely and the lights were twinkling and he was turning her beautifully, all this despite his leg.

As they passed everyone a third time, Annabelle began to wonder how he could dance so well with a bad leg. It was probably painful. She looked up at him, and he did indeed look pale, as if in pain, so she asked quietly, "Would you be thinking of taking a rest, Mr. Norris?"

He smiled and shook his head. "No, thank you." She wished she hadn't said anything, because she didn't want to begin a conversation and now he suddenly looked as though he might. He pulled her close, and she began to push away slightly, but right away he said, "You have a lovely accent, Miss MacBain." She blushed at that and kept her head down. But he drew her in once more and she smelled the spice and closed her eyes.

"Thank you," was the shortest reply she could give. But when a few seconds of awkward silence followed, she thought better of her curt answer. "'Twas my mother's gift to me." But she used the words as an opportunity to try and draw away from him again.

"Extraordinary." Then he said, almost too quietly for her to hear, "In fact, it makes your gift of song unusually beautiful."

Her face grew hot. She certainly would not thank him for that.

When the dance was done, Annabelle excused herself from him quickly, made her way through the crowd and stepped out on the front porch. Mr. Malachi Norris had spoiled her evening entirely by making plain reference to her on the cemetery hill. How dare he remind her he'd listened to it all—all her private songs and prayers and weepings. She was hurt to the core.

Soon Sally was by her side and then Sarah came out a little breathless. Annabelle pulled her friends close to her and hugged them, thankful they'd come out right then so that Mr. Norris would not follow her. She looked behind her to make certain he was not there and then, satisfied, turned her eyes back to the yard.

The moon was still bright, though not as full as two nights before, and at that hour it sat among the treetops of the stand of maples in the old schoolyard. The young ladies stood for a while silently watching it, and Annabelle began to notice that whenever the wind caused the leaves to flutter, the moon was passed back and forth above the branches like a bright silver ball in the hands of children. She became mesmerized by the silvery glow and breathed deeply of the night.

But the smell of his spice lingered in the lace of her dress, and Annabelle shook her head.

Officers had posted their fine horses in among the maples in case they were called out, so whenever the wind carried the sound to them they could hear the low snorting and whinnies of the horses above the sound of the crickets and cicadas. The beauty of the night made Annabelle ache with loneliness for her father. Somewhere out there he tended a sick soldier. Somewhere out there was a battle, a raid, an arrest, a burning, but here, for a brief moment, one could forget the war and lose oneself in dancing and music. On a night like this, one might even forget the petty rules of etiquette and the back-biting that plague small-town life, but it hardly seemed fair she and the others could be so alive and full of youth.

Annabelle broke her lonely silence by whispering to Sally, "What a kind fellow Lieutenant Alton seems."

Sally lowered her head and nodded with a smile then threw her head up in a bounce. "He's asked if he may come calling!" She looked to each of them expectantly and Sarah and Annabelle smiled in reply.

Then Sarah said, "Good for you, Sally, but you'll make him bring his colonel with him, won't you?" And they giggled. Then Sarah turned and put her arm around Annabelle. "And you did wonderfully well in there, you know. We know you'll be fine, Annie. You just needed some rest, eh?"

Annabelle felt a twinge of irritation. To have the pity of towns-people was one thing, but it was really too much to have one's own friends place the same burden upon you. Yet Annabelle only nodded to Sarah as she thought, *Bear up, little thing, it won't be long before everyone forgets it ever happened.* She mumbled, "That's right. I feel much better already, really I do."

"Yes, it was obvious when you danced the last dance," Sarah said with a wink. "Who *is* he, Annie?"

"The Widow Brighton's nephew, Malachi Norris."

"Malachi Norris, Malachi Norris. That sounds so familiar." Sally stared at Annabelle. "Oh, I wish I could remember..." Sally was famous for remembering the smallest details but notorious for being late with the information. Sometimes weeks would pass and then one day they would all be knitting quietly by the fire with the original conversation long forgotten, and Sally would suddenly say, "Sam August! *That* was the fellow who borrowed Mother's carriage that day! Sam August!" And they would laugh and shake their heads.

Annabelle looked back and forth at the two and smiled.

They heard a strange popping sound in the distance then, and before they could even move aside, the porch was filled with officers and men. They heard the words, "Artillery... Found our pickets... Feeling out our position..."

In the same instant, the fellows rushed back inside to say their good-byes and buckle on their swords. The whole thing was dramatic and exciting to the ladies, several of whom swooned. Others burst into tears on the spot. People began to file out to their carriages, even though some of the officers insisted it was nothing and that they'd return shortly to finish out the reel.

Then James Alton came to Sally with a fearful look on his face. Before Sally could say good-bye, he pulled her to him, kissed her full on the lips and then was gone.

Sally stood there blushing for a moment and then, quietly, she began to cry.

FOUR

We hope for the best and so do all
Whose hopes are in the field,
And we know we will win the day,
For Southerns never yield,
And when we think of those that are away,
We'll look above for joy,
And I'm mighty glad that my Bobby is
a Southern soldier Boy.

From the song,
A Southern Soldier Boy

The next morning the news traveled the road like a windstorm; the pickets were attacked the night before and the wounded brought to the female academy where the dance had been held. Lieutenant Alton, Sally soon discovered, though not wounded, had been called away to headquarters to report on the skirmish.

At noon, Sarah and Sally and Annabelle returned to the academy, no longer in their finery but in common calico and aprons to see what they could do for the lads. They carried in baskets of food they'd spent the morning preparing.

At the door, Annabelle saw Hannah Brighton coming out and she quickly made way for her. She looked at Annabelle in passing and then looked sharply at her as she came to full recognition. "Best thee be getting home to rest, Annabelle," she said.

Annabelle flushed and turned and followed Hannah Brighton down the steps of the school porch.

"Ma'am," she said furtively, catching up with her, "I feel I must apologize to you personally. I can understand how my... my actions might have upset you, but you should understand my position. I know you and Mr. Norris would want to..." She searched for the words. "To be discreet. I want you to know my lips are sealed."

"Thy lips are...? My dear girl, what can thee mean?"

Annabelle turned pale as she said with a gulp, "About... about Mr. Norris digging... digging..." She lowered her voice and looked around. "Oh, please don't make me say it."

"Digging what, Annabelle? Thee still believes someone has touched Samuel's grave?" Her eyes grew wide, then narrowed into slits. "That *my nephew*...? Annabelle, go and get thee some rest, young lady. I will certainly have to write thy father."

"No, no, ma'am, you needn't. Your secret is safe with me. I'll take it to my..." And she blanched to think of what she'd almost said.

"Annabelle MacBain, it is certain thee has need of help. Yes. I'll write thy father this very afternoon." She turned away brusquely, continuing to speak but now to herself, in little bursts and fits, even as Jane escorted her into the carriage.

Annabelle stood in utter confusion in the suffocating heat of the road as Widow Brighton's carriage rolled away.

The whole of it left Annabelle confused and frustrated. Thinking it out, the only thing that made any sense was that Hannah Brighton was protecting herself by acting as if she knew nothing, and then perhaps she was threatening to write Annabelle's father as a way of warning off the girl from speaking of it anymore.

Just then Sally came to tug on her arm and lead her back into the school. And so Annabelle looked up and shook her head and did her best to turn her thoughts to the wounded soldiers lying inside. This would be Annabelle's first experience at nursing, and she was prepared to take her role quite seriously.

Annabelle, Sally, and Sarah stood in the hall briefly before they found someone they could ask for information. One busy, officious looking fellow finally saw them standing there and said, "We thank you heartily for the food, ladies. Leave the goods in the kitchen, if you please."

"But we came to help with the nursing, sir," Annabelle told him.

He smiled and looked at his shoes a moment. "No, miss, thank you, but, no. The food is most appreciated, but I believe we have enough females in the rooms at the moment as would make it possible to reopen the school." He laughed at his own humor and then turned on his heels and went up the stairs with an efficient clip.

The girls looked at each other in profound disappointment, but Annabelle shared her sorrows aloud. "I don't believe I'll ever be a nurse!" she said as they walked toward the kitchen.

A private standing behind them in the back hall spoke up, half-joking, "I wouldn't say that, miss. If you're wanting to help, you should wait for General Lee and the boys coming back from Pennsylvanie. Plenty of work for all of you then, ladies."

Annabelle whirled on him. "What do you mean, sir?"

Sarah and Sally pulled in close to her as the soldier replied calmly, "It's just, uh, we heard there's a whoppin' load of wounded comin' down from a battle fought upwards around Gettysburg... seventeen miles, they said. They're retreatin' now, comin' back."

"Here? They're only seventeen miles from here?" Annabelle's head began to throb.

"No." He coughed. "Seventeen miles of wounded soldiers in ambulance, miss. They're a-comin' back, but thing is we don't know when or where they'll cut across the river."

Annabelle grabbed hold of her friends' hands and looked at one and then the other of them. "Was it very terrible?"

"Yes, miss, 'fraid so. Æ Iss a bad loss to both sides. Worse loss for us... the Cause, I mean. We were wantin' to stay up there and keep fighting. Give 'em the what-for on their own ground."

Annabelle's eyes grew large. "Are you certain about the line of wounded?"

"Wish I weren't, so help me." He shook his head slowly. "Wish we could give them fellows up there half the goods we got here today."

Annabelle felt a pang in her heart so strong it made her wince where she stood, and she wished beyond all wishing she could go to her father. "There must be a way to find out where they'll come across the river."

But the fellow politely shook his head.

The sisters thanked him and tugged on Annabelle's sleeve to bring her to the kitchen. There they took the baked goods from their baskets and laid them on a long table, but Annabelle's thoughts were far away.

She could think only of her father, how exhausted he must be, whether he were hurt or even captured. It was painful not to know, not to be able to go to him, to help him somehow. What if he were imprisoned and sick with no way to tell her?

To head home, Sarah and Sally had to pull on Annabelle's sleeve again, for she was deep in thought. And as they walked back, Annabelle began to list a host of reasons why she should try to go to him. The town would certainly be glad to see her visit him. *They're practically expecting it, if not hoping for it. Shilla and Thomas are able-bodied and loyal and would protect our property while I'm away.*

There was a closet full of her father's medical supplies and she could carry a considerable amount to him... to them. *Yes, and Father must be desperate for them. Why, the entire army would be thankful I came,* she thought grandly.

As a final thought—a crowning glory to her lofty wisdom—she realized how much she would love to be rid of the glances and the whispers of her neighbors, the accidental meetings with Hannah Brighton and Mr. Norris, and the pity of her friends. To take Lucy and be away from here—it would be like running the straight stretch all day long to be so free.

In a short time, she had completely convinced herself of the need to go, and the pain in her heart quite suddenly disappeared.

What she refused to dwell on was the danger in the ride, the fact that she hadn't a pass to travel through Confederate pickets, let alone the Federal lines she may encounter, and lastly and perhaps most important she hadn't a clue as to where to find the army. But these all seemed trifles; she had a fist full of good reasons to go. Go. That is what she would do.

Her thoughts were brutally interrupted then as they heard the noise of a dozen horses in full flight as a group of cavalry came up behind them like thunder, making carriages and wagons sway in their wake and horses rear up in fright. The soldiers waved revolvers above their heads like swords at the ready as some of the finest horses Annabelle had seen in years moved the body of yelling men through town like a steam engine afire. Some of the neighbors thought to cheer them on their way, but the girls barely reached the side of the road in time to avoid being trampled.

A fleeting glimpse of gray was all there was to reveal the fact they were Rebels. Headed east at their furious pace, they were soon out of sight completely.

Now the girls squeezed each other's hands and blinked in wonder and shock. Soon people were in the streets talking about the rushing troops, and then they heard shooting to the southeast toward Purcellville.

"Did you hear that, Annabelle? They say those were Mosby's men!"

"Really?"

"Federals burned a barn toward Purcellville, and those fellows are after them... that's what everyone's saying."

"Oh," said Annabelle faintly. "The Gray Ghost..."

Major John S. Mosby was the head of a group of cavalry men called "Mosby's Rangers." Folks nicknamed him the Gray Ghost because his men could hit a picket, a camp or a convoy with deadly efficiency and then disappear into the woods and hills. Although they appeared as apparitions to their victims, their bullets were found to be quite real.

Today it looked as though Mosby's Rangers had yet again caught up with the purveyors of blue justice. And three girls came near to being trampled in their path.

Annabelle had so hoped the war would stay on the other side of the mountains, south or north of them, anywhere but here, but here it was. And so Hillsborough was as dangerous a place to be as any soldier's camp, and with that thought, she cast the final vote to go.

Soon they were at Annabelle's home and as her friends walked her to the door, she quietly told them her plan. Immediately, Sarah and Sally began to try and dissuade her, but she dismissed their worries with the assurance that she would be fine, that no one would harm a woman on the road, that it wouldn't take long to find the camp. They told her to take Thomas along, and she replied, "Maybe I will. Yes, maybe I will." They were still trying to convince her not to go when she kissed them on each cheek, gave them a firm hug and said good-bye in a gentle but determined manner. They said they would pray for her and she gave them her heartfelt thanks, then shut the door behind her.

And when she was alone she allowed herself to shiver, just once, in reluctant recognition of their fears.

But she left her empty basket where she stood and made her way up the stairs to pack her things, deciding to first fill her saddle-bags with as much quinine, morphine and chloroform as she could reasonably expect Lucy to carry.

When she heard Shilla Flannery coming upstairs, she quickly shoved the goods under the bed and began carefully rearranging her hair.

Even as she told Shilla about the wounded at the Ladies' Seminary and mentioned the news from Gettysburg in passing, she watched Shilla's eyes and thought what a stupid plan this was. How could she leave Shilla and Thomas?

Shilla Flannery was a heavyset woman with thick red hair and green eyes, and though Annabelle judged her to be well into her fourth decade, there was not a strand of gray upon her head. The normally cheerful woman found herself still blessed with the pink cheeks familiar to Irish hill country, though she'd lived in America four years. She was an excellent baker and cook, and she had patiently taught Annabelle everything she knew. Annabelle owed to Shilla a gratitude for teaching her the patience and the humor to be found in housework, but she was the most grateful for her friendship.

Now with a sudden discomfort Annabelle looked away from her. How could she hurt this woman by leaving this way? How could she put her own self in such danger? And she knew her father wouldn't want her to go.

But he needs these supplies, and I can help him, and I need him.
But it was pure stupidity to go on her own. At the same time, it
thrilled her beyond reason, well beyond reason. *I could take Shilla.
Then again, if Shilla came along she would only slow me down...
Slow me down? She would tie me down to keep me from going!* And
she knew Thomas wouldn't let her go, but he was in the fields that
day and not an immediate problem. *He might try to follow me, but,
with his poor eyesight, it'll be nigh on impossible for him to find me.*

Shilla was silent, and Annabelle felt an odd quiet in the room.
"Yer taking the news of the battle right well, miss," Shilla finally
said.

"It's just... I know the Lord will take care of him, Shilla." She
had chosen a comment Shilla was certain not to argue with.

Shilla nodded and left the room, and Annabelle took a long
breath and busily finished packing. Should she wait until dark to
leave? No, that was no good. No time. She would have to leave in
daylight, but without Shilla noticing her.

And so then how would she know where to go? If she could
only know the area in which the troops were traveling, she could
follow the river up and down and find them when they came over.
Mr. Henry came to mind as the one who might be able to tell her
something. Wasn't he often seen at Weaver's Ordinary down the
road? Yes, she would go there.

Quickly she changed into her thickest cotton dress, the russet
brown plaid, thinking it could stand the hard travel. Then, when
Shilla went out back to the garden, Annabelle hurried downstairs
and out the front door, across the road and down the street.

To her relief she saw Mr. Henry at the corner window in the
front. She tapped on the window for him to come out, but to her
dismay he beckoned her to come in. Reaffirming her purpose, she
then set her jaw and whispered to the glass, "All right, Mr. Henry,
I will." And for the first time in her life she walked into a tavern.

All eyes caught on her as she came in, but she raised her chin
and turned to Mr. Henry's table and, to her relief, the men looked
away.

"What is it now, Annabelle?" he asked in a surprised voice.

She sat down at Mr. Henry's corner table, and he sat down as well. Keeping her voice low, she asked, "Mr. Henry, I wonder if you happen to have heard about the battle fought at Gettysburg?"

"O'course."

"Would you then happen to know where they'll be coming down... across the river, I mean?" she asked timidly.

"Why, no, Annabelle." He laughed. "Only the angels and General Lee know that, I'm sure."

"Mr. Henry, I'm desperate to know. I want to find my father."

"I'm sure that's true, Annabelle, and I really wish I could help you." He patted her hand in a most fatherly way, then looked over at Tom, the bartender, and asked if he had any chamomile tea. He then stood up and walked over to the counter to ask again, as Tom had trouble hearing above the tavern's clientele. Annabelle knew he wanted the tea to calm her down. She wasn't sure he would tell her anything, but he stayed at the bar and waited for the tea, and she hoped he was considering an answer. As she sat there in the dark corner of the tavern, she rested her head in one hand and began to pray quietly—for strength to carry out the task, for protection and most of all for wisdom to manage the ride so she could find her father. Raising her eyes to the window, she looked into the sunlight and took its warmth on her face for one peaceful moment but then redirected her gaze to a movement at the door.

She pulled back from the light as she saw Malachi Norris step into the tavern and up to the bar. He put in his order and then looked to his right, and for one frightful moment she thought he would see her, but he was concerned with the fellow next to him at the bar, a Mr. Cummings who had made his money on the railroad east of this area. A solid Confederate. Mr. Norris smiled at Cummings and then said something which made the fellow laugh.

Mr. Cummings lived west of town and well outside of it, but Annabelle's father had tended to him now and again, and so she knew of him. As she watched them, Norris caught Mr. Cummings' eye and then opened his coat briefly to show Mr. Cummings something in his inside pocket. Annabelle's curiosity caused her to lean out of her chair to see what it was, and so, hiding her face with her bonnet, she caught a glimpse.

It was a little white book.

Norris pulled his coat closed.

A white book. A little Bible. Mr. Norris read the Bible. That was nice. But it was white like a lady's Bible, and just like the one his uncle carried. A shock ran from her head to her toes. It was Samuel Brighton's Bible, the one they buried with him. Everyone knew he was buried with it, but as it held no particular significance, Annabelle hadn't remembered.

Until now.

Mr. Cummings nodded at Norris, and now the men made their way to a table on the other side of the room.

She pulled further back into the corner and lowered her head in thought. When she was a little girl, she had noticed Brighton's odd Bible because on visits with her father, he took it out often to read passages, and she'd believed it peculiar that a fellow would own a lady's white Bible.

With the delightful simplicity of the eight-year-old female mind, she had laid the problem out in front of her, put the pieces together and figured out the answer all by herself: *If men in the Quaker church carry little white Bibles, then Quaker women must carry the big old black Bibles, and of course, we Methodists do just the reverse, and that must be why we worship in separate buildings.*

By the time she was old enough to know better, she had found that the mystery of Brighton's little white Bible was even easier than she had imagined—it had belonged to his mother.

And he always kept it in his wide breast pocket, just as it sat in Norris' pocket now. Annabelle had a sudden headache trying to take in this new thing.

The clink of a teacup on the table brought her back to the present as Mr. Henry gently sat a steaming cup of chamomile in front of her, but her mind reeled with the robbing of graves, how Hannah Brighton had acted as if Annabelle were crazy, and how this fellow now had Samuel Brighton's Bible and was using it as some sort of secret... something or other. Could this still be a part of something his aunt had asked him to do? What in the name of heaven was going on?

One thing was certain—she wasn't about to ask Malachi Norris anything about it.

But Mr. Henry was staring at her.

She cleared her throat, thanked him for the tea, and drank from the steaming cup as quickly as she could without burning her lips. She then whispered to Mr. Henry so as not to alert Mr. Norris of her presence, "Can you help me?"

And he whispered back, as if speaking to an inmate in a mental institution, "No - but - I- think - you - should - rest- and - we'll - write - your - father - all - about - it." The look he gave her as he spoke the words almost made her laugh out loud.

She nodded with a little smile and said she would indeed rest, and then she stood up and tried to move to the door as inconspicuously as possible. She glanced at the far table as she went out and saw with some relief Mr. Norris' back was to her. *Yes, I will rest, Mr. Henry, just as soon as I find my father,* she told herself while shutting the tavern door behind her.

The street was only mildly busy, with a few carts and wagons parked or moving about and two or three people carrying things to and from the stores. A couple of men loitered at the hotel down the street, but there was no sign of soldiers, rushing or otherwise, at the moment. Although the heat was sweltering and the humidity near to intolerable, the main road was quite comfortable to walk along, for Hillsborough had long enjoyed the miracle of a well-planned avenue. Maple and oak trees planted on either side of the street a hundred years before had grown up along with the town and now intertwined overhead, creating a leafy, shaded tunnel for passersby.

Annabelle strolled slowly away from the tavern under the shade, index fingers poised at her lips, trying to think whom she could go to next for information.

She lowered her hands as she decided to head back to the academy and try her luck there. But as she gathered her skirts to quicken her pace westward, her forearm was gently taken by a warm hand.

Mr. Norris was at her side, and with the shock of recognition, she gave him a look of wonder, but he just smiled pleasantly in reply. And so she slowed her pace and they began to walk past her church as he asked her quite calmly how her day had progressed. She had no reason to believe he'd seen her in the tavern.

But as he spoke she did wonder at the taking of her arm in escort. The road was not busy at the moment, and so she needed no polite form of protection. He was certainly no friend or lover, and so she couldn't imagine what to make of his behavior. She also noted that his limp had disappeared as they walked. Very strange. Very odd.

She watched the faces of people they passed on the street and blushed self-consciously, wrapped as she was in the youthful certainty they were being whispered about.

"Very well, thank you," was the smiling reply she gave to all his veiled inquiries as they passed the stone church, hardly knowing if her answer fit the questions. It was considered rude for a gentleman to ask a question of a lady outright, and so although she wondered at the taking of her arm, the rest of his manners seemed intact. "I was just heading for the academy," she said, "to see if... I could lend a hand."

He smiled. "With all the help they have up there, surely you have time to stroll down by the water? I haven't been down there since I was a child." And then he gently steered her to their left down the path toward the creek.

Now she didn't care for his behavior at all. It was most improper.

She began to pull her arm from him and decline his invitation when he stopped a few feet down and interrupted her in an angry whisper, "Just what do you mean by spying on me back there, Miss MacBain?" All show of manners was gone.

He had changed nature so suddenly she couldn't think at first how to reply, but he was watching her and waiting with a look in his eye that made her wish she had a good answer. "Well, I, I wasn't intentionally doing so, Mr. Norris," she finally stammered, feeling confused and offended all at once.

He released his grasp and crossed his arms to continue in controlled anger, "Well, I'd appreciate your leaving things well enough alone... as you promised. No need for you to play the spy."

"Yes, yes. I mean, no. Mr. Norris, I hardly know where to begin. Shall I apologize once more? I only came to the tavern to ask Mr. Henry a question." But she wondered why he kept using the word spy. She wasn't spying, was she? Was she?

He gave a short laugh to her reply and she knew he didn't believe her, so she added with irritation, "Mr. Norris, I've stated my business to you plainly, although I hardly expect you could explain your recent rendezvous to me."

At the word "rendezvous," his mood changed once more. His arms dropped a little and his eyes studied her. As she stared back into his rigid face, a rather brilliant thought popped into her mind: perhaps *he* was the spy that he could accuse her so readily of spying. As her father liked to say, "To a hammer, everything is a nail." The grave, the rendezvous, the Bible, the mystery of them all; yes, his odd behavior might find an explanation in the word *spy*.

Her eyes narrowed. The fellow was suddenly uncertain, and the way he stood there waiting for her to continue—well, it made her feel positive she was right, and then the sense of power she suddenly felt caused her to almost burst out laughing. Her lip curled slightly. "Yes. Your *rendezvous*." And although it was indelicate to point, and although she was nervous in the delivery of the words, with her pinky she touched the place on his coat where the little leather book rested.

Having given no forethought to what she really might have seen at the tavern or, for that matter, what a few words to a potential spy could do, she could hardly have anticipated his response. He grabbed her arm as if she'd given him a fatal blow, threw his face into hers and said under his breath, "What do you want, then? What's your part?"

It struck Annabelle that she had gotten herself into something awful and deep, like stepping into a sandbox to play only to find it filled with quicksand.

Annabelle gulped and her eyes flew open wide as honesty became her only defense. "I hoped Mr. Henry knew where my father... I just want to find my father, Dr. Ludwell MacBain, Assistant Surgeon to the 43rd Battalion. I want to go and find my father!" She tried to yank her arm away from him. "You may let me go, sir!"

He looked at her with a strange mix of anger and raw energy. He hissed, "It is for certain I'm owed a better explanation than that. Come down the hill a ways, please." And he walked her firmly to the back corner of the church. She followed him meekly at first, but then with more strident steps as she realized this was the fellow who might have the very information she needed. Then he stopped and turned on her. "There. You may have your arm back. Now explain yourself if you can."

She returned his glare and did not blink. "I went into the tavern to discover where the troops coming from Pennsylvania are heading, but I found rather a different bit of information than that for which I'd been looking. And now that I've thought upon it, I believe *you* could answer my question better than Mr. Henry or anyone else in town, with the exception, perhaps, of your Mr. Cummings."

He smiled slightly and surprised her with a quick reply. "How in heaven's name should I know where your father is?"

But his lower lip twinged slightly, and immediately Annabelle felt he knew exactly where her father was, and all her fears left her.

FIVE

I met Mr. Catfish comin' downstream,
And I says, "Mr. Catfish, what do you mean?"
Took Mr. Catfish by the snout,
And turned Mr. Catfish inside out.

From the minstrel song
Turkey in the Straw,
by Daniel Decatur Emmett

Annabelle was quite calm as the next move in the now danger-ous game formed in her mind. "If you don't tell me where I can find my father, I'll be happy to tell the Widow Brighton who you are, and who you're not, and you can explain to her yourself how you came to have her husband's Bible."

His eyes remained steady, and then he lifted his shoulders toward her slightly and said, "She gave it to me." He brought his shoulders down as if that were the end of the discussion.

"Now I know you are a liar," she replied with equal calm. "We all know he was buried with it. And it'll only be a small matter of a question to Hannah Brighton for me to discover the whole of it."

"You don't know anything more?" he asked plainly.

Carefully she answered, "I believe I know enough."

He stared at her, pressed his lips together and then slowly pulled out the Bible. She looked at it and felt sick to think where it had been not so long ago. As Norris looked upon the volume, he said calmly as if noting the time of day, "Then, Miss MacBain, I believe you have compromised the situation enough by your ignorance; it is time you knew a little more. You are true to the Confederacy?"

"I am," she said in wonder.

Annabelle had heard of spying, bribery, and the like, for the

Cause. Friends she knew had flirted with Federal officers, and in their own way, scouted for information, sometimes succeeding in getting what they were after. It was all quite wonderful to hear about it, but now that she was being drawn into it herself, it did not seem so thrilling. He was a spy after all? Truly? *What have I gotten myself into?* she wondered as she stared at him.

He glanced at her as he turned the Bible over in his hands and lifted it up. "Samuel Brighton's Bible." Annabelle shivered and gave a slight nod. "What you perhaps don't know is that Brighton held a list of tried and true men who would help when needed—written within. You didn't know this?" Annabelle shook her head, deprecatingly. "None of the men knew anyone else on the list," he continued. "They only knew Brighton would call them when they were needed. You see? I came here to find the book, by any means necessary. Do you understand now?"

"I think so. I had no idea. Then his widow doesn't..."

"She doesn't know I've *retrieved* his Bible. No."

Annabelle licked her lips. "She really does think I've lost my mind, then, and with good cause."

He smiled wanly. "I couldn't understand myself why you didn't tell her I dug him up. I suppose I'd begun to agree with her."

"I thought she'd asked you to dig him to retrieve something from his... person perhaps she hadn't wished buried."

"Aah. So simple, and so very proper. Of course. I should have thought of it." He leaned against the stone wall of the church, placing the sole of one foot against the wall and rubbing his thumb across his bottom lip in further thought. "But of course, there's no reason Mrs. Brigh... Aunt Hannah should hear of this."

Annabelle looked back up the hill to the road as she wondered aloud, "But a Quaker man, Mr. Norris? I don't understand."

"He is... was, of course. Perhaps he became involved when his sons joined up."

"Ah."

"I had to be discreet in asking after this book, but I found out from the servants with little enough trouble."

Annabelle pressed her palms together, looked down, then

opened her hands and smiled. "When you could have asked anyone in town and they could have told you, but I suppose that
would have drawn suspicion."

"Just so," he replied.

They stood in silence for a while. Annabelle listened to the birds
and the crickets and the sound of the creek bubbling nearby and
wondered how life could get so complicated so quickly when
nothing like this had ever crossed her path before. Annabelle
looked up finally to find him staring at her.

He said gently, "And now that your curiosity is satisfied, we may
let it go at that."

Her face grew hot then cold. "No, we may not."

His voice grew more stern now. "What possible good will it do
you to know your father's position?"

Position. She didn't like the military sound of his question. It
made her stomach tighten, but she raised her eyes to him. "He was
at Gettysburg." He nodded once, and his mouth visibly tightened.
"And I want to help him, if I can. He needs me, I'm sure, and so I
have to find their camp."

He shook his head. "If he needs you so badly, how come you
ain't there already?"

His question burned her through and through. She looked
down. "I'll be taking medicine for him."

There was a long quiet before he finally said with a note of irritation, "Well, it isn't possible for you to get to him without getting
yourself killed. Does your daddy want you killed?" She ignored the
question. And so he said a bit more loudly, "Look. They're being
followed by General Meade's entire army. And could be... *will be*
attacked at any moment. Do you hear? They'll be in the thick of
things again any day now."

"Well, once General Lee crosses the river, they'll be safe," she
answered stubbornly.

"Safer anyway, perhaps, but they can't cross. The river is too
deep from the flooding."

Annabelle started toward him. "So you do know! Tell me.
Please!"

"No, I don't! The whole river's flooded."

"You do know. You do know! You have to tell me." Her eyes grew bright as he stared back at her. "Or I'll tell Hannah Brighton, and they'll be after you for robbing the grave."

"For a little Bible? Try not to be so ridiculous. I tell you I don't know anything, Miss MacBain, and so I can't help you." Then changing tack, he added, "You wouldn't call out the hounds on me, would you?" He smiled uncertainly.

But Annabelle's sixth sense was working wonders for her that day, for she brushed aside his reply, and stared him down once more. "I can follow you to him."

"You couldn't," he said, losing all pretense of a smile.

"My Lucy was best in the Hunt last year, Mr. Norris, and she rides even faster for me. Do you want to take that chance?"

Unable to hide his anger any longer, he said, "You don't understand. What I'm doing is for the Cause, Miss MacBain, and while I'm sure the paltry sum of medicine you could take on a long, dangerous ride, likely gettin' yourself killed on the way, would please your father just no end..."

But Annabelle interrupted to tighten the noose about his neck. "I don't give a fig for the Cause, sir. I only care about my father, and you will tell me where to find him." He looked briefly as if he wanted to strangle her, which scared her enough to add, "But why should I go all the way to Brighton House with my information? I could just go up this hill and tell people your secret. Or..." Her eyes flashed. "I could stand right here and bring them to me in an instant with one cry for help." Her cheeks burned with energy as she looked at him.

He pushed himself from the wall. "Why, you little..." But he seemed to check himself when Annabelle stepped back and opened her mouth as if she would cry out. And then he began to pace—up the hill five steps and then down the hill five, up and down, clenching and unclenching his fists and muttering under his breath.

Annabelle crossed her arms and watched him, with every intention of calling out in the next instant if he wouldn't tell her. She had made her choice and felt oddly exhilarated by it all. She wanted to burst with... what? Tears? Laughter? Ah, she had him. There was only one thing in her mind, and that purpose justified everything. He may work for the Cause, but she, too, wanted to do something for the troops. Why should he stop her from going? She was just a girl, for goodness' sake; it was impossible she could foil his task, whatever that may be.

But as she watched, the horrid thing she was doing to this fellow, now pacing before her like a caged animal, began to eat away at her. She stepped toward him and said as mildly as she could, "Mr. Norris, please. I'm only a girl. I want to see my father. I want to take medicines to him. What harm could there be in telling me where he is? After all, if you don't tell me, you know I'll only find out from someone else. I'm going to go to him no matter what you tell me, even if I have to start on the road without knowing."

He stopped pacing and looked at her for a very long time, seeming to weigh his decision this way and that before his shoulder slumped and he replied. "And you would, wouldn't you?"

"Yes, I would," she said firmly.

He looked up, shook his head and let his mouth drop open as he took a deep breath. Then after seeming to clear his mind, he dropped his head forward and nodded. "All right. I'm going to take a risk, Miss MacBain. The risk is that you'll start on this trip, but you'll have sense enough to quit when you're in over your head."

Annabelle pulled her hands together pensively and nodded.

He went on with controlled emotion, "And I will tell you if you promise me two things. You must wait for them to cross the Potomac, and if you see or hear cannons as you wait, you will get yourself behind the nearest mountain, because the cannon's shell tears apart anything it finds, Miss MacBain, irrespective of man, woman or child. And if you think that sounds overly dramatic, I can assure you no amount of description could disappoint..." But he looked up the hill as he spoke the last words and let them fall away from him even as he wiped his hands on his lapels.

Annabelle could see he knew whereof he spoke.

He looked down, took a breath and sighed. "Your father would want you to take care of yourself, wouldn't he? I presume he wouldn't want to find you in a lineup for his services at the surgery tent or have the displeasure of never finding you at all."

His words struck a fearful chord in her and she agreed with a strong nodding. "I promise."

"Very well. Secondly, if anyone, *anyone*, asks you where you got this information, you must not describe me to them in any way. You will forget who told you."

"I promise."

"Yes, but can I trust your promise?" He shook his head and laughed a little, obviously disgusted with his predicament. "You see, my life will depend upon it, and that is the possible harm you speak of so inconsequentially, Miss MacBain."

Annabelle thought carefully for a moment. "I can give you a sign of pledge. I'll give you my father's ring."

She took the school ring from her skirt pocket, a souvenir she'd tucked there, thinking to take it to her father, and she handed it to Mr. Norris firmly. She would have given him her mother's ring, but she couldn't bear the thought of removing it from her finger; it meant too much to her.

Mr. Norris examined the ring and smiled. "The College of William and Mary, eh?" Annabelle nodded. "My father, too," he said, and Annabelle smiled briefly in reply. Then he tucked the ring in his breast pocket. "All right, then." He looked up and down the hill. "They're camped on the Potomac above Harper's Ferry across the river at Williamsport, Maryland, probably praying the water will go down before Meade can get at them again."

She felt a sense of calm triumph at hearing the words. She could be there tomorrow. She could be with her father tomorrow! For this she was more than glad, but the image and the awfulness of war came again to her as she thought of the waiting wounded and tired troops, defeated in body and soul, camping by the flooding water. Michael could be there among the wounded, or he could already be dead. Her father would be working around the clock for days, she knew, and it hurt her with a physical pain to think how he must feel. Her eyes filled with tears. She had to go and help.

"Do you have any idea how hard it will be for you to get up there?" he asked.

"My mind is made up, sir."

He shook his head. "That may be, but the armies may force a second opinion on you. Your maid won't be enough escort. You should hire a field hand, someone you can trust who's good with a gun."

She smiled lightly and nodded, swaying her skirts ever so lightly.

But he was watching her eyes and, suddenly dropping his arms to his sides in amazement, he said, "I don't believe it. You're going to try and go alone, aren't you!" He laughed. "Are you insane?"

"Well, now, I'd only be living up to everyone's expectations, sir, since I'm the young lady thinks she sees graves dug up in the middle of the night." She smiled demurely as he shook his head. But even as she gave such a flippant reply, the audacity of her actions struck her full in the face and caused her to blush.

He said under his breath and without humor, "Your father lets you take a wagon out alone?"

"Certainly." She smiled, but then added, "No wagon. On my horse. My Lucy."

He grunted and said, "On Lucy. Of course. You've been out alone quite often, then?"

"Yes," she said confidently.

"With no thought for your reputation, I suppose?" His eyes swept her up and down as he spoke.

She blushed with anger and snapped, "I take Lucy out riding, that's all. I can't very well take her for a run with two people on her back, now can I?" But he had struck a sore point, the subject of many arguments with her father. Why couldn't she continue riding Lucy as she always had? She was a better rider than ever. It didn't make sense to give it up just because "ladies" were supposed to ride in wagons. She was a lady, but she happened to like riding a horse.

He crossed his arms and gave half a laugh. "Well, then, and when you are out riding, what do you do when you see Federals?"

Quickly she put her head down.

"I said, what do you do when you see…"

"I heard you, sir. It's just... I've never run into soldiers on the road." Then she looked up. "But they've always been polite to us when they've come around for food. They have nothing to fear from me."

He put his hands up to his face and let out a sigh. "They have nothing to fear." He dropped his hands and looked at her again. "You can't... you really can't go by yourself, Miss MacBain. You do understand that, don't you?" He looked at her with exasperation as she stared blankly back. "You... you really don't understand, do you?" Annabelle said nothing and his irritation grew. "Look, if soldiers meet you out on the road, sometimes they'll be polite, yes, sometimes they do as they're ordered. And sometimes they'll take you in and interrogate you. You must know that much, with the provost marshal nearby. Do you understand me? I'm not even sure you could trust Confederates."

She shook her head. "Our troops have thrown out the provost marshal from Harper's Ferry!" she said obstinately. She didn't want to understand.

"And then there's bushwhackers."

She looked away. "I'm going to my father, sir. That's all. My father needs me."

He gripped his hands together and laughed. "Well, well. Your father needs you." He looked heavenward. "How can I argue with that?"

She blushed and began to feel a pang of remorse for her stubbornness. She thought, here was a man whose purpose it was to help the stranded troops, gathering resources to save them, her father among them. What a fool she was to have threatened to harm him; the madness of the moment had overwhelmed her good sense, and she was greatly ashamed. "But I'm sorry I have been a burden to you, sir. Go and save my father, please, sir, and God bless you."

"Only God can save your father, Miss MacBain," he said, pulling himself up straight.

She tensed but then smiled and nodded. "My father has said the same many times. Let me say rather you will be in my prayers, sir. Godspeed."

"You will be in my prayers, too, Miss MacBain."

"Thank you." She looked down and said shyly, "And I'm... I'm glad to see your limp has... improved."

"My limp?" And then he burst out laughing which made Annabelle look up at him and stare. "Yes, yes, my limp. Much improved. Absolutely." But he was still laughing, and hearing it completely unnerved her.

She blushed and ran back up the hill, but halfway up he called out, "Miss MacBain!"

She turned to look at him.

He said rather stonily, "I asked you before, do you know what to do when you see Federals?"

She bit her lower lip.

"The answer is, you don't. All right? You don't see them and they won't see you. You even think you see blue, you head for the hills. All right? And you do the same with the boys in gray. And any men you may see, for that matter."

She nodded quickly and then turned and finished running up the hill. Now she felt as though something were finally going right. The journey would go well; she was sure of it. All would be well.

But when she got back to the house with her hopes and expectations full, Shilla deflated her happy thoughts by greeting her at the door to tell her Birdie had gotten out of her stall at Brandenburg's. Annabelle had come home victorious, having played the spy and won the game, feeling a new sense of purpose and ready to embark on a wonderful adventure, and now their old horse would keep her in town looking for her, possibly for hours.

The situation was ridiculous. "Can't you get her for me, Shilla?"

"No, miss, if you please. Ye know Birdie runs away from me and bites me when I catch her, and I'm due to take this stew to Mistress Hattie, and she has some sewing she wants me to do. Sure'n it'll have to be yerself and the Brandenburg boy. I'm already late, miss, from waiting to tell ye."

That was all true enough. Annabelle knew Thomas could wrestle with Birdie, but he was already in the fields. She also knew someone would bring Birdie back eventually, but something might happen to the old nag before then, especially with so many soldiers about, and although Birdie wasn't much of a horse at her age, her father had a love for her as a favored animal. She hated the thought, but she would have to go and find her.

But then she realized this could be the perfect means to leave without raising a suspicion. Shilla would think she was out looking for Birdie. It was perfect! On the other hand, she would actually have to find Birdie, and quickly, before Shilla returned from Mrs. Humboldt's. For once in her life, she prayed Mistress Hattie would detain Shilla for the rest of the day.

As she walked to Brandenburg's in a determined march, she remembered that although it was late in the season, it was still likely Birdie had gone hunting for strawberries at Mr. Jacobs' farm. She shook her head with dismay. Mr. Jacobs had his nerve planting his strawberry patch not fifty feet from the road, and so he deserved to have it served up to the animals. Last year, she'd politely suggested he move it back from the road, and he had replied to Annabelle in his halting stutter, "N-n-n-now I can't be, uh, uh, bothered. You keep a better eye on that there horse!"

Two weeks later, Federal soldiers reaped Mr. Jacobs' harvest. She couldn't believe he'd let the stand come up there again this year, but he had. People didn't like to change things much, not for war or any other petty inconvenience.

She saddled Lucy and then asked the Brandenburgs' youngest son, Will, to help her find Birdie. Will was always game for adventure, and so the two headed east and then turned south toward Jacobs' farm.

But as they traveled, she realized something was wrong along the road, and then she remembered the skirmish from that morning. She knew they shouldn't have come this way by themselves, but she'd never seen the results of these fights before now and curiosity, morbid and inglorious as it was, made her suddenly spur Lucy onward. Will gave her a knowing look and followed.

Her gaze was drawn to several holes in the stone fences along the way. That probably meant artillery or cavalry had passed through. The homes held an eerie silence, and Annabelle had to think on it before she realized there were no animals to be seen or heard. At the Howard place, she turned Lucy and went up through a scraggly hole in the stone fence to see more closely what had happened. She came to the side of the house and found herself staring at the chicken pen.

Feathers were scattered there. And her stomach lurched to see a gory hog's head, pale and bleeding, lying in the hot sun. Flies had gathered there and on the dead chickens. Her stomach turned again and again, and she decided not to investigate more when she saw something out of the corner of her eye at the house. She was paralyzed with fright before she recognized Mrs. Howard at the front window. It hadn't occurred to her the family would still be here.

"Are you all right, Mrs. Howard?" she called out shakily.

"Yes, Annabelle, but they've killed all our livestock. Retribution, they said, for Mosby's raid yesterday south of here. But Mosby came through after them, bless God!"

"Yes, I heard. Oh, but I'm sorry to see this. May I help?"

"No. No, thank you. Sam's due back soon with some help. I wouldn't want you dirtying your dress, dear. You go on. You know we'll manage."

Yes, everyone is getting good at managing, Annabelle thought angrily *whether they like it or not.* She pulled hard right on Lucy's rein and returned to the road. A tingling fear began crawling up her spine as she moved toward Mr. Jacobs'. She wondered if they'd hit his place, for he was as much secessionist as the Howard Family. She didn't have long to wonder. She saw his burned out barn as soon as she came to the bend in the road, so she trotted Lucy toward the place. Will kept up behind her without a word.

Mr. Jacobs and some of his children were in the side yard cleaning up the mess. When he heard Annabelle ride up, he straightened and stood solemnly watching their approach. Lucy stepped side to side as Annabelle and Mr. Jacobs watched each other for a long, sad minute. He finally said in his familiar way, "Bu-Bu-Bu-Birdie went to eat them. Shu-Shu-She picked a bad time to hunker for them berries, Annabelle."

A bolt of fear struck her as she looked over at the strawberry patch. At the edge of the last row lay a dead horse.

Annabelle dismounted and walked over to Birdie slowly, carefully. She saw the wounds in the neck and the head as she approached, and the tears sprung to her eyes.

She hadn't realized Mr. Jacobs was behind her until he spoke almost in her ear and put his hands gently on her shoulders as she cried. "F-f-f-fellow said, 'This, uh, uh, this one ain't worth takin', boys,' a-and he just shot her. He ups and shoots her! N-n-n-no good Yank had n-n-n-no right." He squeezed her shoulders.

Annabelle pulled her hand to her mouth and leaned back on Mr. Jacobs, biting down hard against her knuckle and crying great rolling tears.

Birdie was the most gentle, loving horse they'd ever had. Slow, yes, but oh so gentle. Her father had planned to retire her, but the war came up and she had had to keep on serving them. She was just a horse, but that's why shooting her was such a pointless, common thing to do. Annabelle looked at Mr. Jacobs and wiped her tears as he said, "There, there, Annabelle. We'll take, uh, uh. We'll bury her n-n-n-next to this here, uh, uh. Right here, if you like."

"She would like that, I think," Annabelle said with a little smile. "So very, very kind of you," she managed before bursting out with, "Oh, Mr. Jacobs, will it ever end?"

"D-d-d-don't know. Uh, uh, uh, only good thing. There ain't nothing good about it! Dang. Least there a-a-a-ain't nothing left to take."

Except what's left of our dignity, Annabelle thought but she kept the morbid words to herself. As she looked at poor Birdie, she felt even more strongly it was time to go to her father. She'd never felt so unsafe in her life.

Will Brandenburg interrupted her forlorn thoughts. "Kin I help bury him, Miss Annabelle?"

Annabelle sniffed. "Thank you, Will."

Will immediately went to find a shovel.

And in our small world, Annabelle thought, *this stupid war cre-*

ates a cast of thieving marauders wandering about dressed as soldiers, spouting orders to justify their deeds. It was true Major Mosby's men were the only ones to keep any sense of order and law in this part of the state, for in the towns, there were no banks, no schools, no markets, no commerce of which to speak. Annabelle thought of the man in a nearby town living in a house he didn't own, all because the bank shut down while he was trying to buy it.

She mounted Lucy and thought all in all it was a crazy, fool hard life for everyone around here. As Annabelle stared at Birdie lying still on the ground before her, Lucy pulled toward the old animal and made a snorting kind of snuffle that caused tears to spring to Annabelle's eyes once more.

Yes, she desperately needed her father to tell her everything would be all right.

She galloped back to town and drew up short at Brandenburg's stable where she dismounted and walked quickly to the tack room. She took her father's English saddle—Birdie's old saddle—from the wall and loosened her own sidesaddle from Lucy's backside. Throwing her father's saddle across Lucy, Annabelle noted that Brandenburg had kept it well-oiled—the leather shined with age and beauty—and in a trice the polished saddle was strapped on. She smiled as she remounted. A hundred times she'd wondered what it was like to use a "real" saddle. Now there was no one to stop her from finding out.... Well, no one, that is, once she was out of the town.

And so she rode Lucy in a pretend sidesaddle down the street as patiently as she could.

She rode Lucy around to the back of her house and worked to catch her breath before reentering their home. Opening the kitchen door slowly, she called out for Shilla, but received no answer. "Thank you, Miss Hattie," Annabelle said with a smile and a sigh.

She ran upstairs and packed the rest of her belongings in a whirlwind, filling the saddlebags with the last little things she could think of that might bring her father comfort: a change of clothes, a couple of surgery aprons, and a flask of good brandy. Since she'd never been west of Harper's Ferry in her life, she took her father's old map from the wall, carefully folded it and placed it in her waist purse. She tied the purse at her belt, and then she removed the crinoline she wore. "I won't be needing hoops where I'm going."

When she was done, she took a look around; she hadn't emptied the medicine closet by any means, but she had a considerable load to carry. And she must hurry.

She flew downstairs to the kitchen, and the grim thought occurred she might never see this place again, and so she looked about the room for a moment.

Plastered and whitewashed, the kitchen was once a log cabin finished to look equal to the home; even the ceiling beams were white, so that the whole of it, blessed with a good number of windows, was filled with light and a sense of cleanliness. The dried herbs and apples and the clutter of crockery on the open shelves, and the huge black stove that came out from the wide stone fireplace—in those few spare seconds Annabelle saw that the kitchen was the heart of their home, a thing she never would have considered just a few years before. Now staring at the table in the kitchen's center, she thought that although there was no work quite as hot and nasty as jarring, there was also nothing quite as lovely as seeing jar after jar and row after row of glass burdening their long table when a jarring day was done. In the late afternoon, the sun would crest the Short Hills Mountain and shine through the double windows and light those jars from within as they lay out to cool. The blueish jars would glow with gold, amber and ruby. Peas looked like emeralds and tiny onions like brilliant pearls, and Annabelle could look on their work and feel incredibly happy: there was the work of their hands before them and it was beautiful to behold.

But there was no end to jarring until every bit of food was done, every last bit. For there was little money to supplement their garden, which was fair enough since there was no food at the stores asking to be bought. And now Shilla would have to do the jarring alone for a while. The thought depressed Annabelle terribly, and she almost sat down at the table and gave in to it.

But she looked up to the ceiling beams, blinked back the tears and shook her head. "No, I can't stay here, either. Home is with my father."

She made herself walk about the kitchen to gather a small store of foodstuffs, enough to last about three days. She trusted nature to provide for Lucy. Then she placed her straw bonnet on her head and tied the ribbon in a nerve-stricken but determined way.

Finally, she wrote the note.

With a trembling hand she told Shilla and Thomas she was taking medicine to her father, that she knew exactly where he was, that it would be a short trip and she would be all right (she prayed the same even as she wrote), not to worry and not to follow her. She signed with her love, underlining with a scroll the word "love" as if somehow that little gesture would make everything all right. No, it was not enough.

"I am in God's hands," she wrote below it all. She placed the note on the kitchen table, then snatched it back up. The living room mantel would be best. It would take a little longer to find.

She walked to the living room and picked up the heavy saddlebags. She knew Thomas would come after her, but first Shilla would have to find him in the fields. Thomas would then have to discover where the troops were, just as she had, and he'd have to find someone to go with, and so she was fairly certain he would not find her, or at the least he wouldn't catch up with her.

Just a bit younger than Shilla and strong as an ox, Thomas O'Brian worked their gardens and handled the animals. In the fall of 1862 he had begun to hire himself out to local farmers. He was, as the farmers would say, a strapping man, with a long face and rolling shoulders. He had a perpetual farmer's tan, and the deep brown of his face caused his clear blue eyes to leap out at you with their light.

Thomas always had a smile for Annabelle and she in return thought he was the most gentle giant she had ever met. The only reason Thomas hadn't been pressed into armed service was his poor eyesight. But this was a thing that mattered little in the fields and backyards that were familiar to him, and Annabelle had more than once and rather selfishly thanked God he'd been cursed with those eyes.

She felt a twinge of guilt for causing trouble for Thomas, but it was only a twinge.

Then she was off.

Now riding Lucy slowly west down Main Street, Annabelle greeted people in her most ladylike manner. A few took a curious look at the pack behind her, a pyramid of saddlebags and bundles cinched together with a belt that circled her waist, but she only smiled pleasantly in reply. Most town folk would assume the goods were for the wounded up at the school. Soon enough they would all know she had lost her mind, and soon enough she wouldn't care in the least what they thought. She was leaving the long rows of buildings, their stone and log and frame, the quiet smoke rising from chimneys, the sound of the axe and saw, and the hum of the grinding wheels of the mills; she was leaving the carts and horses and commerce waiting for their owners to push them into service, but most of all she was leaving their owners—the wives and daughters and husbands who whispered as Annabelle walked by.

And she was more than glad to go.

As the last home was well behind her, she straddled Lucy, then struck her flanks, throwing the horse forward into a lovely canter.

She would head northwest toward Harper's Ferry and continue north along the Potomac River past Shepherds Town toward the river at Williamsport.

A mile outside of town, she slowed Lucy to a pace just to take in the view. The fields rolled out to either side in a quilt of rich colors and cloth; green and gold, corn and corn stubble, hay and grass lay in patchwork all the way to the Blue Ridge Mountains a few miles distant. She sighed. Her father told her this view was very much like the hills of her mother's Scotland; she wished fervently she could be in Scotland with her father now—wished, in fact, she could be with them both there. She paced Lucy into a trot as the "hills of Scotland" brought pleasant memories to mind—her father's story of how her parents first met.

The son of a prominent Virginian doctor, after he had graduated from college, Annabelle's father was sent like many other privileged children of the time on a grand tour of Europe. But unlike others in his group, he wanted to see Scotland. To visit the medical school at the University of Edinburgh "in honor of the family name, boys," he said cheerfully, but his friends could not understand why he cared to see "the backward state of Scotland."

He parted company with the tour and headed north to Edinburgh, half hoping to find some of his own clan. Well, in a sense he did meet family, Annabelle thought wryly. On his way back from Edinburgh he met her mother.

In those days, it was acceptable to stop at someone's home and ask for a night's lodging. He was an hour from the Scottish town in which he planned to rest when he heard music from over a hill of heather.

"Like in a dream," he would say, *"I walked toward the sound and found a cottage nestled in a vale. The home looked more like something from a fairy tale than anything I've ever seen. I was so sure little fairies would open the door for me if I knocked that I brought myself to the window instead and peeked in to see if it was real."* Then he would wink at Annabelle and say something to the effect, *"Most rude of me, most rude, but quite lucky from your point of view, I suppose. There was your mother, curls brushed to each little ear, and a face bright with concentration, drawing forth musical nectar from the yellowed keys of an old pianoforte. I stood at the window for at least an hour, afraid if I moved I'd break the spell. I watched her as she played and I came to know her there—her brilliance as she played the masters, her cheerfulness with a jig, and her empathy with the songs of her own people. I even caught the look in her eye when she played a lullaby. At the end of the hour, I checked my heart and found that it was gone from me."*

Annabelle smiled as she rode along, and a tear trickled down her face.

Her father would end the happy tale by saying, *"And when she finished her music, she startled me by turning to the window where I stood and furnishing me a curtsy with a charming sweep of her gown.*

When she rose up, our eyes met, and... she... well, she consented to be my wife, didn't she?"

Annabelle wished she'd also heard her mother tell the story. She wanted to know how her mother had felt about it all; when her mother had known her father was listening and what she thought when she found out the listener standing entranced at her window was an American. And how she came to love him. This much she knew: the only way her father could cause her mother to leave her family was by promising to bring her to Virginia's Loudoun County where she would find green, rolling hills so like her home she wouldn't be so homesick. Then and only then had she consented.

Perhaps some day she'd find the courage to write to Aunt Fiona and ask exactly what her sister had thought of the bold American. Better, it would be wonderful to visit Scotland and see that little cottage for herself. Then she was certain she would understand.

Annabelle crossed the top of the Shenandoah Valley and moved on to the Blue Ridge Mountain road before she pulled out her pocket watch and saw that two hours had passed. Harper's Ferry was now no more than an hour's ride.

She knew the Confederate troops were holding Harper's Ferry at the moment, and she thought she could probably bribe them with a few medical supplies. Then she remembered Mr. Norris had told her to avoid soldiers of either color and the sadness in his eyes as he'd said it. She determined to avoid the pickets by going northwest past the town. She would follow the Shenandoah River to the bend where it turned south and try to cross the water there.

Two more hours passed as she rode along. Harper's Ferry was behind her and she was looking for a path down the mountain to the river when she heard a noise in front of her.

Crackle and shot and then the echo of shot.

The guns were firing fairly far away, around the bend in the road, but it took only a second to realize the noise was getting louder.

They were coming her way.

SIX

Oh, say, Bonnie lass,
Would you lie in a barrack,
And marry a soldier and carry his wallet?
Oh, say would you leave baith your
mither and daddy,
And follow the camp with your soldier laddy?

From the old Scottish ballad
Oh, Say, Bonnie Lass

She stopped Lucy with a jolt and stood terrified, wondering if she should hide in the woods and let them pass or if she should turn around. Soon enough she could hear the shouts. It sounded like ten men or so, one party in pursuit of another, and there was no time to take to the woods. She turned Lucy and drove her heels in hard to go as fast as she would along the road. She didn't care to know who was pursuing whom; the bullets flying in her direction wouldn't be particular about their target.

Lucy met the challenge well, although she probably carried weight equal to the burden of a cavalry horse. If she could not outrun those who ran for their lives just behind them, she was at least keeping pace with their retreat. Annabelle knew Lucy would soon tire, though, so she decided to try her luck down a mountain trail she saw to her left toward the river. It was wide enough for a carriage, and in a second they had veered off and down the path easily, Annabelle still holding Lucy to a wild run. She began to slow Lucy as they descended so she could listen for the horses. They were halfway down the mountainside when she heard the men pass by on the road. But not all passed. Someone had peeled off from the pack and was coming her way.

Annabelle kicked Lucy's sides once more and headed for the river. When they reached the water's edge, they were running toward Harper's Ferry, and Annabelle thought with horror they would soon find a picket if they didn't stop. She pulled back on Lucy as hard as she could, and Lucy reared to a stop that made the mud and leaves fly up before them. Then they bolted into the woods, rode up the hill a piece and halted as soon as it seemed safe. Immediately on the path below her came two riders in gray, and she was greatly relieved to see them continue down along the river. There was no one in pursuit of those men, near as she could tell, but for a few moments, all she could hear was her own heart and Lucy's frothy breathing through flared nostrils.

She patted Lucy's sweating neck. "I'm sorry, girl. I knew you'd be up to it, but I'm sorry I pulled on your bit so hard." She slid off and looked Lucy over for abrasions, soon finding a small cut on her upper left shoulder. When she went to the saddlebag for iodine, she noticed she'd torn her sleeve. She looked at the rest of her person and found she'd put a fine rip along her skirt, as well. She took off her straw bonnet. All was well there. At least she had remembered thread and needle for mending the tears, and then she shook her head and said aloud, "So these are the silly things that run through my mind when I dodge bullets—an inventory of my apparel." But her legs were shaking and she was soaked with perspiration. She dabbed some iodine on Lucy's shoulder and then dug around for the needle and thread, and still her hands shook. She tied Lucy's leads to a tree and finally sat down on a mossy spot to recuperate and try to mend the rips.

This wasn't the way things were supposed to happen. She admitted to herself she hadn't thought it all through, and she briefly wondered if she should turn back. No, it would never do to show she'd given up. That would never do.

After she'd mended the tears in her dress, she took a little supper and rested a while longer. Then she stood up and stretched and decided to walk Lucy for a bit. As they walked along the Shenandoah, she noticed the waters looked high. But hadn't Mr. Norris implied that the troops would be able to cross the Potomac soon?

And so she assumed she could cross the Shenandoah somewhere, since it was generally more shallow than the Potomac. The sun was already behind the mountains, and she took in the sights and sounds with pleasure. Then she mounted Lucy and kept on the trail another hour and the more they walked, the more she realized that the water was even less passable than before. *What was I thinking of?* she wondered morosely. She chided herself for coming all this way and for not watching the river more closely. A pang of fear jangled her nerves, causing her to suddenly begin to pray.

Just then a brown square up the hill caught her eye—an old log cabin. Pulling up on Lucy's reins, she stared at it for a moment. With no glass in the window and one shutter hanging limp over the broken eye, it looked deserted. The walls were leaning, the ridge pole of the roof was bent, and shingles were scattered about. All in all the cabin looked as though it had been struck on the head by a giant... hard.

It grew darker even as she stood there, and she wondered if she shouldn't spend the night in the cabin, and further wondered if the roof would hold.

She slid from Lucy, led her up the brambly path to the front door, and more from polite training than because she saw any signs of life, said meekly, "Hello?" She creaked open the door and shivered as the old wood groaned beneath her hand. She still held Lucy's reins in a tight fist and she actually considered pulling the horse in with her but then thought better of it and let go of the reins.

With a deep breath she stepped inside. The air was musty and the room dark, but she could see a few scraps of furniture to one side. She took another step, looked around the room and then heard a voice call out to her.

The hairs on the back of her neck rose up, and she took a faltering step backward when she heard the voice again, saying, "Annabelle, s'me. I tole you boys she'd come. She's come. Annie, s'me." She recognized the voice but couldn't exactly place it, and she stood still because she wasn't afraid of it.

Then her eyes focused on a disheveled looking creature standing before her. He was tall, bearded and thin, and the distinct odor of peach brandy lay about him in a cloud.

"Michael? Is that you?"

"Yea. Yea, it's Michael, Annabelle. You've come." He swayed a little with the words as he was overcome not by the emotion of the moment but the sweet brandy from the hour before.

"What on earth are you doing here, Michael?" Annabelle whispered. "And drunk, besides." Michael looked back to the wall with a smile, and Annabelle leaned to her left just enough to see two other soldiers sitting on a bench looking equally down and out.

One of the men had a gun lazily slung across his lap and an empty bottle at his side; the other man held a mostly empty bottle in one hand. Both grinned at Annabelle as if they were seeing a heavenly vision. The fellow to the right interrupted his gaze to burp and then resumed his grin.

She surmised these three were likely to have left their regiment, and the thought made her stomach lurch. She would have to leave quickly, but how? Annabelle straightened up to look at Michael, who had taken a step closer and now stood uncomfortably near. She asked straight out, "Have you left your regiment, then?"

Michael concentrated on the question, and then lifted his fine eyebrows. "Why, yes, we have, my love, my Annie-belle." She always hated it when he called her that. He swung his left arm back and said loudly, "These gentlemen and I have decided to become rich instead of to die. Ain't that right, men?" And they nodded as best they could. He slung his head back to face Annabelle, and leaned in to her to say, "If that's all right with you?" He was so close Annabelle could almost taste the brandy herself.

"I won't trouble you on your journey then," she said tersely, but Michael grabbed her by both shoulders and she froze.

"You wouldn't think I'm a coward, Annie—*hic*—belle. I'm not a coward. Not. You gotta' unerstan' what we been through. We just been through the mouth of hell, that's all, pardon, sweet Annie. We just... you gotta unerstan.' I gotta' tell you. Cap'n was gonna' make us charge straight on across a bridge." He looked past Annabelle now, seeming to remember with extreme effort why they were there. "He told us to just be brave and fight for Virginny and cross that accursed bridge, and I thought to myself, 'Virginny ain't gonna' thank me for this. No, sir. An' I'll be dead.' There were three hundred blue bellies 'cross that bridge waitin' to cut us down. See? You see now, don't you? Cap'n done lost his mind, and it weren't right." The boys behind him heartily agreed, and Michael concentrated on Annabelle's face once more. "See? And now you're here. It's perfec... perfect." He burped. "You can come with us, see?"

She stepped back. "I wish you all the luck, Michael, but I won't be going with you." She pulled away from his grasp and actually made it to the open door before Michael threw himself forward and grabbed her by one arm. He pulled her around to grab the other arm and so they stood again in the doorway.

Anger and fear and humiliation tore through her, but they could not give her the physical strength she needed to get away.

"Annabelle, come with me. You've left your home, now, don't you see? You were meant to come here."

"No!" she cried, but when she tried to pull away again, he tightened his grip and squeezed her arms together like a vise. Then he picked her up, swung her back into the cabin and placed her in the center of the room as neatly as a bundle of sticks.

"Don't be like this, Annie!" he said angrily, and now she was simply scared.

The fellow with the gun stood up. "Maybe she don't want you no more, Delaney. Maybe she wants me."

And the fellow to his left wheezed a coarse laugh and looked past them all. "I jesh want the horse," he said, but Michael wasn't listening to either of them.

His eyes were bloodshot and although he was reasonably drunk, he was not so drunk he couldn't manage her little frame. He began shaking her by the shoulders. "You'll come with me, Annabelle, right? You'll come with me this time. You're all growed up now." But she was too afraid to say anything, too terrified to move, and all she could think was that her father had been right.

Her father took her hands in his as she stood there trembling with anger and fear. "Annabelle MacBain, listen to me, now. Listen. Michael's request is a selfish one."

"Selfish?" she cried. "But he loves me, Father!"

He closed his eyes and tried again. "His is a selfish request, Annie, and the Lord knows my decision may be a selfish one as well. But I wish to spare you pain. And if Michael loved you he wouldn't ask you to marry him now." And his eyes looked at her so sadly.

"You think he doesn't love me?" she whispered.

He nodded grimly, and though she continued to cry she took herself to bed without another word.

But she'd seen Michael again just ten days later, the day he was due to leave town for his regiment. Wishing to at least tell him good-bye, she set herself on the road and made a bold movement toward him as the group of local boys came near. The war was barely six months old, and these young men had finally convinced their families they were old enough to fight.

Michael stopped when she approached him that day, but at first he would not look into her eyes.

No place for delicate good-byes, she knew it was the last time they'd see each other for a long while if ever again, and she wanted it to be a quiet time with no tears. But Michael, tall and sturdy, with his father's strong face and deep brown eyes, could not say good-bye. He was still angry; his pride was hurt in the extreme by her father's refusal.

And when Michael was angry, he kept it to himself until it boiled up and over the pot, and so it was a quiet time there on the road but not a peaceful one. And when Annabelle finally steeled herself to speak, the pot boiled over. With a look that made her suddenly fearful, Michael interrupted her farewell to say he was sorry she was not woman enough to make up her own mind about her future, and that he deeply regretted ever wishing such a child would become his wife.

And then he had walked away from her down the main road of Hillsborough in the very coat she had pieced and sewn for him, hours and hours of fine cutting, and thousands upon thousands of stitches. She remembered the loving thoughts and prayers she'd sewn into its gray seams. They brought a bitter taste to her mouth now as she watched him walk away through tearful eyes. And so, immersed in her humiliation, she told herself, "If he loved me, he wouldn't have asked." But then she let the words die in the air, thinking, all in all, she was suddenly relieved to see Michael Delaney go.

The fellow behind Annabelle was speaking now, "You know, I ain't seen a woman so likely since Dolly's place, and I'll be danged if some yellow belly gonna get her first. I don't care if you know'd her first, it's my turn."

Michael was concentrating on Annabelle with such intensity he didn't see the fellow come up beside him with his gun.

Fright has a strange way of telescoping your thought and sight into a living, breathing nightmare, and now Annabelle watched as in a split second that lasted an hour, the fellow raised up the butt of his rifle and thunked Michael in the head so hard it sent him careening to one side of the room. Immediately, she lunged for the door and passed under the attacker as he tried to catch his balance from the weight of his swing.

Out of the cabin and up on Lucy's back in an instant, she hoped beyond hope the fellow wouldn't shoot her in the back as they ran.

She was a thousand yards away before she wondered how badly hurt Michael was and decided she was not going back to find out, and then she was a mile away before she slowed Lucy down and realized through her fear they had no horses on which to chase her. And so she stopped and listened.

She heard the rolling river, a hoot owl, a bevy of crickets. Nothing else. She was soaked with perspiration, and her clothing and even her skin felt gritty, but she let herself breathe deeply, and she thanked the Lord for her rescue. Then she fell forward onto Lucy's mane and let loose her tears. She cried for Michael's sake, and the sake of his family, but mainly she cried for herself, that she could have ever cared for him. They were probably back there killing each other, she thought ruefully. She had heard of men like this, created by the battlefield, men that roamed the area to pillage what they could before leaving, some to go home, some to go west. They were the very sort Mosby had cleared off the mountain behind their home. Somehow she had assumed she could avoid bushwhackers, but it was obvious now she'd avoided thinking about it at all, and she deeply regretted her decision to come.

She realized she'd had luck this time. No, not luck. Grace. The mercy of God.

And so she decided to keep going east and make Hillsborough by morning. At least she'd have the cover of darkness. She decided she could suffer the humility of returning to town as long as she didn't have to face anything like those men again.

As it grew dark and she found it harder and harder to see the trail, she finally determined to take the first road up she could find. Just as the moon edged up over the hill, she spotted one. The darkness fit her mood as she tromped up the hill with Lucy; she was sorry she had come, sorry she was tired and aching, and knowing she had only herself to blame. She felt pretty miserable about her poor choices right then. The thought occurred to her that if she'd had her way—if her father hadn't kept her from it two years before—she'd be the wife of a coward right now. She shuddered.

She made it to the main road and had turned Lucy east toward Hillsborough when she heard a noise ahead which startled her until she realized it was only conversation. She walked Lucy over to the woods against the mountain and waited for the voices to come nearer. When they didn't, she tied Lucy's reins to a large oak and went to investigate.

As she came to the curve in the road, she could make out two fellows sitting in a wagon. For one terrified moment she thought they might be the men from the cabin. She calmed herself down as she realized it couldn't be them, and so she leaned up against a wide tree to observe. "A fine time to sit in the road and talk," she said under her breath. She couldn't see whether they wore uniforms, but after running into Michael she wasn't about to take any chances.

Then she heard a groan which sent a tingle up her spine. The men turned quickly to the back of the wagon, and one of them hopped over the seat and attended to someone lying in the wagon bed. The fellow in the wagon bed was throwing up. A concussion could cause a person to vomit—a concussion from the swing of a rifle—and so she froze there and listened.

An old man was saying, "He's gettin' worse. We got to get over to town."

"Well, we gotta get some liquid in him first," a younger voice replied angrily. "He's gotten rid of everything, so far. Don't you die on us, Sid, we got enough to worry about."

Sid! He said Sid! It isn't Michael. It's all right, she told herself.

She listened for another moment to the two anguished men, their conversation punctuated by the moaning of their patient, and her sympathies were aroused. Then she remembered the medicine. She had medicine.

But thinking about the man in the wagon also brought Michael Delaney clearly to mind once more, and then the horrible thing she had done by leaving him back there held her fast. Tears brimmed in her eyes as the force of the incident hit her.

Placing her hands on the tree, she leaned her head against its rough bark as the fierceness of regret swept over her. She should go back. They might have beat him further. They would leave him there. He might die. She gripped the ridges in the old oak and prayed for guidance and forgiveness as she wept, and as she prayed, her course became clear.

She would offer medicine to the men in the wagon, and perhaps they would then be willing to go back for Michael in trade. She lifted her head. Sniffing and then wiping her nose indelicately on one sleeve, she decided the men in the wagon were the answer to her prayer. She wiped the rest of her tears away with one hand as she headed back to get Lucy and the medicine.

SEVEN

When a woman will, she will
You may depend on it,
And when she won't, she won't,
And that's the end on it.

**Poem from the diary of a
Confederate girl of Leesburg, Virginia,
Miss Mary E. Lack,
November 1861 - November 1862**

She placed herself in the saddle lightly and moved Lucy forward in a measured pace. As she approached the wagon, she saw the men still busily tending to the fellow lying in the back. Apparently, the sick one wouldn't take anything they were trying to give him. They heard her coming and the older man called out to ask Annabelle if she could assist.

She replied that she would be willing to try.

"Heaven sent an angel," the young man said drily, and the words made her blush.

She rode up close to the wagon and stared into the pale face that lay in the wagon bed. In the lamplight she saw the white complexion and bloodless lips of a man with only enough strength to moan.

"Dysentery," the older man said and she quickly slid off Lucy and went to the bag for the powders they would need.

The younger man offered his arm as she returned to the side of the wagon, and it was then she looked up to see it was Malachi Norris.

She was shocked to see him again, but neither said a word as she took his hand and firmly stepped up into the wagon. The three then began working the medicine into the man with cups of luke-warm canteen water mixed with the powder, and all the while Annabelle kept her eyes averted from anyone but the patient.

As for the patient, he was not well at all.

In fact, "Sid" was skin and bones, with cheekbones oddly pronounced and hair receding from a large forehead. And so, after they had forced him to take down a good dose of powder, they watched and waited pensively until he finally dozed off. Then the three able bodies stepped to the back of the wagon to take a breath of air.

Annabelle avoided further embarrassment by quickly helping herself over the side before Malachi Norris could offer his hand. Only the thought of Michael Delaney at the cabin kept her from fleeing the minute she alighted.

When the three got down and moved away from the wagon, Annabelle filled the uncomfortable silence by asking after the patient's condition. Then she said quietly and to no one in particular, "Parched lips. Muscle fatigue. Already chronic."

The older man, a slightly rotund fellow in civilian clothes with large white sideburns hanging bushily on either side of his ample face, asked quite plainly how she would happen to know, and Norris turned to him and replied that she was the daughter of a doctor. Raising his eyebrows in amazement, he began to look back and forth at the two. Norris swallowed hard and introduced Miss MacBain to the fellow, a Mr. Bartholomew of Bolivar, the town just west of Harper's Ferry. The fellow in the wagon, he said, was Bartholomew's assistant, Sid Mathews.

"Well, Mr. Bartholomew, it looks as though the medicine may come too late for your Mr. Mathews," Annabelle said slowly. Mr. Bartholomew nodded and his lower lip pushed forward with dismay. They stood there an awkward moment, and suddenly Norris began to pace, a trait quite familiar to her now, even as Bartholomew bowed his head in thought.

As she watched the pair, she decided this was a good time to discuss going to the cabin for Michael. "Gentlemen," she whispered, "it may be too late for Mr. Mathews, but I know of another case." And then she told them how she was heading west when she stopped at a cabin where a fellow had been struck by the butt of a gun. She wasn't sure how badly he was hurt, but she came back along the road to find help.

Mr. Bartholomew was listening intently, but Norris, in mock wonder, spoke up, saying, "The lady who can diagnose illnesses looks at the fellow long enough to know he's been hit by the butt of a gun but doesn't look at him long enough to know his condition? The doctor's own daughter doesn't stay put and help him? Or does she leave due to her inordinate need to travel the roads alone?"

Annabelle stared at him with wide eyes. This she had not counted on.

"… But she comes rushing for help… *walking* her horse?" he added.

She nodded stupidly, wondering how much more she should say. "I don't know that I can explain everything simply. There were reasons I couldn't stay to discover his condition, and there were reasons why I was walking Lucy just now, but neither are pertinent to the fact a man needs help down there!"

"Did he hurt you?" Norris asked boldly.

She crossed her arms and squeezed them together, unconsciously replaying Michael's vise-like hold, but then she shook her head.

He stared at her. "Well, I say we don't go down there," he said blandly. "Despite the look of an ambulance wagon here, we have important work to do ourselves." He leisurely turned, stooped and yanked a box up from the ground and placed it on the side of the wagon.

She swung around to Mr. Bartholomew.

But Mr. Bartholomew just shrugged. "I am not captain of this crew, my dear."

She turned back to Norris. "Mr. Norris, what could be more important than saving a life?"

He smiled. "I couldn't say."

She knew he was making a vague reference to his confidence

work, but his arrogance irritated her. "Then I'll take the medicine with me."

Norris turned and stared at her again and then burst out in a laugh. "Well, I recognize this game from here on out, but you're not in Hillsborough anymore, and just across that bridge is all the medicine we need. I'm just curious, now—are you still trying to reach your father? Or have you decided to take up medical practice on your own?"

A fierce pride rose up in Annabelle as he asked the impertinent question and made her rethink her choice to return home, although to imply that there was much thought in her decision would be a gross misuse of the language. "Yes, I'm still going to my father," she said and pressed her lips together with a sudden resolve.

"And just how were you planning to pass the soldier at the corduroy bridge?" he asked sullenly.

"I wasn't planning to cross the bridge. I am going to go west and then cross over the river."

He looked up at the stars and sucked in his breath. "She's going to... Of course." He turned back to the wagon and pulled a leather buckle up around the box, speaking all the while. "Yes, General Robert E. Lee is more afraid to cross the swollen river than little Miss Annabelle MacBain. He'd rather stay and fight what will surely be the last battle of *his* glorious career, yet this little lady would cross a river just as deep?" He looked at Mr. Bartholomew and added with a wink, "She's an angel for a certainty, didn't I say so? She's gonna' sail right over the water on gilded wings." He fluttered his hands for emphasis as Bartholomew let out a low chuckle.

Annabelle's face reddened and her cheeks tingled. "All right, Mr. Norris, surely you've put me in my place." And although she could say that much, still she could not admit she'd just been heading home in defeat caused by that high river. Instead she said, "But if I give you more of the medicine, will you get me through the picket at this bridge?"

"Miss MacBain, go home," he replied tersely, and he yanked on the leather buckle for good measure. Then he turned away.

With that, Bartholomew and Norris mounted back up into the seat of their wagon. Norris tipped his hat to Annabelle. "We do thank you for the medicine." He nudged Bartholomew and then leaned toward Annabelle, adding, "If you decide to go on down the road, be sure'n fly careful over the rapids. The winds are right fierce this evening." He sat back and they laughed once more as Norris snapped the reins and the wagon began to trundle down the main road toward the corduroy bridge that crossed into Harper's Ferry.

Anger rolled through her at his words. She would get across that bridge, even if it killed her. There must be a way.

Now it was her turn to pace as Lucy stood in the road patiently waiting for her. Nervously rolling her mother's ring upon her finger as she walked, she rolled it and rolled it until her finger began to redden, and then the plan came to her and so she stopped and looked at the golden band. It would be risky, but she laughed at the challenge, a challenge that made her tiredness suddenly flee. It was worth the risk, because if the truth came out, she wouldn't be arrested anyway. Someone would eventually know who she was, and by then she'd be well on her way toward Williamsport.

She got on Lucy and leaned forward to whisper in her ear, "Be just as quiet as you can, girl. Follow that wagon to the river." The sound of the river and the wagon wheels would keep Mr. Norris from hearing her, and she made sure if he did happen to look around, she'd be difficult to see. After all, she wouldn't need to approach them until they were right to the picket. As she began the descent now, with a pang of guilt, she remembered Michael and determined to tell a soldier in town to send help for him. And what would she say? That he'd been abducted? Abducted by Federals, and that she'd seen the blue coats run off? Yes. That way they wouldn't know anything about his desertion. But it was not called abduction, it was called taking a prisoner. Taking a prisoner, that was it. The thought satisfied her and she was pleased with herself for being so downright smart.

The road was steep as it wound down to the riverside, with many a tight turn to keep her out of their sight. Finally, through the woods, she saw the river, and then the bridge of sturdy logs stretched out before her in the moonlight. "What Lee wouldn't give to move that bridge to his troops tonight," Annabelle whispered sadly. But a flash of light caught her eye and she looked to the wagon to see Norris had lit their lamp again.

Then she heard a distant "Halt! Who goes there?" and watched the wagon come to a stop. They had found the soldier on picket duty at the bridge.

So now was the time. With a deep breath, she steeled herself for her performance.

Annabelle clicked her tongue, tapped Lucy's flanks and sent the horse rushing toward the wagon. "Husband! Husband!" she cried and waved one hand wildly above her head.

The look on Malachi Norris's face as his jaw fell open was worth any embarrassment.

The picket was at least as surprised as Norris and raised his gun toward her at the last second. "Halt!"

Annabelle immediately complied with the order but gave a pitiful sob as she stopped Lucy short.

The poor, confused picket lowered his gun a little. "What is the meaning of this?"

Annabelle raised her eyes and directed a loving, tearful gaze at Norris. "I'm sorry, my darling, but I... I've finally come."

Norris writhed in his seat as the picket looked back up at him expectantly. "I don't know the woman!" he said through clenched teeth.

This caused Annabelle to wail, "Oh, he doesn't know me! He doesn't know his own dear wife, and we two married only yesterday. How can you be so cruel?" She began to sob again and then blew her nose into her handkerchief.

The picket looked back at Norris. "I tell you I don't know the woman," Norris said again more firmly.

Now the picket looked at Bartholomew, but Bartholomew just shrugged.

"Woman, stop your crying," the picket cried out in utter frustration, "or I'll place you under arrest!"

Annabelle stopped but looked at him sorrowfully. "Sir, my own husband refuses to know me. Jail me if you must. Surely I cannot suffer more than I have this day."

Norris' eyes rolled in his head. He turned back to the picket. "Jail her then. She's obviously insane." He slapped the reins to try and get the wagon rolling.

"HALT now!" the picket cried with a pitiful whine in his voice.

Annabelle saw the fellow was so confused she would need to force the issue if they were ever to cross the bridge. She got the attention of the picket again with a wave of her hand. "Sir, I can tell you with utter truth I followed my husband here because this morning he begged me to follow him to the city, and I was too proud to come. He humiliates me by his response, and I stand duly humbled for my behavior, truly punished, dear husband." She cast large, doleful eyes at Norris. "But you asked me to come to the city with you, so you did, and although I am late I am here. If it is not true, tell the man I did not make a pledge to you yesterday. Tell him you don't have my father's ring for pledge."

At these words, Norris's back visibly stiffened. The picket searched Norris's hands with his eyes, then said uncertainly, "Well, it don't look like he's wearing no ring, ma'am."

"Of course! Of course. It must be fitted! But he carries it upon his person. College of William and Mary, class of '43. Look for yourself! Look!" she said with another dramatic wave of her hand.

"Ma'am? That's not… I don't know… I can't." And as the soldier spoke, he raised and lowered his gun several times, desperately trying to come to some sort of decision. Finally, with an anguished twist of his mouth, he said, "I-I'll have to take all a' y'all to the Captain."

Annabelle lowered her head, smiled to herself and waited.

Then Norris sighed. "No need, sir. I have the ring." Annabelle raised her eyes to Norris in smiling triumph, but he returned her gaze with the saddest eyes she'd ever seen. Momentarily lost in their blackness, she forgot her smile. "All right, Annabelle," Norris said sadly, "come along with us, if this fellow will allow it." Hearing her name in the midst of her performance stung

Annabelle with sudden shame as she realized that Norris had some sort of duty to perform and she was making his job infinitely more difficult. Possibly she was even interfering in something that could help Lee's army and her father, and she was suddenly very, very sorry.

The picket pulled his right hand away from the gun stock and unfolded two crumpled pieces of paper he held there. They all stood in silence as he read. Then he shook his head. "There's no allowance for a woman here, but…"

"It was a sudden commitment." Annabelle interjected.

"Very sudden," Norris added, crossing his arms.

The picket looked at them and squinted his eyes briefly. "All right," he said carefully. "I'll make allowances for a honeymoon, I 'spect." He smiled and half-winked at Norris.

Norris grimaced.

The wagon rolled forward and Annabelle brought Lucy to walk behind it. As she passed the picket, she stooped to say, "Thank you, sir."

But he tipped his cap and replied, "Not at all, Miz Patton, not at all." And so, of course, Annabelle stared at him as she passed by with a look that surely made him question her sanity once more. Behind her, she heard the fellow muttering to himself.

As they crossed the corduroy bridge, Annabelle's ears filled with the sound of the rushing water and the creaking of wet logs beneath Lucy's skittish steps. She watched the logs rise and fall precariously under the weight of the wagon before her, the river rising and falling beneath the wheels, and she became excruciatingly aware that the boats to which the logs were lashed were all that separated her, and them, from the rushing torrent.

By the time they were halfway across, she was terrified, and she could feel Lucy tense under her and begin to sidestep. Lucy sensed her fear and in Annabelle's present mood the horse would soon bolt if she continued to allow the experience to overwhelm her. Then they would have an unpleasant bath in the river forced upon them. And it would be their last.

Annabelle made herself relax, brought her lips together and prayed the rest of the way over.

She took a deep breath when they finally arrived on the other bank and then wiped a sheen of sweat from her brow.

The city of Harper's Ferry was relatively quiet. Only a few soldiers in gray were on guard here and there. *Must be midnight,* Annabelle thought tiredly, and then trotted Lucy up beside the men in the wagon.

When she caught the young man's eye, she suddenly asked, "Why am I Mrs. Patton?"

He looked at her and then swung his eyes back to the road. "I can only presume it's because you have a tendency to get what you want before you know what you've asked for." A little irritated puff of air came from his nose. "And I suppose you'll have to *be* Mrs. Patton until I get us out of this town."

"No," she said stubbornly. "I won't be in your way. I can go on now."

"No, *Mrs. Patton*, you most certainly cannot." He tossed his finger toward the mountain and then swiped at the air. "Up that road are a dozen men who are only used to seeing a certain type of lady riding alone in the middle of the night and there are a dozen more who will want your horse." Even his tone of voice had grown insulting.

"But I'm surrounded by Confederate soldiers." She thought of Michael and his companions. "True soldiers. General Lee has ordered anyone shot who would offend a lady."

"*Lady?!* I'm just telling you," His voice rose steadily as he spoke. "*Ladies* don't ride alone, in a city of soldiers, in the middle of the night!"

"I'll... I'll just follow the wagon, then." she answered meekly. But again she remembered Michael. "But who shall I tell about the fellow in the cabin?"

"NO ONE!"

And she was too stunned to reply.

They rode for a way and cut up the middle of town, heading for Bolivar, she presumed. Five minutes passed, and wanting somehow to smooth things over, she said, "I'll just follow you all up the hill. Then I'll go on, you see. I'll not be any more trouble to you."

Norris didn't turn his head as he quipped, "Tired of the marriage already, my love?" Then he jerked his chin toward Bartholomew. "What, no honeymoon?" And both men snickered. Humiliated by this final remark, Annabelle was ready to move up the hill without them, but when she pulled forward he turned toward her and said with a twinge of anger, "Mrs. Patton, you are trouble enough for any man, and so I will, more gladly than any fellow on the face of the earth who ever had the misfortune to be called a husband against his will, release you from the shackles of matrimony at the top of this blasted hill."

"The General should have you shot."

He and Mr. Bartholomew laughed at that, and then he said cheerfully, "I'm sure he should, but, I'm sorry, I was almost certain the situation called for rudeness. Please forgive me, *wife*." He twisted the last word and he and Bartholomew laughed again.

Annabelle's eyes smarted, and rather than let him see her cry she simply said, "I'm sorry." She kicked Lucy into a run then and headed up the hill into the darkness of the warm night, away from all lights and wagons and cruel looks.

But even through her tears and to her horror, she could see on the road ahead a knot of soldiers rising up and moving to intercept her, and so with a little cry of anguish, she yanked Lucy hard right and ran back down the hill.

When she was almost back to the wagon, she slowed Lucy to a pace and, averting her eyes from Norris's look of chagrin, waited as he stopped the wagon. Pulling Lucy up behind, she dismounted and tied her reins to a hook on the back of the wagon. She tussled with the leather there, then mounted her horse again and laid her head down on Lucy's withers. The wagon started up again, and clasping her arms around the horse's wide neck like a drowning soul to driftwood, Annabelle cried.

At the top of the hill, somewhere along that high road, Harper's Ferry became the city of Bolivar, and Annabelle quit her crying.

Norris stopped at a little one-and-a-half-story home with a wide front porch, jumped down and walked back to Annabelle. She had almost fallen asleep, but when he touched her arm she brought her head up quickly, nodded and sniffed, then slid off Lucy.

Norris turned back to the wagon bed to check on Sid Mathews, and Mr. Bartholomew came to Annabelle's side. She blinked, swayed with sleepiness and grasped Lucy's harness to steady herself.

It was utterly quiet and very dark in the middle of that town. Mr. Bartholomew nodded toward the dark street, gave her a kind smile and whispered, "He was only concerned for your safety back there, Miss MacBain."

She straightened her back. "You needn't try to excuse his rudeness, Mr. Bartholomew. It's what I've come to expect."

"Well, I just thought you ought to know. Rudeness is sometimes a man's way of..."

She blinked and cocked her head.

"Well, when a man has a job to do, he's rather single-minded and, although he would in other circumstances find... He might respect the lady, and yet... Well, manners, they sometimes fall by the wayside."

"When my father has a job to do, he does it gently. A true gentleman would hold his tongue."

He coughed into his hand and nodded. "I'd say that depended on the job, miss."

"My father saves lives, sir. It is the most important job I can think of."

"That's so," he agreed. Apparently he'd reached an impasse in the conversation, and so he changed the subject. "Well, I hope to meet you under more pleasant circumstances one day, Miss MacBain."

"And you, sir. Thank you."

Bartholomew walked away and to Annabelle's embarrassment Norris came around the other way and whispered, "May I have a word, Miss MacBain?"

"Yes?" she said tentatively.

"I... I'm sorry I was hard on you back there. I let the situation ride me, and I hope you will consider accepting my apology."

She looked toward Mr. Bartholomew, wondering how in the world they could have discussed the matter between themselves so quickly only to realize with a blush that Mr. Malachi Norris, now Mr. Patton, had come to apologize all on his own. Her eyes swept the ground and she nodded. "It's all right. I'll..." But the word became a yawn. "I'm sorry, too. Mr. Bartholomew said you have an important job to do."

"It is," he said bluntly. "Most important."

Something in the way he said it sent a shiver down her back and she looked up to stare at him wide-eyed. His eyes seemed troubled and sad and caring all at once and it made her gulp hard and look away. For lack of a better thing to say, she mumbled, "I'll leave a cannister of the medicine with you, if you like."

"You can stay here, you know." His voice was as warm as velvet as he motioned to the little house and it sent a shiver down her spine as well, but not with fear. But before she could work her feelings into thought, he added, "With Miz Bartholomew. Then you could wait for the troops to cross if they haven't already."

The feelings fled. "That's very kind," Annabelle replied, "but I may as well go on."

Stiffening slightly, he said, "You seem an unusually intelligent woman, but it's difficult to reconcile your methods with your... Haven't you seen enough to know you aren't safe out here?"

"Safe!? But, that's just it, Mr. Norris, Patton, whoever you are, I don't feel safe anywhere, and I don't believe I'll be safe again until I find my father." She stepped back to Lucy's saddlebags and took out a cannister of the powder they had used. As she handed it toward him, she lowered her eyes. "You know, you should keep a little for yourself. If you've been eating with him, you're bound to catch it."

He bowed slightly, and smiled. "Yes, doctor." Annabelle's cheeks reddened at that, and he added, "I suppose you haven't thought out how you'll make it through the next picket."

"I'll find a way."

He looked down and searched the ground with his eyes as his lower jaw came forward in obvious irritation. "Miss MacBain, I am hoping that the lack of concern for your safety does not extend to those around you. I want you to remember your pledge. If you leave right now, you must never describe me to anyone. You must not explain how you crossed that picket."

She gave a half-laugh. "Obviously my concern does extend to those around me, sir, or I would keep that cannister for my father's use, and of course I recall my pledge as I never make a pledge I cannot keep, and how could I possibly describe you, sir, when I'm not at all certain I even know who you are?"

He smiled. "The last is quite true," he said and his words sent a little shock through her.

"So you're not Mr. Patton?" He kept on smiling. "Are you really Malachi Norris?" But he kept on smiling. "Well, I suppose it hardly matters, anyway," she said slowly, but still he made no reply. They stared at each other for another moment before Annabelle turned in disgust to remount Lucy.

He offered a foothold for her remount by clasping his hands together but as he stooped he swayed backward, and Annabelle asked, "Are you all right?"

"Fine. I'm fine," he answered brusquely, and he held his hands out again.

She accepted the offer and placed her foot in his hands only because she wanted to be gone from there. When she had gotten up, she turned and said more gently than she expected to, "Well, whoever you are, I still will pray for you. Despite what you think of me, sir, and despite my own doubts about the trip—yes, I've almost turned back—I see somehow the way has opened for me to continue, and so I think the Lord is with me in the venture. I will believe that until He shows me otherwise. He will protect me."

The fellow passed his hand over his forehead which Annabelle took as a sign of irritation. "You think the Lord had anything to do with you becoming Mrs. Patton for an hour or two?"

She answered slowly, "Well, I think Scripture asks Christians to be wise as serpents but innocent as doves."

"Yea, well, I think you've stretched the interpretation to suit your needs."

"Well," she said with a little smile, "just between you and me, sir, I think you're right." And with that, she turned Lucy and kicked her flanks lightly to trot away.

EIGHT

Mother you must not think so
hard of the Rebs for they are human
beings. They think they are doing
right. If they should all be where
you wished they were, there would not
be any more fun for the Soldiers this
summer...

Respectfully your son,
Geo L Payne

**From a letter to home, George L. Payne
17th Pennsylvania Cavalry**

It was one or two in the morning, she guessed, but somewhere in the last half hour Annabelle had passed through the point of exhaustion and actually felt as though she'd already slept.

The city of Bolivar began to scatter itself along the road into little clumps of homes and stores until soon there was only farm land and rolling hills. The thought struck her there would likely be another picket at this western edge of town when she'd pass near Bolivar Heights. So Annabelle decided to walk Lucy along the forest edge south of the road until they found the picket or until the picket found her.

Then she wondered if a picket here would be sympathetic to her. Perhaps he would know her father, perhaps even take her to him.

As she rode along beside the woods the scent of moss and honeysuckle drifted to her whenever the night breeze flowed through the undergrowth. She caught the sweet odor more than once in a deep breath and thanked the Lord for the respite from the heat. As she gained peace of mind from the quiet of the night, she prayed for Norris—Patton or whoever he was, for Michael, for her father and for wisdom on her journey, and then for... what was his name? Sid Mathews, Assistant.

Her mind then easily strayed from prayer to question the strangeness of Norris, Bartholomew and Mathews, their purpose and their journey. *I wonder how Mr. Mathews assists Mr. Bartholomew and I wonder why the young man is captain to Mr. Bartholomew? They could all be spies. They must all be spies,* she decided. *He said his job was most important... most important...*

Soon she was thinking about Norris-Patton more and more. She was attracted to his directness but repelled by his rudeness. "He thinks I'm unusually intelligent," she whispered to herself, "but he's rude to say so!" It reminded her of his whistling. She shifted in the saddle. He shouldn't have been whistling, but she liked it. No, she adored the tune. And she should be offended at his direct compliment, and yet the praise felt good... no, wonderful. She shook her head.

No, I shall not like him, she told herself firmly. *He's a spy, for goodness' sake.* And being an agent was not considered a high calling in either army, she remembered her father telling her. *And why is that? Ah, yes. Weem said the money tempts them to betray their trust, and too often they become double agents.* The thought intrigued her and she wondered if this Norris-Patton fellow could be a double agent.

But Norris held a sense of duty and purpose that was quite appealing. Strength. He exuded strength of purpose. She wished she could hold firm to her commitments in the selfsame way.

But, of course, it was when she ran headlong into his purpose that she felt the most guilt-ridden. The look of sadness he'd given her at the bridge was one she was only just now understanding. His eyes had said, "You have jumped and now look below you to find the quicksand. It is too late." Although the night was still warm, she shivered. Those eyes were painfully honest with her then, no matter what he said or by what name he was known.

Doesn't matter, anyway, she thought. *I'll never see him again.* At least she'd been honest with him, too, in the end.

She was well away from Bolivar now. But where was the picket? She scanned the dark horizon for any sign of human life and finally, her heart leapt as she saw an odd lump on the small hill to the right and in front of her. The picket's camp?

She walked Lucy toward the lump and as she approached she saw the barrel of a rifle leaning against it. Of course, when she rode closer she saw that the lump was actually a man, and he was snoring loudly. She looked toward heaven and murmured, "Thank you, Lord." This solved every problem. She would leave a message beside the sleeping picket about Michael Delaney without having to explain anything more. She slid off Lucy as quietly as she could, took some of her drawing paper from her pack and wrote with a bit of charcoal from the dead fire a short message to the sonorous soldier. In the note she carefully detailed the location of the cabin in which they could find a Private Michael Delaney, "apparently ambushed by bushwhackers."

Well, that wasn't a lie, she told herself.

She rode an hour more, then found a mossy spot under a tree, and sitting down for a moment to rest, she immediately fell fast asleep.

Late the next morning, she pulled herself up on the horse once more and they headed over the knoll and back up along the road to Shepherd's Town. The day was already hot and so she left her sleeves rolled up, realizing formal conventions were pointless at this period in her life. She'd already broken all the rules she'd ever known in her short spread of years, for heaven's sake, and so she may as well keep cool.

Soon she heard a cart approaching and while she prepared to head for the woods she heard the voices of children. With relief she realized it was a family's wagon and she rolled her sleeves back down as they pulled nearer. She rode past them then, smiling and nodding, but the only response to her gesture was from the gentleman who touched the brim of his hat politely. His wife turned her eyes away and told the children not to look at her, and Annabelle bowed her head in sudden embarrassment. A woman alone on horseback was considered of questionable character, Annabelle knew, but somehow she thought folks would see that she was just a nice young girl. They did not.

How dare they judge me! she thought. *I'm only riding to...* But then she reddened. She'd grown so used to straddling the seat she hadn't even remembered she wasn't riding sidesaddle as a lady should.

Well, sidesaddles were a stupid, useless, dangerous method of travel, anyway. What was wrong with riding a horse this way? Everything on her was well covered. If the Lord had meant for a lady to ride sidesaddle, why did he give her two legs for balance and why did he allow horses a fear of snakes and water? Of course, if she made such arguments to men, they would tell her a woman probably shouldn't be riding at all. "Stuff and nonsense!" And she kicked Lucy into a run.

Every once in a while, she saw an empty home, a burnt-out barn, a lone chimney, and unplanted fields—too many unplanted fields. The landscape had changed dramatically since the war's beginning. And the faces of the people she passed were somber and tired.

She was soon at Shepherd's Town, and at the northeast edge of town she came upon a knot of houses strung together by a myriad of fences. As she passed the row, a door opened and a gaggle of ladies, young and old, emerged from the doorway, sewing bags in hand. Annabelle was reminded then of her sewing circle back home, and how much she hated it: the closed minds and open mouths. She hated it, because she was a part of them.

She decided this must be a wealthy town that they still had needles and cloth with which to sew for their boys, for her circle had stopped being able to sew for the Southern soldiers half a year ago.

But then followed the horrible realization that she was not in the South.

She was in fact traveling through the newest state in the union, *West* Virginia! Those women were Yankees! Indignation and fear rose up in her as she glanced back at the knot of women heading down the road. They were doing the very thing Annabelle and her friends had done, but the cloth… the color of the cloth would be blue. The thought brought a fire to her cheek, and she snapped her head around and tapped Lucy into a trot as the righteous indignation propelled her through the town.

As she rode, her original purpose edged back into her thoughts, and she realized it was time to look at the map. She halted Lucy and took her map from her waist purse, but saw immediately that it was old and outdated. Then she read the tiny lettering along one edge: "1839."

"Drat!" she said aloud. She had been in too much of a hurry while packing to look at it closely. She stared at the road ahead of her. There had to be a straight path north, she reasoned, and she would simply have to ask someone for help.

Coaxing Lucy into a trot along the westward road, she soon saw a wagon coming toward her, and when it passed Annabelle slowed and turned and brought Lucy alongside the driver's seat to ask him about a north road to Williamsport.

The fellow jerked his thumb behind him. "Shore, miss, there's a new payeth t'the right of the elm up the hill. Can't miss it and it'll take you to the river up theyuh." She thanked him kindly and trotted over the hill toward the elm.

In the beginning, the road seemed no more than a trail in the woods, but the path grew wider as another road met it from over the hills. She slowed Lucy to a trot and finally calmed her to a walk.

But as they passed through some brambles, Lucy jerked her neck down and kicked out her hind legs, almost throwing Annabelle into the bushes. She pulled up hard on the reins. "It's all right, Lucy, it's all right. I'll find the trouble."

She slid off quickly and it took only a minute to find the stray branch from a raspberry bush grasping the blanket that rubbed Lucy's flank. Annabelle went to the saddlebags for a small grooming brush, but as she undid the leather strap, she stopped to listen…. Voices up the hill?

She listened half a second more, and then in a coarse whisper of fear, spoke the verdict out loud. "Bushwhackers!"

NINE

How dreadful to hold everything at
the mercy of the enemy and to receive
life itself as a boon dependent on the sword!

David Thomas Dortch, ca. 1885
Confederate Veteran

Two words. She heard two words that took her breath away:
"guns" and "ambush."

Gingerly she stepped in front of Lucy up the hill, and at once
could hear the conversation as if she stood next to them, for the
woods amplified every sound.

A deep-throated fellow was saying, "That's right. Come on. I
got my sights on you."

Another voice croaked, "You git the fat one, and I'll pick off the
skinny little nit."

Yet another said, "Don't miss and kill the animal, Flint. Looks
mighty tasty, and I been lucky lately."

It sent prickles up her spine to hear them.

"Id-yit, that's a horse," the first retorted.

"What's yer point, Ty?" And they chuckled.

She tied Lucy to a tree as quietly as she could, licked her lips in
nervousness, and took a few careful steps into the woods to determine the bushwhackers' location. They were up the hill and far to
her right, too far to see and far from the path. And so she came
back to the path and crept up the road to see who they might be
about to ambush.

As she moved, she lowered herself to the ground and finally slid
along on her belly to look over the hill. A wagon was coming
down a road on the mountain far off to her left about five hundred

yards away, and it met her own road within the clearing one hundred yards in front of her.

Very soon the fellows to her right would have a clear shot. Any second, in fact. Looking over to where she'd heard the voices, she caught the glint of a rifle. The bushwhackers lay in the woods about one hundred yards off.

Seeing the rifle made her throat grow dry, and quickly she looked back to the wagon, now about four hundred yards away, and she promptly broke out in a cold sweat. "What shall I do? Please, Lord, tell me what I should do?" The thin fellow in the wagon had a gun propped against the seat while the fatter man held the reins.

And then with a horrible sinking sensation she realized it was Norris and Bartholomew!

But Norris was swaying in his seat a little as if he were unwell. And then she understood why she hadn't recognized them at first; they both looked sickly pale. "Dysentery," she said to herself, but she realized that in a matter of a few moments the bushwhackers would take these two far from all the pain and trouble of this world, unless...

Suddenly, she raised herself to her knees, shut her eyes and yelled as loudly as she could, "TURN AROUND! AMBUSH!" She opened her eyes to see Bartholomew pulling the horse left and away from the woods and Norris snatching his rifle up to his shoulder. *Good, good!* She thought wildly.

"GO!" she yelled.

The bushwhackers opened fire and both men ducked forward in the wagon seat. Norris held his rifle unsteadily but shot back toward the puff of smoke in the woods to her right as Bartholomew began to run the wagon over the field toward Williamsport.

In a short lull in the firing, she heard someone crashing through the trees beside her. They were coming for her. She didn't know how many there were or if they had horses. She ran back to Lucy in stumbling bounds, jumped on her as best she could and kicked her into a blind run down the path. Soon a shot exploded behind her and hit a tree nearby with a thud. Then another. The next bullet had a strange whiz and thud as it hit a hollow tree to her left. She held fiercely to Lucy's neck as the horse lunged forward at a mad pace.

They ran and ran and finally she turned Lucy into the woods and rode her up a hill a hundred yards, came down off the saddle, and slumped into a heap on the forest floor. Shaking from head to foot, she noticed as she sat down that her hand still held the grooming brush. She would have died with a grooming brush in her hand. In the woods. And no one would have ever known. She laughed and then began to weep, all the while shaking uncontrollably there on the mountain by the weary feet of her horse.

When she was done crying, she stood up a bit unsteadily and got a bite to eat from the saddlebags as she tried to decide what to do next. She was afraid to go forward and she was afraid to go back.

How could she steel herself to go back up that hill? They could be following her even now. She sat there eating, letting a tear fall onto her hard bread now and then, ardently praying for guidance. The answer came half an hour later as she heard men's voices on the trail below her. She froze and gripped her skirts. What if Lucy neighed? Quickly, she stood and grabbed hold of Lucy's nose, holding her nostrils shut to keep her from whinnying. Lucy fought the hold with a yank upward and then another, but Annabelle held her fast.

It was indeed the voices of the bushwhackers, and they were talking about their lost opportunity in terms that made her blush. It seemed there were only three bushwhackers, and with a great relief, the voices finally disappeared down the trail. She let go of Lucy's head and sat down, leaning her head into her knees and thanking God for taking such good care of Norris and Bartholomew, and for protecting her, as well, and even for putting a thorn in Lucy's saddle. She remembered St. Paul's thorn in the flesh, and the verses came to her, "And he said unto me, My grace is sufficient for thee: for my strength is made perfect in weakness. Most gladly therefore will I rather glory in my infirmities, that the power of Christ may rest upon me." *I am weak, Lord, but you are strong. I cannot do this without You.* And then she realized how the Lord had made subtle changes in her since the trip began. She smiled and thanked Him again. She went on to pray for the men and surprised herself at the depth of her feelings as she thought of Norris. She longed to know if he was all right, if they had medicine and who would care for him if he were ill.

She was suddenly appalled at the way her mind was wandering. Certainly, she could hope to meet up with them along the road. They were both sick and needed help, but the goal of reaching her father was uppermost, wasn't it? "Besides, these men are used to taking care of themselves, Annabelle," she sputtered to herself. "Don't become a little fool for romance like a Sophie Sutter."

Sophie was a member of her sewing circle and looked to be a quiet little mousy thing with dark curls and rounded eyes, from constant amazement, her friends joked. Sophie's conversation in Hillsborough rarely strayed from the serial romances she loved to read in magazines, and she never failed to irritate Annabelle with summaries of their content. Annabelle had often thought Sophie might actually find romance, for she could be charming in conversation when she wished, if she would just bring herself to live life outside her tiny world of sewing circles and magazines. Quietly, she laughed and said to herself, "Oh, Annabelle, how very pompous you can be. You're 'living life,' eh, girl? And wouldn't you rather be home with your nose in a book? Yes, yes, *yes.*"

She wondered just how far it was to Williamsport by now, for she was tired and sore, and then it slowly occurred to her that the army may not cross the river right at town. Williamsport couldn't be far, but Lucy was too worn to keep up this pace. Perhaps she should head for the river now and follow it along the banks. Seeing a likely path, she turned down toward the water's edge.

They walked and walked for hours along the riverbank, and then she looked across the water and her heart gave a wild thump as she spied a flutter of white on the hillside.

Hallelujah!

It was a grouping of tents and a nest of soldiers, but there were only a few hundred men camped there next to the water. The rest, she reasoned, must be stretched out over the hill northward, toward Hagerstown.

She watched the boats pull up along the far shore, and her heart leapt to think they were already ferrying men across, but then she remembered the order of things: it was prisoners, not wounded, who would come across first.

Those were prisoners. She squinted and looked more closely at the bank and saw they were collecting logs and planks; they were going to make a pontoon bridge. Her eyes then searched the groups camped there, seeing if any were being attended to by surgeons or nurses, but with great disappointment, she saw that her father was not among these. Of course, his wagon would be behind all those who could still march. These across the river now were the healthy ones. The workers.

Prisoners first, then the healthy, then the wounded.

How presumptuous she was to think she would just find camp and find her father. More than half the Confederate army had gone with Lee, and so she realized with further dismay it could take quite a while to locate her father after they crossed the river, if he could be found at all. Hundreds of thousands of men along and behind those hills waited to cross, and only one of them was her father. Only one.

And when would they cross? It was now July 11th. She had enough food to last a couple of days, but it might be quite a while before she could even begin her search. She slid off Lucy and dropped to her knees by the waterside. "Lord, please hold me up, now that I've come so far. What shall I do now?" She wished she had her Bible, wished she could read its promises to make her feel better, but in her hurry she had left it. She thought of her favorite verses: "Cause me to hear thy lovingkindness in the morning; for in thee do I trust: cause me to know the way wherein I should walk; for I lift up my soul unto thee. Deliver me, O Lord, from mine enemies: I flee unto thee to hide me." She found a melody running through the words, and she sang there by the river as she rested.

She watched the soldiers scurrying around, crawling over the trees, cutting away branches and then dragging the great things down to the water's edge, and she felt as though she were watching ants upon an ant hill as the day progressed. But hadn't Mr. Norris said General Meade was after them? They didn't seem like men in fear of their lives. The log and plank pile grew and she finally pulled out her drawing pad.

As she drew, her mind wandered to the bridge at Harper's Ferry, the one General Jackson had destroyed in the first year of the war. That bridge was once Hillsborough's lifeline to commerce, and with its destruction the town began to feel the first consequences of the conflict.

"There's a sad picture to draw, Annie." And her father pointed to the ruins of Harper's Ferry and then to the remains of the bridge that lay across the Shenandoah River south of town.

"Nothing left to draw," she had said somberly. It was hard to comprehend the force required to level a covered bridge, a building, an entire city; she'd seen a shell once, and it had looked very small to her. But then, many things about the war defied logic.

She had stared intently at the remains of Harper's Ferry across the water. She understood why each wanted it: Harper's Ferry was an armory from the Revolutionary War, and so, with its rich store of weaponry and equipment, this federal fort was attacked by Rebels within the first month of the war. Before fleeing, Federals had burned the factory and as much of the town as they could. When the Confederates finally entered, they packed up anything left and sent it to Richmond to make arms for their soldiers. What Annabelle couldn't understand was why they kept taking the place from each other now when there was nothing left to wave a stick at.

"Weem," she had said impatiently, "why does each side keep taking Harper's Ferry from each other now?"

Her father smiled and shook his head, then shrugged and replied, "Strategic, I suppose. The train, or what's left of it. I'm no general, Annie, so I really couldn't say." And he laughed good-naturedly, but Annabelle shook her head and wished there was an explanation.

She stopped drawing now. Why hadn't she been sensible and

stayed home? The sun began to hide behind the mountains, and she remembered more of their visit to the camp that day.

"Well, don't let on about your talent with a pen, Annie, or the officers will line up to pose for you and you'll never be done."

She and her father had laughed all the way home over his prophecy, for indeed, the officers had lined up to have their portraits drawn.

But within the week those same troops were sent to the Battle of Sharpsburg—what the North called Antietam—and she knew because her father had told her that most of the men she had drawn that day were now dead.

She had not offered to draw a soldier's portrait since.

By nightfall, a few boats had ferried men across. She walked closer to the river and squinted through the trees. Prisoners. More important than the wounded. It made her angry. But each boat made it to her side of the river without incident and well above the place she had chosen as her camp, despite the fast current. She considered asking if she could go across with them when they returned to camp, but it had grown dark already, and so it would be impossible to find him. Besides, the current looked so violent, she would never trust a boat—even a flatboat—to take her across.

After supper she pulled Lucy up into the woods where she spread the horse blanket on a mossy spot on the hill. She fell asleep thinking that tomorrow she would find her father.

When she awoke the next morning she raised her head to look across at the camp, and a thrill passed through her as she saw men by the bridge-dock making ready to send a boat filled with men and heavy ropes. Bridge builders! Quickly then she saddled Lucy and packed up the saddlebags, for it was time to go and announce herself.

Annabelle watched the boats float down like so many twigs pulled along the current, but she knew from the strength of their paddling motion and the shortness of the journey they would soon arrive and they would be below her. She tethered Lucy to a tree and walked down the path to meet them.

Not far down the path, she met the men from the first boat

walking up the trail, and so she put on a brave face. "Good morning, gentlemen!" she greeted them heartily.

Every one of them stopped to stare at her. The oldest Annabelle judged to be in his thirties, and the youngest about seventeen. Startled to find someone on the bank besides themselves, and startled further that that someone was a friendly young woman, they stood as statues until one fellow ventured, "Well, I'll be."

The oldest, obviously in charge, simply said, "Ma'am?" She gave them an enthusiastic smile. "I am the daughter of Dr. Ludwell MacBain of the 43rd Regiment, and I've come to wait for you all to build this bridge so I can cross over and find him."

"Well, I'll be."

The large man in charge whose wide face and small eyes Annabelle was looking into so innocently shook his head and then crossed his arms. An imposing man, he stood well over six feet tall, with a balding pate and sharp green eyes, and he looked grimly at her as he asked in a deepening voice, "And just why would your father be over there, miss?"

"You all were with General Lee at Gettysburg, were you not?"

"And how would you know all that?"

Annabelle lost her smile. "Sir? I'm not sure what you mean. I was told this was where I could find my father."

"Told by whom?" he shot back.

The question profoundly surprised her. All at once she saw that the fellow doubted who she claimed to be, that he couldn't know her father or he would believe her, and that most unfortunately she was unable to answer his last question. She looked down at the leaves at her feet. "Actually, I can't tell you how I know." Then she raised her eyes to him. "But that hardly seems important, because I *am* Annabelle Shannon MacBain, and if any man among you knows my father you know I speak the truth, and, to be frank, sir, I am not accustomed to being spoken to in such a manner." She looked at their faces intently, hopefully, but received no response.

One fellow came sliding past the others, looked back over the water at their camp and then whispered loudly to the head man, "Cap'n James, now we don't really know who she is, eh? And she talks funny, don't she? Couldn't be here if she weren't a spy, eh? Cap'n, so..." He let his meaning fall away as he cocked his head slightly toward Annabelle.

She backed up on the path and said with an edge of fear in her voice, "I am Dr. Ludwell MacBain's daughter—and he'll have you... General Lee will have you hanged if you... if you..." She didn't know quite how to continue.

The large man, Captain James, held his arms out and told the fellow to be quiet, and she was immediately grateful. "There, now, no one's said anyone's going to harm you, miss. I am Captain Reynold James, and these, my men. Good men. Billy, you poor sot, that's a Scottish accent like Matheson's."

She nodded and said with a gulp, "That's right, sir. Captain Reynold James, is it? Then all that remains is for me to wait for my father to pass here when your bridge is complete or go over myself." But she couldn't hold back the tears, and when he saw it the captain apologized again for the men.

"The bridge'll probably be done this afternoon, but you'll be needing to stay with us from now until it's done."

"Of course." Then the captain nodded and began to escort her back up the hill. "I thank you for your protection, sir," Annabelle said, "but it's a sad thing I should need protection from our own army. I thought General Lee said a man could be hanged for insulting a woman."

"So he did, miss, but it's not for your protection but our own that I ask you to stay near."

She thought for a moment and then whispered with the barest laugh, "You don't mean, on the chance I may be a spy?"

"On exactly that sort of chance, miss."

She thought of Norris-Patton and decided it was very odd to have the shoe on the other foot.

TEN

"How to Judge a Horse...
If the color be light sorrel, or chestnut,
his feet, legs, and face white, these
are marks of kindness... If he is
broad and full between the eyes, he
may be depended on as a horse of good
sense, and capable of being trained
to anything."

**From *Inquire Within, or
Over 3,700 Facts For The People*, 1857**

As they neared the place where Lucy was tethered, Annabelle pointed her out and explained the horse belonged to her and that the bags were filled with medicine for her father's use. Captain James ignored the emphasis, saying loudly, "A horse! By heavens, you're Heaven-sent, miss. I can use this horse."

"Lucy is no draft horse!" Annabelle sputtered.

The captain just smiled and neatly took the reins from her hand. Jerking his head toward his men, he said, "Well, Miss MacBain, before the war this fellow here was a postmaster, this one a shoemaker, I myself used to be a carpenter, the fellow with the rude tongue was a do-nothing, that fellow was a field hand, that man a lawyer, but today General Lee says we're all bridge builders, so by jing, today I think we can turn your Lucy into a draft horse."

Annabelle looked around at each of the men as he spoke. The reminder of their former callings caused them to straighten up their wet selves and grin a little at her. She looked at them and then back to Lucy. "All right. After all, Captain, you have me playing the spy for a day, and that's as far from my routine as I can imagine. By all means, let us all be who we are not for a day."

And at that peculiar bit of logic, the captain gave her a large smile and then a laugh that echoed out into the empty woods.

As they continued up the hill, she reminded him about the medicine, and he nodded thoughtfully. "The wounded need this medicine, sir. You should let me take these to my father as soon as possible."

"We'll see, we'll see."

With Annabelle and the captain leading, the group finally came to a clearing by the water directly across from the camp. Captain James gave command and the men organized themselves and began to secure the ropes.

Across the water, men worked their way along these ropes to tie boats in place one at a time toward their side of the river. When all seemed to be running smoothly, without word or ceremony, Captain James began to empty Lucy's saddlebags of their contents. She watched in silence, sure that as he found all the medical supplies he would know she was telling the truth. He pulled out the brandy flask and looked at Annabelle while raising his eyebrows.

"My father's favorite brandy, sir. His initials, there, on the flask." She pointed meekly.

For a moment he looked about to pocket the thing but then thought better of it and laid it aside. Her face burned.

He nodded approvingly when he had looked through everything, but then he glanced at her waist. "What do you have there in your pocket, miss?"

"Just paper," she mumbled, and without hesitation, she untied the waistpocket from her waist and handed it to him.

The first thing he pulled out was the map, and he gave a little grunt as he examined it closely. "1839. Useless." But then he found her drawing pad, raised his foot up on a tree stump and flipped through it as it lay upon his knee.

When he came to the pictures she'd drawn the day before, he shot her a glance that made her blush deeply. "I like to draw, sir," she replied to the unasked question.

His mouth twisted a little. "You like to draw encampments? Ladies draw flowers and portraits, not encampments." He wagged his head. "Only folks I see drawing camps are field reporters, and I don't know any female reporters. You men know any female reporters?" They laughed at the joke, and a shiver went up her spine. A strange silence descended as all the men stopped working and stared hard at her again. Billy took a step forward, but Captain James without even looking at him said, "Shut up, Billy, or by Jimminy we'll lay you down for a log on that bridge." This made a few of the men chuckle.

Then they all waited silently to find out what Captain James would do with their captured spy.

He stared at the pictures some more and then leaned his arm upon his knee and began to rub the stubble of his chin. "I believe I'll be putting you under temporary arrest 'til we can find out more." She sucked in her breath at the words. Then he asked her to sit in the first flatboat so they could watch her. She obeyed, but only because she was certain eventually they would find her father or someone who recognized her as a MacBain, and then she would be all right. From the boat she began again to watch them work. And she prayed and prayed that everything would be all right.

All this time the men had been trying to use Lucy to pull this way and that on a rope along the bank, but they found out soon enough Lucy turned stone deaf to anyone who tried to coax her.

Annabelle watched the proceedings, rising up from her seat quickly and crying out when it looked as though one fellow would strike Lucy on the nose.

Captain James yelled, "Halt." The fellow left his hand in midair, and James then turned to Annabelle. "Do you think you could do something with your stubborn cow there?"

"Certainly I could," she replied, adding loftily, "I told you Lucy is no draft horse. And she's not stubborn. She simply does not suffer fools gladly." She said it only loud enough for Captain James to hear.

Annabelle walked briskly over to Lucy and whispered a little encouragement in her ear. She tugged gently on Lucy's harness as she spoke and the horse began to strain with every muscle she possessed, pulling the rope taut the way they wished.

After that, Captain James and his men left Annabelle at Lucy's head to work there along the bank with them, but James gave strict orders that no one was to have conversation with her. That suited her well, as Lucy was the only company she wished for, anyway.

Two long hours they worked, tightening the ropes and struggling to keep the boats in line, and when Annabelle saw that it looked as though no boats would slip from the line, she pressed Captain James once more to see if she could cross the river, but he adamantly refused.

As the day grew long, the sun poured down on the backs of the workers and at times Annabelle wished she were working there on the river; the men could take a dip now and then to cool off, but she worked in a clearing that had become a choking pool of dust. She wished she could at least roll up her sleeves, but she dared not in the company of men.

Every once in a while a worker came over to their side of the water, and Captain James would have to explain about his "prisoner spy" and who she claimed to be. Some had heard of Dr. MacBain which made her hopeful. But sadly no one knew if he were alive or dead, let alone where he could be found. And, to add to her dismay, no one had seen Dr. MacBain personally; it would be obvious who she was, if anyone had, since the two looked so much alike.

But General Lee had a large army across the river. She kept hoping.

As the day wore on, though, Annabelle's heart grew cold with fear. That not many knew her father was a strange disappointment to Annabelle; she had somehow thought everyone would know him. That no one could tell her if he were alive or dead heightened her fear to near frenzy at times. And, although Captain James' constant reference to her as a spy invariably made her angry, more than once she caught the look of awe that passed over the men's faces at the word "spy," and it gave her a strange thrill. There certainly was power in that word. She wondered how she had appeared to Norris-Patton as he had let on that he was a spy. She blushed to remember how it elevated him in her eyes. "Go and save my father, sir," she had said to him rather gloriously. Or words to that effect. What foolishness.

Remembering the spy suddenly brought to mind his warning about cannon shells. What would she do if a battle began right there? She decided she would unhitch Lucy and ride over the mountain but wondered if one of these men would beat her to the saddle.

In the late afternoon, the captain went to stand at the river's edge. He looked intently across the water, and when Annabelle followed his gaze, she took a gulping breath as she clearly saw a trail of ambulance wagons being brought to the riverside, to the ferry skiff they'd used earlier. Just as she was thinking it, Captain James said it aloud. "Well, I'll be. They're gonna bring the wounded over beforehand."

Surely this was an answer to prayer. "I ask you as a gentleman, sir," she called out to Captain James, "will you help me find my father now?"

He turned to stare at her. "You may ask after him as they come over." And Annabelle was finally satisfied.

As the first ferry came over, so, too, came the sound of moaning. Louder and more focused it came as the men crossed the water. Now Annabelle heard an echoing scream as an ambulance thumped and bumped down the hill toward the water. Annabelle hugged her shoulders tightly and dug her nails into her arms, holding back the urge to scream and flee.

She turned to Captain James, every fiber of her being throbbing. If she did not do something, she was bound to turn and run from the place. "I have to cross the river now, Captain. I have to. I have to go and find him. He needs my help."

"Just wait," he said sternly.

As the first ferry touched the shore, she rushed up to the driver to ask after her father. But the skipper could tell her nothing. Men straggled past her, asking for food or water. Litter bearers carried the rest. She shook her head and apologized to the soldiers over and over again, for every time she asked after her father she received a bevy of requests for her attention.

From the second load, a man finally answered her inquiry. "Lud MacBain? Yes, miss. He's a couple of miles back over there with the 43rd, I think."

Annabelle backed away for a second. Could it be true? She heard herself ask if he was well.

He looked at her in amazement. "He was all right this morning, miss. Miss?" Annabelle could hardly contain the flood of relief that engulfed her.

She felt strong arms go around her as her knees gave way, and Captain James asked, "Miss MacBain, he's well, isn't he?"

"Yes," she sobbed. "He said yes." And that was all she could say for a long while as she wept grateful, tired tears. She went to sleep that night under a tree, but she slept well. The bridge was done, and her father was alive.

On the morning of the 13th, as soon as the sun began to rise, the first troops crossed the bridge. Annabelle was so busy checking over the rafts and ferries as they came across, she almost missed the words.

"There he is," Captain James said in a reverent whisper.

"Who?" Annabelle asked but suddenly she knew. "General Lee?"

"Yes."

Annabelle looked, but all she could see was a worn looking older gentleman, felt hat in hand, with a fine looking white horse. They were the first to cross the bridge. "That man?" Annabelle asked in a whisper.

"That's him," he said, "the gentleman himself."

She stared at the fellow as he passed in front of them, but the general did not look to his right nor left. An officer came up beside him to ask a question, and soon they were out of sight, swallowed in the mass of humanity that followed him across the bridge.

Captain James now stood beside Annabelle and her weary horse and together they watched the men come across, regiment by regiment. The tattered flags they carried told their story as easily as words. After watching these faces in the hard light of day, Annabelle began to feel such grief she had to lower her eyes more than once to keep from crying. But at least these men were whole. Their feet were often bare, but they could walk, they could breathe the air. Captain James said nothing as they came and kept coming and Annabelle was glad for the silence. All day long they watched and Annabelle waited.

The sun began to dip behind the mountains and the cool evening breeze seemed to liven the men a bit as they marched. Here and there she heard conversations and light laughter, an occasional song. Thousands upon thousands had crossed the bridge by then, and hundreds of the wounded had been ferried over, and the darkness brought a growing fear she would never find him.

She finally turned to Captain James. "Must I keep waiting on this side, sir? Surely I can ride over the bridge to look for him now."

He pushed his cap back on his head. "No, miss, that wouldn't be wise. The wounded will be spread out all over the hills over there, but every last one of them has to cross this bridge or come by ferry eventually. It's best to stay here, although I must say I'll have to return soon."

A chill went through her to think of being left alone out there. "Oh, Captain, I was hoping you'd stay with me until we find him."

"Did you? Well, never you worry. I've never intended for you to be left alone out here." She felt some relief as he said it, but then he added, "No, I expect you to come with me."

Through sheer will she held her tongue. She bowed her head and prayed silently for a few minutes and finally heard the words float through her mind, *The Lord wouldn't bring you this far to have you fail, Annabelle.* And she looked back up at the waves of troops passing through the night, talking low to each other, laughing or singing songs among themselves.

It would be all right. They would find her father soon. She was sure.

When the foot soldiers and cavalry had passed, then came the cannons, their caissons, and limbers filled with ammunition. The smell of powder and hot metal accosted her as the wagons filed past, and the odor made her vaguely nauseated. Then she caught sight of wagons filled with soldiers following the artillery, and quickly she said to the captain, "Other wounded?"

He looked over and laughed a little. "No, that would be stragglers, filling up the wagons that used to be filled with ammunition."

"Oh," said Annabelle.

Next across the bridge was a long line of sutlers' wagons filled with provisions, forage from the rich hills of Pennsylvania, Annabelle presumed. They were slow going, for the mules had to be hand-walked along the logs even more carefully than the horses.

It was now the middle of the night and Annabelle was growing tired. She was falling asleep right where she stood. She fell against Captain James at one point which embarrassed her no end.

He made light of it by saying, "Glad you're not on my picket, miss."

"Oh, I am sorry. I must keep awake. How do the men stay awake on night watch, Captain?"

"Fear."

"Fear?"

"They know they'll be shot if they fall asleep."

Annabelle was suddenly very much awake. "You don't mean as a punishment?"

"Yes, miss. I lost a good man that way only recently."

Annabelle's mouth dropped open and she replied with a tremor, "But aren't they better to you alive?"

"Well, that ain't up to me, really," he said quietly.

She looked back at the wagons, but her vision blurred with tears even as things unspeakable came clearly into focus in her mind. She was sure no one had gone looking for Michael. No one. Drawing her arms together, she pinched her tired muscles in a vicious grip. Oh, how she hated this. All of it.

When she had wiped her eyes, Captain James said, "I have to be back to my regiment by daylight."

"You can't keep me away from my father, now. You can't. You wouldn't."

His eyes grew sad. "No offense, miss, but what I truly need is your Lucy. If you'll give her over to me, I'll let you stay."

Her throat went dry.

"See, one of my jobs is to secure horses for the troops," he said flatly.

Annabelle grew cold and felt the tears come up, but she held them back. "She's my horse."

"I only wish she weren't such a fine one."

"Yes," she said slowly with rising bitterness. "Well, I would have brought our nag, but the Yankees shot her."

"I am sorry, miss, but you have to understand. I'll give you a note for her to be reimbursed by the government."

She laughed aloud, walked over to Lucy and began to smooth her mane and withers. Nothing would replace Lucy. Nothing. "I had begun to think you a gentleman, Captain James."

"In another life, perhaps," he said under his breath.

She continued to smooth Lucy's mane. "Will she be used for more work?"

"No. Oh, no. Cavalry. I've looked her over. Definitely cavalry material."

And then a light flashed before her eyes as she said, "You only delayed me to acquire my horse."

"Well," he joked, "I have to show something for my time. And now everything's come out right. You'll be with your father soon, and I'll have something to show for my trouble."

"Yes, true enough. That is a good thing," she said with a smile, but in her mind she had carefully decided what she must do, and she acted quickly. "And let me thank you for your kindness, Captain James." She stepped to a saddlebag and drew out her father's fine flask of brandy. "To your health." And she handed him the silver vial.

With undisguised delight, he took it eagerly. "Well, I do thank you." He quickly twisted the cap off.

"I'll just remove the saddlebags, then," she said.

"O' course." She turned to the saddle then to hear him say behind her, "To *your* health, Miss MacBain."

And when she presumed he had tipped it to his lips for a good, long draught, she said under her breath, "My health was never better." In the next moment, she jumped on Lucy's back and kicked the worthy horse into a run along the river path.

To her utter delight, she heard the curses of Captain James fall away into the night air behind her, and she couldn't help but laugh into the empty woods as they ran.

ELEVEN

Get out the way, ole' Dan Tucker,
You're too late to get your supper.
Supper's over and the breakfast's cookin',
Ole' Dan Tucker just stands there lookin'.

**From the minstral song *Ole' Dan Tucker*,
By Daniel Decatur Emmett**

She soon felt the uncertainty of Lucy's canter on the narrow path. Though dawn was about to break, it was still dark in the woods and so she slowed the pace a little.

"You've been this way before, Lucy girl, remember?" Annabelle said as she fell upon her neck.

Afraid it would be too easy for Captain James to catch her if she tried to cross the bridge, she decided to wait by the road and go out to the line of wounded and find her father after he came across.

She blessed God for the waning moon that kept prying eyes from noticing a young girl on horseback by the soldiers' line. Annabelle carefully crossed to the other side of the road, and let Lucy walk along the side as best she could to avoid the mud.

She saw an older gentleman driving an ambulance and came up beside it. "Is the 43rd still behind you?" she asked.

The fellow glared at her. "Don't know, gal, an' I kin tell you for a truth I care less."

Annabelle pressed her lips together in consternation and turned Lucy aside as the wagon slowly passed them.

She decided to look for a friendlier face before she asked again.

The next driver had a fellow sitting next to him and they were chatting comfortably and laughing. She drew up alongside their seat and asked after the 43rd once more.

"Forty-third, 43rd. Weren't they one of those what got attacked by raiders?" the driver asked the man beside him. Annabelle's heart lodged in her throat, and she looked to the other man.

He shook his head. "Na-a-a-w, that weren't the 43rd." Annabelle pressed shut her eyes, said thank you and turned Lucy away.

When she stopped to ask yet another wagon, she was so surprised at the answer, she asked the fellow to repeat himself. "I said, yep, they're still behind us—next crew back."

"Thank you!" she yelled to the poor man, and then she pulled Lucy away to kick her into a run. But she halted and drew Lucy back as she asked the fellow, "Do you know Dr. Ludwell MacBain, then?"

"Sure do." He smiled. "He been working hisself most to death lately."

"I imagine so," Annabelle said softly. Then, "Well, thank you, again!" And she turned Lucy about and renewed her search with vigor.

Asking after her father came more easily after that. She was soon dashing around the wagons and had come up close to the bridge.

She asked yet again at a covered wagon, and the driver said simply, "Yea, Lud's in the back."

Just like that.

"Lud's in the back?" Annabelle repeated because she could hardly believe her ears.

"Yep, 'workin' on a boy."

She felt suddenly light-headed as she moved Lucy slowly to the back of the covered wagon. Walking Lucy behind the rolling wheels, she peered into the lamplit back bed and focused on the silhouettes inside. A soldier lay on a cot between two fellows on their knees. She brought one hand to her mouth and blinked back the tears. Her father was to the left of the cot, while an assistant of some sort was to the right.

She watched them, knowing not to interrupt as her father removed the bandages. The assistant then soaked a handkerchief in chloroform and placed it over the soldier's nose and mouth while her father took out needle and thread and sewed up the fellow's arm. All this was done to the uncertain rhythm of the swaying wagon.

For what seemed like an hour, she stared at the profile of her father in the wagon as he worked. His arm was silhouetted by the lamplight, and she could see that he was as thin as he'd ever been. His apron was covered with blood, his gray beard was mottled and matted dark brown, and his arms moved jerkily, puppet-like. He was past exhaustion.

She longed for him to finish so she could let him know she was there. As he tied off the string, he peered around for something and then looked at the assistant. "Lem, there are no more bandages," he said in a dry, choked voice.

Annabelle turned quickly in the saddle and dug deeply for the rolls of bandages she had brought. She took two of the precious rolls of cotton wrapped in muslin from the bag and brought Lucy up close to the back of the wagon. "Here, sirs," she said, and held out the bundles.

Lem crept back, took them from her hand and mumbled thanks, but her father kept his eyes on the bandages and didn't even look her way.

Dr. MacBain tore a new bandage and wrapped the fellow's arm. Then he finally sat back into the canvas, brought his face to his hands and rubbed his eyes and cheeks. Now staring at the muslin and the bandages, he said aloud, "My thanks to you, young man. I don't think I've seen bandages good as these in quite a while. Couldn't have wrapped them up better myself."

"You did wrap them yourself," Annabelle said playfully, causing her father to look in amazement to where she rode.

"Annabelle? Annabelle! I've lost my mind."

Annabelle shook her head and smiled.

"Lem, it's my daughter, Annabelle! Oh, girl, come here, come here! My land, what are you doing here? I know I've lost my mind completely."

She jumped off Lucy and scrambled up the back of the wagon, still holding Lucy's reins as she hugged her father's tired form. He rubbed his face and laughed and hugged her again, and Annabelle wept and laughed.

When they were through hugging and laughing, Annabelle looked at her father and asked him when he had last slept, and he replied he had no honest idea. "Actually, I was planning on a nap right after this fellow got sewn up."

"He says that every time, and then they bring us another one," the assistant said.

Her father nodded. "Annabelle, this is Lemuel Walker, my assistant. Lem, this is my pride and joy, Annabelle. And what in the world are you doing here?"

Annabelle shook her head. "You're too tired to ask me questions, Father. When you wake up, I'll tell you how I came to be here, and you can make me go home if you wish, but I couldn't forgive myself if I kept you from a rest right now. Please lie down, Weem." She patted the pallet next to where she knelt just below the wounded soldier's cot.

He looked as though he might argue the point, but the pallet caught his eye. He moved to it without another word and lay down, then looked back up at Annabelle. "Good night, my dear."

"Good night, Weem." And she bent down and kissed his cheek.

When she came close he whispered, "You know, I love you, Annie." He smiled and laid his head on the rough cotton pad. And then he was asleep.

Annabelle tied Lucy up to the back of the wagon and then sat down where her father had worked just moments before. She took off her bonnet, and her thick hair slid out and down her shoulders. Apparently the rough ride had loosened all her hair pins.

Lemuel Walker stared at her and his mouth dropped open just a bit. He was staring as only a man who hadn't seen a woman to speak to in months could stare. And so she blushed and quickly brought her hair back into a knot.

In the darkness, she had trouble at first seeing past the spattering of blood that covered his face, but she squinted and looked carefully to see he had a fair complexion, blonde hair, rather large pale eyes—probably blue—and a face as smooth as a child's. He looked to be about Annabelle's age. She glanced down at his blood-smeared apron and noticed his fingers were long and delicate, like a woman's, but mostly like Shilla's whenever she butchered a hog, for his hands were covered with blood.

Then she looked around in some shock to see that blood was everywhere, covering the canvas behind her, behind Walker, and they were kneeling in it. Her dress was wet with it already. She looked again at Walker and shivered slightly, and so he self-consciously began to wipe his face with the muslin from the bandage roll.

"I... I have a clean apron you can use," she said in a whisper.

Walker whispered thanks but added he hoped he wouldn't need it until after he'd had some sleep, too.

She looked down at her father sleeping and let out a deep sigh.

"Your father talks about you all the time," Walker said. "I believe you're the only thing kept him going these last few days. Now I... I can see why."

"Well..." she smiled sadly, "he's what keeps me going, too."

Walker smiled and cocked his head. "If I may ask, what is the significance in calling him 'Weem'?"

"It means 'winsome' to me... to my mother..." Annabelle couldn't suppress a yawn. "Mother used to call him Winsome, and I couldn't pronounce it." She smiled. "So I called... call him Weem." She yawned again. "I'm... I'm so sorry."

"No, no, I'm supposed to watch this fellow 'til he wakes up, Miss MacBain. Why don't you sleep, too, now?"

"Are you certain?"

"Yes, miss. I'm used to it." And so she went to lie down next to her father at the bottom of the wagon. She curled up there and didn't think another thought until she awoke.

At first she didn't know where she was.

She saw the end of the flatbed a foot from her nose and the rope tied to the side of the canvas. She felt the rocking of the wagon. Then she saw the spattering of blood on the canvas and remembered, but she lay still as she heard Walker whispering to her father, "Your wife must have been quite handsome."

"Thank you, son," came the cheerful reply, "I do give full credit to her mother."

"Yes. But I didn't mean…" Walker stammered. "I didn't mean to imply…"

"No matter." Her father laughed.

It was so good to hear her father's voice. She sat up and rubbed her eyes and noticed her hair had fallen down her back again. She knotted it up as she gave her father a good morning smile and then a more shy greeting to his assistant. She turned her head to the cot to see that it was empty.

"Well, she's awake," her father said. "Annabelle, you bring good fortune with you. The other surgeon heard about your visit and decided to let us all sleep a good long while, and he's not the sort to hand out favors."

Her smile faded as she raised her hand to her lips. "Oh, Weem, I brought medicine. I should have told you."

"You don't think we could have kept the men from looking in those fat saddlebags, did you? They distributed the goods hours ago, Annie."

"Oh, thank Heaven. And how is the fellow you sewed up last night?"

Her father took in a breath. "He took complications."

"Oh, I am sorry." She wondered how they managed to take him away, and realized she'd been more tired than she thought.

"Annie, where's Thomas?"

Annabelle looked at her father and then at Lem Walker and back to her father. "I came alone."

Her father's eyebrows rose. "What!" he yelled, which startled her considerably.

She straightened her back. "I said I came alone. They wouldn't have let me come, and I had to come."

"Heavens to Betsy, Annie, haven't I taught you anything?" He put his face in his hands. "You were out on these roads by yourself. Surely God watched over your soul. You could have been killed or harmed a thousand ways."

"I'm sorry, Weem. Yes, you taught me better, and I regretted this trip a hundred times after I started it, but I always found a reason to go on, and they were good reasons at the time... I thought."

He looked at her gravely. "By the Lake of Kinchyle, what... *what* could have made you think you should come?"

Annabelle slid next to him and held his arm. "For one, I missed you so horribly I thought I should die, and then I heard about the battle in Pennsylvania, and I thought perhaps you finally would need me."

"I always need you, child, but sometimes I need you to be safe or I need you to run the household while I'm away. I certainly don't need you to endanger yourself like this."

"Oh, Weem, don't chastise me. Don't. You don't know what it's like. Hillsborough's no safer than anywhere."

"What do you mean?" he asked quietly.

"Well, Federals are punishing folks for taking care of Mosby's men. They burned up Jacobs' barn, a host of barns, and they killed livestock, and they've taken people on the slightest whim for questioning. Oh, I can hardly bear to tell you..."

"Shilla and Thomas all right?" he said suddenly.

"Oh, yes, but it's Birdie."

"Birdie died?" he said sadly.

"Shot. They shot her for a useless nag, Father."

His mouth curled in disgust and he spat into the corner of the wagon, but he gained his composure quickly and patted Annabelle on the head. "Well, I suppose it was her time, eh? We should have retired her before this. But, Annie, you're my main concern." He shook his head, raising his voice slightly, "I left you in Hillsborough because Thomas and Shilla could watch out for you. I thought you understood that. I can't believe you took off like that." His lips pressed together as he asked more gently, "But you came here safely?"

"Yes, but I hardly want to tell you how. I'm sorry, Father. I'm sorry for the danger I put myself in. I just didn't see it so clearly." She looked out toward the wagon behind them, feeling ashamed and utterly stupid. All the freedom she had felt on the road couldn't make up for the sorrow she felt right then.

"But you're all right. All right. You're here. That's all I need to know." She was grateful he didn't ask her any more questions. They rode along in silence for a while and her father finally said, "You know Thomas will be out looking for you."

"I thought he might."

He pressed his lips together. "Won't stop 'til he finds you. You know you've put him in danger, too."

"Oh, I..." Tears came to Annabelle's eyes. "I didn't think... I didn't think about that...."

She leaned against her father's arm and he patted her head as she cried. "Aw, you didn't think, Annie. You didn't think at all, but it's all right. It'll be all right. We'll send word to Shilla. Maybe he'll double back to look for you at home soon. We'll send word." But Annabelle felt little comfort in his words.

And then they spent the afternoon caring for the wounded.

Annabelle carried supplies from one cart to another and brought water for the men, getting her first true taste of nursing. But the first time she watched the removal of a bandage and blood spurting up thickly from the wound, she felt tingly and light-headed. On her knees in the cart, she caught herself with her hands before she fell on her face. She knelt there, breathing deeply and feeling disgusted with her weakness.

When the nausea passed, she firmly decided to do better the next time. But the next time, she began to faint again and was instantly caught up by Walker, who held her a little longer than was proper as she straightened herself and thanked him. The soldiers helping around her smiled and nudged each other.

"My pleasure," Walker said with a smile and she believed him.

What personal retribution could not do, public humiliation accomplished for her in that instant, and Annabelle never again felt faint at the sight of blood.

But for all the strength her embarrassment had given her, the task before her was impossible. Enormous in scope, with the count of wounded rumored in the ten thousands, she could see why her father was getting no sleep. There simply wasn't enough help and there weren't enough supplies. Soldiers constantly stopped at homes along the way to take clothing for bandages and liquor for painkiller, and Annabelle watched as they clearly removed more than these necessities. Strangely, she could see the soldiers' need to reward themselves, as it were, for what they'd seen and for what they might see tomorrow. What they may never see again.

But Annabelle had little time to notice what anyone else was about, for she found herself constantly running, taking messages, medicines, helping here, getting water from there, and trying hard to remember who needed what. Priorities. Her head became so full of the duties and the earnest cries of the men, she began to feel separated from it all, suddenly able to ignore the blood and broken bones and work steadily, with no breaks at all. "Miss, over here, please, miss," she heard four hundred times that day.

Her father put a piece of bread in her mouth as she passed him and she ate. She took some water as she ladled it to the men.

By the end of the day, she even found herself in the back of her father's wagon calmly watching him amputate an arm.

But something broke within her as she saw the well-muscled arm, tanned and firm like a farmer's, suddenly become a lifeless thing, swept quickly into a metal tub next to the cot. Her cheeks began to tingle and she got out of the wagon as fast as she could to lose her meal beside the road.

She had found her limit that day, and it occurred to her that she was never meant to be a nurse, and the thought made her angry and sad all at once. She stood there, wiping her face and cheeks and mouth, and regretting that she'd ever dreamed of helping her father, when she began to overhear a small but important conversation between a doctor and a soldier not twenty feet from her. She looked toward them through the bushes by the road and as she listened she forgot her self-pity for a moment. The doctor was a fellow her father happened to dislike by the name of Watson Prang. She remembered his name easily for two reasons: It was near to the worst name she'd ever heard, and secondly no one could have fit the name but him. Little squinty eyes behind fussy gold spectacles and a nose that looked perpetually pinched with thin lips drawn up under it. He was telling the soldier, "Absolutely not. We've enough to work on already. You tell your Sergeant Brasted we'll not waste medicine on strays and vagrants, wounded or otherwise."

The soldier knew not to argue and he nodded, turned and walked away. Annabelle straightened her back. Maybe there was a purpose for her being there, after all. Her father could not be everywhere at once, and so at times she could represent him on this earth. She strode past Dr. Prang and soon caught up with the soldier he'd dismissed.

"Private?"

The fellow wheeled about. "Yes, miss? May I be of service to you, miss?"

"Thank you, no, but I have a message for you. By the authority of my father, Dr. Ludwell MacBain of the 43rd Virginia, I may tell you this ambulance train will care for anyone found sick or wounded. Anyone. You go and tell your sergeant that."

"Yes, miss." He smiled and promptly disappeared into the crowded march.

TWELVE

And early the next morning,
We were called to arms again,
Unmindful of the wounded,
Unuseful to the slain.

From the Confederate song
The Battle of Shiloh Hill

Scouts ran further south along the road from the wagons looking for a building in which to set up a hospital, and finally they returned with good news of a large estate to the southeast that was already in use but had room for more.

It was late afternoon when they finally came to it, and Annabelle, tired though she was, drew in her breath with awe at the sight of a huge sweep of grass encircled by a drive that led around to the steps of a magnificent wide stone mansion. This was perhaps the largest home she'd ever seen, with columns parading down a long porch across its long front.

But there was something odd about it. Furniture in wide variety—shining sideboards, huge armoires, a fine corner cupboard and decorative chairs—lay all about the yard in the tall grass. Some had been thrown, some carried out and placed there. The estate looked less of a hospital and more of a widow's sale.

As soon as the wagons stopped, doctors and able soldiers began to unload the wounded and carry them into the now empty parlor room in the right wing of the home. It was a Confederate's home, she'd heard. Stepping into the grand parlor, its long walls painted a bright shade of robin's-egg blue, Annabelle's eyes were immediately taken by the paintings still hanging on rich roping from the moulding there, but she winced as she looked down at the floor. Around the edge lay discarded family treasures; clocks and china, figurines, bowls and candlesticks that had fallen as the furniture was taken out.

Some of the men were looking the items over, and so she took it upon herself to gather up the small valuables to hide them for the owners' return. She used her apron like a basket and went around the room. Then she went about the house to find a spot to hide them.

She soon discovered that the only room that did not hold sick men was the kitchen, and so she walked there with her apron weighted heavily down. She quickly perused a likely cupboard and hid the items well to the back of it. A boy servant, a slave, had the nerve to laugh at her, and Annabelle did not stop to rebuke him but only shook her head as she left.

Back in the living room she found the once polished floor almost entirely covered with the litters of some fifty wounded men. She was at least thankful they were all in one place, as the stress of running from wagon to wagon in the last two days had made nursing as difficult as she imagined it could be. She rolled her sleeves up for the work ahead.

Funny how something as improper as rolling up one's sleeves no longer mattered to her. No longer mattered to anyone at all, in fact.

She let the noise of the shuffling and talking in the room fade to the back of her mind, and she looked out the front windows. More wagons were pulling up outside, and in the hallway she heard heavy tromping and muffled groans as men carried men up the steep staircase. Soon the house would be full.

And then she set to work.

As the day wore on, Annabelle confined herself to helping her father and Lemuel Walker with the patients in the parlor. She didn't think she could bear to know more than these. During the wagon train she had watched men die, but because she hadn't known them somehow it was easier to accept. The very first soldier she saw die had passed away in his sleep in the back of a covered wagon. When Lemuel Walker had pulled the blanket up around him and then up over his face, Annabelle said, "What?" before she realized why he'd pulled it there.

By that evening, she had come to know many of the men in that house. Those who could speak told her of home, family, people they knew, people they wished could be with them, sweethearts, mothers, sisters, and when two of those men began to die that night, Annabelle wondered if she could bear it.

It was after the second one had passed away, when the sun was going down and the rooms had taken up the softer light of candle and lamp, she first admitted to herself she hated everything about this. She wished she were far, far away. Her father had come and put his arms around her as the boy died in spasms before their eyes. "This is too much to see in one day, Annie," he said gently. "Please. Get out of here for a moment, take a walk, take time to pray. It's all right." She nodded mutely and walked to the front of the house.

The fresh air hit her like a bucket of ice water as she opened wide the front door. She hadn't realized how the foul smells of infection, gunpowder, blood and medicine had permeated her senses.

She stepped out onto the long porch and breathed in deeply, catching up the faint, sweet smell of honeysuckle entangled in a bush nearby. It was dusk and the fireflies lit up around her now and then in their lazy flight while crickets and cicadas chirped their summer's song. She watched as fireflies settled on the shining top of a sideboard. Most of the other furniture had been taken to the barn by then, but this lovely piece of mahogany, with its fine inlay and handles of polished brass, stood alone, looking out of place, cast out despite its finery. *Like your owner,* Annabelle thought sadly.

She looked out over the vastness of the yard, past the rolling hills below, to the far-off distance, and the dip in the hills where the Potomac River must lie. Smoky mist lay along the hills beyond the river, and the sun set to the left of it like a glowing seal marking the end of this strange day. "What you have seen this day...," she told herself as she shook her head slowly and began to pray.

Soon she was interrupted by Lemuel Walker who stepped out to stand beside her in the twilight. They stood together in the pretty silence as Annabelle watched the mist move above the mountains by the river. "That must be the group they left behind for Meade," Lemuel Walker said casually.

"Pardon?" she said, wishing he hadn't ruined the silence.

"The smoke." He nodded toward the river. "A thousand or so men were left to fight General Meade when he came to the Potomac. They were right behind our wagons. Looks as though they're having a time of it." She stared at the mist and wondered why she hadn't noticed how strangely the fog moved upon the air. Dense. Dark. Smoke and fire. A battle just over the hills.

She shuddered to think that what she'd taken for a romantic vision of mist on the horizon was just another fight too far away to be heard. Men were dying again when she thought she'd gathered a moment of peace.

There was no peace.

She rubbed her arms. "And who will take care of those wounded, I wonder?"

"God 'n the Yanks," he said somberly, "'though more'n likely, it'll have to be God."

She thought with bitterness about how the Yankees treated Rebels, but she found the thought made her tired. She would not pursue that angry thought. She was too, too tired.

She watched Walker wipe his hands carefully on his apron. Those hands would more than likely make him a fine surgeon one day. He said, as if in answer to her thought, "I'm glad to say your father has accepted me as his intern, Miss MacBain, after this conflict is settled, of course."

"Oh, yes, that's fine, Mr. Walker," she said distractedly, but then she turned to him as she understood the words. "I believe I already thought you were a full surgeon."

He blushed. "No, my studies were interrupted by all this." He waved his hand toward the home, and Annabelle nodded.

"Well, then, I must say from what I've seen you'll make a fine surgeon." She reddened. "That is, if my father has chosen you as an assistant, you must be quite proficient."

"And you make a fine nurse." He rocked on his heels with satisfaction.

"Thank you." She looked down. "But I think I found today 'tis not my calling." She turned away and looked back over the yard again, thinking what a bitter disappointment it was to have found that out. Since childhood, it was all she had ever thought to want.

"Yes, indeed, the work's too hard for a woman. A woman was made for better things—happier, gentler things, I think."

If she were less tired, the remark might have irritated her, but all she said was, "Yes, happier things. I believe I'll go back in now."

When she came into the foyer, she noticed her father had set up an amputation theatre at the end of the broad hall beneath the spiral staircase. She froze to see him laying out his tools and she wondered which man... Clayhill? His arm had been bad all day. But then so was Benton's. Perhaps both. She lowered her head. Secondary amputations—those done after the first twenty-four hours—were nearly always fatal.

She heard sounds from the room to her left, across the hall from the living room entrance. Suddenly she wished to step in that room to look around. More than anything she did not want to stay and find out who would be brought to her father's table.

She creaked open the door and peered in. Beautiful portraits set in carved and gilded frames were hung along the melon-colored walls, fine moulding and plasterwork detailed the ceiling, and a large crystal chandelier hung from the center of the room.

The floor was filled with men. For a moment she wondered if her father's wounded were moved here, for their positions, their bandages and the sounds they made were strikingly familiar, but she looked over their faces and saw they were indeed different.

She opened the door completely then and found about twenty men lying about the room. A large table was pushed to the right side of it and various bottles and bandages were lying there.

Immediately, a fellow saw her. "Water, miss," he cried out.

She nodded and went to get the pitcher from the parlor. When she returned, she slaked the man's thirst, then went around the room with the water. When she came to a fellow by the window who was turned away from her, she almost passed on because of the stench. Dysentery. "Would you care for some water, soldier?"

she made herself ask. He groaned and rolled to his back and she looked intently at his pale, drawn face.

It was the spy.

Annabelle's hands grew sweaty as she looked at him and the pitcher almost slipped from her hand.

Norris lay before her there in as much disarray as the assistant, Sid What's-His-Name, had a few days before. He doubled up in pain even as she bent over him, and she looked around frantically for the attending surgeon. No one was there. And this man was certainly about to die. She stumbled out to the hall to find her father.

Her father was at the surgery table under the candelabra and Annabelle stopped short. Three men held down a patient while her father raised a small saw above his head. Sickening at the sight, Annabelle held her breath as she waited. She could see by the stripe of the man's pants that it was Eli Morton. At least they had given the poor man chloroform, and so at least Eli wouldn't remember any of this, if he lived.

Annabelle gulped hard and looked up at the thick, bright candles in the chandelier above her father's head. Her eyes focused on one sparkling crystal as she heard it begin. The saw was quick and though the moments seemed to last an hour, it was only a minute before the leg fell into the bucket with a slap. She looked down to see her father applying a tourniquet while directing the men on bandaging.

Without looking at the table, Annabelle walked forward. "Father, please come quickly. There's a man in this room with severe dysentery. Chronic. Please come see him, and I'll find the powder."

He looked at her blankly, wiping his hands on a bloody towel. "Annie, dear, we don't have any more. And I'm not really done here." He glanced back to the table.

"No more," she repeated. "But there must be something."

"Does he have fever?" He was staring down at his patient while the men wrapped the stump of the leg. Suddenly his brows furrowed. "What's this? Look here. Take that away." He redirected the men's work for a moment.

"I don't... I don't know."

"Don't know what, Annie?" her father said, finally turning back to her.

"I don't know if he has fever."

"Who? Oh. Right. Dysentery." He stretched his back and blinked. "Let's see. We still have chloroform but we need every bit of it. Little of anything else. Nothing for pain. I'm sorry, Annie. Find out where you could send his effects, if he has any, but there's nothing more we can do."

She shivered to hear her father speak of him as if he were like anyone else here. She had seen three men die that day. She didn't want to watch this one die. "Father, I think... I think this is Malachi Norris. Samuel Brighton's nephew."

"Norris? Malachi Norris?"

Annabelle grew hopeful and wanted to stir his memory. "Yes, you and his father went to William and Mary together?"

He looked at her blankly. "There wasn't any Norris at the college."

"Hannah Brighton's brother, Alfred Norris?"

"I remember Alfred, but Alfred Norris wasn't at the college. There were too few of us for me to make that sort of mistake."

She grew nervous at his reply and waved her hand. "Never mind. Never mind. I'm sorry to go on about it. I'm too tired to think, I suppose." Her father nodded and she thought, *So, perhaps the fellow groaning in the other room is not anyone he's ever claimed to be. Still and yet, he'll die if we don't help somehow.* Finally she asked, "What about... isn't there a root or an herb or something that will help him, Weem?"

He smiled. "Just like your mother." he said wistfully. "You never give up. Yes, herbs'll do. Let's see, there's jimsonweed. I don't know if you can find it around here, but wait... there's maypop root—that's good for pain."

"I'll go and look."

"Good girl."

She ran down the back hall toward the kitchen where she found a servant, a thin black slave girl, standing at the fire in the large fireplace. "I'm looking for a plant, missy," she said. "Do you know if you have a flat-looking plant with wide leaves like a eucalyptus, you know, wide-fingered, that hide a white flower below them when they bloom in May?"

The servant turned her eyes to Annabelle. She was short with large expressive eyes and neat hair pulled back tightly from her brow. Gray streaks were evident, which surprised Annabelle. It was not a girl but a woman.

"Maypop?" the woman repeated quietly. Annabelle nodded. She had assumed the woman wouldn't know the term. "We had 'em, but de blooms is all gone now."

"Yes, that's right, the blooms are gone."

"Den look at the tree toes to find 'em."

Annabelle nodded and moved to the back door but hesitated there. "Did you say tree toads?"

The woman half-smiled. "No, miss, de toes of de tree. Look at de feets of de trees, 'specially de sad ones."

"Ah." Annabelle pretended to understand as she turned and walked uncertainly out to the backyard garden and then to the edge of the woods.

"Tree toes. Tree toes," she repeated, but she closed her eyes and prayed the Lord would grow some maypops instantly there under the big oak. But when she opened her eyes, she scoffed at her silliness and looked down to see a bank of ivy. Then she began the search in earnest, brushing aside the long willow branches as she passed through them to look down at the willow's trunk.

And magically, or rather in answer to her prayer, she saw a wide spread of maypops under the willow. "*The sad ones... the willows!*" Annabelle smiled. "Now I understand." Quickly she tore up the roots and dashed back to the kitchen, all the while thinking of the task at hand and being afraid it was too late.

The servant silently helped her work the roots into a bitter paste, but as Annabelle brought the bowl close to her nose when they were done, she snapped her face upward. "I don't believe I could even make a dying man eat this mush." And so the servant brought a little milk and worked it into a greenish white liquid whose smell was not quite so repugnant. Then she threw in a handful of what looked like herbs and stirred.

"What are you doing?" Annabelle asked sharply.

"It'll make it taste sweet."

Annabelle eyed her suspiciously and took a taste with her finger.

The woman nodded and Annabelle, with wide eyes, nodded back. It was sweet and minty. In fact it was almost delicious. "All right." Annabelle pulled the bowl away, hastily thanked her, and almost ran down the hall with it to Norris' room.

The door creaked as she opened it, but her heart took a hopping jump into her throat when she saw he wasn't there by the window where she had left him.

She looked around frantically and soon found they'd only removed him to a table where a doctor was trying to get something down his throat. The doctor was Watson Prang.

He would not doctor these men well, and she was glad she'd come.

Norris was well into a fever as Dr. Prang and two soldiers attempted to give him a bit of quinine, but he wouldn't take any. She observed the scene with growing irritation. Her father thought there was no quinine left, and yet here was a full bottle! How predictable of Prang to withhold medicine for his own use.

But Norris was a more severe concern at the moment. He swung his head back and forth as he tried to roll free of the nurses, all the while clutching at his stomach in obvious agony. The doctor had obviously had enough. He was waving the bottle over the man and cursing.

Annabelle took a breath and scrambled forward, stepping over the other men and almost falling headlong into the table when her foot caught in a blanket. The bowl she held so tightly came down on the table edge with a horrendous thump which gained Dr. Prang's attention, and so quite quickly she stated her purpose. He looked into the bowl with some disgust as she described her remedy, but one of the nurse soldiers said meekly, "I've heard them maypops work."

The doctor waved his hand. "And it may well be that a little boiled bat's wing will work magic on him, too, but you won't get either of 'em down the throat of a lunatic."

"But may I try?" asked Annabelle quietly.

"Well, be my guest, Miss MacBain, 'cause he's gonna die anyway." And with that, he shoved himself away from the table.

She could not keep herself from speaking as he passed. "Now that you're free, Dr. Prang, perhaps you could take the time to tell my father about the quinine you have." His only reply was a slamming of the door as he left.

In a moment Annabelle was beside Norris' head and busy with her work. The patient's mouth was white and parched despite the quinine they had tried to pour down his throat. It seemed the liquid had only found its way to his shirt.

She leaned in close and began to whisper in his ear, rather like the way she had coaxed Lucy into working one long day ago. And at the sound of her voice he began to quiet down. "It's me, Annabelle, Annabelle MacBain," she said over and over. "I've brought you some medicine. And you have to take this, now. It's sweet. Good for you. You have to take this to get well. Come on, now." As she spoke she brought a ladle of the liquid to his mouth and he did not resist but let it fall in and through his lips.

She got him to take another spoonful and then another, and she whispered to him all the while, but she never called him by name there in the crowded room. For she wasn't at all sure she knew his real name, but she knew he was a spy, and then there may be no point to knowing him at all if the disease would take from him all that it wished.

After the mixture went down, she got him to drink some of the quinine, and then ever so slowly he eased off into a deep sleep. When he did, they moved him back under the window and then Dr. Prang came up behind her and asked who the patient was. She answered only that she thought she'd met the man before but couldn't quite be sure.

But the doctor pressed her. "We're all wanting to know who he is. Someone found him by the road near here. The goods on him made us think he might be one of us. He seems to know you, don't you think?"

"Oh, no, I don't think he knew me."

"Well, what do you think his name *might* be?" he asked, but not politely.

"I can't remember." She shook her head in frustration. "Besides, I'm certain this isn't the man. I really am quite sure I don't know who he is." She said the last with the utmost sincerity.

But the doctor wouldn't leave off. "Well, think hard on it, please, because we have to account for everyone, and he may die on us before we can get it from him." When she didn't answer, he said, "You more than likely wasted your time with that potion. Likely to be a deserter, you know. Wouldn't that be something? Healing him up so the boys could administer the punishment?"

Annabelle's cheeks burned.

"Know where the fellow was from you thought you met? Sure you haven't met him? Took that green slime like a baby from you." He leaned forward. "Sleepin' mighty well, though." He knit his brows. "Too well, maybe. Maybe he's poisoned. Maybe you picked the wrong roots, eh, Miss MacBain?" Prang laughed but none around him joined in. "Don't you think he knew you, miss? I think so." He looked around at the men at his feet. "Don't you think the fellow knew her?"

"I'd take poison from her if she asked me," one soldier said and the others around him smiled, but Annabelle only half heard it. It had suddenly dawned on her that the upstart was irritated because she'd done his job for him and caught him with the quinine, besides.

"I think you could try to remember his name," Prang continued to press. "Any name, really, so's at least we can tell the next of kin." He chuckled. Annabelle only raised a corner of her mouth in wry judgment; she couldn't help him with that information. She knew many facts about the man lying there, but his name was not among them.

"Leave off, now, Wat," a soldier lying nearby said. "She did good and you know it." And finally the disgruntled Dr. Prang turned to walk away. Over his shoulder, though, he said one last thing, and the words made her tremble. "Well, I think you should try hard to find him out, Miss MacBain, because by all rights, he's your father's patient. I would have left this piece of dross by the road, but a fella' said your father gave authorization to bring him in."

THIRTEEN

War is the work of the element, or
rather the sport and triumph, of
death, who here glories not only in
the extent of his conquest but in the
riches of his spoil.

David Thomas Dortch, ca. 1885
Confederate Veteran

In an hour or so her father squatted down beside her and looked
the patient over. "If they can forget their pain for a while they
heal better," he said under his breath. "It's good to knock 'em out,
so to speak. There's a saying, *Give the body rest from pain and the
body will heal itself.*" He looked at Annabelle. "Is this the Norris
boy, then? Must say he doesn't look like his father at all."

She hesitated a moment. "I thought it might be, Father, but
perhaps I was mistaken."

"Hmph. Well, this jack-a-daw's sleepin' well enough. Think you
could come back over and help me for a while, Annie, if you aren't
too tired?"

"Yes, I'm sorry I took so long here." But when her father rose
she lingered another moment. Then, when she finally looked up,
he had a curious expression on his face. She smiled awkwardly. "I
suppose I just wanted to find out how the home remedy would
take. My first patient, so to speak."

"Ah," he said. "Well, I do believe your experiment worked."

"Good." And she stood up and came away to work in the other
room.

It was almost dark before Annabelle finished her rounds. The
number of wounded in the house swelled to one hundred during
the long day, and now every bedroom, nook and cranny was filled
with bodies, equipment and medicines. Their work had just begun.

That night the colonel in charge offered Dr. MacBain and his daughter, with apologies, the only lodgings left on the premises—one of the slave quarters at the back of the house. Officers had taken all the slave quarters but one.

Even as he made the offer, Annabelle yawned, and her father laughed and gently nudged her toward the back door.

They walked through the backyard laid out with a large rose and herb garden in the center, and Annabelle shivered as she entered their new quarters, the first "house" on the right in the double row of slave quarters. The little room was dark and smelled musty. When she lit a candle they found the space was hardly larger than their pantry at home, with a small fireplace at the other end and straw ticking for a bed laid simply on the dirt floor. One chair was the nearest thing to furniture.

"Look here," her father spoke up. "There's not room enough for both of us, and I believe I prefer to be closer to my patients. You take the room, Annie."

"Alone!?"

"Come now. You've a row of officers behind you. You'll never be safer. I'll inform the colonel."

"All right, Weem, if you insist."

"I do." And he kissed her on the forehead and disappeared into the darkness.

When he'd gone, Annabelle dragged the ticking out the little door, shook it, and shook it again and then looked it over carefully by candlelight; finally it seemed free of bugs and she dragged it back in to lie upon it.

But she couldn't sleep. In her mind they paraded before her: the men with stumps where their arms and legs had once been. All day long she had seen them: brain injuries and mangling wounds to stomachs, backs and hips. More than once she had almost passed out as she worked over those wounds. How was it possible that her father could stand it day after day?

She had watched men die, and few had passed on peacefully. Horrible images came to her now. The blood didn't fall as it should, and it wouldn't stay on the table. The wounds refused to be neatened by bandages. Men refused to die quietly. They told her they yearned to be home and it broke her heart. They wanted to see their wives, their children, before they died.

One fellow wanted to ask his father to forgive him for leaving his mother to go to war.

Annabelle had replied, "But you should take comfort that she has your father in these trying times."

His eyes looked back at her with hurt. "Aw, no, miss. My father's dead, you see, an' I shouldn't never have left her in the first place."

It was the last time she tried to give advice that day.

She thought again that she was certainly not meant to be a nurse. It had come to the point that she grew butterflies in her stomach every time her father asked for help, and the eye for detail she imagined would be useful for nursing—that helped her to draw so unusually well—could not get past the blood and the smell and the raw pain these men were feeling. She couldn't even bring the proper words of comfort some had learned to dispense as easily as bottled medicine. And she was ashamed for her weakness.

Where would the men go from here? she wondered. Back to their families or to another battleground? What pain had they endured and what pain had they yet to endure before they could live again?

Yet, despite their situations, their injuries, disease and lack of common goods, the men joked when they were able. She thought of the older man who had asked her for bread earlier in the day. She told him they'd run out of bread, but instead of complaining, he said he would just pull out some of his old hard tack.

"S'wormy, but it'll do." He nodded and smiled.

His friend lying next to him had added, "And I'd give you mine, Jake, but my biscuit up and crawled off about an hour ago."

She had smiled then, though she wanted to cry, wanted to tell them how proud she was to serve them, but words had failed her so many times that day it was all she could do to smile.

Finally, she knew she wouldn't be able to sleep, and so she put on her dark plaid dress once more. She was glad it was a russet brown. It hid the bloodstains well.

The crescent moon gave off a soft light, just enough to keep her from stumbling as she walked to the garden edge. The mistress of the house had been asked to leave with her family, and Annabelle felt a pang of sympathy to see the woman's garden lying in disarray, the roses bowed with the weight of uncut flowers and the herbs growing wild.

She began to walk around the edge.

The roses made a foursquare in the middle of the garden, with the bushes wide and simple and neat in their design, but it was the herbs that set the garden off. She didn't dare prune roses in the dark, but with her bare hands she thought she could harvest some of the luscious herbs.

She gathered up a large bunch of spicy lemon verbena and then the low-lying mint to its side. She pulled up smaller bundles of thyme, tarragon and chives, and soon she had ten fingers and two arms full of the scented greens. She carried the greens through the kitchen door, laid them carefully in the dry sink and lit a candle for herself. Then she found some twine hanging from the rafters and set to work bundling. After hanging the bunches gently from the nails in the beams, she looked at the two fine rows and felt very good, as if she'd been jarring, even if it were such a small thing as bundling herbs. The poor woman would appreciate the thought when she returned, Annabelle told herself.

Annabelle was hanging the last bundle when she heard footsteps in the hall.

The slave woman entered and stopped to stare at Annabelle. She glanced upward. "Din't have to do that, miss," she said. She moved to the fireplace and began laying logs in the wide space.

"I thought your mistress might appreciate them when she returns. It's the least I can do while we're here." Annabelle wondered why the woman was up at this hour. It must be three or four in the morning.

The slave turned to stare at Annabelle for a moment and finally smiled. "Well'n, miss, if'n you want to do sumpin' for Mizz Reed, you coulda' cut her roses, but de herbs is mine for de cooking."

"Your herbs?" Annabelle said in wonder.

"Laid 'em out mysef, yes, I did. They's all mine." Her smile disappeared and she rubbed her hands angrily on her apron before turning back to the fireplace.

"Well, I shouldn't have bothered them," Annabelle said, dumbfounded. "I'm sorry."

"Das all right, miss." Her voice was a cool echo as she leaned into the brick hearth. "I know you din't mean to do a favor fo' me, but we been a might busy lately, and I've a mind to thank you anyway."

The woman's frankness caught Annabelle off guard, and she cocked her head and stared at the little woman before her. Then the woman's two almost-grown children, the lanky boy Annabelle had met before and a girl, came silently into the kitchen and began their chores on either side of the fireplace. Then, for the first time, it occurred to Annabelle these three were up in the middle of the night to get breakfast started, a breakfast to feed everyone in the house including herself.

"All right. Well, all right. Yes." But Annabelle realized she was speaking to herself, and she shook her head as she stepped down the hall. Then, as long as she was there, she decided to look into the dining room to see if Norris were resting well.

But as she walked along the empty corridor, a low moan came from one of the rooms and it caused her to tiptoe the rest of the way. She cracked open the dining room door and looked over to the window. He was still there, she thought, but she couldn't see much more without going in. Then, as soon as her foot passed over the threshold, a fellow at her feet asked for water and she stepped right back out to find some for him. She returned quickly with a pitcher and a mug for him and then stepped over the fellow and gingerly made her way toward Norris.

The moon cast shadows among the blankets and cots and sacks and sleeping forms and so she made her way slowly. A man near her feet moaned, and Annabelle turned back to get him water, too.

Finally, she stood at Norris' side. His face was turned to the window, but at least he was breathing. Trembling, she peered over his cheek to see how he fared and held her breath from the sudden stench.

At that moment, much to her shock, he turned and met her gaze.

She let out a little gasp, fell back on her heels and sat on the floor. He smiled ever so slightly at that.

But he lost his smile to ask for water in a dry and rasping voice, and she moved quickly back to borrow the pitcher and the mug. Then she knelt and brought his head up with one hand and poured some water on his lips with the other, for he was too weak even to hold the thin mug. After a couple of attempts he was finally able to drink and she was glad for that, but she noticed his hair felt matted and greasy under her hand, and she was shocked at how thin he had become. And she surmised no one had changed his soiled clothes in many days. She was breathing through only her mouth to avoid the putrid smell.

He closed his eyes and drew in his breath as if it took all his effort, and then he focused his gaze on Annabelle. "Ah, A-a-annabelle. You... you found your father well?"

"Yes, but please don't speak. You'll be needing your rest." But she needn't have told him for he had already closed his eyes and passed into sleep again. She rose, satisfied that he would at least live to see morning, and when she returned to her bed she was finally able to oblige her body a modicum of sleep in what was left of the dark hours.

When she awoke, Norris was on her mind and she thanked the Lord he was a little better. She dressed and a few moments later, walked into the sweet smell of baking bread in the kitchen. She nodded to the slave woman, took a roll from a basket on the table and stood by and ate it quietly. She knew a group of men had gone out foraging last night, for five hams and six geese hung from the rafters and at least ten sacks of flour were stacked neatly on the floor. Success.

Annabelle was enjoying the roll very much, and looking at it closely, she saw there were seeds throughout. "Whatever do you add to your bread, Auntie?" Annabelle asked appreciatively.

"Honey and car'way, chile."

"Well, it's a wonder." Annabelle took another bite.

"I knows it," the woman said, which made Annabelle cough as she swallowed. She'd never met such a forthright, self-confident slave; it shook her preconceived notion of what they were supposed to be like. She immediately decided the woman was odd and dismissed her from her thoughts.

Annabelle took up two baskets of the rolls to take to the men and excused herself. She wondered how well Norris would be this day.

When she entered the dining room he was half-propped up on a sack roll and looking a shade less pale. She had instructed two soldiers to change him into her father's clothing, and though the cuffs were short on him and the clothes quite dirty, at least they smelled of nothing worse than river mud.

She thought Norris saw her as she entered, but he made no sign of recognition. *Perhaps he doesn't want to seem to know me, still playing the spy,* she thought, and so she began to pass out the rolls, going around the room slowly, with a "Good morning" and a smile to each fellow and coming to Norris only in his turn.

But he would not look at her. She greeted him and handed him a roll. He said nothing.

"Feeling better today?" she asked, becoming concerned at his despondency.

He nodded but kept his eyes averted as he began to eat.

Maybe he was afraid she'd given him away somehow. She looked about her and, seeing there was no one looking their way, she leaned toward him. "I haven't called you by name and I never will," she whispered. "No one knows who you are, not even my father. I haven't said a word about you. I've kept my pledge."

He was eating the bread all the while she whispered these assurances, and when she was done speaking, he licked his thumbs, worked his way down to lie on his pallet, and rolled on his side with his face to the wall.

As she stared at his back, she stiffened. Why was he acting this way? What had she done or said? Perhaps the illness had affected his mind. But, no, last night he had called her by name and asked after her father. He'd been all right then.

Another few moments and still he did not turn back to her. *Well, what could he have to say to me, eh?* she thought. *I've merely saved his life, that's all.*

She turned away, finished passing out the bread and then walked out of the room, trying to ignore the butterflies that floated within her. Across the hall she found her father and asked for assignment of the rest of her daily duties. But as her father smiled and greeted her, she found herself wishing she could tell him about Norris. She wanted to speak to someone about it all, but, no, that was impossible.

She busied herself with her work then and kept herself from thinking on Norris until that afternoon when she came around his room with the water pitcher once more. He took the cup and turned away from her yet again when he passed it back, and though she gave a heavy sigh as he did, still he would not look at her.

As she continued with her duties, she realized it was likely she would never understand. She glanced around the room and was glad to see her work there was almost done, for the air had suddenly become unbearable. She was giving water to the last four men when Dr. Prang entered and strode purposefully toward Norris. Annabelle froze as he passed behind her. The doctor pulled Norris up and made him sit against the wall and then began to question him.

From across the room Annabelle heard the calm reply to Dr. Prang's inquiry: he claimed to be Purchase Patton, a sutler whose wagon and goods were stolen from him on the road when he fell ill with dysentery. As in his conversation with Annabelle, Prang was not convinced, and so with unflagging zeal he continued to pepper him with questions. What did he carry in the wagon? Who attacked him? How many had attacked him and with what weapons? And what had his dysentery to do with it? As Annabelle listened to the tense conversation the butterflies turned to hornets within her.

She spilled the cup of water for the next gentleman as she tried desperately to think what she could do, wondering if somehow she could right the situation by saying something: say she saw the man pass by with his sutler's wagon a couple of days before, for instance, but then she wondered if the doctor might think her comment suspicious since she'd said she hadn't recognized him, after all. She tried to tell herself that he must know what he was doing. But why couldn't he just say who he was? After all, he was as much a Confederate as anyone there, and he had to be carrying his identification, even if it was to carry on as a spy. At least he had to have something on him that said he was this Purchase Patton fellow. That paper from the bridge. Surely he still had that. But they hadn't found anything on him, had they? Prang said they hadn't.

Then a shock went through her as she realized that whatever papers he had carried in his other clothes were probably gone now, in the bonfire of trash from this morning. He had no proof of who he was, and it was all her fault. And the Bible. They must have burned the Bible with its list of names. No wonder he was angry with her!

A full sweat broke out on her face as she wrestled with her thoughts. And it was becoming obvious Norris was saying less and less, which only made the doctor more vociferous.

Just as she turned to the men, ready to explain she'd had his clothes changed, that the man's papers were lost due to her error, Norris made a seemingly brilliant move; he simply fell asleep in the middle of a particularly lengthy question. Would it work? She tensed and waited to see. Now Prang tried to shake him awake, and then actually yelled in Norris' ear, but the patient would not budge nor bat an eye. The hornets settled down in Annabelle's stomach and she smiled as she poured another cup of water for a waiting patient. She knew full well it was a ruse on Norris' part, but, oh, it was rare.

In another minute, the disgruntled Dr. Prang stood up and tromped out of the room. Annabelle gulped down her laughter but blushed as the soldier she was serving smiled knowingly.

"If Wat could surgeon as well as he can jabber, he might make himself useful around here," he said and Annabelle chuckled despite herself.

She realized she hadn't laughed in a great long while. It was so oddly uncomfortable to make the giggling sound it was almost as if her voice had forgotten how to let a gurgle of laughter come.

In the next few days, there was little to remind her of laughter as the hard work took its toll. By the end of the week, Norris was sitting up all the time, and on Sunday, he even took some halting steps around the edge of the room. But his rudeness toward her never changed. Granted, he hardly spoke to anyone, but that fact didn't lessen the slight for her and she felt it keenly. She wanted to apologize for making his situation so uncomfortable, but there never seemed to be a good opportunity.

As for Norris' fellow patients, the soldiers accepted "Purchase Patton, sutler" at face value, and when it became clear to them he wanted to be left alone they obliged him and so dwelt there with him in recuperative harmony.

Annabelle began to wonder if she had only imagined him kindly asking after her father in the middle of the night. Twice during the week she'd almost come to tears at his rejection, but both times she'd walked to the stable and leaned against Lucy for a while. The second time she released her frustration and anger in the most brisk grooming Lucy had ever felt.

And in that fierce grooming session, she realized what she wanted from the wretched man was thanks—thanks for saving his life. She wanted to be able to say, "All right, I had your papers destroyed, but, really, it's been twice I've saved your life, sir. Won't that even the score?" She would tell him how she'd foiled the ambush, too. Wouldn't he be impressed, she thought, wouldn't he thank her then? She imagined his gratitude, the humbled spy.

But when she walked back to the house she saw there was not a fleck of humility in him for her or for anyone else, no gratitude for anything or anyone.

At the beginning of the second week, she was taking up herbs again, bending next to a tall, fragrant bush of sweet lilac, when a figure coming from the kitchen caught her eye.

It was Malachi Norris Purchase Patton.

He made his way along the kitchen wall, leaning his hand

against the stone as he moved. It hurt her to watch his face as he worked and she drew in her breath and held it at the sight. And it was work for him; he was soon drenched in sweat from the effort. Though her father's clothes were muddied and a little short for him, still he hadn't appeared so well clothed since the night of the ball. He moved around to the side of the house now, then pressed his back against it to rest and drew one leg up behind him. *Just as he leaned against the church a few weeks ago,* she thought mildly. *It's good he wants to come outside. Perhaps he is coming around to himself, after all.* The thought gave her courage and she decided to approach him again. She would apologize for having his things destroyed and then ask about Mr. Bartholomew, a reasonable excuse for conversation. But as she came around the side of the house, she heard him singing softly to himself and the tune sounded pleasantly familiar. He hadn't seen her yet, and so she listened for a moment. Soon enough she realized it was the tune he had whistled on the mountain road, but now he gave it words.

"Angels bring my angel home to me,
Carry her gentle on that day,
Carry her in a boat of clouds through the pale blue sea,
Have her to sail on home to me.

If there ain't no watermen among you,
If there ain't no cloudy boats to ply,
Have mercy 'pon a poor lad and lend her your wings,
Have her to fly on home to me.

If no wings can be spared for this good service,
And the ones she wears can't be made to fly,
Then lend her your harp and teach her a song,
And have her sing it just for me."

His voice was sweet and strong and true; how he must ache for the one he sang it for. And she wished for one sweet moment in time that it was she.

Then all was still, and Annabelle felt the strange sensation she had evened the score between them after her humiliation at the graveyard. Her face grew flush with embarrassment. At that moment, he limped from around the house, still leaning on the wall, and stopped short to look her full in the face.

She drew her arms together and pinched them nervously. "I'm sorry. I shouldn't have stood here without announcing myself." His grim silence caused her to feel the pain of it all the more. She wanted to rush back inside the house and for a moment her body swayed toward the door, but she thought she might at least show she had a good reason to draw near. She looked around to see if anyone was listening, then asked, "And how is Mr. Bartholomew?"

"Dead," he answered flatly. "Bartholomew's dead."

"Dead. Oh, my goodness, I'm so sorry." She looked out over the garden. "You're getting along better. Is your leg all well, then?"

"Sh-h-e-e-w." He laughed bitterly and rested his head on the wall. "Well, yes, Miss Annabelle, my leg is just perfect. It's all there. It's absolutely healed and feels just wonderful."

She felt her face grow red and they stood awkwardly for a moment until he growled, "If you wouldn't mind moving, I might could like to go back in, now."

How the tears stung her eyes to hear the anger in his voice and, oh, how she felt it. "I'm sorry. I'm the one had your clothes changed," she blurted out. "It's my fault, my fault entirely that you lost your papers."

"And the Bible is gone."

"And the Bible. Gone, too. Yes. I only meant..." She gulped, and though the humiliation of the moment was almost unbearable, she pressed on, "I only meant you to be more comfortable, and I'd forgotten... I forgot who you were. I'm sorry. But wait..." A horror passed through her. "Was my father's ring in your clothing?"

He looked to his hand pressed against the wall. There, on a bony finger, sat her father's ring.

"Oh, yes, indeed," she said quietly. "How wonderful you still have it."

"Wonderful."

Silence grew between them and Annabelle bowed her head. She knew the anger must be building up inside him. He must be pulling himself up this very minute to the full height of anger he could feel and soon he'd burst with it. And she deserved it. She should have thought before she acted. *By all means, tell me I'm a silly chit. No, no, he'll have much worse to say than that.* She waited to hear the words but when finally she had the courage to look up into his face, what she saw there was not at all what she expected. He was simply examining her with his eyes—which held no anger or malice. His face held more of a look of curiosity than anything. But so certain was she of her guilt, so deserving of his anger, she next wondered if he were sick—if he had misunderstood. "I've told you plain. I lost your things. They burned all the clothes in a bonfire. But I've kept our bargain. I've never said anything about you to anyone, except, of course, as a nurse." Her voice grew flat with the word, "nurse," but she quickly added, "I haven't even asked after your things for fear of a suspicion." She didn't think she could bear any more of that strange silence, and fearfully, she said, "Have I destroyed your work, then? The list. I've ruined everything for you, haven't I?"

Now he gave a reaction. He laughed. He laughed, but he shook his head. "No, Miss Annabelle MacBain, you have not destroyed my work."

She was both relieved and humiliated by his laughter, and when he had quieted, she said, "Then, I suppose I'll be wanting my father's ring back, if you please."

His jaw grew slack and he leaned heavily against the wall. She stepped toward him, but he held out his arm and slid down to sit on the path. He rubbed one hand against his face and said quietly, "No."

She leaned over and said breathlessly, "Why ever not? I've not told anyone who or what you are. The least I expect from you is my father's ring." No answer. "When you leave, then," she said suddenly. "Give it to me when you go." Still no answer. "Send it by post, then."

"No."

Stomping her foot, she stared at the top of his head. With vehemence she spat, "If you will not honor your promise, at the very, very least I should think I could expect a word of thanks for saving your life!"

In a small voice he answered, "Seems to me if I sit here long enough, the least you'll expect from me is nothing at all." He laughed. Then without emotion he added, "Tell you the truth I don't think I'm gonna' thank anybody for saving my life. Nope. Nobody asked me if I wanted to keep on livin'."

In disbelief, Annabelle straightened her back and shook her head as if she could clear the odd words from her ears. Inside the house were men whose bodies they had worked over for days—some had died, some had lost arms or legs or both. There were those who would give anything to be able to go home again as this man would when he was able. Without thinking, she said in a hiss, "There are men in there who would give their souls to be as healthy as you are, as you will be! You're ungrateful to God!"

His chin came forward. "It's true I am alive, but I have no..." He paused and smiled grimly. "No soul, and so I don't choose to be grateful." His words, twisted out from that unkind smile, would have drawn ice upon warm water.

Shocked, she stared hard at him, and yet he had simply told the truth—the truth as he knew it. She could only presume he had come through something horrible and grotesque, some torture that had removed him from himself. And then she realized if she stared into those eyes a moment more she might fall into that sad abyss as well, and she stepped away from him as she groped to find a proper limit to her sympathy.

Her lips moved once, twice, but she was at a loss to know what to say. She wanted to shake him, to somehow wake him from his nightmare. She threw back her head and said uncertainly, "Well, then it's your soul I'll be praying for." She meant it to accuse him, to sting his conscious, but he did not blink.

"Then there'll be no work in it for you," he said plainly.

He looked away from her, and she turned and took herself back inside the house.

That night she knelt beside her pallet to pray for him. In the days before, she'd prayed a hundred times that a man might live despite the state of his body, but this was the first time she'd prayed that a man would want to live despite the state of his soul, and she found a soul was much harder to pray for.

In the middle of the second week, Annabelle came to the dining room to make her rounds, and she looked to the window where he usually sat and realized he was out walking again.

She thought to go and seek him out, but then thought better of it and stayed put. Instead she crossed the room to see if Dr. Prang needed help changing a bandage. When he saw her he said nonchalantly, "That fellow you treated with root took off." Then he smiled.

"Took off?"

"Yea. Deserter. I knew it," he said rather viciously as he pulled at the poor man's bandage. "I knew it all the time, dang it. Nobody listens. And nobody's got the time to go get him and string him up. But, oh, you did a good job for him, didn't you, Miss MacBain? A fine, dedicated job." Some of the men laughed uncomfortably, but Annabelle was only half listening by then.

"A deserter?" she whispered. She could not comprehend the words.

She began to tremble as the doctor continued, "Yea, but he was an ungrateful cuss, wasn't he, boys?"

The fellow getting a new bandage said with a laugh, "The fool. Shoulda' waited for pay due when we get back to the regiment, then he coulda' jumped—" He sucked in his breath as the doctor pulled the bandage away from the wound.

"And you're a fool for thinkin' we'll ever be paid," another fellow said.

Some of the men snickered, and the fellow to his left rejoined with, "And what if we are paid? A pack of Confederate dollars is as useless to me as a brick in my roll."

"Now that's unfair," another said, "that brick would be worth a lot to you in a fight hand to hand." They all broke up laughing at that.

But one man lying on a litter near the door yelled out, "Y'all shut up—no offense, Miss MacBain—shut up, now. Hurts to laugh."

Everyone settled down, but Annabelle had already turned away and was walking out to the garden, trying to take it in. Was he like Michael Delaney, after all? With all these brave men about her, why is it she always picked out the ones who would flee? What was wrong with her? She felt slightly sick and sat down heavily on the garden bench.

So he was a deserter. Well, it was possible he would return to his regiment in the east. These men didn't know where he came from. But, then, he wasn't Malachi Norris, was he? And he wasn't Purchase Patton. He was a spy. He would simply disappear. She laughed bitterly; it was now the second time she'd dressed a man up and had him leave. And she wasn't likely to see this one again, either.

Perhaps he means to sell my father's ring, or will it be buried with him? She shivered. No doubt he'd sell it or use it to bargain for information, just as she had. She was sorry she had given it to him, sorry she had ever met him. He had taken something more from her than just her father's ring: he had stolen her trust.

For her honesty, he gave her lies, and for saving his life, he offered no thanks. It was as if he said to her, "What you trust in is worthless, what you believe in is not worth believing," and the betrayal cut her to the bone. Michael had killed the naive and childish love she thought she'd felt for him, but this fellow had stolen a portion from the woman she had become, and for that she was more than angry. She was afraid. She wanted to run to her father and tell him everything, hear his reassurance that the world was not ending, that she would still find good here, but she held herself back. She thought again of her father's ring, and she fingered her mother's gold band as she sat on the bench. An afternoon shower was about to fall, but she stayed on the bench a moment longer.

I will not allow him to take this from me. I will trust. I will trust in the Lord, since no one else can be trusted. And, for my part, and for as long as that man has my father's ring, I will keep the last por-

tion of my pledge. Lord willing, I will not speak of him to anyone.
This strengthened her heart and she felt better for making the
decision. Then she rushed into the house as the drops of rain grew
quick and heavy about her.

She went about her work that day, keeping to a sort of schedule
and trying hard not to think about the man who had left, but it
rained all day and the heaviness of the heat and the mist caused her
to dwell in the depths of despair; everything reminded her of loss,
of dying and death. And her heart was far from the men she
served.

Late that afternoon, she tried to get one fellow to take a sip of
water, coaxing him, saying, "Come on, Will. Come on. You have
to take some water and food, now, if you want to get home to see
your little girls again."

But the fellow next to her quietly said, "Miss MacBain, I believe
William Cole is dead."

Annabelle looked at the patient and her tin cup rattled to the
floor. She laid the fellow's head back down and stood up as the
room swirled slightly around her. When she gained her balance a
coolness came over her and she began to shake all the way to her
bones.

Someone called out for Dr. MacBain. When he arrived someone
handed him a Bible, and just as he had done a dozen times before
in the last few weeks for lack of a preacher, he read a passage from
Scripture over the fellow's body and led everyone around him in a
short prayer.

When he was done, two soldiers carried the body away, and
Annabelle leaned heavily on her father's arm. "This is the oddest
thing," he said as she tried to steady herself. "What do you think of
it, Annie? Somebody just handed this to me, and I happened to flip
to the front, and look here, this is none other than Samuel
Brighton's Bible!"

FOURTEEN

She went away and took another,
Heigh, ho, you rollin' river,
She went away and took another,
Away, I'm bound away to the broad Missouri.
From the song, *O' Shenando*

When she came to, she was in her father's arms. "Anniebelle, you've been working too hard," he said.

The men gathered around and voiced their concern as well. She tried to smile and tell them she was fine, but she couldn't seem to speak. Instead she turned her head into her father's shoulder and began to sob, feeling she had nothing to give anyone anymore and no portion to hold herself up with, either. She could only cry.

When she was able to walk, her father gently led her outside, sat her on a chair and tried to comfort her. Soon he whispered that he and the other doctors had decided to move to meet the regiment once more. He asked her if she would return to Hillsborough.

She thought about it and finally asked, "Would it make you very happy, Weem?"

"Yes, it would, Annie."

"Then I'll go home."

He hugged her so hard and so suddenly, she almost cried out. He was grinning ear to ear. "Annie, child. I believe..." Here he stopped, for his voice had grown full of emotion.

"What, Weem? What is it?"

"I believe you're giving it all the signs now, of growing up."

She gave him a slow smile and fell against his shoulder. They rested there awhile, and then he hugged her once more. "But perhaps nursing isn't the calling you thought it might be, eh, Annie?"

She sniffed. "Is it so obvious, Weem?"

"No." He shook his head. "Actually, until this moment, I hadn't seen past your good efforts."

"My heart isn't in it," she said sadly. "My heart just isn't in it."

"It's all right, Annie." He drew her in for a hug and a kiss to the forehead. "You know how happy I was to see you, you know how much you helped, although I'd have never let you do it, I'm glad you did. Whatever else you've done, and it's been considerable I'll tell you, you saved my life coming when you did. Mosby's been riling the Federals rather severely of late, I hear, so it's probably a good time to send you back, but of course I can't let you go back alone."

"Oh, will you come home for a little while? It'd be so nice!" And she began to smile again.

"No, no, I'm sorry. They're not gonna' let me go just yet, but Lem Walker has offered to escort you."

Annabelle's heart sank to her shoes. "You couldn't be spared even for a few days?"

"Can't really spare Lem, Annie, but he insisted on taking you, and I couldn't think of anyone I'd trust more," he said half-cheerfully. "B'sides, he'll be working with me when this fool war is over, and it'll give him a chance to see our little village, eh?"

She nodded. It was really quite heroic of Lem to offer to escort her, and he was a perfectly nice boy. And so she agreed to his escort.

The next morning, Walker hooked Lucy up to a wagon from the mansion's stables and brought it around to the front door where Annabelle and her father stood saying their goodbyes. Her father patted Lucy's flanks as they chatted. Then Annabelle heard Lem calling the herb woman's son to the side of the wagon. He wrote something on a piece of paper, and with a flourish of his arm he handed the sheet to the servant. "This says the Confederate Army has removed this wagon from the property and will pay the owner accordingly for the goods."

Annabelle's father shook his head at the display. Her tongue went dry and tingly as the thoughts came to her. *Weem knows the army isn't good for it. The army cannot pay, just as those men were joking the other day. Just as my father hasn't been paid in months. We aren't going to win this war.* She hated to think they'd chosen the losing side.

Her father helped her up into the wagon and now she looked intently at his smiling face, imprinting it on her mind. Just in case... Just in case.

No, she thought obstinately, *We will win, and Father will be home soon. Surely the Lord hears our prayers. There will be a miracle. England or France will support our cause, or we will break the blockade of the ports and sue for peace, and my father will come home safely. Some good must come from all I've seen. Please, Lord, let there be some good from it.*

Her father pulled a little white Bible from his coat pocket. "I'll be darned if I know how it got here, Annie, but why don't you take this back to Friend Samuel for us? I can't imagine how it ever got away from him."

She shivered as she took the little leather volume. "Oh, Weem, I'm sorry to have to tell you. Samuel Brighton. I forgot to tell you before. He passed away early this month in a hunting accident."

"Ah, no. That's a shame. That's a cruel shame, Annie. Such a man, such a good, good man." He stared curiously at the Bible. "A hunting accident, you say. He had this with him all the time... It's a wonder he wasn't buried with it, eh?"

She blanched and nodded. "Yes, odd that it's come to be here, but I'll take care of it. But it's luck you found it." She quickly tucked it away and nodded at Mr. Walker to tell him she was ready.

"Luck?" her father said doubtfully, but Annabelle leaned forward and kissed his forehead. He smiled and gave her a wink. Then he stepped away, and Walker started the wagon off.

As they trundled down the drive, Annabelle looked back to blow a kiss to her father and noticed that the slave had let Mr. Walker's piece of paper flutter to the ground on the steps of the house as he walked without hesitation back up to the front door.

Annabelle's thoughts wandered to the Bible in her pocket and, with a little thrill, she remembered the list of names it held somewhere inside. The list of tried and true. She burned with curiosity, and as soon as they came to a flat piece in the road, she drew the Bible out and leafed through it page by page.

Brighton had underlined many passages, but she saw no writing in the margins.

There was no writing anywhere.

She wondered if the list were in spy ink or something of that sort, and she began to go through it once more, but she found nothing unusual. She came to the last page and left the book open on her lap in dreary disappointment. It was then she saw the tear along the binding.

Well, there it was. Or rather, there it was not. *Well, of course he removed the evidence. He's not an idiot. Still, the list must have burned along with the clothes. Suppose it isn't surprising the soldiers chose not to burn the Bible.*

She sighed and put the Bible away. She couldn't possibly give it to Widow Brighton, as her father would expect. But she couldn't destroy it, either. Losing it or leaving it out on the road seemed a sacrilege, as well. Burying it over the grave would be... No, that didn't seem right, either. She got a headache thinking on it.

By the afternoon, her headache had grown to a dull aching thud, and Lemuel Walker was doing nothing to improve her state. His indecisiveness drove her to distraction. She would say, "Would you care to stop at the creek and rest?" or, "Shall we take some bread now?" And he would reply, "If you would like," and then when they had finished resting or eating she would look up to find him staring at her. She tried to hold conversation with him, but he was tongue-tied on every subject. By dusk, she had decided Lemuel Walker was a puppy, unable to entertain an original thought. It seemed the one purpose he served that day was to force Annabelle to look forward to coming home, and, by nightfall, she looked forward to it with a vengeance.

They arrived in Hillsborough around ten o'clock that night, and Annabelle was never so glad to see the little town. It was unchanged as far as she could tell. *Well, of course, it isn't changed,* she told herself, *I've only been gone the better part of a month!* This line of shops and homes was still Hillsborough, still her home. A few folks stood outside of the taverns that were open, and she could see pale lights through the wavy glass of various homes and shops. It was a great comfort to see such familiar sights, and she realized it was a miracle that they had arrived there safely.

In front of her home, Annabelle jumped down from the wagon and ran up the steps. Shilla must have heard her for she met her at the door with a cry of joy and hugged her wildly.

Finally, Shilla held her at arm's length and shook her and told her how angry she was at her for leaving, and then in the next second she was hugging her again and laughing and crying at the same time. Annabelle then asked after Thomas and to her relief Shilla told her he was all right, though he was taken by Rebel soldiers on the road and had to put in a week of hard labor before he could escape. By the time he returned home, Shilla had received the letter from Dr. MacBain saying Annabelle was all right.

"And where is Thomas, now?" Annabelle asked.

"Asleep, Lord bless him."

"I'll let him rest for now, then, but, oh, tell me everything, Shilla."

But Shilla was staring over Annabelle's shoulder, and with embarrassment Annabelle realized she'd forgotten about Lemuel Walker. After introducing him, Shilla lit some candles in the parlor and made them sit to catch up with the news. Walker seemed content to sit and listen, and so Annabelle ignored him for a time.

Shilla then told Annabelle the soldiers pursuing Lee had come through about a week after Annabelle left town, and that she was glad she'd buried all their important goods, because these men thought nothing of coming onto private property and taking whatever they wished. Some of the neighbors had taken their horses up to Jockey's Cave and so escaped the forage, and Thomas took their cow and some chickens up the hill to avoid the soldiers, spending the night up there with the animals, bless his soul, she said. Oh, and Revo Lewis had been arrested for pro-Confederate activities, but a group of Quaker men had talked him back out of jail. May Nance had had her twelfth child, Shilla added brightly, but then she shook her head and said old Samuel Roop was killed in a wagon accident, and finally with a lopsided smile she said, "And I believe Miss Sally Drum has something to tell you."

"She's engaged to James Alton, isn't she?" Annabelle asked merrily.

"Maybe she is, and maybe she isn't. You'll have to ask her yourself, miss."

Lem Walker then haltingly suggested he should go and seek a night's lodging. Without hesitation, Annabelle recommended the best one in town and gave directions to it, but he was visibly disappointed. She realized he had half hoped to stay at their home, but that would never do. Annabelle was never more relieved to see a person go as when he excused himself for the evening. When he finally left, Shilla rolled her eyes heavenward, and Annabelle saw she understood the situation entirely.

The word Annabelle used to describe him was one she made up on the spot; he had a certain "puff-ed-up-edness" about him, and Shilla nodded in complete agreement. Out of politeness, Annabelle had suggested to Walker he return for morning tea, hoping he would say he must get back to the regiment, but he had accepted her invitation without hesitation. Well, at least she could work in a visit with Sarah and Sally in the early morning, before the boy-man returned.

Before she took herself to bed that night, she knocked quietly on Thomas' door. He opened it and yelled out with glad surprise. Then he plucked her off the ground and into the air to give her a great hug. She blinked back tears and though he was squeezing the breath out of her, she said into his ear, "Thomas, I'm sorry. I'm so sorry I put you in danger."

And rather than telling her it was nothing, rather than pretend, the giant of a field hand said gruffly, "Say no more about it."

It was good to be home.

In the morning, she sat up in bed and drank in everything about her room—the look of it, the pale walls, the smell, the light from the windows. Then she turned her head slowly and stared at the door to her world. She stared hard.

She did not look forward to the millions of questions she would have to answer that day. Of course, folks would be dying to hear every detail she could provide about outside events, for newspapers were almost impossible to come by these days.

Also, she did not look forward to the late morning tea with Lemuel Walker. Well, it was only tea and then he would be gone, she reasoned.

What she did look forward to was a visit with Sarah and Sally, and having to dress for the occasion. She jumped out of bed and threw open the door of the wardrobe. Four dresses. She had only four dresses left, now that the dark plaid was stained and torn beyond use. She took out her summer dress, the white lace she'd worn to the ball, shook it out and then found the gauzey shirtwaist, high-necked and long sleeved, that fit under the bodice for the sake of modesty.

Shilla called her down for breakfast but Annabelle was too excited to eat and asked, instead, if Shilla would come up and help her dress.

And so, with great ceremony, she and Shilla laid out her things, and with more of Shilla's help, she bathed and then readied herself to put each layer on.

Her stockings and pantaloons came first. The long chemise was then pulled over her head and then came the corset and the little corset cover, and Annabelle began to wish the clothes could put themselves on, for Heaven's sake. She had forgotten what it felt like to be dressed in layers like a pastry crust. And she felt appropriately oven-heated, too. She then stepped into and tied on the hoop skirt—the one item that would help cool her as she walked—and then came two thin cotton petticoats over the hoops. The shirtwaist was next and then the dress itself, and lastly the choosing of a ribbon for her waist and finally it was done.

Ah, but then there was the fixing of her hair. Shilla carefully slicked her tresses to either side of a sharp part in the middle, brought her hair to a neatly braided bun in the back and pinned it in place. Then the felt boots were pulled on and laced up the sides, the gloves, parasol and bonnet were chosen and a ribbon tied around the bonnet to match the color at her waist. She hung her purse at her belt and tucked a handkerchief there and then walked gracefully to her father's room to look at herself in the long mirror on the far wall.

From the doorway Shilla said, "Traveling has done ye good, lass. There's some color in yer cheeks, now."

Annabelle laughed. "Say what you mean, Shilla! I've been sunburnt!" And Shilla laughed and clucked her tongue.

But then Annabelle looked around her father's room, and a tight sort of feeling came into her throat. She put her head down and said a quiet prayer for her father and then looked up to find Shilla's eyes filled with tears.

She gave a little self-conscious laugh and Shilla smiled.

"Yer not thinkin' of runnin' off agin' are ye?"

"No, Shilla. No. I miss him terribly, but I... I know what it's like for him out there, and I know what he wants of me here."

"I'm one to be glad to hear it," said Shilla.

Just then Annabelle's stomach growled. The dressing process had taken an hour and a half, and Annabelle winked at Shilla. "I hope my corset strings aren't so tight I can't eat my breakfast! I have missed our kitchen most of all." And she followed Shilla down the stairs.

It was 9 A.M. when Annabelle decided it was time to leave—a little early, yes, but she knew her friends would understand. They lived on a beautiful estate west of town, and Annabelle thought the walk would do her good. But the twenty minute walk took an hour and twenty minutes after Annabelle stopped and reported the news to Ritter Estes, Mrs. Brimble, Fanny Day, the old men in front of Pease Dry Goods, the ladies doing wash in the Smith's side yard, and finally Molly Parker who, it turns out, was really more interested in telling her what she knew than listening, and so Annabelle reluctantly heard everything the Parker family had done in the last three weeks.

She was exhausted when she reached the door of the Drum house, but Sarah and Sally's company soon revived her. Right away Sally announced her engagement and to Annabelle's shock she told her the wedding was the next Saturday. "I was praying you'd be back in time, and so you are! It's wonderful."

James Alton was promoted, Sally explained, and was now a full colonel, but with the responsibilities came a new regiment and a new placement in the field. He would have to go with his men soon, and so they had decided to marry before he left. Annabelle noted the tremor in Sally's voice, and she was secretly sad for her decision. But any fellow smart enough to get Sally Drum was smart enough to dodge bullets and shells, she reassured herself. She did not express those thoughts in words, however.

Sally ran upstairs then with a servant to put on the dress she would wear to show Annabelle, and while she was gone, Annabelle told Sarah about some of her traveling adventures.

"Any news of Michael?" Sarah asked, and although Annabelle should have prepared herself for just such a question, she was caught completely off guard and blushed violently. Sarah cocked her head. "What is it, Annie?" Then, much to her horror, the truth was out of Annabelle in a moment, and she fell into Sarah's shoulder with the tears she had held back all those days and nights. Tears for the humiliation of meeting him in the cabin, tears for Michael, for the loss, and worst of all, for the not knowing. Sarah listened and patted her head and told her she had done the right thing.

"I suppose that's all I've wanted to hear," Annabelle sniffed. "I did leave a note at a picket for them to go and check on him. I told them he'd been bushwhacked, but I found out later they shoot men for sleeping on picket, so I'm sure the note was never shown to anyone. Sarah, you mustn't tell anyone. Not a soul."

"Of course not. Of course not. Well, I've never wanted to say how little I thought of Michael, knowing you cared for him so much, but I can tell you now he's quite lived down to my expectations, Annie."

Annabelle nodded. "I never really knew him, did I?"

"No," said Sarah, "but your father did."

Sally returned just then and Annabelle drew in a long breath. The dress was a pale blue shot silk with fine lace set around the collar and cuffs and a dainty row of mother of pearl buttons running all the way from her delicate neck down the front of the dress to the floor. The skirt was pleated evenly around the front but grew fuller and longer in the back, in keeping with the latest style.

Sally awed Annabelle with the story of how they had gathered the materials to make the gown; paybacks and back-scratching and goods brought through the blockade long ago, needles sent through the mail, and lace and thread purchased as if they were buying gold. She wasn't sure if it was the stories or the sight of Sally in the dress or some combination thereof, but a lump grew in her throat that did not leave until she made it home.

Then she waited with growing irritation for Lem Walker to arrive.

FIFTEEN

"You flatter me," said a thin exquisite,
the other day, to a young lady
who was praising the beauties of his
mustache. "For mercy's sake, ma'am,"
interposed an old skipper, "don't
make that monkey any flatter than he is."

From *Harper's Weekly*, 1857

When Lemuel Walker came to the door, he stood speechless as he looked past Shilla to view Annabelle in all her finery. Annabelle glanced down and blushed, wishing she'd had the sense to change her clothes. He surely needed no encouragement.

Annabelle showed Mr. Walker her father's offices, and was quickly reminded he was unable to carry on artful conversation of any sort. In her father's upper office, she turned to him. He'd said so little, she wondered if he'd been listening at all, but instantly she regretted looking at him, for now he was staring at her with that lost look of his—the very look she detested. Annabelle brought forward her chin and curtly asked if they might now move to the parlor for tea before he left. He nodded and they moved silently downstairs where he took a seat on the sofa. Annabelle carefully took the chair. She wished Shilla would hurry with the tea.

She sat with a cold smile and finally brought up the subject of his internship. "My father's offices are small. I suppose it will be difficult for two to work there. You are probably used to something more spacious."

"Your father has some fine old equipment," he said, and for the first time he seemed able to focus on something other than Annabelle. "Those pots, they are somewhat large for blood-letting."

"They're for boiling water to clean Father's instruments."

"Oh, that old saw. Yes, well, I believe your father had to face facts in the field. Boiling water doesn't do anything but waste precious time and energy."

She pressed her lips together and forced herself to be silent. She knew full well Dr. Benjamin Dudley's theory was sound, and that her father boiled the instruments every chance he got—even in the field.

But Walker brought up the office again. "Yes, the whole of it could use some rearranging. Perhaps an addition could be built to the back of the house." Annabelle bristled. She was in charge of organizing her father's offices. Still, this was the fellow her father had chosen for an intern. Walker shook his head and laughed. "I thought I'd never see a one-eared stethoscope again. That's really quite something. Yes, I believe I can round out that inventory somewhat and bring him up-to-date."

Carefully counting to ten, Annabelle took a deep breath and pressed on. "Well, I'm sure you will enjoy Hillsborough. Like my father's offices, we are small and seemingly antiquated, but we have everything we need, that is, when war is not at our doorstep."

"Yes, I am certain Hillsborough has everything I would need." And he blushed a mottle of red patches over his fair skin that made Annabelle squirm in her seat. "It is a quaint little town, and I hope to live here a very long while." He was looking at Annabelle with those lost puppy eyes of his once more, and she looked away.

She hated the word "quaint," and she hated those puppy dog eyes. *Where is Shilla?* she thought with irritation.

"Miss Annabelle... if I may address you as Miss Annabelle," Walker said uncertainly.

She nodded. "Of course. You will be my father's partner."

"But I should hope to come to know you *very* well while I am here. I think so highly of your father, and you must know you dwell in the upper reaches of my esteem, as well. Such respect and admiration flows from me unbidden by your fair voice, I realize, nevertheless, though it's been such a short time since our meeting,

I find you to be a woman among women, a woman that a man might come to treasure as life itself."

Thinking perhaps he had read one too many romantic novels to make such a puddle of words at her feet, she almost burst out laughing, but she quelled the impulse. "Mr. Walker, I'm not sure you know me as well as all that, to think anything of..." But he was looking at her so intently, she knew he wasn't listening. "Now, where can Shilla be?" And she rose up on the pretense of checking on her. But as she passed him, he had the audacity to grab her hand. "Mister Walker?!"

"I cannot eat or sleep or think of you, I mean to say to think of anything but you, but I... uh." And he blushed to hear his own jumbled wording.

He was, of course, ruining his chances of ever enjoying his internship, but Annabelle was fairly certain she couldn't tolerate him under any circumstances, anyway. She pulled on her hand but he held it firmly. She wanted to shake him out of his daydreams as quickly as possible, so she gulped, "Mr. Walker, you hardly know me. May I remind you the first time you saw me—a *woman among women*—I had come all the way to the Potomac River unescorted? Suppose... Suppose I like to hunt or drink. You see, sir..." She tried to laugh. "You really don't know me at all."

"If you hunt, I would call you the most beautiful huntress on earth, and if you drink, I would cause you to drink of me, and if I don't know you now, that's as it should be, for I will give my life to knowing you completely."

He has obviously caught his breath, Annabelle thought, *but he is certainly not catching the point.*

"I could never wonder at your actions, my dear, sweet, Miss Annabelle," he went on, still pressing her hand. "For I know your father well enough to be assured of the quality of his offspring."

His last offering was too much. As if she were a prize cow at the fair! With vinegar in every word, she said, "Mr. Walker, this has really gone far enough, please! You do my father insult to provide this... this sort of display without his consent!" And with some violence she snatched her hand from his.

He hesitated for a moment, and then he coughed. "I, I didn't really mean to say so much. It is too soon. You are right." They were silent for a moment and Annabelle was about to excuse herself to the kitchen when Walker added, "It's just that, in these uncertain times, one never knows if one will have a tomorrow in which to say such things. I do apologize."

This much Annabelle could understand, and her heart softened somewhat.

"I should have spoken to your father." He wearily rubbed his hands against his face for a moment.

The room was silent for a great while, and then she clasped her hands together. "Actually, I suppose I'm glad you've finally spoken your mind. I believe I was growing tired of thinking for you."

She thought she saw a little flash of hurt pride come to his eyes, but then he smiled and nodded. "I see. I suppose I have made a pretty fool of myself these last few days." He stood up and bowed. "But I hope with time to prove myself worthy of your admiration." He looked into her face. "It is, if I may be so bold, what I will live for."

She swallowed and then tittered, "If only you will speak your true mind more often, I'm certain it will be the more pleasant for everyone; I'm sure you wouldn't keep your good opinion to yourself in the surgeon's tent."

"Oh, no, of course not. Not with *him*," Walker said grandly, and somehow Annabelle was angry all over again. He certainly had a knack for making her angry.

And then, to her great satisfaction, he said he would have to be going. With polite goodbyes at the door, Lem Walker asked if he might correspond with her. She agreed, saying she would be glad to so he might know all about Hillsborough before he was to be her father's intern, but she hoped the war would end soon so that he might learn these things for himself. But when she saw the light in his eyes, she quickly regretted saying anything of the like. Then he bowed and was gone.

As she turned from the door Shilla came out with the tea things, and Annabelle informed her they could share the tea together.

"Already left then?" Shilla said. "He's got eyes for you, hasn't he, miss? Two great bulgy eyes." And she winked.

Annabelle giggled and shook her head. "I believe his estimation of my worth has placed me somewhere between a prize cow and a good meal, and, now that I think on it, that puts me squarely in a cattle cart bound for market, doesn't it?" Annabelle rolled her eyes and they had a good laugh, then Annabelle repeated much of the conversation to Shilla and with unmerciful flourishes repeated his last dramatic words: "It is, if I may be so bold, what I will *live* for..." And she had Shilla in tears of laughter when she was through. Oh, but it felt good to laugh again.

Annabelle turned her thoughts then to Sally's wedding. For a wedding gift, Annabelle decided to give Sally the pillowcases she had embroidered and placed within her own cedar hope chest years before. She took them out and worked Sally and James' initials into the circles of embroidered flowers on each one.

Sally was even more quiet than usual in those days before the ceremony, and Annabelle could see her decision to marry was weighing heavily on her.

On Saturday morning, in the first week of August, Annabelle walked to the church with Shilla at her side. But, as she came through one set of doors, a little thrill of horror touched her to see Michael's family, the Delaneys, enter through the other doors. They nodded politely, and Annabelle could only think that their calm faces meant they'd heard nothing at all about Michael. She took a seat and kept her eyes forward.

All during the ceremony, her sad feelings led her to ponder her own future. What was she supposed to do with herself? Why wasn't she called to do something with her gifts? And when would a man like Sally's come into her life? A Lemuel Walker who had an opinion? A Michael Delaney who would love her for herself? A dashing fellow like the spy, but with a heart? A man with a sense of humor and kindness like her father's? Was there a man like this? Perhaps it was too much to ask. And would a man with all these attributes be willing to love her? And if there were such a man, would he be alive after this war?

She vaguely heard Sally and James making their vows to one other, and she fell to judging herself intently for her past mistakes. She'd shown strong-headed stupidity in trying to find her father, and put her life in danger—the one thing her father feared the most. She didn't much like the way she'd treated Lemuel Walker, was horribly uncomfortable thinking again on the problem of Michael Delaney, and she hated herself for being unable to tell her friends everything she'd gone through. She also allowed a few kicks to her soul for getting in the way of the poor spy. Perhaps she'd ruined his mission altogether, and he was only polite to say it wasn't so.

Oh, how she hated herself just then. She couldn't see a man taking her as she was now, but at least she was repentant—yes, she was very sorry. But she didn't know what to feel past that rotten, sinking feeling that had settled in her soul, and so she sat there feeling wretched. She breathed deeply and asked the Lord to forgive her, and she knew that he did and yet, there were people to make amends to, people she may never see again, and so she couldn't feel completely right.

And then they were married, and the congregation came away to the Drums' home for the reception.

During the festivities, Sarah struck up a conversation with Annabelle that made her forget all of her self-pity. She said, "By the way, I have a bit of a mystery for you. This morning Sally said she remembered the name and where she'd seen it. Norris' name, I mean."

Annabelle took a deep breath. "What exactly did Sally remember?"

"Alfred's only son was from the 33rd regiment, wasn't he?"

"I think so."

"Sally said she remembered seeing the name on the list of casualties of war the month before he came. Jedediah Norris."

"But it wasn't Jedediah, it was Malachi."

"There's the mystery!" said Sarah with a cry of delight.

Annabelle pulled her hand up to her heart.

"Is it possible that handsome fellow was a spy? You know

Hannah Brighton—she can't remember her servants' names from one day to another, and so she took this Malachi fellow for her nephew, and don't you wonder what he came around looking for?" Sarah ran on cheerfully, but Annabelle was barely listening.

Soon after, she took herself away from the reception and walked all the way home. She had to think.

She had always known he wasn't really Brighton's nephew, hadn't she? She really had always known it; he'd said as much, but to hear the plain fact he was an imposter somehow turned the whole thing sinister once more. Worse yet, the Widow Brighton had been duped into thinking her nephew was alive, while the War Department was right on their mark. What a cruel trick to play on an old widow woman.

Now she thought of her father working himself to nothing near to and within the battlefields with no guarantees he would survive. She had just watched her friend marry a man who would more than likely die. She'd heard officers were more likely to die. And spies were more likely to die. At the reception it seemed all anyone had spoken of was this cousin or that uncle or brother dying at such and such a place. She was sick of it—utterly sick of it all. As a result, the rest of August was marked by a suffering despondency in her soul that Annabelle could not shake.

By the end of August, Shilla and Annabelle and Thomas worked hard to jar the vegetables and fruits in the oppressive heat and humidity. With their neighbors, they traded work for cornmeal and buckwheat. Flour was nowhere to be found, unless you took the oath of allegiance to Lincoln's government. If you took the oath, you could buy your wares straight from the blue devils or have them handed to you in rations. And while Annabelle bravely stated she would rather starve than take the oath, in fact, the theoretical choice had already become a real one for many of her neighbors.

In early September, the town received news of Michael Delaney. He was listed as missing in action. Annabelle knew better, of course, and allowed herself to feel completely wretched knowing she couldn't say a word about him, not even to tell his parents she saw him alive, but then she couldn't guarantee he was still alive.

Daily life was beyond her control, ever changing and she changing with it, as from within her a gnawing sense of survival supplanted all her former dreams and hopes.

She didn't like the feelings she felt now, the fear of the unknown and the raw and violent energy that sprang up in her bones whenever people talked about Yankee soldiers coming, Yankee soldiers burning a nearby mill, blue bellies putting a torch to a family's barn, stealing the family silver, a friend's dowry. No one spoke of winning anymore. All talk was of survival.

It took all her energy to manage her anger and keep herself from the fear that wrangled her afterward. Hoarding their food as best they could, Thomas and Shilla also began performing drills in the dead of night in case the enemy came through to steal or kill their livestock.

Thomas made a secret path up the hill that curved well up into the woods toward the cemetery. On the drills, he would hold Lucy's halter in one hand and a lead for their old cow, Priss, in the other and head for the henhouse. There he would gather three of their best hens and place them on Priss' shoulders and rump and tuck the chicken's necks down under their wings, which caused them instantly to fall sleep. Then, after tucking his favorite rooster up under his arm, he would gently guide his little menagerie up the hill and through the fence—all to keep their livestock and horse from the soldiers.

Whenever Annabelle watched Thomas by lamplight, she wished she could draw Thomas and the animals because each and every time it made her laugh—each time, that is, until the autumn day it ceased to be a drill.

The soldiers in blue came through on a cool morning right after first cockcrow. Luckily, Thomas had been awake the hour before.

Four Union soldiers and their regimental doctor pounded on the MacBains' door until Shilla unlocked the thing. They proceeded to push their way in. The doctor took two of the soldiers with him to Dr. MacBain's office and proceeded to relieve the shelves of everything there, including the one-eared stethoscope. When the other two soldiers asked Shilla where the silver was hidden, she lied and told them soldiers had taken it already. Still, they proceeded to go through every room of the house looking, presumably, for money. Annabelle came down the stairs in a rage, but for Thomas' sake and his sake alone, she held her tongue. She stood in the doorway of her father's office, and in an angry silence, watched them ransack his things.

Thomas was safely up the hill by then, and Annabelle wished to keep everything as quiet as possible. No trouble. The doctor and the soldiers who smelled of dirt and gunpowder didn't know to ask or look for medicine beyond her father's shelves, thank Heaven, but the other soldiers managed to take every bit of food in the pantry and the root cellar—all the jars they'd stored for winter, save the ones, of course, in the cache below the smokehouse. The group would have taken every morsel and left them with absolutely nothing if they could.

Annabelle sighed in relief when they prepared to leave but then held her breath as they decided to look through the outbuildings.

It seemed like an hour, but it was only a few minutes before the soldiers finally left the yard. Annabelle then walked around the home in a daze, checking what was gone and trying to be thankful for what was left. Shilla followed with a dust rag and went on and on about how they could do this or that to last out the winter, that everything would be all right, but Annabelle finally had to ask her to please say no more.

But after about an hour the shock of it had passed and then came anger, tight-lipped and brooding, and it began to work its way up within her to a boiling, passionate rage.

She paced about the house until they heard the soldiers had left the town completely, and then she had to get out, to release her frustration somehow. And so she ran up the hill to the cemetery and walked calmly to her mother's tombstone. There she gathered her fists into tight knots and screamed to her heart's content, to the empty forest walls, to the rug of autumn leaves under her feet, and to the odd furniture of silent tombstones. And then she listened to her echo as the sound died out.

And when she was done, she felt better.

Winter came, and the cold was at least as cutting as the year before. The snow soaked one's boots, and the wet winds sliced through fabric more easily than the steel blade of an Arkansas toothpick.

The soldiers camped dutifully to last the winter out, but Major John S. Mosby never did like standard procedures, and since his favorite weapon was surprise, what could be more of a surprise than wading through a foot or two of snow to raid cold Union soldiers whose only thought was to stay warm?

And so, around midnight on the snowy night of January 9, 1864, Annabelle was awakened by the sound of dozens of horses marching through town. She saw the ostrich plume on the hat of the lead rider, and realized it was Mosby and his crew. She'd heard of the group of about three hundred Yankees socked in for the winter up the Harper's Ferry Road at Loudoun Heights. Apparently, Mosby had decided to do something about them.

The next day, Mosby's men returned through town. From the looks on their faces the fight had not gone well. As the town gathered bits and pieces of information, it was discovered Mosby had lost about seven of his finest men, and worse yet some had mistakenly died at the hands of their own comrades.

Still, to the Confederate cause, it must have been deemed some sort of success, because it was rumored Major Mosby would soon be made a colonel.

The town talked about the raid for a week, and the rumors began that the Federals were on the prowl again, looking for Mosby's Rangers. One cold afternoon, Sarah, Sally and Annabelle were knitting in Annabelle's parlor, chatting about the soldiers' raid, their conversation highlighted by the clicking of their needles in a rhythmic titter, when Sally ventured she was glad to have something to do to keep her hands warm. It reminded Annabelle of how cold it was the night of the raid, and she told them she'd heard men had lost fingers and toes to frostbite on that venture.

"The Rangers surely suffered that night, but they seem to keep warm enough most of the time," Sarah said. "You know, it's said John Mosby will go anywhere for a cup of real coffee."

Annabelle rejoined, "Well, then Hillsborough won't expect the pleasure of his company anytime soon."

"Oh," said Sally, "I heard he carries a pouch of grounds with him all the time!"

"No!" Then Annabelle shrugged. "To the victor go the spoils. At least he doesn't imbibe."

"He mayn't, but his men certainly do," Sarah said. "Just the other day Captain Murphy and one of his aides came into town to call at Dottie Lansing's. They stayed the whole of the afternoon and they could hardly get back on their mounts afterwards."

"Really!" Annabelle said with disgust.

"Yes, and they had the finest horses and outfits I've ever seen. Honestly, it looks as though they've become soldiers just to have something to wear to a dance, with their fine uniforms and polished leather." Annabelle and Sally shook their heads in dismay. "And you know," Sarah went on, "for one horrible moment I thought the fellow with Captain Murphy had taken Lucy for his mount."

"Don't frighten me, Sarah," Annabelle chided. "You'll make me go out to the shed to check on her for fear."

"It wasn't Lucy, of course. It wasn't Lucy, but it could have been her twin, and this James fellow practically pranced her down the road as if she were a show horse, that is, before they'd visited with Dottie."

"You met them?" Sally asked.

"Well, yes," Sarah colored at the question. "But only because Captain Murphy saw me."

"Where have I heard that name, James?" Annabelle asked.

Sarah laughed and Sally smiled. "What?" said Sarah. "Do you have Sally-itis, now?" And they all laughed.

Annabelle smiled but lost her smile as the memory grew clear in her mind. "Now I remember. I met a James. Remember how I told you I almost lost Lucy at the river? It's funny you should say a fellow named James rode a horse like Lucy, because the fellow who tried to take her was named James. Reynold James, I think."

"Yes!" cried Sarah incredulously. "Reynold James! Is he built like a lumberjack?"

Annabelle nodded. "Balding? With green eyes?"

"Yes, green eyes, I think, but he was wearing a hat." Sarah paused, thinking. "You know the Rangers require a man to bring his own horse when he joins up with them. Maybe…"

"Unless Mosby gives them one from the spoils," Sally corrected.

"Yes," said Sarah. "But I was going to say, perhaps this James wanted your horse so he could ride with Mosby."

"I think you must be right." Annabelle put down her needles and shook her head. "To think he might have been riding my own Lucy into town." It was an awful thought.

"He may have ridden in, but I don't believe he would have ridden out on her," said Sally, so boldly and with such venom it made the girls look at her in mock amazement. Sally just trilled a laugh to see their faces.

"You would have shot him on the spot, eh, little sister?" joked Sarah.

"Half a minute older is hardly cause to call me little sister, Sarah."

Sarah cocked her head and smiled impishly. "I was referring to your size, dearest."

"You!" And Sally threw the nearest pillow at her.

But Sarah caught it in midair and laughed. "Poor shot!" Then she settled the pillow behind her and turned back to Annabelle. "Tell me again the story of how you got Lucy away from him, Annie. Now that I've seen the brute, I'll listen more carefully."

And so Annabelle repeated the story, and the needles all fell silent as she spoke.

Further diversions for the girls that winter were the letters from Lemuel Walker. Annabelle chose to read them to her friends and ask their advice on how to reply. Sarah always said he sounded absolutely wonderful and that Annabelle should marry him, while Sally kept saying it was too much of a decision to base on letters alone. His missives at first all sounded as he had, reverent, utterly smitten and yet somehow detached. But as time wore on and she replied to the letters one by one, they grew more natural. Then Annabelle began to actually like them a little. She began to wonder what he looked like now and she took more care with her replies. The girls saw the change and gave each other knowing glances.

Sorrow came to their circle when Mrs. Drum took fever and died in March. At least, thought Annabelle rashly, it brought their father back to them for a time, to settle things with his girls before leaving home once more. Annabelle almost wished some cataclysm would befall her that would bring her father home, but just as quickly she reprimanded herself for thinking like that. But, oh, how she worried for him, and, oh, how she missed him, too.

After the funeral, when friends and relatives were gathered at the Drums' home, Colonel Drum shocked his daughters with the news he wished his girls to go to their Aunt Agatha's home in Richmond for the duration of the war.

He told them they were not safe in town any longer, and of course they could not refute him. He suggested that Annabelle go with them, but when she politely refused, he proceeded to humiliate her by saying no proper father would allow his child to care for a home under these circumstances. Annabelle was ripe to argue, but out of respect, she held her tongue.

After he walked away, Sarah and Sally immediately asked her to reconsider. But she could only shake her head. She knew she would miss them horribly, but she couldn't imagine her father coming home to an empty house. "But you might write him, Annie," said Sarah, "and he would come straight to you in Richmond."

Annabelle thought it about and finally said, "I have a confession to make. You must believe it when I say I want to be here, now. I am glad to have learned what I've learned, on my own, and so I don't mind the dangers." She looked at them. "Can you understand?"

To her surprise both nodded back. "I understand, Annie," Sally said. "Ever since my wedding day, all I've wanted is a home to care for—our own home."

"Father treats us like children," Sarah clucked. "He doesn't realize how we've managed things while mother was ill." She looked at her father far across the room. "But, of course, we would never dare refuse his wishes."

"I know," Annabelle said softly. "I know." And then the three friends entwined their arms in sad but certain understanding of it all.

In April, her young friends left for Richmond. The day after they left, a large group of Mosby's Rangers came through and gleaned the goods from stores and farms. To Annabelle's relief, they seemed determined to pick only on Quakers and Union sympathizers. She felt badly for Hannah Brighton when she heard they'd taken her last wagon and most of her crops. Hannah had tried to remain neutral, giving to both armies when they asked, as many of the Quakers did, but it seemed inevitable one side would eventually become irritable about it.

As summer approached, Annabelle and Shilla began to care for Mistress Humboldt more and more. The two women could not induce her to come and live with them, but she was more than willing for them to come by her place as often as possible. And so they would clean her house and fill her pantry and fix things that needed fixing.

In June, Lemuel Walker sent a recent photograph of himself. He looked older, had grown a handsome moustache which fell nicely to either side, and his face seemed to have filled out somewhat. He hinted rather boldly at marriage in his letters, and now Annabelle didn't seem to mind so much. She could do worse, she reasoned, and quite literally had tried. The least she could do now was think about it—to try the idea of Mrs. Lemuel Walker on for size.

By early summer of '64, Mosby's Rangers had grown to a size numbering several hundred men grouped into various companies. Their activities within "Mosby's Confederacy," the counties of Loudoun and Fauquier, had of course grown in proportion to their size and so the Federals were becoming desperate to dispose of them. Yet Mosby's Rangers were so confident, and the discretion of the local people so reliable, the whole of company B made itself comfortable in the taverns and homes of Hillsborough for the entire first week of June without unreasonable fear. The soldiers amused themselves with cards and dancing and music, but early on Annabelle discovered Reynold James was in this very company and so she stayed well away.

One night, long after supper, Annabelle had a hankering for buttered bread before going to bed. For once in many months they had real bread and real butter to enjoy. The flour was a gift from the Drums, sent up from Richmond. "Lord only knows where they got it from in Richmond," she wondered aloud as she padded down the back stairs in her dressing gown. Her stomach grumbled loudly and soon the bread knife was in her hand. She cut a thick piece of bread and realized with slight irritation that she would have to go out to the spring house for the butter. But it was well worth the trouble.

In the springhouse, she was bent over and looking down the row of crocks in the stream to find the right one when she thought she heard something move to her left. Thinking, *Rattlesnake!* Annabelle froze.

But then she heard a little voice. "Miz MacBain, doan you tell on me, please."

A child's voice? It was Pella.

"Pella, that you?" She peered into the darkness and raised her lamp to see.

The pile of baskets in the corner moved slightly. "Yes, miz. But doan tell 'im I'm here, please."

"Pella, step out here now," she said firmly.

Clearly frightened, Pella complied, but, as he came toward her, she saw he held a large stick in one hand and raised it as he walked.

Annabelle's back straightened. "No need for that. No need for that, child. Tell who, Pella, Mr. Marsden?"

He stopped and nodded once.

"What's the stick for?"

He was silent.

"You know you don't have to be afraid of me." But the stick did not move. She hunched her shoulders forward with dismay. "You know Marsden'll punish you if you try and run away from him, and that stick isn't near big enough to keep him from you."

"I ain't a goan back, tonight, miz. I ain't. Doan' you try and make me, neither."

Annabelle couldn't think what to do. Harboring a slave, even one so young, was against the law. The Emancipation Proclamation hadn't meant much to the slaves in Loudoun County thus far, and Mr. Marsden would be within his rights to... well, she didn't care to think about it.

"But, Pella, you know you have to go back," she whispered. Now he looked terror-stricken and he brought the stick up as if to hit her, and so she stepped back. "All right! All right. Wait." She licked her lips. "You know you can trust me, Pella. Tell me why you're so afraid of him tonight."

He hesitated but finally answered, "Marsden, he drunk. Mighty drunk and swears to sell me to a soldier man. But I won't go." He lowered the stick somewhat. "I tell you. I ain't a goan. Mr. Marsden, he's jis drunk an' off his coot. He be all right tomorrow, and he forget all he done dis night. And de soldiers be gone tomorrow. So, Miz MacBain, kin't I stay here tonight?"

She knew Pella well enough to believe him. She knew Marsden well enough to believe every word Pella said. Marsden would threaten to sell him to a soldier just to enjoy frightening the child. Then again, he might. If he were drunk enough and the mood struck him, he very well might sell Pella off. She shuddered in the coolness of the stone room and wiped her forehead, trying to think what to do. "Lord, help me," she pleaded in a whisper.

And what would Father do? she asked herself. *I wish he were here.* But a voice rose up inside her. *No, this is your decision now, and you must ask what Christ would do.*

Swinging the lamp out toward him then, she looked into his frightened eyes. "Pella, you may stay."

"Thank you."

"But you understand they will hold me responsible if you don't return in the morning, so I'm counting on you. Will you return then? Promise?"

He nodded.

"Good." But a thought began to rankle her mind and they both stood for a moment until she had wrestled with it. "Do... do you want to stay indoors?" If he were caught in her home, she knew she'd receive abuse from her neighbors at the very least, but if Pella stayed out in the springhouse and were caught at least Annabelle could claim she hadn't known he was there. She was surprised Pella took so long to answer, and she looked up to see him staring at her.

"No, miz. Out here'll be fine." And she let out a breath she hadn't known she was holding. She was too glad, much too glad for his answer.

"I'll go and get you some blankets, then."

"Horse blankets be fine, miz." Lowering his voice he added, "You know de house blankets won't do."

Startled, she looked up at him, for she realized he had kept perfect pace with her thoughts. "Thank you, Pella, I'll get them."

On the way back down the stairs, she wondered if Samuel Brighton had ever taken Pella in on a night like this. She wished the little boy weren't owned by such a man as Marsden. But then she sighed. If it weren't Pella, it would be some other poor child, and at least Pella had sense enough to stay away from him when he needed to.

She gathered the blankets from the pantry, and when she returned to the springhouse, Pella took them and laid them out in the corner behind the baskets. Annabelle wiped a stray hair from her forehead as she watched him. "Pella, do you still miss Samuel Brighton?" she asked gently.

He turned and nodded sadly.

"He was a good man, wasn't he?"

He nodded again. "He watched out for me, Miz MacBain, but now I got's to watch out fo' myself."

"God watches over you."

"I guess," he said quietly, and she nodded to his honest answer. She went back to the house and spent a long while praying for him.

In the morning she found the blankets neatly folded in the

corner of the springhouse, and she walked to the creek past Marsden's place to try to find him. She wasn't afraid he was gone. She was afraid he'd been caught somehow, afraid he'd been punished. To her relief as she passed the back kitchen of the tavern she saw Pella chopping wood. He looked up, they nodded, and that was all.

And life returned to its pace, each to his own.

SIXTEEN

My homespun dress is plain, I know,
My hat's palmetto, too,
But then it shows what Southern girls
for Southern rights will do.
We've sent the bravest of our land
To battle with the foe,
And we will lend a helping hand,
We love the South, you know.

Song, *The Homespun Dress*

In July of '64, Shilla and Annabelle were working hard once again to put up for the winter, packing their hiding place with goods to keep from losing most of it to soldiers as they had the year before. Thomas built a bookcase in an unused doorway and made the bottom kickboard empty under a removable shelf so they could keep their silver inside and hide it at their ease. At a church supper, an old school chum informed Annabelle her family had lost their buried silver when soldiers decided to bayonet their yard. Annabelle had Thomas go out to the yard the very next day and bury her father's medicine even deeper. Everyone did what they could to prepare for the worst, but they were bone tired of the effort.

Annabelle missed her father. It had been almost a year, though it felt like forever, since she'd seen him. She was forgetting the sound of his voice, his laughter. She was forgetting all the little things, and at certain times of the day missing him could loom larger than life itself.

There were skirmishes around Hillsborough east and west as the Federals pursued Jubal Early and his men retreating from Washington. The days Annabelle could see smoke or hear artillery from her home were too numerous to count. The year before, everyone would always run to their homes whenever soldiers were near, but now they cast a weary eye toward the noise and pretty much kept about their business.

In August, life changed for everyone again.

A new edict was given to wipe the scourge of Mosby's Rangers from the land. General Ulysses S. Grant had given instructions, people said, to destroy and carry off the crops, animals, slaves, and any men under fifty-one capable of bearing arms.

In September, when the orders were still not carried out, Annabelle and Shilla begged Thomas not to go to the fields for harvest for fear he'd be taken. He just shrugged off their worries, reminding them of a hundred such rumors in the past and how nothing had come of any of them in Loudoun County. He went to the harvest. Nothing happened. Loudouners began to think again it was only rumor, and yet Annabelle thought it was all rather too good to be true.

Then, in mid-October, the Federals captured and summarily executed six of Mosby's men in a retaliation. Miss Sophie Sutter, Annabelle's overly romantic school chum, happened to be in the town of Front Royal, Virginia, when the Federals brought such heady revenge on their foes there, and she wrote Annabelle about every horrible detail of what she'd seen and heard. Knowing Sophie as she did, Annabelle might have believed the story was created from Sophie's rich imagination: the execution of two men beside a church wall, their bodies left in bloody heaps for all to see and learn from; the tale of the mother whose young son had ridden for the first and last time with Mosby's Rangers the morning of this ill-planned raid, only to be brought home by Federals and shot before his mother's eyes while she begged for his life. The stories sickened Annabelle just as they had sickened her poor friend. "Such cruelty I had never seen," Sophie wrote, and Annabelle cried for her and for them and worried over what was to come.

In late October the news came that indeed a formal order had been given to "scorch and burn" Loudoun County to purge the area of Rangers. People had seen the document at the provost marshal's office in Harper's Ferry. "They're just trying to frighten us," they told each other when they gathered on the street. "You see nothing's happened." And they were right—until November when the Union army gathered enough men to carry out the task.

Even as the weather turned to a bitter chill, the order came down, and so one day Annabelle came back to the house after hearing about it to tell Shilla and Thomas. She told them somberly, instructing Thomas to please stay close to the house now. He nodded gravely.

In the last week of November, the tempest came.

The clear winter sky turned black with smoke, and people streamed from their homes to point and stare and curse the day. Those who knew distances could tell that Hamilton, southwest of Hillsborough, was burning. Then they saw fires from Purcellville, eight miles south, and then gray snowflakes of ash began to fall on their own shingled roofs. They watched as the fires grew closer and turned the world gray, and now people took time to reconsider their allegiances.

Some packed their things in wagons and headed out of town, but this seemed a foolish idea to Annabelle, for with the likes of these brutes about, the road would surely have its own danger.

And would they burn the outbuildings and barns within Hillsborough? everyone asked themselves. Rumor replied they wouldn't, for fear of catching the homes on fire. At least they hadn't yet taken to burning homes, people reassured one another. With that in mind, Annabelle left their goods under the smokehouse. Although it was a difficult decision, she could think of no better place to take them unless it was up the hill to bury them, too much of a task in the cold of winter for already the ground was hard as ice.

It was painful waiting—the most painful time of all of Annabelle's life—not knowing what would come but seeing the destruction so clearly in the sky.

Then a huge billow of black smoke rose from the southeast, very near to town, and Annabelle grasped Shilla's hand as they stood in the upper window watching. When they saw the haystacks lit on the surrounding fields, Annabelle said, "They are here."

Shilla nodded and with eyes hollow and lips drawn said, "I'll go to see about Hattie, then."

"God help her," Annabelle whispered.

"God help us all." And Shilla walked away.

Within a quarter of an hour the Yankees had arrived on the main road of Hillsborough.

Rows of men in blue overcoats rode into town on horseback just as they had the previous autumn. A marching group of soldiers arrived and quickly their officers arranged them, barking orders as they divided their duties. People came out of their homes and begged them to stop. Annabelle heard mothers and their children screaming down the road. She knew those voices, and listening to them made her weak.

From the guest room window she watched and gripped her stomach. As if in a trance, she stared as an officer pointed to one house and then another and another. Soldiers banged on the doors of each one and shouted orders, while other soldiers ran directly to the outbuildings and lit them without announcement. She shook with anger and fear. She watched as they torched Marsden's outbuildings and she was half glad for it.

She watched it all and she waited, staring at the swirling flames reaching high above the rooftops, the burgundy and orange of a searing heat formed in broad daylight.

At least her own home was secure, she told herself, but the knowledge didn't make the knot in her stomach go away. Thomas had gone up the hill with Priss and Lucy, and Shilla had gone to settle Hattie Humboldt's nerves. Although the troops were unlikely to bother an old woman, nonetheless Hattie would need comforting, but now Annabelle wished Shilla had stayed with her.

Then Annabelle watched the soldiers come to the Humboldt door and she sucked in her breath. The soldiers went in, and in a few minutes, to Annabelle's utter amazement, she heard them pulling down the rail fence in Hattie's back yard. She rushed to the back of the house and down the stairs, her heart pumping. "How *dare* they destroy an old woman's property!" she cried aloud as she came.

She ran out the back of the house full of righteous indignation, her thin parlor shoes crunching in the cold, dry grass, but she stopped short when she saw Hattie point a crooked finger toward her. Hattie, her eyes wide with fright and her neck stretched taut, looked every inch a snapping turtle just then. Shilla stood beside Hattie, staring hard at the old woman.

Annabelle was too frightened to think what was happening. Shivering, she felt a cold mud puddle seep slowly into her shoes.

Hattie gestured shakily to the officer in blue, and now a look of horror crossed Shilla's face. Annabelle's heart skipped a beat as Mistress Hattie pointed up the hill to where Thomas had walked just an hour before.

"Oh, no," Annabelle whispered, her words becoming mist in the cool air and floating slowly away from where she stood. "No!"

The officer gave a sharp command and three men in blue pulled away from him and broke into a run toward Thomas' hiding place. With their rifles held out before them, they moved stiffly up the frozen hill, up and up, toward Thomas.

Annabelle held out her hand as if that would hold the soldiers back but then cried out, choking on the words, "NO! Don't do that. Don't do that!"

Now they crossed up to Annabelle's hill and were driving hard toward the fence line.

She had to do something. Thomas' tracks would be obvious over that fence. They would get him. He would fight. But he would lose.

Suddenly Annabelle began rushing up the hill behind the men, slipping almost to the ground at first, but rising to run once more. As she struggled up the hill, she realized she would be too late unless she called out, and so she gave in to it all.

"Thomas!" she screamed. The men slowed to look back at her. "Thomas!" echoed into the woods. "Come down, Thomas! They know you're up there!" The soldiers stopped mid-stride and turned to stare at her and then they looked to their officer. He nodded, and so Annabelle yelled again for Thomas to come down, and then she listened to the thud of her own heartbeat in the silence that followed.

She couldn't believe this was happening. They were going to lose everything.

Soon came the slow tramp of animal and man and Thomas was leading them down, his face as gray as ash. Annabelle gripped her stomach and turned away, and the officer stalked over to her yard, but though she heard his steps she kept her head down and would not look at him.

"This is the house of a Confederate doctor?" he asked fiercely. He was an Englishman, or had been, and somehow that fact angered her all the more. They hadn't even sent a true Yankee to do their dirty work.

She remained silent.

He turned back to his men. "Kill all the livestock. Take that horse. Take him away."

Annabelle felt the world swing and sway, but with some effort she stood her ground. Shilla began to weep but Annabelle could not weep with her. She could only stare at the mud below her feet. Her mind could not take in the sound of the animals as they died. She would not look and she would not listen. She could not bring herself to say good-bye to Thomas, to Lucy.

Shilla screamed to Thomas that the old woman had betrayed him. What look Thomas gave Mistress Hattie Humboldt, Annabelle did not know, but she heard Shilla saying, "That's right, that's right! After all we done for ye! Ye better get into your fine house and stay there, ye wicked thing! And all good people have done with ye!"

At this point, the officer standing next to Annabelle told Shilla to be quiet and leave off threats or she'd be taken away, as well. Annabelle looked up at the officer then to see his lip curl and she thought, *Surely the world has turned upside down.*

Shilla threw her arms around Annabelle and sobbed, and the two women began to plod toward the kitchen door, their arms wrapped around each other's necks.

And all seemed silent and done with as they walked, but as they reached the door, the officer yelled out, "You there! Will you take the oath and spare your buildings?" Annabelle stopped for only one second, but then opened the door to her kitchen and went in. She sat at the table and Shilla sat across from her, as the men busily set fire to the chicken house, the shed, and then the smokehouse.

Within a few minutes, a knocking came at the kitchen door. Annabelle nodded, and Shilla rose to answer. It was the officer. "We spared the well house as it was too close to your home. My men are coming in now to search. You'll understand the orders are carried out here to keep Mosby from foraging in this area, to discourage you people from assisting him in any way."

Annabelle clasped her hands and set them on the table as calmly as she could. "Well, you've just burned the forage, sir." It was true. They'd not left enough in the home to please a wee mouse, and all the rest of the goods had been under the smokehouse.

But he brushed past her and the soldiers went to their work like hounds to the fox. That they had done this three or four hundred times before was obvious by their efficiency. They found no food in the kitchen or pantry, and other soldiers had already removed the accumulation of twenty years of doctoral practice. Curses filled the air, and Shilla rose from the table when they heard the trace of an Irish accent from one man. She walked to the office door and yelled to him something about the mother country.

He looked at her with bloodshot eyes. "Whill' now we know where they kip the cutlery." And the men around him laughed. It took all Annabelle's effort to sit at the table, and she quietly asked Shilla to please sit down.

What the soldiers couldn't carry they smashed on the floor with seeming delight. All the things her mother had brought with her from Scotland. The things her father had inherited from his family. "To keep Mosby from foraging," she repeated to herself with dry humor.

As they worked, Annabelle felt her spirit break within her. And this, she was sure, was the true and ultimate purpose of it all, and this they did better than all else.

Soldiers moved through the kitchen, looking through jars and covered pots, jostling past the two women at the table and quickly finding and entering Thomas' room. They came out and searched the dining room, then the parlor, taking any small belongings that caught their eye. Annabelle was glad she'd hidden her mother's portrait in the attic in her own hiding place against the ceiling, for they threw more than one picture to the floor to break the glass and look for... what? Hidden money, she supposed.

They broke furniture, and if they found a locked drawer they shattered the wood. Twice Annabelle offered to unlock a drawer and twice they broke through before she could even rise from her chair.

The men were laughing and talking now, easing their pace as they went upstairs. Their work was almost done.

Somehow she wished they'd take it all. Burn the house down. She didn't think she could bear to see it all left broken. She laid her head on the kitchen table and felt Shilla come over and move her hand across her hair gently. Now Annabelle understood the story of Job and what it felt like to have your life taken out from under you. Like Job, she said to the Lord, "What have I done to deserve this?" But she couldn't hear God's voice as she sat there at the kitchen table. Life had never seemed so empty of meaning and purpose. Nothing, absolutely nothing, made any sense at all.

The officer came back through to the kitchen as the group made ready to leave and he reached up to take Thomas' rifle from over the back door.

This was too much.

"Sir, I believe you've forgotten to cut off our hands," Annabelle said quietly.

"What did you say?" the officer asked in his clipped English accent.

Annabelle spread her hands slowly on the table before her and stared at her fingers. "You have taken our man-servant, the gentleman whose gun you're holding. You have taken all the food from our pantry. You have taken my horse, our livestock. You have burned our cache of food for winter. Our neighbors have nothing. With hunting our only hope of survival, if you take that gun—" She looked up at him for dramatic emphasis. "If you take that gun from us, you may as well remove our hands, for we will be unable to feed ourselves. We will not have a fair chance. In truth, we will not have a chance at all."

He ground his jaw and spat back, "You could take the oath, young lady."

She stared at him coolly. "And you could take yourself back to England."

He looked down at his shoes for a moment. Perhaps it was the shock of what she'd said—the harsh reality of what the burning raid would mean to Annabelle and all of her neighbors—or maybe it was the way in which she spoke her mind, but whatever the reason he quite suddenly laughed and returned the gun to its place on the wall. As he passed them at the table he said, "So be it," in a lofty tone, and then to a fellow soldier he murmured, "Never let it be said Captain Henry Taylor denied someone a fair chance."

The soldiers left the house, finally, through the front door. Annabelle watched the last soldier waddle through the door, a porcelain cherub candlestick stuck carelessly in each pocket, and then she continued to stare at the back of the door for half an hour more.

SEVENTEEN

They was poore looking Devils.
Ragged and starved to death.
They are so poor they wont Blead.

W.A. Payne

**1864 letter home from a
Union soldier concerning a recent
skirmish with Confederates.**

The two women sat at the kitchen table for two hours or more, and only once did one of them speak.

It was Shilla who braved the silence. "I'd like to kill that woman, after all we done for her." Annabelle did not disagree but only laid her head in her arms at the table again. She was overwhelmed and tired, beyond tears and well beyond sleep.

That the soldiers hadn't found the silver or the bulk of the medicine was her only comfort. These could be bartered for food to last the winter. And the furniture may have to go for firewood. A bitter curl came to her lips to think at least she wouldn't have to suffer the pain of breaking up the furniture with her own hands. The furniture. Ah, she was too tired to think of picking up. She was too sad to wish to discover all they'd taken or broken.

She finally told Shilla she had to try to sleep.

But when she came up to her room, she saw the broken furniture, her clothing spread like rags across the floor, and she brought herself to the window. And there she stood, leaning against the window well all night, staring out to the charred remains of their outbuildings.

Where a working yard had stood yesterday, there now lay piles of ashen logs and glowing charcoal, as if soldiers had made camp there the night before and left their bonfires to die.

The shed had fanned out as it fell, and so, although it made the largest scar in the earth, little of it was burning by nightfall. But the orange glow from the chicken house seemed very much alive. The waves of rippling heat within the logs gave Annabelle the odd sensation of watching breath. Something was trying to live, it seemed, but it was writhing in the heat and dying just the same. Now and then the wind would stir an orange-red ember into flame, wrench it from the wood, and it would fly across the yard only to be thrown to the cold ground to die. Toward morning the rest of the smokehouse roof caved in, and the sound of it thudding against the frosty hill made Annabelle straighten up where she stood.

All night long, she kept her eyes away from Humboldt House. She wasn't afraid of what she might do to that woman. She was simply past caring about anyone or anything at all. Past caring even how it had come to this. Another time she would have walked to the cemetery and had a good cry, but even that was beyond her now. It seemed she had only enough energy for thought—and only for one thought at a time.

Daylight brought December to her sleepless eyes. When the light again revealed the destruction in her room, she stared blankly about her from one thing to another, making a halfhearted inventory of all she was missing. She looked to her table and saw her books were gone. Moving her eyes upward she saw they'd taken her pictures from the wall, as well. All her favorite things. Some would be lost on the road. Some would be broken up for sport. Some would no doubt lie in a Northerner's house one day with the new owner unaware of the memories they held for a young girl in Virginia whose world had burned to the ground.

A mild vision formed in her mind; it would actually be pleasant to take Thomas' gun from the wall, walk to the nearest Yankee camp and shoot the first soldier she saw. That would feel good right now, very good.

But the bitter thought ended in a yawn.

Then Shilla called up the stairs, but Annabelle asked her to let her be for a while.

As the morning wore on, still trancelike, Annabelle got up and dressed. She pulled her clothes up from the floor and heaped them into one side of the wardrobe, the side they'd torn the shelves out of. But then she sat down on the bed, feeling completely drained and believing there was nothing else to do, anyway.

The sun had been up for a couple of hours and she was still sitting on her bed when she heard a far-away knocking, then a wild and angry thumping that she soon realized was the front door. She heard Shilla moving quickly to the door and then listened to the noise of gruff voices below. Annabelle's heart shot through with fear, for surely there was nothing left to take now but themselves.

She heard Shilla say loudly for Annabelle's benefit, "Medicine, ye say? Well, there's no one here to ask about medicine. Miss Annabelle is gone. Ye know fer yerself yer soldiers have been here before and taken it all." But an argument followed.

Soon there were boots against the stair. But Annabelle was already running with light steps to the attic. The nooks and crannies were wonderful for hide-and-seek when she was a child. More recently, Annabelle had taken to "hiding" there to read or draw or wile away her hours. Boxes were once piled on and around old furniture in heaps and layers and even up into the rafters, but the soldiers had scattered them in every direction. Still there was the desk in the corner, the desk where Annabelle kept all her drawings. The soldiers had pulled some of the drawers open and dumped them, but she didn't need the drawers just then.

She ran to the desk, quickly stepped up onto the top, reached up and took a great breath, then pulled herself up onto boards that lay across the rafters some eight feet from the floor. The effort strained every muscle in her body, but she had made it up more easily than she imagined she could, from sheer fright. She quickly curled herself into a ball, tucked her skirts up around her and waited in the cold.

With her nose to the wood, she smelled the raw pine of the planks and their cold pressed against her shoulders through her thin dress. She felt a trickle of sweat roll down her forehead and she listened to her own breathing as she waited.

One pair of boots came up the attic stair. One soldier walked the boards. She heard him looking around, moving boxes, and looking, looking. He walked to the desk, and she held her breath. She peered through a crack between the boards and stared at the top of his head.

Go! Go away! But time began to tick more slowly, and soon it seemed not to move at all. The soldier was looking at the open drawers in the desk and examining her drawings.

Just then he reached out his hand to where her foot had stepped on the desk and with a jerk of his head he looked up.

He stared up to where she lay as though the floorboards between them were made of glass. And a rush of unbelief passed through her as she looked through the crack into his face.

The spy.

She wondered at what the spy was now doing in a Yankee private's uniform, but just then he yelled down the stairs, "S'all right, Sully. She's not up here. I'm just taking a look around for supplies."

"Need any help, Potomac?" she heard from the stairway, and the name was not said kindly.

His name is Potomac, now?

"No, Sully, I don't," he answered testily. And then more evenly he added, "Nothing up here—be down in a minute." But the boots on the stair came up anyway and walked to the desk.

"Why you need a minute?" the fellow asked gruffly. "You wouldn't be keeping something good from me, now woudja'?" Annabelle's body shook uncontrollably with cold and fear, and she hoped her shaking would not give her away. The man walked away from the desk to look around the attic for himself. "Now what's up there?" And Annabelle knew he was pointing to her hiding place.

"Boxes. You need spectacles, Sully?"

"None of your mouth. Help me get up there to look around," the man said, and Annabelle held her breath.

"I ain't helpin' you up there," he said, calmly shuffling through the pictures once more.

"What do you mean?"

"I mean you've already taken enough today." He looked up at Sully now. "And if I see you slippin' another thing in your haversack I'm gonna' explain the situation to Forrest."

"You try it, and this'll be the day you die, Potomac."

The tension held as the two sized each other up.

The spy said more quietly and in steady measure, "Tell you what. You put your paws back in your fat little pockets, and I won't submit my report from yesterday."

In a few more seconds the man quite suddenly laughed. "All right. All right, but you're a..." And here he spat on the floor as a means of finishing his description.

Annabelle pinched her eyes shut with relief.

"So what you takin'?" the man asked.

"Just some drawings, Sully, hardly your cup of tea." Annabelle looked down to see Sully's bald head as he walked up to the spy.

Sully looked at some of the drawings. "Pichers of graybacks, eh?" He spat on the floor again, then turned and walked back to the stairs. "I could teach you a thing or two about foraging, you..." But the last of it was lost on the stairwell as he made his descent.

And then the man called Potomac looked back up to where she lay hidden. "Hello?" he said softly, and she almost jumped out of her skin.

When her heart had slowed its ka-thumping, and she'd caught her breath, very, very slowly, she brought her face over the edge of the boards and they looked at each other. "And who are you now, sir?" she asked with a cold, dry voice, and a little smile flashed across his face. He had filled out some; his hair was clean and brushed back neatly to his collar. His deep blue eyes were as she remembered them.

But he did not answer her question. Instead he said, "We'll be gone soon."

"We?" she shot back.

He hesitated and shook his head. Then he took a deep breath and removed something from his pocket. He set it on the desk. "I'm... giving you back your father's ring," he whispered.

"You... You a Yankee?" she said, barely grasping the situation.

"Yes."

"Were you always?" she asked hoarsely.

"Yes."

A gross horror took hold as she gripped the boards and her nails dug into the wood. She wanted to kill him. She truly wished to kill him just then, but he held all the cards. If she came down, the other soldiers would find her. For a moment, she thought it might be worth the fight, but instead she held her place.

"Perhaps someday I can explain it all to you, Miss MacBain, but I have a duty now," he whispered. "Will you need assistance getting down from there?"

Her eyes narrowed. "Certainly not from you."

He nodded curtly, turned and walked down the stairs.

Her head began to ache and she trembled with fury. All the implications of his words flew about her and she felt a cold dragging in her heart as though some other person had entered her soul. Some other person was feeling the humiliation she should be feeling. And it was some other person who decided she would have her revenge when the time permitted.

He was a Yankee and he was a spy and he had always been these things, and she was a very young and very stupid girl. That is all she could think while the hate welled up in her. He had used her, toyed with her. And she had saved his life—twice—for pity's sake! He'd had a good laugh at that, she was sure.

A loud conversation was coming from downstairs, and then she heard the soldiers leave. She slid down out of the rafters and stood for a moment there in the attic. Her father's ring lay on the table near her hand and she snatched it up. She looked out the attic window and saw Shilla beginning to clean up the charred mess. She placed her father's ring in her pocket. *Well, if God gives me opportunity, and if there's any justice in this life, I will not save your life again, spy.*

When she reached the landing, a movement in her father's study caught her attention. Potomac was sitting at her father's desk. The desk was gone through earlier, and so some drawers were already dumped, and her father's papers mingled on the floor with the books that were tossed down from the shelves, a testimony to the maniacal efficiency of the men in blue.

She felt tingly all over as she watched him going through her father's documents in the remaining drawers. He was reading the files! Reading her father's privy information as if it were his right! What he was looking for or had found she didn't know, but it was in keeping with who he was, someone evil and base. A Yankee spy. He needed to pay for what he and the soldiers had taken and destroyed.

She stepped softly down the back stairs, pulled a stool to the door, stepped up and took Thomas' rifle from its perch. She found the shells in the salt box by the door and carefully worked powder and bullet into the rifle's boor. She checked the barrel quietly and muffled the cock of the trigger with a bunching of her skirts. Then she tiptoed back up the stairs to the doorway of her father's study, pulled the gun to her shoulder and calmly aimed it at the back of his head.

So it wasn't a fair fight. Men died walking their picket all the time. A soldier should always be on his guard. It wasn't her fault if he didn't see her, didn't assume her capable of this. It was really as if he had come to be sitting here for just this purpose. Fortuitous.

Just then, he turned his head slightly and looked to his left.

Now one second of her life became an hour as she glanced to see what he saw. He was looking into the mirror and the mirror was looking at her. For a second she saw his face, but with her mind made up she stepped forward and leveled the gun again.

But in the brief moment she had looked into the mirror she had seen him and now her mind brought his face to her and his eyes to her and she could not shut the image out.

But he didn't move.

She swallowed and looked again at the mirror and now she saw herself standing there, fully prepared to kill a man. She wanted to finish it, but instead she stared at the dark circles under her eyes, her tangled and matted hair, her thin frame wearing a homemade dress and holding that rifle.

She hesitated a moment more.

"Annabelle," his voice cracked. "Go on." Then she looked back to him, while her jaw slackened and her mouth tingled. She licked her dry lips and gulped while she held on firmly to the rifle.

"Let me make it easier for you." He swiveled her father's chair to face her. His brow was sweaty and his face pale, but his eyes would not let go. "Self-defense, you see?" *He has not made it easier,* she thought.

He lowered his gaze to stare at the long barrel of the gun and licked his own lips as her finger twitched on the trigger. She watched a trickle of sweat come down his nose and rest at its tip. He said very slowly, "And if you unbuckle my belt when you're done, my own commander will think you've done a brave thing. Heaven knows, they expect it of me."

"Quiet!" Annabelle said shakily. "I want you to be quiet!" With a strained voice, she added, "You should know. I've saved your life. I've saved your life twice before this. More than anyone else I've a right to take your life now, don't I? Don't I?" Her voice rose nervously as she spoke.

He looked into her eyes. "Once I told you I wanted to die. If it's twice you've saved me, then, yes, this is fair and square, and so I'll say it again. Go on." He shut his eyes and just as his lids closed she remembered the words of the English officer: *Never let it be said Captain Henry Taylor wouldn't give a Confederate a fair chance.* She released the trigger ever so slightly.

Then came the words she could definitely not shake. She even moved her free shoulder as if to shrug them off, but they would not leave her: *"Revenge is mine," sayeth the Lord. "Revenge is mine," sayeth the Lord.*

She shrugged again. *He wants to die; I'm only granting his request.* But the moment of violent temper had passed, and she looked again at herself in the mirror. Beyond the bleakness there, some spark of Christ as Lord remained.

Annabelle lowered the rifle and let it swing down in one hand as she raised the other hand to her face. She stood there for quite a while unable to believe what she had almost done. Finally she sat down against the wall in a heap on the floor, letting her shoulders fall against the door frame and laying the rifle on the floor beside her. And she began to cry.

She cried as if there were no one in the world left to cry but she. She gulped and hiccuped and cried still more, for all her pain, all the pain that had led her to this place.

Finally, when no more tears would come, she looked up and with surprise saw he was still sitting there—still sitting in her father's chair—but with his face in his hands. "Why are you still here?" She'd cried so hard the words were pocked with hiccups. "Please g-go, be-fore I change my mind."

He didn't move.

Annabelle's nerves were jangled and tense. "We-well, take what you-you want. I d-don't care anymore. I wa-nt you gone. Would you like the silver? Perhaps you'd li-ike some of the furniture to keep your fires bright?" She wiped her cheeks furiously with each sleeve.

He stood up and shook his head. "I'm sorry. I had nothing to do with that."

"And aren't y-you a Yankee?" She sniffed.

He ignored the statement. "You said you saved me twice?"

"It (hic) doesn't matter, does it?"

"If it doesn't matter, then tell me. Tell me and I'll go."

He made her tired, and she wanted him to go away, and so she answered, "The am-bush. It was I-I who yelled to you from the bushes." She sniffed again.

His eyes widened and he straightened his back. "You!"

"Yes, and I wholeheartedly regret the decision, be-believe me. Now, if you have nothing else to look for, and wh-ile this is still my-i father's house" She clenched her fists. "I want you (hic) *out!*"

"All right." And he walked to the door. "But thank you," he added before walking down the stairs.

"So, he didn't really want to die," she whispered to herself. "And it's only that a spy has lied to me again."

She stood up slowly, then took herself to bed and slept for a very long time.

She woke up shivering late in the afternoon, remembering what she had almost done and wondering what could have possessed her. She slid to her knees beside the bed and began to pray. Her head wagged as she vividly remembered the hate that brought her to it. So much hate, it had seemed to have a life of its own within her, its purpose to destroy. Just like the Yankees. She was really no better than they. And if she had killed him, it would have destroyed her as well. Somehow, by some miracle, she hadn't followed through. It was a miracle she hadn't killed him. "Thank you, Lord," she said aloud.

"Lord, I ask forgiveness for the state of my heart. Take away the hate, take away the hate." For a time, this was all she could say, and she thought after a while that she felt a peace pass through her, and it calmed her to where she rested her head in her arms on the bed.

Suddenly she wanted to find Shilla. She rose up and went downstairs and sought her out, drew her into the parlor and sat her down on their settee; she was so glad to have someone to tell it all to she hardly noticed the large rips along the old silk cushions. First, to Shilla's amazement she explained what she had almost done earlier that day and how she had just now prayed about it all and found herself forgiven. Shilla immediately nodded. "I had as much murder in my heart toward poor old Mistress Humboldt." But then Annabelle told her the whole story of who the fellow was and how he had come there and Shilla could only say, "Poor Hannah Brighton has lost a nephew, too, then. Who is he really?"

"I have no idea, but they called him Potomac. The way I feel now, with all forgiven, somehow I wish I'd asked him forgiveness for what I almost did and for what I said. Lord, I can hardly believe what I said to him—as if his life were mine to take."

Suddenly a furtive knocking came at the door, and they both looked to see a face through the side transom. "It's him? It's him!" Annabelle said in wonder.

Indeed it was, and he held something large and obviously cumbersome, struggling with it as he stood there in the gathering dark.

EIGHTEEN

My great concern is not whether God is
on our side; my great concern is to
be on God's side.

Abraham Lincoln

They stared at the blue-coated figure through the sidelights of
the door. "Do I let him in then?" Shilla whispered.

"Yes, Shilla, yes!" Annabelle nervously stood up, and so Shilla
stepped to the door and opened it.

In came the spy, Potomac, carrying the burden of a body.

"What's this?" Annabelle asked with a gasp.

The burden groaned as his carrier said, "Another of dysentery."
Potomac held the man in a stiff embrace against his knee. "Miss
MacBain, you were the only one in town I knew could help."

They looked at each other for what to Annabelle seemed an
hour.

*Uncover the medicine? Lose it to the soldiers, completely? They'd
come for it earlier. Was this a trick?*

She glanced at the body. Well, if the man were acting, it was the
best acting she'd ever seen; his face was pale, and he smelled of it.
She knew her father would never refuse such a request, and she
looked at the man who held him and checked her soul and with
mild surprise found no hate there, none whatsoever.

Then she knew she wouldn't refuse him either. "Lay him on the
couch here, and, Shilla, get the medicine."

Shilla started for the back door. "Ten paces west of the maple?"

"Yes, and deeper than a bayonet," Annabelle yelled as the
kitchen door shut.

The man Potomac laid upon the couch was not a private, that
much was obvious from his relatively clean uniform. As Potomac

drew the patient's cloak from around his prone form, she glanced at the rectangular gold braiding upon his shoulders to see he was a lieutenant. *A Yankee lieutenant. They dress their officers well,* she thought. Now glancing at the spy's own crisp uniform, she added to herself, *and their regular army, too, while our men dress in rags.* Annabelle turned then and ran to the kitchen for water. As she returned she asked, "Is there no medicine in your camp for a lieutenant? Where is your camp?"

He took the glass from her hand and brought it to the officer's lips. "Shouldn't have gone out," Potomac muttered under his breath. "He knew he was sick."

"You haven't answered my question." Annabelle bent her head toward him.

"That's right, I haven't."

She watched him as he tried to get his officer to drink the water, and it slowly dawned upon her he was a Yankee who couldn't tell a Confederate what he was doing in the area. She had asked a perfectly reasonable question but had forgotten the circumstances, and his answer was a bitter reminder of everything that stood between them. Annabelle shook her head, and went to fetch a clean horse blanket to place under the lieutenant, thinking wryly she'd have no use for it now with Lucy gone. On her way back into the parlor, she grabbed a pillow from the settee for his head.

Soon Shilla returned with a cannister of medicine in her cold and muddied hands, and Potomac and Annabelle quickly worked some of the powder down the man's throat. Shilla ran out again and returned with two bottles—one of brandy and one of morphine. They gave him the painkiller and then poured the brandy down his throat, too, in hopes that he would sleep.

And, in all this time, Annabelle found herself growing more and more afraid to look at the spy.

When the lieutenant finally began to nod off, Annabelle stood up and wiped her hands against her dress, just as she used to when she was last a nurse. She looked down at the pale fellow and it dawned on her he was no longer a Yankee in her mind, but simply a sick man in need of medicine and she had done at least as much for him as her father would have. "Do you want to take the rest of the medicine for your camp?" she asked the spy and then held her breath in surprise at how easily the words had come.

"Thank you," was his simple reply.

She checked her heart again, and was once more surprised to find she didn't mind serving a Yankee, she didn't mind giving them medicine, she didn't mind helping this fellow, this spy. Forgiveness had washed through her like a tide and taken all the bitterness away. And then she thought, *Fancy that! A Federal lying to a Rebel!* Somehow the whole thing seemed so sadly ludicrous she almost laughed out loud: she'd been perfectly willing to kill a man all because he'd hurt her pride. It hadn't a thing to do with the war. It all boiled down to a question of pride.

And so she found she had regained her senses completely, and now her curiosity about the man before her was uppermost in her mind. She was no longer afraid to look at him.

He interrupted her thoughts by asking if she had a room on this floor.

"Yes, Thomas O'Brian's room, but he's gone." She shot a glance to Shilla, but Shilla was staring at the lieutenant.

"Perhaps we could move him there?" She almost smiled to hear the sound of a gentleman's indirect question. Etiquette seemed all too out of place.

Annabelle grabbed the lieutenant's feet while Potomac took his shoulders and they lurched and swayed with him down the hallway to Thomas' room off the kitchen behind her father's doctor's office. He was surprisingly light, but Annabelle noted that Shilla had not offered to help, although she did follow behind them with the medicines.

Thomas' room had, of course, been ransacked, and it was only as they entered the mess that Annabelle realized Shilla had cleaned the parlor, dining room and kitchen with no help from her that day. But Shilla hadn't had time to clean this room, or perhaps, hadn't had the heart. They shoved things aside with their feet as they moved the patient toward the bed. The bed was skewed, but they lowered him onto it before righting it from either side.

While Shilla began picking up the drawers the soldiers had pulled to the floor, the private and Annabelle removed the lieutenant's boots and jacket, but the movement brought up such an unbearable odor from him, Annabelle quickly offered a change of clothes. Then she blushed to remember the turmoil she'd caused at the hospital due to a simple change of clothes.

But the private merely nodded at the suggestion, completely intent on the lieutenant's bed covers at that moment.

Annabelle then told him to take from Thomas' wardrobe, only to realize his things were now spread about the floor.

"Thank you," the private said. "I'm sure I'll find something."

Then she and Shilla left the room, and Annabelle walked back to the parlor and grabbed up the little pillow and the water while Shilla busied herself in the kitchen. Eventually Thomas' door was opened, and the private nodded to her. She went in and laid the things down on the side table, looked at the sleeping lieutenant and then tucked the pillow under his head.

Shilla had followed her and was continuing to pick up Thomas' things when Annabelle quietly said, "Would you like me to do that, Shilla?"

She looked up at Annabelle, her eyes edged in red. "No, miss, it's good to be doing something for Thomas, it is."

Annabelle nodded and quickly turned her head, leaning down to look again on the lieutenant. The tears pooled and fell to the sheets as she blinked.

The lieutenant was pale, but his lips still had some color to them. He smelled of vomit and Annabelle quickly brought her head back up as her stomach lurched. Across the bed, the private bent down on one knee and arranged his officer's boots and then wiped his brow slowly, obviously thinking hard on something or other. The spy was still on his knees when Annabelle asked him, "And what name do you go by now, sir?"

"You won't believe it."

"Oh, I'm not so sure." She smiled. "I've come to believe many impossible things recently. Only this morning I would have believed I was capable of murder." He watched her but said nothing. "This afternoon, a miracle has occurred and I find I am forgiven and have forgiven." She bent down and picked up Thomas' collar box, its lid clearly flattened by a soldier's boot. "We'll have to find glue for this," Annabelle said as Shilla took the box from her hand.

"Yes, but there won't be enough glue in Loudoun County, I dunna think, for all the fixin' needs doing in this house." And with that Shilla walked slowly out to the kitchen.

The lieutenant's uneven breathing was now the only sound in the room, and Annabelle walked to the window to look out back.

With her breath on the glass and a catch in her throat, she said, "Truly, and it isn't easy to ask, and don't think I underestimate the gravity of this morning. But this... I have to ask forgiveness. For my wounded pride, I almost killed you."

"But I asked you to."

"Please don't make light of it," she interrupted. "You lied in the asking." She looked at the pile of blackened boards where the smokehouse had been.

"All right," he agreed and then said firmly, "I forgive you, if you'll forgive me the lie."

"All of them?"

"I'm fairly certain all but one were made in the line of duty."

"Ah, duty," she said unhappily.

"But duty had nothing to do with treating you as I did in the field hospital. For that I ask forgiveness."

"You weren't well."

"You're right there, not in body, nor mind, nor spirit. I'd suffered a reversal of fortunes, you might say, and I was feeling none too kindly to the world." A moment elapsed. "Miss MacBain, I was angry with you then because you forced me to rejoin the living when I wanted to die. But it was a good thing you did, and I appreciate it, now, though I couldn't properly thank you at the time."

"Ah, well then." she said shakily, "I forgive you, Mr... ?"

He stood up and laughed but the laugh gave way to a stretch and a sigh.

"Abraham Lincoln, is it?" she asked with a smile and she listened to the soft plunk of brass buttons as he unbuttoned his coat.

She continued to wait, too embarrassed to turn around.

When he finished he took a deep breath. "My name, my true name, mind you, is P.D. MacBain."

She jerked her head back towards him. "You're joking!"

He smiled and shook his head. Shilla came to the doorway, then, her eyes wide with surprise.

Annabelle said with half a laugh, "Capital M-a-c, capital B-a-i-n?" He nodded. Shilla's mouth had fallen open as she continued to stare at him. Annabelle looked down at the officer. "And I suppose he's a MacBain, as well?"

MacBain laughed a bit but then grew somber as he stared at the bedridden officer. "No, this is my commanding officer, Lieutenant Forrest. Uh, and I thank you for taking him, uh, us in."

She smiled. "Well, whoever you are, you took a risk bringing him to me, didn't you?"

"Suppose so." He sniffed, but then he shifted his weight to the other foot. "But how is your father?"

Annabelle lowered her eyes. "My father is well, as far as we know." She was remembering her father's words, *They're not gonna let me go just yet,* and said somberly, "I haven't seen him since..."

"Since the hospital? I am sorry."

She heard the sincerity in his voice and then, as she glanced at the lieutenant once more, she thought of how her father would treat these same gentlemen. "Well, I don't know if it's another ruse, pretending you're a long lost cousin, but I suppose we should feed you. Are you hungry?" But then she felt a little shock of remembrance. The soldiers had taken everything worth eating.

"We have some food."

"Yes, well, it's probably ours." She was amazed to find she could make such a joke. Shilla nodded without humor, but he laughed a little and even nodded.

"Then we'll share it, eh, cousin?" And he walked out of the house and down the front steps to their horses.

"He's a MacBain, miss?" Shilla was clearly dumbfounded. "Do you really think so? T'would be strange indeed." She shook her head so that the red ringlets bobbed.

"Should we believe him?" Annabelle asked. *It is too strange not to believe,* she thought to herself. "Well, whoever he is, he's bringing us food. Shilla, we should invite Hattie to eat with us. Could you do that?" The question was not asked lightly.

"If yer askin' me to, I will, miss, but it won't be for wanting her company."

"I know. I know it right well, but perhaps we would have done what she did if we were old and frightened." Annabelle rested her hand on Shilla's shoulder.

"You know how angry the town is, miss, and she'll be tellin' everyone you have soldiers here and of a certainty there'll be trouble."

Annabelle hadn't thought of that. "As the Lord wills."

Shilla shrugged, then grabbed her shawl and left the house to find Hattie Humboldt.

P.D. MacBain was taking a long time to come back, and Annabelle's stomach growled ferociously as she stood in the kitchen. Finally she walked to the parlor window to see what was taking him so long.

With a shock she saw that the soldiers' horses were gone.

"So, he's left again!" she said bitterly. "And he'll return when his lieutenant's well, and he's only used me once more!"

But before she could continue this line of bitter reasoning, MacBain came around the side of the house, walked briskly up the steps and grabbed the two saddlebags that were lying on the porch. Annabelle gulped and opened the door for him and almost apologized for what she was thinking as he entered, she was so grateful he had returned.

He set the saddlebags in a chair and silently began to draw the items out, laying them one by one on the parlor table: four loaves of fresh bread, three large rounds of cheese, two bottles of wine, a dozen potatoes, and a cloth bag dumped out to make a mound of dried apples, raisins and figs. Annabelle held back sudden tears as she watched him. She hadn't seen so much fresh food in months. It was a feast.

As she looked at all of it with wide eyes, she whispered how she had asked a woman next door to come join them since she had even less than they. He nodded and gathered up all of it again and walked back to the kitchen where he laid the items down on the table. Then he began to stoke the fire in the kitchen stove to warm the room.

"And where are your horses then?" she asked meekly.

"In the upper room of the well house, if you don't mind. It's the only place, you know, while it's still dark."

"Of course."

"Trying to avoid a chill," he went on. "I laid some straw down out there for them and brushed them down."

"Ah." She stared at the fellow, and she wouldn't admit to anyone, but she was impressed.

When Shilla returned with Hattie, the old woman looked more like a snapping turtle than ever, but there was no fear of being bitten by her now. She looked quite dazed. Shilla would only shake her head, making Annabelle wonder what in the world had happened between them. After settling the woman down at the kitchen table and introducing her to MacBain and bringing her some food, Shilla pulled Annabelle into the dining room.

Shilla had had to look for Hattie and finally found her huddled and shivering in one corner of an upper room. "She really thought I might kill her, miss, but it did make my heart sick to find her like that. She'd been hiding there since yesterday. I told her she'd be eating with a Yank, but she said she was too hungry to care." And from Shilla's humor Annabelle knew the woman had purged her own anger, too.

Annabelle drew her into a good, strong hug and whispered, "We will forgive, Lord willing, and someday we will forget all this... all this."

"Yes, good Lord in Heaven, I pray it's so."

MacBain was the last to sit down at the kitchen table, and the four of them ate together in silence under an uneasy truce. From the looks Hattie Humboldt gave MacBain as they ate, it was certain she had never intentionally eaten with a Yankee in her life, and Annabelle realized it had taken a fierce bit of starvation to bring her there. Then, at the end of the meal, MacBain asked Shilla to wrap some of the food to take back over with Hattie, and so she began to roll some bread and cheese into a cloth.

It was then the old woman looked around and finally spoke. "I was afraid of the soldiers, Miss Annabelle, Shilla. I've done a horrible thing. I'm sorry. How will your Thomas... How will..."

Annabelle came and drew one arm around her. "We forgive you, Mistress Hattie, if forgiveness is what you're wanting. But when Thomas returns, you'll have to speak with him." Hattie nodded and took her parcel, and she and Shilla stepped out the back door.

Annabelle watched them go and said to MacBain, "She told them where our man Thomas was hiding, up in the woods with my horse and our cow and the chickens."

"I know." He tiredly wiped his eyes with his hand.

"Oh?" She turned to him with a glare in her eye.

"Lieutenant almost put me in the detail, but I told him why I couldn't. I told him you saved my life."

"Oh." She blushed, but then she thought for a moment. "Why then did he send you here for medicine?"

He looked at the floor and drew his arms behind his back. "My fault. I mentioned your name and Lieutenant Forrest knew of your father. Knew your father was a doctor. He figured you might have medicine." He kicked at the table. "He thought maybe you'd be willing to give me the medicine." They both smiled at that. Then he stretched his arms. "But he didn't want to waste time looking for it, so when we couldn't find you, earlier today, he let the whole thing drop."

"But you did find me."

"But you didn't want to help us." He eyed her.

"Because I had the medicine hidden."

"I figured you'd probably taken most of your medicine to your father, anyway. May have been a false assumption, but it eased my conscience some."

Annabelle smiled again. "It was a good assumption. On the other hand, I suppose you should know Mistress Hattie already told the soldiers about my father. That's why they chose to burn our outbuildings, I think, and that should ease your conscience as well."

"Oh. Oh, of course. Right." He moved his weight from one foot to the other, coughed and went on, "Well, then Forrest, he brought me with him on a scout to the rear of the battalion as they moved back down the county, and he took sick when we came up just south of town."

She sat down at the table and breathed deeply. "I must say it's refreshing to get the whole picture of a thing for once."

He sat down at the table, too. "When the lieutenant's a little better, we'll move on. I am fully aware of the danger we put you in by staying here."

"Danger to yourself," she retorted.

"Yes, that too." He put his head down. "Nevertheless, I need to ask if we can keep him here tonight." He stared at the candle on the table and began to push a little at the warm wax at the base.

Her eyes stayed glued to the remains of the bread as she replied, "Of course. He can't be moved, yet. I'm not sure you should take him tomorrow, but I wish my father were here to take care of things."

"But you are his nurse."

"No. I don't believe I have the gift."

"I have lived to disagree." He laughed. "You'll be a doctor, then?"

Incredulous, Annabelle looked at him. "I think I've had enough of Yankee humor for one day, thank you."

He lost his smile. "It wasn't said in jest."

Her eyes narrowed. "I didn't think it would be necessary to tell an educated man a woman can't be a doctor."

His lower lip came forward as he nodded. "Can't be a doctor in the South, that's for certain." And he began pushing at the wax once more.

She brought a hand to the table and rested it there. "You have female doctors in the North?" she asked with a pure and open surprise.

"More than one. More than one in our army, too—at least two that I know of. Dr. Mary Walker, I've met her myself. Sharp as a tack. Last I heard, she was captured in Georgia, though."

"We... the South doesn't..." She shook her head. *They only let us nurse them for lack of anyone else they can trust,* she thought. She stared at the floor. "Female doctors." He couldn't have known how overawed she had become. But he had asked her a question. "Well, I don't want to be a doctor or a nurse." She waved her hand and let it fall into her lap. "I don't care for the work."

"Well, that's another thing altogether." He pulled the old wax from the base of the candle holder and began to roll it in his hands. "Patients too difficult, I suppose."

She smiled. "Too often they wanted to die."

"Ah." He nodded. "I understand. And so you have other plans for yourself."

She cocked her head. "Ladies do not plan." She blushed to her roots to realize what she was saying. "Well..." She glanced at him. "It's really no business of yours, is it?" Now she thought he must be trying to humiliate her.

But MacBain smiled and completely ignored her answer. "You've never asked yourself what you want to do."

She looked at him and her mouth dropped open. Whatever did a man care what a woman did as long as it was what he wanted her to do? He was a strange bird, indeed and she wasn't at all sure he was in his right mind. That or he was teasing her unmercifully. She shut her mouth and looked back to the candle.

They sat at the table for several minutes more and then P.D. broke the silence. "A professional artist then?"

She blushed again and shook her head. At least it was certain he wasn't romancing her, for a man who asked so many questions concerning a woman's career could not be thinking of her as a lady or as a woman. But the last thought made her blush even more.

"Your drawings. You're very good."

"Thank you." If it was boorish to compliment a lady outright, why was she so pleased to hear his words?

"Not at all. I thought the drawing I found of my face to be very accurate, although the likeness of a scarecrow might have suited, too. But you had to have drawn that from memory."

She nodded and looked at the table again. She'd never really thought about being an artist, but now somehow it sounded vaguely delicious. But certainly he was teasing. This was the way soldiers frittered away their time, teasing and flirting without a conscious thought, without a conscience. Quickly she changed the subject. "So, will I never hear the story of why you first came through town?"

He put aside the ball of wax and picked up half a cheese, shaved off a slice for himself and shook his head. "I suppose, I suppose you'd have to take the oath of allegiance."

"To Lincoln?"

"To the Union, yes." He put his knife down and watched her reaction.

"I see." She laughed sharply. "Ridiculous. You must think I'm as steady as a dry leaf to give up my allegiances so easily." Annabelle looked around her and shook her head. He was making her nervous.

"But you took us in today," he countered.

She shrugged, unable to find a simple way to explain her actions.

"But what if your allegiance to the South was lost in a fair fight?" He then smiled slightly, picked up the knife and shaved off another piece of cheese.

"What do you mean, sir? You mean the way they're settling it now? There's nothing fair about it."

"No, I mean by argument. I consider you able to hold your own in an argument."

"A Yankee compliment," she replied sarcastically. *Surely, he's baiting me,* she thought.

"Well, I was raised in Virginia, where everyone always speaks the truth." As he spoke, the butt of the knife tapped the table. "Most *especially* when no one wants to hear it."

He was awfully smug. "Aren't you afraid you'll give away more of your secrets?"

"I haven't told you anything you didn't already know. Besides, I have nothing better to do at present than argue with a Rebel lady, but..."

"But?"

"Two things. One, I'd like to dispense with a conversational formality I happen to detest."

She cocked her head. "And, pray, what would that be?"

"The rule requiring a gentleman to beat around the bush rather than ask a lady a question straight out."

Annabelle's brows rose in amusement. "Well, if I'm not mistaken, sir, you've already dispensed with that formality."

"Then I suppose I'm asking if you mind?"

"No. No, I don't mind." It occurred to her she rather liked his directness.

"Good." He smiled broadly and Annabelle shifted in her seat, uncomfortable that she'd pleased him so well with her answer. "Then the second item is simply this: If I win the argument, you'll take the oath."

"Now I know you're teasing." She rolled her eyes. "I know well enough a provost marshal is required for official documentation, and you may be many things, but you are *not* the provost marshal."

He smiled. "Ah, yes, but I know of one who owes me a favor, and he would sign it for me after the fact."

"You're serious? You're serious." She laughed. "And pray tell me who would be deciding who has won and who has lost?" She pointed to the knife in his hand. "You argue very well when you're holding the knife, sir."

He placed the knife carefully on the table. "I can make my points without it."

"Oh, save me from your humor, please." It was entirely too easy and pleasant to talk with him. She didn't know what to think of herself.

"All right." And he wiped his hands together. "Since I have nothing to lose, you decide when the argument's done, but..." Annabelle leaned forward, mildly intrigued with the game. "You must decide these things with your mind and heart. Together, they must agree."

The mind and the heart.

She thought of her pride and how it had brought her to the edge of insanity that day, and she nodded slightly. So be it.

NINETEEN

Our Dixie forever, she's never at a loss,
Down with the eagle and up with the cross.
We'll rally 'round the bonny flag,
we'll rally once again.
Shout, shout the battle cry of Freedom.

From the Southern version of the song
The Battle Cry of Freedom

A nd so by the light of a few candles and the warmth of the kitchen stove, P.D. and Annabelle began their debate. Quite methodically, he raised each issue that had brought the country to war, and they argued there at the kitchen table while the candles burned and the lieutenant slept and Shilla settled Mistress Hattie in her bed.

P.D. and Annabelle argued concepts and details, they argued persons, states, and countries. Shilla returned and sat down to listen. Then they argued over words that held two meanings, like "states' rights," "union," and "economy," and then over words that had a thousand meanings, like "property" and "souls." Eventually Shilla yawned and took herself to bed. And the debate continued.

Annabelle found she enjoyed their sparring and thought quite possibly she'd never had a more interesting discussion in her life.

Occasionally there was a silence as one would get up and check on the lieutenant. Then that person would return and they would begin the debate where they left off, now heading down one tunnel of thought, now backing out and heading down another.

Since the beginning of the war, she'd held several of these discussions with Northerners, and she'd won every argument with searingly brilliant logic. But, of course, those discussions had always taken place within the safe confines of her own mind.

But, here the imagination was turned real, and to her dismay she was not winning on all points—not by any means.

When their conversation had begun to die down somewhat, they talked over the points that had bubbled to the surface most often and finally Annabelle asked, with some exasperation, "Why do you refuse us our states' rights? Tell me again!"

"Perhaps I didn't put it plainly, but a country simply cannot hold itself together based on a concept of states' rights. From the beginning of this war, your leaders have argued over whether to share their armies from one state to the next. Your President Davis is at his wit's end—a rather short walk to begin with—to hold together an alliance, because the states won't cooperate with him. And why? Because each state says they have a right to determine their own destiny! There's biting the hand that feeds you! Your Confederate government is a set of medieval fiefdoms, each territory with its own little army and its own little goals."

"And is that so horrible?" *Indeed, it sounds horrible,* she couldn't help thinking.

"Well, if you don't mind the poverty and ignorance enjoyed by medieval England, no. But the point is moot. We are arguing about the Cause, and that is not the Cause—the true Cause being to force the Union to recognize states' rights to allow slavery here and out in the territories."

"It has nothing to do with slavery," she said. "The North only wishes to become rich at our expense. They know our economy is based on cotton and tobacco and make no concessions to us and our ways, and so I believe they wish to destroy us to make their own selves rich."

He pulled forward. "But that's the whole point of a democracy! To implement the will of the people through the laws which they themselves create to establish order!" He became so intent in the conversation, he laid hold of her hands.

Her eyes widened with sudden fright and she stared at his hands over her own. She shook her head, but he was so involved in the conversation, he'd gone right on. "Why in heaven's name would we wish to destroy our cousins, our brothers, our uncles? The

South chose its own means of economy. No one forces them to own slaves!" And as he went on in this very spirited way, Annabelle shut her eyes and began to pull her hands out from his, slowly, deliberately.

When her hands were safely back in her lap, P.D. MacBain grew quiet. He was staring into her face when she opened her eyes.

"I'm sorry," he said.

She looked away. Besides the blush his touch had brought to her cheek, he was being all too persuasive, and she was glad for the interruption. So many things he'd said had rung true, and she'd grown terribly confused about her feelings. Actually, she was losing the argument, and her heart was feeling rather queazy, as well.

"What was I saying?" asked MacBain.

She couldn't tell him. The memory of his hands was uppermost in her mind. "I believe... I believe the discussion has ended."

He took a deep, long breath and let it out in an unnerving sigh. "If for one moment you allowed your conscience to guide you, Annabelle, this discussion would indeed be over."

Burning with sudden indignation, she replied, "Mr. Lincoln made slavery an issue, not us. We will abolish slavery in our own time and in our own way. The North offers them no better life. You all are taking our slaves from us right now, and what are you using them for? Labor."

"At least it was paid labor, but that's not true anymore."

"You see," she said smugly.

"They're fighting now," he said, trying not to smile.

"They are?" she said weakly. "I... I'd heard a rumor to the like, but I didn't believe it."

"Believe it. They are, and they're impressive. I can tell you that from experience, too. All they wanted was a chance to show what they can do. That's all. That's only fair, but your proposed system of government will never allow them a chance, fair or otherwise. If you can't see a man rise above a slave you can always think of him as a slave. Yes, sir, slavery, the first perpetual motion machine," he said with a sneer.

"And I suppose you'll be having them vote in the very next

election," she replied cattily. "Such a handy way for Mr. Lincoln to hold on to the seat of power."

"That'll come in time, too."

She let out a harumph. "In time. You think the women of the South will allow their own slaves to have a vote when they cannot? In time. Pish."

"And you say you'll rid yourselves of slavery in time," he replied angrily, "but would you say to a murderer, 'One day we'll bring you to task for your behavior, but meanwhile do as you like?'" The fever of the conversation drew him to lean in toward her, all manners aside and forgotten for the moment. But at least her hands were safely in her lap now.

Her mouth tightened. "My neighbors treat their people well." But she gulped after saying the words.

He gave her a crooked smile. "Like Pella?"

"Like Pella." Annabelle thought of the boy's cheerful face.

He shook his head. "You know his master beat him."

"Well, I myself was given the hickory stick more than once as a child, and deservedly so."

"I have no doubt," he chided, but quickly grew serious once more. "But did your father ever beat you to the point of welts upon your body, welt upon welt, enough to make a forest of ridges on your back?"

Annabelle grew quiet and then began to tremble. He had hit the mark now, and hit it hard.

"Yes, I've seen Pella's back, his legs. Marsden is the one who ought to be horsewhipped, treating a child like that. Horsewhipped and hanged."

If he went on, she was going to cry, and so, rather than suffer that humiliation, she chose a cowardly reply. "You are only trying to arouse my sympathies. Pella runs away now and then, and..."

He took her words like a slap in the face. "Have you any sympathies? By heaven, I've tried to appeal to your heart, but it won't give answer!" With wide eyes, he pressed his lips together, but then shook his head and quieted his voice. "No, it's worse than that. Worse than a lack of sympathy. You're ignorant, ignorant of the facts. Have you ever seen a slave child sold away from his mother? Ever seen a husband torn from his wife on the block? And the traders down below them cool as ice?"

Annabelle was angered by his tone, but she had to shake her head.

"No, of course not. I've never seen a white woman watch a slave auction. Too indelicate, they say." He laughed as he folded his arms. "Indelicate, my eye. If they did watch they'd make themselves sick with it. But it's all right to let your men deal in human flesh. It's all right for Pella to be beaten down as long as his master keeps the scars well covered. Well, if you don't believe me, you can go and see Pella's marks for yourself, but you'll have to go to our camp to see him, because he's our regimental drummer now." He sounded triumphant.

She looked at him and blinked.

"Yes, he's free. And what do you think of that?"

She couldn't hide the pleasure his words brought, and she squeezed her hands together with relief. "I'll admit it. I'm glad to hear it. I… I've spoken to Mr. Marsden before about how he treated the boy, but I didn't know… I didn't know."

"I suppose I can only hope you feel something for Pella and his race."

She nodded miserably, and now the tear she'd held back slid down her cheek. She brushed it away quickly, hoping he wouldn't see, but he did. She looked into his eyes, and, with surprising clarity, saw herself reflected there.

"You see more in them than property, don't you?" he whispered. "Don't you?"

She nodded slightly as a memory came to her. *"Annabelle, keep your eyes to the front," Weem had said. But I wanted to keep looking back—all the way to the back of the church and up into the loft where the slaves sat. They were silent when we sang, but I'd heard them sing before. They sang the way I did, with my eyes shut and trying hard to be adult, but they sang it real, with feeling. That was the word. "Daddy, Colonel says his slaves don't have souls. If that's so, why does he let them come to church? And why don't they sing their church songs here like they do outside?" "Hush, child, we're in church. I'll answer little ears and eyes when we get home." But he never did.*

P.D. MacBain's eyes were watching hers. "I believe they have souls," she mumbled, and the words brought a fierce burning to her cheeks for she had never admitted it to anyone. And suddenly she faced a black hole of guilt that she dare not fall into, and she was afraid. Quickly she shook her head. "But a Christian's task in the New Testament is to bring people to the Lord, not to abolish slavery."

He smiled. "I believe you've painted yourself into a corner there. Let's look in the New Testament. Have you a Bible handy?"

She gulped and got up to walk to the dry sink. She opened a lower drawer and reached way into the back. "What?" MacBain asked in surprise. "Are Bibles contraband around here that you have to hide them?"

Annabelle's face was bright red. "I believe this one might be considered contraband." And she held out Samuel Brighton's little white Bible.

"Omigosh." He took it from her hand. "Omigosh. Brighton's Bible. I'd completely forgotten. Well I'll be doggone."

She had meant to shock him. Guilt was the object she had in mind—to temper the feelings of guilt she'd had the last several minutes. She wanted to say aloud, *"Remember where you took this from? Remember how you used it to dupe me? Remember?"*

And so she was not at all prepared for his response.

"I suppose it's only right we should use it properly for a change, eh?" He flipped through the pages while Annabelle stared at him. He found the place and crossed a leg over one knee. Then he pushed his chair back on its hind legs, and was ready to read from it when he looked up and caught her eye. "What?"

"I can't believe you're..." But there weren't words to express her strange feelings at that moment. "Well, you are a wonder." And she took her seat with a thump.

One corner of his mouth curled up, but he made no reply to that. "Let's look here at Philemon, verses 15 and 16. Here. After Paul tells Philemon that his slave, Onesimus, has come to him and become a Christian, he says, 'For perhaps he therefore departed for a season, that thou shouldest receive him for ever;... Not now as a servant... *Not now as a servant...* but above a servant, a brother beloved, specially to me, but how much more unto thee, both in the flesh, and in the Lord?'" He let the verse sink and then he read the next line. "And verse 17, 'If thou count me therefore a partner, receive him as myself.'"

"Let me see that." She took it from his hands ungraciously. "Our pastor gave a talk on Philemon, but he read this differently. He talked about him being a servant, not a slave." And she reread the words for herself. "Well, it says *servant*." she countered.

"Isn't that what we call them in the South?"

She resented the remark, especially because it was true. She looked to the verses again and shook her head.

"Yes, he was Philemon's slave, a runaway. I'm afraid that's fairly obvious if you read it through. Now your pastor may have read it differently," MacBain said with a laugh, "if he owned slaves. He may have read it differently if he doesn't believe a slave can have a soul, but we both know better. We are all equal in the sight of God."

She smiled faintly. "But that's not something I *know*. It's something I believe. You believe, and so we have left logic by the wayside."

He let his chair fall forward again. "Well, I'll tell you, politicians love to argue points of logic, but men are never sent to die over points of logic, are they? Men are never willing to die for anything but a belief, and while the South is fighting to preserve its ragged hide, I'm out here 'cause I believe it is good to try to preserve the Union." His voice rose as he spoke. "And I believe Lincoln was right to issue the Emancipation Proclamation, and if you'd seen the look on that boy Pella's face when we told him he was free, you'd be out in the streets and ready to fight for it, too. And that's why I'm here." He slammed his fist on the table, and the noise made Annabelle jump in her seat and stare.

Annabelle tried to order her thoughts, but they would not be ordered. In truth, they were scattered and huddling in the various corners of her mind like frightened children.

She fidgeted as she struggled with her soul, but then MacBain opened the discussion once more. "Tell me this, what do you think your life would have been had you been born a slave?"

The question was ridiculous. "Well, I haven't been born a slave, so it's impossible to answer you."

"Did God paint your soul white, you think?"

She blushed. "Don't speak of Him like that, and no, well, yes. He intended for me to be white, didn't he? He didn't make me black."

"But couldn't He have? Scripture says nothing shall be impossible with God. Would you disagree?"

"Please make your point, Mr. MacBain."

"Galatians says, 'There is neither Jew nor Greek, there is neither bond nor free, there is neither male nor female; for ye are all one in Christ Jesus.' To God our souls are on a level plane."

With a twinkle in his eye he pressed on, "Now do you think my high intellect provides me with a better soul than the next man? Closer to home, Annabelle, do you think your pretty face makes you more worthy?" He didn't wait for her to answer. "No. It is the state of our souls that matter to Him."

Oh, but he was irritating beyond belief. She pursed her lips. "You are impertinent and purposefully trying to fluster me. You ask far too many questions and ask them rudely. I will not discuss this with you further."

He grinned. "Ah, you change the subject."

She bent her head. "Of course I change the subject. You are much too personal, and you bandy Scripture about as if it were any book. Even this—Samuel Brighton's own Bible—you show it no more respect than a book of receipts."

"All right. All right, Annabelle. Don't listen to me then, but promise me one thing. Promise me you'll read your Bible for yourself from now on and not rely entirely on the opinions of preachers. God did not give you such an excellent mind to toss it aside. You should think these things out for yourself. You should know these things for yourself."

Her eyes grew wide as she stared at him. A good retort would have been, *I'm through making promises to the likes of you, Mr. MacBain!* and yet she held her tongue. Never had a man said such things to her. They looked at each other and Annabelle gulped and nodded and then laid the Bible on the table rather gingerly. She rubbed her face in her hands. "Well, I still can't take your oath. I agree with much of what you say. Yes, I'm humbled enough to say it, but I still can't take your oath."

"Because?"

"It would be a dishonor to my father," she said in a hushed whisper.

"Don't you have a mind of your own?" he replied in a burst of restrained anger.

"Well, of course I have, Mr. MacBain, but we are, all of us, required to honor our fathers and our mothers!" she replied tersely.

"Not if they go against the will of God, we're not."

"My father is a God-fearing man."

"You're old enough to think for yourself."

"Why do you care whether I think for myself? You're only having this discussion to pass the time."

"Not true! I do care."

"Why?"

"I care because..." He spread his hands on the table and then let out a sigh. "Because," he repeated, and paused once more to take a breath. "Because I believe in it, and I want.... Because it's true, and, well. That's all. I believe in it." Then he gave one nod, shrugged, and pushed away from the table as if that explained everything.

She looked away from him and all was silent for quite some time. For reasons Annabelle couldn't quite understand, she was afraid of the empty space in the conversation and thought desperately for something to say to lighten the burden of the unnatural atmosphere. "Well, you argue quite effectively, sir," she said carefully, "but the last of it I cannot do."

"I think the last is to ask what God may call you to do," he pressed.

She turned her head away and her chin came forward slightly. Pushing her chair back from the table, she kept her eyes averted. "I'm not at all certain my God is the same as yours." And then she rose, walked past him and made her way up the stairs.

TWENTY

The Union forever, Hurrah, boys, Hurrah!
Down with the traitor, Up with the star;
While we rally round the flag, boys,
Rally once again,
Shouting the battle cry of Freedom.

From the Northern version of the song
The Battle Cry of Freedom

Dawn's light fell on the charred waste in the yard, painting all the black soot and dry grass with a pale pink glow. *A rather nauseous glow,* Annabelle thought wearily, *as if someone bled there and another came along and tried to clean it up without success.* She wondered at the images it brought to mind, the image of a charred and shattered world, a world so fragile one fire could take it out. As she looked upon the waste, more and more unpleasant feelings rose up in her.

She dressed and took herself downstairs, but she paused at the last step to overhear P.D. MacBain talking to Shilla.

"Yes, a couple of months ago we had a preacher come to camp and I accepted the invitation to take Christ as my Savior. Used to be I did my work and wished to die early, in a blaze of glory, I imagine. Every time I went out on scout I'd expect to be picked off. But I never was." He paused. "Haven't been yet, I should say. But when I took Christ... Well, when I did that, I believe it was the first time since the day I signed up I was not afraid to die."

Never had she heard a man bare his soul like this. She was amazed at his willingness to tell it and then horrified to think how close he came to dying. But Shilla was answering, "I don't know as I've met any Yank who's a real Christian."

"You have now."

"I'm still to be convinced." And Annabelle heard Shilla push open the other door to leave the kitchen.

Annabelle stepped into the kitchen, then, and their eyes met. "Were you so unafraid to die yesterday morning?" she asked with a sad sort of smile.

She took in his eyes, his hair, the way he held his head, and then tried to condemn herself for feeling unaccountably attracted to this Yankee. They watched each other for a moment. Then he turned his head slightly and smiled a wide, slow smile.

"It's the truth," he said. "I'm not afraid to die." He raised his eyebrows. "However, I do have my preferences as to how I'd like to go."

She looked toward the door Shilla had exited and then whispered, "But you asked me to shoot you!"

He laughed and said with a twinkle in his eyes, "Well, what was I supposed to do? With that wild look in your eyes and your finger an itch away from my demise, the only thing I could think," he shook his head as he remembered the moment, "was that this woman hates me so much, if I might tell her to do one thing, she'll do the opposite just to be irritating."

Annabelle blinked in wonder and let out a gasp. "That is the strangest thing I've ever heard." She shook her head. "But who knows why I stopped. What you did, it might have worked." She thought about it briefly. "And it's true I hated you right then, but I think I hated you most for lying to me all along."

"Ah, well, that, as I said, was all in..."

"... the line of duty, yes, so you say, but don't go on about it anymore, please," she said tiredly, "because I'm never going to hear the real reasons you were in my father's office, because I'll never take your oath." She nodded toward the window. "If I did, it would mean Thomas and the livestock and our outbuildings were taken for nothing, and that seems too cruel a joke to play."

"Thomas took his chances staying here, and the others, they're only things, Annabelle. Besides, our troops did more damage to Quaker and Union farms than Rebel sympathizers'."

Annabelle's eyes widened. "Why ever would they do that?"

MacBain shook his head. "Sounds strange, I know, but those are the places Mosby steals from first, you see?"

"Well, you've all gone insane and that's the whole of it. Your army is let loose on us like a great swarm of locusts, and now we're going to starve here, you know," she said matter-of-factly.

"I'll bring you more food."

She blinked back her tears and said with a half laugh, "If I take your oath."

"No. I said I'll bring you food. You've kept your food hidden and never intended to give it to Mosby. Lieutenant Forrest will allow for that."

"Is that so?" she said angrily.

But he looked at her awhile, and even while her eyes rimmed with tears, she couldn't turn her gaze from his. A tingle crept up her spine, and finally her cheeks grew red and hot.

Abruptly he said, "You know, I think I can tell you some of it, at any rate. Despite what you say, I don't believe you'd..." He grasped at the words. "I believe I trust you. I need to trust you."

"You need to trust me? What does that mean?" She sniffed and felt a twinge of pride to hear him say so.

He looked down. "I need to ask you some questions, and I need to explain why I looked through your father's files."

"You don't have to tell me."

"I want to."

She stood up and walked slowly across the room. She brought a pot of sarsaparilla leaves down from the cupboard and set it carefully on the table. She stared at the pot lid. "It's not true you can trust me. I know you for a Yankee spy, and I now know Mr. Cummings is probably a spy for you, and Mr. Bartholomew."

"... is dead," he interjected, and Annabelle immediately regretted her words.

"Yes, I remember," she said quietly.

"But I know you won't turn Cummings in."

"Do you?" She turned on him suddenly. "And how is it you know me so well?" But her cheeks burned and her voice had lost its edge.

He walked toward her. "I don't know," he said gently. "I just know, Annabelle. There's no logic in it."

She tingled from head to foot as he came closer. She didn't like the feelings he brought up in her. How could she be attracted to this man? But she was attracted, deeply and utterly attracted, and now the guilt took hold to shake her from dreaming. To get him to quit walking toward her she spat, "And what if I told your lieutenant that you gave a secessionist information in trade for a gold ring?"

His jaw tightened and he stopped short. "No doubt he'd believe you."

Just then the lieutenant groaned and they went quickly in to attend to him.

Forrest had pushed himself up to a half-sitting position in the bed and was looking around him in confusion, his head wobbling on thin shoulders. He was blonde with a thick moustache and he might not be unpleasant to look at if he were well groomed, though he did have a slightly large nose sitting roundly in the middle of his face. Most noticeable, however, was his hair, which had bent to compass points all over his head from drying on his pillow, and MacBain hadn't shaved him yet, and so the fear she might otherwise have felt for his military office melted away at the sorry sight.

MacBain slowly explained the situation to him and it didn't take much for Annabelle to see the lieutenant didn't think much of MacBain. Then P.D. introduced the lieutenant and Annabelle to one another.

"Miss MacBain, I knew your father before the war," Forrest said quietly. "I grew up in Lucketts, and..." He grabbed his stomach until a pain passed through him, then leaned back against the bed and with effort finished with a little smile. "I had a lot of respect for him, and I... and I..."

Annabelle nodded. "Thank you," she said with discomfort.

But the lieutenant grabbed his stomach once more. "Potomac, get me... Excuse me, Miss Mac... " And Annabelle left the room as fast as she could.

When MacBain finally returned to the kitchen, he stoked the fire for a while without speaking, and Annabelle laid out some of what they'd eaten the night before for breakfast. As he worked, he began to whistle, and immediately Annabelle recognized the tune from their walk up the hill a year and a half before.

She smiled a little, but then stared at him as he helped to lay out the plates and spoons upon the table. The sight of it confused her. Never had she seen a man help in the kitchen, and it seemed so inappropriate, it unnerved her. Like watching a hen milk a cow. She wondered just what sort of "fetching up" he'd had that he knew how to handle a stove and bothered to help women in the kitchen. And then the only solution came to her: he must have been very, very poor.

She tried to take over the tasks, but he gently pushed her hands aside. The sensation from the sweep of his hands frightened her now just as it had the night before, and she stepped back from the table and let him alone.

When her nerves had settled somewhat, she asked after the lieutenant's health, hoping MacBain would understand that his duty was elsewhere. "Well, Lieutenant tried to get out of bed, but he folded in a heap, so I'd say the decision was made for him. We'll stay put another day."

She nodded but had to think to hold her tongue from saying, "Good." She was embarrassed by the feeling of gratitude that had sprung up within her—from where, she did not want to know. "Well then, I'll go and get Shilla for breakfast," she said nervously. "And do you think Lieutenant Woods will eat anything?"

He looked at her and smiled. "Forrest, Lieutenant Forrest." But his smile was pleasant—not condescending.

And her face grew red once more. "Forrest." She did everything she could to keep from smiling back at him. It concerned her very much that she wanted to smile at him.

After breakfast it began to snow. The flakes were small and dense, and so they knew it would be a heavy storm.

All afternoon the snow fell fast and thick, covering the charred ruins of the outbuildings until the black lumps disappeared altogether. At times the flakes fell as large and fluttery as goosedown. *Pretty stuff,* thought Annabelle as she stared out the kitchen window. But she also watched the snow pile up around Mistress Hattie's door. Shilla insisted she be the one to go and check on her and she began to get her shawl. But MacBain said he would go for her.

Before Shilla could make protest, he went out.

When he returned, he went to the stove and began to boil water. Shilla and Annabelle wondered what he was about until he went into Forrest's room and brought out the lieutenant's uniform.

Annabelle offered to wash it for him, but he said he thought they'd done enough for Yankees in one day. Annabelle smiled and Shilla actually laughed. They sat at the table and sewed as he washed. And, to pass the time, they made small talk.

After a lull in one conversation, Annabelle asked him if Potomac were his real name.

He laughed and rubbed his unshaven jaw. "No, it is not."

"A pet name then?"

"Of a sort," he said. "The kind the men give you just so's it'll needle you every time you hear it," he added with a touch of bitterness.

She thought on this and began to surmise something about him that unsettled her, but she couldn't quite put it into words. "Well then, what would the P.D. stand for?"

He turned around to face them, and leaned against the dry sink. "I'm sure you all wouldn't mind a good laugh?" Annabelle smiled and he went on. "So I'll tell you. P.D. stands for Pembroke Decatur."

They giggled.

"That's right, ladies, Pembroke Decatur, the *third*, mind you. Three full generations cursed with the dubious name of Pembroke Decatur." And they began to laugh aloud at his expense.

Shilla finally said, "That mought well be the worst name ever I heard."

Annabelle had tears in her eyes. "No, no, the worst was the boy my father grew up with. You'll think you've been blessed, sir, when you hear. He was named after six rich uncles, for his parents had an eye toward inheritance. They christened him 'Yukson Haben Obergat Teban Ernest Fleming Chalk.'" And then all three fell into a belly laugh.

"Oooh," said Shilla. "An' I thought I'd hurd all yer father's tales!"

"He was the meanest child in town," Annabelle went on. "Everyone picked on him because of that name. Then again, he was rich by the time he was sixteen!" And they laughed again.

Shilla said, "Sure'n it can be said the boy 'arned every penny!"

And as they sat there enjoying themselves, Annabelle thought that Pembroke Decatur had a lovely laugh. He sat on a stool, a hand on each knee, as he gave into it—the laugh coming from deep within him and taking over completely when it came. She was glad he could laugh with them and that she could share in it.

After P.D. lay his clothes out to dry on a string along the back porch, he grew fidgety and finally excused himself to check on the horses.

Shilla raised her eyebrows and said without looking up from her work, "He's a pleasant man, for a Yankee, I'll allow. But for all that, keep an eye on him, miss. Soldiers are not t'be trusted." Annabelle couldn't look at her for the red was creeping up her collar.

"But he is pleasant, as you say," Annabelle said quickly.

He was gone for an hour or two and they had already had lunch before he returned. Annabelle had amazed herself by worrying if he were all right, and she breathed a sigh of relief when he came back in the kitchen door.

But he was carrying his rifle, and Annabelle jumped a little at the sight.

He caught her look of surprise and he lowered his head. "Excuse me. There are no rags out there, and I should clean this."

Why he was there in her house in the first place came back to her with a vengeance at the sight of his gun. She threw her towel into the dry sink next to him and sat down quickly at the table, pulled her chin down and tried to concentrate on her sewing as he cleaned his weapon. But she lost stitches and silently cursed her nervousness.

There was no more joking that day.

"Her Gentleness" had by nightfall laid two feet of crisp snow on the ground around the home. P.D. gathered firewood for them, since the troops had taken most of the cords and the rest had burned as it sat by their outbuildings. Lieutenant Forrest woke up and began to curse loudly upon looking out his window. He felt well enough to sit up in bed, though, and took his dinner and ate rather well, they all noticed.

After dinner, P.D. immediately engaged Annabelle in conversation once more. This time Shilla joined in, and so they discussed much of what they had the night before. Annabelle knew Shilla was really more interested in chaperoning than in debating, but for her part Annabelle smiled more often and listened more and concentrated on MacBain's ability to persuade, his passion for his cause—a thing she envied—and the honesty and respect he gave the women in his presentation.

She couldn't imagine Michael Delaney willing to argue with her over anything. What he said was said and what he said was so: that was that. He expected a woman to follow suit. And she imagined Lemuel Walker would be the same way when the worshipful attitude he held toward the fairer sex gave way to the realities of married life. No, this man was quite different from any she had ever met, and she felt a strange thing well up in her as he spoke.

At first the feeling was intangible, but slowly it gave way to a strength of emotion as clear to her as perfect glass. She actually wanted his good opinion. Stunned with the realization, she shook her head, not believing her own state of mind.

P.D. noticed the shake of her head and ceased his argument with Shilla. "What, Annabelle, now you disagree? But you agreed to the selfsame argument last night."

She looked at him in wonder and realized then and there he wanted her good opinion, too. She gulped. "No, no, I was thinking of something else entirely. I'm sorry."

He looked relieved, and Annabelle determined to listen more carefully to the discussion from then on.

When the clock struck nine, Shilla excused herself, and she looked at Annabelle severely when P.D. had turned away, as if to say, "It would be best if you did the same."

Annabelle smiled reassuringly. "I'll be up in just a moment." Shilla didn't smile back but she did take herself upstairs, albeit ever so slowly.

P.D. stood up and stoked the fire and whistled that tune very low. Outside, the wind howled and caused the snow to drift against the back door. Handfuls of snow pelted the window now and again as the wind whipped around the house, but they were inside and warm. She didn't really want to go up to her cold room. It would take a dozen quilts to become warm enough to sleep, but it was quiet and cozy right here. A candle burned down on the table and that and the light from the stove made everything soft and golden. She knew it was a slightly dangerous thing to stay up with him now, but she couldn't leave just yet.

His left arm was draped casually at his side with his thumb in his belt, while his right arm moved slowly to stoke the fire. He had filled out since the day they'd met. His back was wide now, his legs sturdy, and he was completely at his ease. How different he was from that first impression she had had. She had thought, what? Ah, yes, she had thought he was arrogant. But she understood him now. It wasn't arrogance but a sense of duty that made him stand so straight and tall. Oh, but it felt good to see him standing here now, and she wished the moment would last.

"P.D." she said carefully. He put the poker down and came and sat at the table and smiled at her. "Do you think this war will be over very soon?"

He lost his smile. "Yes. We will win it soon, if by nothing more than amount of men and arms, we will win this war."

Annabelle nodded. "I believe you. This recent burning of towns. It's done its job. It won't starve Mosby out, but it's starved the people's hatred. No one wants to fight anymore. And when it ends, I want to know I'm in the right place. I've thought a lot about things and I..." She hesitated. "I believe I've decided to take the oath." She glanced up at him, half-afraid he might laugh at her.

But he kept his eyes on the candle, nodding slightly to show he'd heard, and for that she was extremely grateful.

He took his sack from the floor then, pulled Brighton's Bible from it and laid it on the table before her. She gulped and put her hand upon it. And he began to say the oath quietly giving her time to repeat it after him.

"Please repeat after me, 'I, Annabelle MacBain, do solemnly swear,'" he said, keeping his voice low.

"I, Annabelle Shannon MacBain, do solemnly swear,"

He smiled briefly. "Shannon. Lovely."

"That can't be a part of the oath," she quipped.

"I'm sorry. Sorry." Then he went on with it and she repeated word for word the following:

"... in the presence of Almighty God, that I will henceforth faithfully support, protect, and defend the Constitution of the United States and the Union of the States thereunder; and that I will in like manner abide by and faithfully support all acts of Congress passed during the existing rebellion with reference to slaves, so long and so far as not repealed, modified, or held void by Congress or by decision of the Supreme Court; and that I will in like manner abide by and faithfully support all proclamations of the president made during the existing rebellion having reference to slaves..." Here he stopped to glance at her and she nodded for him to continue. "... so long and so far as not modified or declared void by decision of the Supreme Court. So help me God."

"So help me God." Then Annabelle took a deep breath and let her hand fall back into her lap.

"I forgot to ask. May I keep Samuel's Bible?"

"By all means," she said.

He placed the Bible back in his sack and then went back to stoking the fire.

The snowy wind continued to shake the window panes, and the fire still crackled in the stove as it had, but as Annabelle sat at the table she began to feel differently about herself, and about the situation at hand. The honesty of what she had done had given her a new sense of herself. She crossed her arms and rubbed her elbows mildly as if she were hugging herself for doing a good thing, and for the first time in a long time she realized she felt good about something and clean, like her soul had had a fresh scrub.

But then a sadness washed the smile away as she thought of her father. *Forgive me, Weem,* she said to herself, and she wished her father were here, but then she didn't.

They sat there in the warm silence for a good long while.

TWENTY-ONE

Nicodemus, the slave, was of African birth,
And was bought for a bag full of gold;
He was reckon'd as part of the salt of the earth,
But he died years ago very old.
'Twas his last sad request, so we laid him away
In the trunk of an old hollow tree.
"Wake me up!" was his charge,
"at the first break of day,
Wake me up for the great Jubilee!"

From the song _Wake Nicodemus_

P.D. stoked the fire for a while more before he laid the poker down. "Annabelle, there were some questions I was about to ask you last night, and now I am twice as ready to ask them. May I ask them now? I don't work for Secret Service anymore, but I do have one task left."

She nodded uncertainly. _He's not a spy any longer?_ she wondered.

"I told you a long time ago Brighton's Bible held the names of men ready to help him." He paused and then smiled. "You may have guessed by now Brighton was sympathetic to the Union?"

"From the fact you had his Bible, yes, but I hadn't thought much more about it, actually."

"Well, Brighton's home was on the underground railroad."

Annabelle was shocked to the core. "What?" she whispered. "Samuel Brighton, no. Really?" _Right here in my own town, an underground railroad for runaway slaves? In Mosby's Confederacy?_ It was too amazing. She knew the Quakers were sympathetic and that some had gotten in trouble over the years for harboring runaways, but she never thought anything like that could have gone on in Hillsborough.

"I was looking through your father's things to find evidence of something, but I found proof of the railroad first."

Nothing he could have said would have confused her more. She drew her brows together. "In my father's things?"

"The notes he has there on his patients—he knew no one would ever look in his files. Apparently, he took care of the slaves that came through on the railroad whenever Brighton asked him to. At least 150 of them in the last few years."

What he was telling her changed the course of Annabelle's mind entirely. Her own father knowing of the railway, abetting the Northern cause? "Are you saying my father is a Northern sympathizer?" she said, numb with shock.

But he shook his head. "No, I think he is a Christian man and a good doctor."

Annabelle remembered how she would go with her father to Brighton's place when she was a young girl and how her father asked her to stay home from the place as she grew older. He had made it clear it wasn't a woman's place to go on his doctor's rounds. He had put it to her as a compliment. *Such a big girl—too big to go on my rounds anymore, Annie.* But she had thought, *So this is what it's like to grow up and be a woman. I don't like it.* But now she realized the true reason her father had asked her to stay home.

Her hands grew animated as she told P.D., "You know, when I was a little girl, Father took me to the Brightons' with him all the time, and I thought they were the most marvelously rich people I'd ever seen, because it appeared to me they had dozens and dozens of black servants." She laughed abruptly as P.D. smiled, but her smile froze as she shook her head. "I never thought before how odd it was. Quakers don't have servants at all, you know, unless they come, like Jane and the others at Mrs. Brighton's, as indentured orphans from the Meeting. But you must know all that."

He nodded.

"Well, then, as I got older he wouldn't let me come with him. He didn't want me to know. When I went there the day you were there, I thought of how many servants they once had and truly believed they'd come to poverty! Still it never occurred to me about the black servants. Free blacks never take on indenture."

"Like freedom too much, I guess," P.D. said mildly.

"Yes, but how strange I knew this and never thought it out." They both shook their heads. "By the Lake of Kinchyle, I just can't believe it. My father, all that time."

P.D. laughed at that. "By the Lake of what?"

"By the Lake of Kinchyle. Haven't you heard it before? You've never? Why, that's where the MacBains come from—the Lake of Kinchyle. When my father's ever amazed at anything he says, 'By the Lake of Kinchyle!'" But her voice drifted off as her eyes rested on his. P.D. was looking at her happily, enjoying her enjoyment, concentrating on her in such a way that she had to clear her throat and look down at her sewing. "In Scotland, our relation, Donald MacBain lost his lands to debt because he came to America to fight the French. You know, a hundred years ago, my father said."

"By the Lake of Kinchyle." he said slowly. "I didn't know that. Hm. MacBain found a higher purpose in war, eh?"

"Maybe he just liked to fight. Most Scotsmen do, so I've heard," she replied impishly. But she wanted to go back in the discussion, so, while still looking at the handiwork between her hands, she asked, "But why were you looking through Samuel Brighton's file in my father's desk, then?"

P.D. pushed his chair back and leaned his elbows on his knees as he shook his head. "I came across something when I was here before as Malachi Norris. It's not something I was looking for, but there it was. When I dug up Mr. Brighton..."

She sucked in her breath and looked down quickly, staring hard at the uneven stitches she'd made.

"I found something strange about the body. Is this too indelicate?"

Annabelle gulped. "No. Please. I want to know. Besides..." She tried to say it jauntily, "I've been a field nurse, for heaven's sake. Nothing should shock me now."

"All right. True enough. Well, I don't expect Mrs. Brighton

suspected anything when she prepared her husband for burial." He turned his head as if turning away could somehow lessen the meaning of his words. "I mean to say, Mrs. Brighton couldn't know what the impact of a certain bullet can do." With all her experience, still Annabelle's flesh crawled as he spoke and her sewing stopped. "But Mr. Brighton wasn't shot through the neck from the front at first."

Annabelle felt herself go pale, and she folded her hands in her lap as he went on.

"You see, I knew from looking at the wound..." And then he looked down and spoke as if explaining it to himself. "I knew what a bullet could do to the neck when it penetrates, and so I knew he was shot from the back as well as from the front, through the same hole, twice, you see?" But she didn't see. "Straight through the neck from the back first, I can only presume, because when you kill a man, you don't bother to shoot him head on if you can help it." He observed her face. She'd almost killed P.D. from behind, but he went on, "I knew then the man had been murdered."

"Murder!"

"Yes. Then, whoever did it, laid the body out to look like an accident."

Annabelle gulped again, and she drew her shawl about her. "That's horrible. That's horrible! Poor Samuel Brighton, murdered?" She drew one hand to her neck. She thought of the man suffering that way. Such a kind, kind man. It was grotesque. Beyond belief. Who would do such a thing?

They were silent for a long while—long enough for her to think things out a little more. She blinked and cocked her head. "But how do you know so much?"

"Well, it's like this. I was looking at Brighton's neck, and something one of Brighton's house servants said came back to me. The old man had gotten sentimental, telling me about the day they found him dead. He said they'd all heard his one shot—Brighton was known as a one-shot hunter, and so whenever he went out with his gun, the servants all waited to hear the shot because they knew he'd be arriving within the hour and they'd prepare something for his return—but when he was more than an hour in coming home that day, they all knew what had happened. Now that old man could have been lying to me, but I chose not to think so."

"And?" she said, leaning into the word.

"And after putting that question to my mind, if there were two shots, front and back, to the same spot in the neck, why was only one heard? I put a lot of thought to it. I've seen a man kill two turkeys with one bullet by waiting 'til they twined their necks together when they fought over a hen, but I've never heard of a man shot once in the same place front and back from two sides of the woods. Made absolutely no sense. So I slept on it, and in the morning, I up and went around the woods looking. I wandered about and finally found what I was looking for. A tree with low limbs where they could prop him up and shoot him again with his own gun. A tree fairly far from where the body was found with a lot of blood about five foot up. You can't very well wash a tree down."

"But the one shot?" She was totally engrossed in the description now, and a flicker of a smile passed over him to see her look of utter concentration.

"Yes, the one shot. That's where being a spy comes in handy. How do you shoot a man twice with the sound of one shot?"

"When the shots are made at exactly the same time." she said intently.

"Yes, but you'd have to be twins to think that much alike—and even then it would take a miracle. There's another possibility."

"Yes?" And her brows rolled together like a dark thundercloud.

"It can happen," he smiled ever so slightly "when one of the bullets makes no sound."

Annabelle's eyes nearly crossed at this, for he might as well have lapsed into Greek.

"I understand your confusion." He sat back. "I'm talking about an air gun. A percussion gun that uses pumped air instead of a powder to"—slap!!—he smacked his hands together causing Annabelle to jump in her seat—"force the bullet out. Works well. Too well. But the gun, well, it isn't considered soldierly, honorable. But a few spies might have them. And spies might be ones to know about the underground railroad, you see? So I went looking for a bullet near to the bloody tree, and here the Lord was surely with me, because beyond all probability I found it. I found it just before I came back to the house and met you visiting with Mrs. Brighton." He smiled lightly. Then he looked down. "Anyway, whoever it was shot him from probably around fifty yards away."

"An air gun," she said vaguely, but suddenly she drew herself up. "I don't mean to be coarse, but with all the murder about why would anyone choose to investigate one murder? Why would you pursue this? I... I'm glad you are, for Samuel Brighton's sake, but it's a bit unusual, isn't it?"

P.D. nodded. "Mr. Brighton was a good friend of President Lincoln's, and Mr. Lincoln asked me to look into it."

Annabelle stared at him with new eyes. "You know Lincoln?"

"Passingly, but he was a good friend of Mr. Brighton's long before the war. Brighton hatched his plan of a secret network of Northern sympathizers out here because there were so many Quaker farmers who were assumed to be neutral but weren't. The President, although he wasn't president at the time, thought it was a good idea, and they cut off contact a few years before the war began. Until this."

"Do you mean Lincoln knew the war would begin when it did?"

"Not exactly. Mr. Brighton had other reasons not to draw attention to himself. About 150 reasons."

"I see," Annabelle said with awe in her voice. "And Lincoln asked you to look into this. Does your unit know about this duty of yours?"

He let out a sharp laugh. "Can't you tell? They treat me just like royalty." He folded his arms. "No, they don't. And I'll be lucky to live long enough to do Mr. Lincoln any good on this. I only told you half-truth in saying we were scouting. I was really sent along in case Forrest needed someone to do his dirty work, like ferreting out a sniper for him, perhaps, by the use of my head."

Annabelle smiled uncertainly. "And why are you favoring me with this information?"

"Because I'd like as much information about Brighton as you can give me; who might have been an enemy, who might have known about the underground—I exclude your father, of course—and what his last day might have been like. Things like these."

"All right." Annabelle checked off the questions in her mind. "First of all, he had no enemies that I know of. I knew nothing of the underground and can't imagine anyone else did or something would have been done about it, I'm sure. Lastly, all I know about his last day is that Pella didn't go hunting with him as he usually would."

"Yes, I spoke to him about that. He said Marsden kept him home that day, but that it wasn't unusual. There'd been some extra work for him."

Annabelle shook her head. "That poor child."

To that he laughed and rubbed his chin. "Not as much of a child as you might think." She cocked her head as he smiled. "Those hunting trips with Brighton early in the morning? Pella wasn't hunting. He was conducting—on the railroad."

"No!"

"Yea!" He chuckled. "Pella was in charge of taking folks up to the next station while Mr. Brighton watched their back and sides."

"No! But why ever didn't Pella escape, too, then?"

"He said he wanted to stay. *Virginia is my home place*, he said. Told me he's looking forward to telling his grandchildren about the days of slavery and how he helped the underground railroad way back when."

They grew quiet as a wind kicked up around the house. "So, anything else you can tell me?" he asked suddenly.

"I'm sorry." Annabelle looked about her. "I'm afraid there's nothing much left to tell. These days, folks keep to themselves a lot. I suppose they won't want to speak to me at all, now that I've taken the oath."

"And how will you manage?" he asked calmly and the suddenness of the thought startled her.

A trickle of fear crept through her. "I don't know." She hadn't a clue what it would be like. "But I suppose I've not seen many friends recently, anyway. My best friends moved to Richmond." *And this, they are not likely to understand,* she thought. She couldn't bear to think about it. She looked up at him. "And how do you manage?"

"Being an outcast among my own?" He lost his good humor. "It doesn't go down too well."

"How did it happen?"

"That's the one story I can't tell you, I'm afraid."

"But I took the oath."

"Yes, but..." He laughed nervously. "Really, the story's not so amazing or threatening to the national welfare, nothing like that, it's just... I can't tell you." He shook his head and gripped his hands together tightly, adding bitterly, "But I suppose I can tell you this much—I gained my poor reputation by earning it."

"I see." But she didn't see at all, but she wanted to. She wanted to know everything about him. Everything. She'd rather believe the lieutenant unworthy than to think MacBain had done something so horrible to deserve such shoddy treatment. Perhaps he had done something the shortsighted Union army couldn't understand.

She wanted to come around to him and hug him and tell him it was all right, that she believed in him. She wanted him to feel better about life, but she shook herself from such thoughts. "Well, I should retire." Her face grew pink when she realized she'd left an opening in her words.

"Should?" he said with a quick glance and half a smile and then he looked at her with soft eyes that made her want to kiss him. She very much wanted to kiss him.

And the thought thrilled and frightened her all at once. But they stared at each other, and the way in which he leaned into the table and the way she let her silk shawl fall from her shoulders just then, they may as well have kissed for both knew what the other was thinking.

They were thinking, as lovers do, that there was no one more beautiful, more honest, more bold, more worthy of love than the one they looked upon at that moment, the one whose look betrayed a perfect symmetry of thought.

Only Annabelle could not bear to let those thoughts take further flight. Suddenly she stood up.

Now he stood, too, and came forward to reach... the chair? Her arm? She stepped back awkwardly. "No!" She was afraid, afraid that he would touch her, afraid she would give in to her feelings completely.

He hesitated. "But, Annabelle."

The candle flickered on the table as the room fell silent.

"I know. I know it, P.D. But as I live and breathe, please don't say anything more." She wrung her hands as if to warm them. Then her hands flew out from her momentarily before she pulled them in, gripping her shawl and pulling it tightly back up around her shoulders. But her hands shook as she looked at the back stair door. Her actions were forced and awkward, and she hardly knew what she was doing, but she made herself walk past him toward that door.

What was going through her mind at the time was that for all the changing she had done in the last two days—and the changes were considerable—the idea of kissing a Union soldier in her father's home was beyond the realm of possibility. She would not. She could not face herself, if she did. But she found the strings that held her to such a bold resolve were very thin, and so she said good night as quickly as she could.

"Annabelle." he said as she passed. His voice was low and resonant and it was lovely to her.

Was it she who turned at the door or was she dreaming? He pulled her close to him then and it was not a dream, and she began to kiss him with a long and longing kiss by the window of the back stair.

And when the kiss was done, he still held her, and she let her head rest in the cup of his shoulder, and the movement was so natural it was as if she'd done the same a thousand times before and she held him tighter. It was all right, now. Everything would be all right. She breathed in the smell of oil and firewood, sweat and gunpowder, and she loved him with all her might. She pulled away to look at him, but he kissed her again, and she thought she would die in the wonder of it. The beauty of it hurt her. Beauty that could not last, and so it stung her all the more.

She pushed him away for a moment and while he still held his arms out to her he said, "You must know I love you, Annabelle."

She nodded. "But how can love come so quickly?" she asked innocently.

He smiled and shook his head. "No, I've thought of you every day since the day I met you."

She let out a gulping laugh. "Aye, every day, and yet I thought I hated you."

He shrugged. "Doesn't matter now."

She smiled and they embraced again.

He rocked her gently. "Annabelle, I fell in love with you as you walked up the hill measuring the music with that carving." He took her face in his hands. "And I said to myself as we walked up that road, *What will my poor father say when I bring home a little Rebel girl?*"

"No! Did you now?"

He smiled.

In nervous irritation at his words she pulled his hands from her face. "Well, then, I'll tell you I thought you were a bit of a snob, so I did, although a very thin and a very ragged one." They laughed. "Are you very poor, love?"

P.D. MacBain cocked his head. "What exactly do you mean by poor?"

She felt herself blush. "Well, how you help us in the kitchen, and wash clothes. I know you must have…" She shook her head. "It doesn't make any difference to me, really, and though I thought your habits strange, you see, I've gotten used to them." She smiled uncertainly.

He let out a laugh. "No, I'm not poor, Annabelle. I'm not rich either. Picked up my strange ways in the army, I guess, taking care of myself in the field, but I'll drop them if you like."

"Oh, no! I think I rather like having a man in the kitchen. That is, if you like... Having you... It's nice..." She felt her tongue tie mercilessly in the last words, and so he hugged her close and laughed again. Then she stood smiling at him with tears in her eyes. "But this is impossible."

He hushed her and smoothed her hair. "Let God do as He pleases. He gave us this. He gave us this. He will work it."

She nodded and gulped. "If we do as He bids. But my pride, my pride is an ugly, hateful thing at times."

"Pride. Well, you won't be fighting it alone. For pride I couldn't tell you how I felt at the field hospital."

"But you were angry with me."

"Oh, yes." He laughed. "I was angry. There I was in the perfect spot to die, a recent failure haunting me and an illness wanting to kill me, and then you came. Against all sense, against the very will of nature, I wanted to get well just so I could look at you. I knew I couldn't have you, but I wanted to live another day to watch you walk around with a cup, blush at a compliment, write a letter for a fellow, or cry with him for his wife and children. Or even to see you trip on a blanket as you crossed the room."

"You were watching me."

"But it was all I could do to keep you from knowing it."

She colored as the memory came to her. "I was watching you. Oh, how I watched you. And when you sang the song."

"I sang it for you, Annabelle."

"The very thing I'd hoped." And they kissed again, a long, soft kiss.

Then Annabelle rushed up the stairs.

TWENTY-TWO

"When he was going, he put his arm around my neck and kissed me, and said, 'I love you, Mollie, you need not be uneasy.' He said once before that he must love anybody very hard to kiss them, so I suppose he loves me hard then. I hope I may never be unworthy of his love."

From the diary of Miss Mary E. Lack

At first she couldn't go to sleep. His kisses still burned in her memory. Never had she been kissed like that, so gently, passionately. Never had she returned a kiss with such likemind.

Michael Delaney's kisses had held all the passion of a waxen seal—always a statement to her she belonged to him—and in her young heart, she had thought that that was love, to be owned and cared for by someone stronger than herself.

But she knew the difference now, and she would never make that mistake again.

Finally, she fell asleep, but she dreamed the strangest dreams she'd ever known and woke up feeling queerly in the morning. And then suddenly she realized, "He's downstairs. P.D.'s right downstairs!" And she hurried down.

He greeted her at the stove with a handsome smile and she blushed deeply and returned the favor. But then he was staring at her collar. He let out a chuckle. She brought her hand to her neck, and her face burned red to find that in her hurry to dress she had bound the first button to the second loop! She turned away from him toward Shilla and struggled to fix the buttons, but then Shilla was looking at her absolutely horrified.

They continued to prepare breakfast and Annabelle and P.D. began to glance at each other and smile. Shilla watched it all unhappily, for the meaning was all too clear. Annabelle caught her disapproving looks more than once and finally came over and gave her a grand hug. Then Shilla stepped back and looked her over from head to toe as if she'd gone mad.

"Everything is fine, Shilla, just fine," she whispered, but Shilla wouldn't smile.

Instead she whispered, "I want them out, miss. Ye know t'isn't right."

Annabelle rolled her eyes. "Hush, please, Shilla. They are our guests until the lieutenant's well enough to travel." But she would not look at Shilla again. *Heaven knows what she'll do when she finds I've taken the oath,* thought Annabelle cheerlessly.

Things grew somber for a time as Shilla continued to make her feelings obvious. The rattling of Shilla's pots was unnerving, as was the occasional wiping of a tear on her long apron, but just when Annabelle thought she could stand no more, she looked at MacBain and suddenly it didn't matter what Shilla thought.

Then Thomas' door opened and there stood the lieutenant, swaying a bit but obviously feeling more like himself than he had in days. He greeted everyone stiffly and they all sat down for breakfast. He, too, began to watch MacBain and Annabelle and was unpleased at their unspoken but obvious bond.

After breakfast, the day passed much like the one before, with MacBain going out to care for Hattie Humboldt and the horses and to gather wood for the fire. Lieutenant Forrest made quiet conversation while MacBain was away and the morning passed.

By the afternoon, Forrest said he might lie down awhile and promptly retired to his room.

Annabelle and Shilla stayed at the kitchen table sewing. When Shilla thought the lieutenant was asleep, she quietly said, "T'isn't right, miss. I've said it before, and I'll say it again."

Annabelle blushed. "Hush, Shilla. It'll do you no good to speak to me like that. Do you trust me so little?"

Shilla put down her sewing. "Dear Annie, it's not you I'm mistrusting, but I'm afraid your romantic notions have stolen your sense aw'y. He's just a soldier, miss, and for all tha', he's a spy."

"Was a spy," she interjected.

"And if he still were, d'ye think he'd tell you? Anyone knows the likes o' that can't be trusted. And for such a one to be makin' bold-faced love to you in plain sight. T'isn't right, and you know it." Her voice rose. "Only think what yer father would say!"

"Hush!" Annabelle said fiercely. "You don't know him as I do." But tears welled in her eyes to think of her father's opinion. She certainly didn't need Shilla to remind her.

With a twinge of bitterness in her tone, Shilla announced she didn't feel well and thought she might lie down herself. But she ruined Annabelle's anticipation of being alone with Private MacBain when she gave another pronouncement. "I know you wouldn't do anything intentional, miss, to dishonor yer father's house. I know that much of ye."

"Well, thank you for that, Shilla," Annabelle said with a catch in her throat. "You're too kind."

As soon as Shilla left, Annabelle quickly walked back to the window to look for him.

She stood there half an hour, but he did not return. She stoked the stove for a while, then sat back down to sew, and finally she noted with disappointment and not a small amount of fear that an hour and a half had passed since he left.

When she heard a door open, Annabelle looked over with shock to see that Forrest was standing at the door but he was very unsteady.

"Lieutenant Forrest, you need to go back to bed."

"I was hoping you'd say that, Mishhh Annabelle." A loud belch followed his words. He swung an almost empty bottle of brandy behind his back.

"Wherever did you get that bottle?" she asked. "You're drunk!"

"'WHErrrrrever did ye git that buttle,' she sez. Gad, I love your speech, mish. Itsh lovely." He sloppily spat the words at her even as he made his way toward the kitchen table.

All Annabelle could think was that Thomas must have hidden

some brandy in his room and this fool had found it. *Trust a Yankee to find the goods,* she thought testily. And then she was immediately uncomfortable to be left alone with him.

But he sat down at the table noisily. "Yer lookin' for him, ain't che? Well, Missh Annabelle, I got sumpin' to tell you." She stood up and began to walk carefully to the back stair. "No. No. I've needed to speak to yer lovely person alone. Regards a certain private."

Turning back, she said, "Sir, P.D. will return any moment, and he will help you back to bed..."

"*P.D.?* P.D. So now yer callin' each other by your Christian names! Well, his name isn't P.D. It's Potomac. Be sure 'n call him Potomac." He hiccuped and laughed. "S'wanna I want to tell you. Know why we call him Potomac?"

"You needn't." She pulled at the fringe of her waist pocket and then halfheartedly smoothed her dress. She did want to know. She wanted very much to know.

Forrest waved his hand in the air and wagged his head, then swung his face low to the table and glanced about the room in a manner reserved for conferring secrets of great worth. The gestures would have been more impressive if his chin hadn't snagged the table top as he began to speak. "They tell me these things 'cause I gotta keep him in line—now everybody in the outfit knows 'bout Potomac."

Forrest looked ridiculous, yes, but his words had piqued her curiosity. And what would be the harm in knowing? After all, she reasoned, if everyone in his troop knew how he got the name, there couldn't be any consequences in telling her, could there?

She came toward him only a little and rested her hands on the door frame to the kitchen.

He smiled. "They (hiccup)... they call him Potomac because thash where he messed things up. Potomac River." He looked away with a soggy glint in his eye. "He was a high-falutin' spy o' some sort, a personal friend of the Baboon's, an' he got some crazy idea into his head right after Gettysburg." *P.D. was at Gettysburg,* Annabelle said to herself.

"Russshhhed down to Washington to tell Lincoln he'd heard Gen—General Meade had no intention of pursing Lee 'lessin' he had help. Lincoln told him Æbout his Quaker, so Potomac up and goes and... he was too late, you shee. I don't want to insult yer... yer sensibli... sensil... dignity, but he had to dig the Quaker up to get a list of names. Ain't that a hoot! I love to think of it... him out there diggin'." The lieutenant stopped to laugh and snort.

But Annabelle was growing pale.

"Anyways, he went to get this dead man's list of friends to help. They were gonna get a little group of us together, blow Lee away from the other side of the river with cannons—cannons bought from some farmer who'd gotten 'em out of Harp-hic's Ferry in '61. See? If he'd a gotten the cannons situated across the river like he was supposed to," he said with utter scorn, "he could a' blown Lee's army straight to Hades and back and the war'd be over. But," he started to laugh, "he got sick. The fool got sick and, and he coun't do it. Ne—never got to the cannons or found soldiers to do 'em, he just got sick. An' that is why we call him Potomac." He spit on the floor. "And I woun't be here if it weren't for that mishcreant." He looked at Annabelle unsteadily and smiled. "But now that'd be a shame, woun't it darlin'."

But Annabelle was no longer listening. She was shaking as she remembered the day she'd gotten P.D. to tell where they were coming across the river; he told her to stay clear if the cannons fired, but he hadn't said from which side of the river the blasts might come. Tears filled her eyes as the truth struck her; at last, those cannons had found their mark, and she felt a huge and painful tear ripping through her soul, and a pit grew within her into which all of her feelings silently fell.

And all was dark there.

"An he kissed you, din't he?" the lieutenant talked on. "Yea, 'course he did. Took advantage of you, din't he?" He struggled to get out of the chair. "Thash how he got all his informashion, courtin' Rebel ladies. Gettin' their sympathy roused with a little limp in his leg." His voice grew whiny now. "'Hep a poor sowdger just back from the war, Mrs. Willing? Sit down and tell me your troubles. Captain Willing's away, you say?' Oh, how the mice will play." With great effort he shook his head. "They call that spyin'. Wish I were a spy." His smile was contorted; his nose was a bright pink from the bottle, and Annabelle immediately backed up toward the stairs again. "Yea, our little Potomac has got a way about him." Then he looked up as if remembering something, and out came,

> There once was a spy named MacBain (burp)
> Whose service was truly profane;
> He'd kiss the girls soundly,
> And when told he was rude he said,
> 'Girls, I'm just doing my duty.'"

Then the lieutenant looked angry again. "Always kisses the girls, but I'm his superior in 'ev'ry way." He lunged for her and then righted himself; it wasn't hard for her to step back and away from him.

At that moment, P.D. MacBain entered the back door, sized up the sorry state of his commander, then turned to see Annabelle.

Now the hate she'd had for him at first was nothing compared to what she felt for him right then. A black, dark hate took hold of her, an iron cord of anger like a noose about her neck, and though it would kill her to give in to it she could no more pull her neck away from the rope than the man that stands upon the gallows with rifles at his back.

But she could turn away from him. She could turn away from P.D. MacBain and she did.

As she walked briskly toward the back stairs, Forrest said loudly, "I was just 'tellin her how you happen to come by the name Potomac."

"You fool, you're drunk." He pushed the lieutenant aside. "If I find you so much as touched her, I'll kill you," he whispered fiercely.

The lieutenant raised his arms in mock surrender. "No, naw. She's all yours, *Potomac*. Ain't they all?" And he laughed.

"Annabelle!" Annabelle was halfway up the stairs when MacBain grabbed hold of her hand on the bannister and pulled.

"Let me go!" she cried.

But he clung tighter. "Annabelle, I... did he touch you? I'll kill him, I will." But Annabelle gave him a look that said much more, and suddenly he asked, "What did he tell you?" as he held on to her hand and came up the stairs below her.

"Keep away from me! You!" A racking sob tore from her throat and as he met her on the stairs she yanked her hand free and hit him in the chest with both fists. "You would have killed my father." She said it again and again and hit at him wildly. He wrestled with her and finally grabbed her arms and pinned them at her sides.

"Annabelle!" he yelled. "Don't. I was only trying to do my duty."

With that, Lieutenant Forrest laughed and began his limerick again. MacBain yelled down to him to shut his mouth.

"Your duty?" Annabelle said with a sneer.

Then Shilla's voice boomed down to both of them from the top of the stairwell. "Take yer hands off her."

They both looked up to see Thomas' rifle steadily held against Shilla's shoulder. Immediately he released her. The rifle that had lain for half a week on the floor of her father's office at the top of the stairs was once more taken up and aimed at MacBain's head.

MacBain backed down the stairs, watching Shilla all the while, and she went on to say, "I see yer lieutenant's well enough to sniff out his own supper, so I want both ye foul rats to clear off."

As she spoke Annabelle backed up the stair toward her.

When he reached the bottom of the stairs, MacBain looked up at Annabelle and tried again. "Annabelle, you can't take it personally. You can't."

"But war is personal, isn't it? A belief, you said? Well then, sir, I *believe* I hate you with all my heart." The words came out with a shudder and a hiss.

"Miss, quiet miss, quiet yourself. And you—" Shilla raised the rifle once more, "—you kin just quit yer talkin' and git yer things and get out of here. Good night to you then."

"I'll bring food for you."

"Don't bother, Yank, we'll manage," Shilla said angrily, rashly. "Now git!"

He gulped and nodded and walked toward the kitchen. Within ten minutes the men were on their horses, although Forrest was none too steady on his mount.

Shilla and Annabelle stood upstairs in Annabelle's room while Shilla watched them from the window with an eagle eye. "Blue devils," she said venomously. "Aye, they'll be going now. And if they come back they'll find Thomas' bullets for a welcome song."

Something in Annabelle wanted to watch them go, but she stood where she was, holding one post at the end of her bed to steady herself.

"There they go," Shilla said, and Annabelle looked up quickly.

Then one long bloodcurdling tormented sound rose to them from the snow. "AN-NA-BELLE!"

A feeling tore through her such as she'd never felt before; it almost wrenched her pale hands from the post, but in another moment it had passed. P.D. MacBain had given a cry as shrill and bone-chilling as the Rebel yell, and her name echoed into the woods, into the snowy branches, up into a cold December sky. A sob rose from within her, but she let it die. She let herself feel absolutely nothing.

And in another moment, Shilla quietly said, "Well, they're gone."

TWENTY-THREE

"Secession has ruined old Loudoun.
She has been between hawk and buzzard
all the time, and between the two she
has been made a wreck. Most of her
people are disloyal and have been broken
up and scattered, and though the war
should end tomorrow, most of them
are beggared."

**From a letter signed Tom,
August 16, 1863**

Later in the day and after the women had sat in the kitchen several hours, Shilla quietly sewing and Annabelle staring into space, Annabelle finally pulled her thoughts together and told Shilla what Forrest had said about "Potomac."

"I wish you'd told me on the stair," Shilla replied. "I'd have shot him for ye, then and there."

Annabelle could only nod.

She had told herself it wouldn't last, and it hadn't. All was illusion. Nothing made sense, and what was the point of things anyway? Shilla tried to talk to her, tried to ask her how they might feed themselves, whether they should sell the silver, but Annabelle could hardly speak. She didn't see much point in food, not much point in anything. The man she loved was merely a spy and a liar. He'd spoken words of love to her because such was his training and his habit—nothing more.

She remembered Forrest's words, and now realized that even MacBain's limp was a ploy to gain her sympathy. All his mild conversation was only to help him discover more about Brighton and his grave that day. She remembered how he laughed in the hospital when she noticed his leg was "healed." It was disgusting. He had deceived her several times over, and now she had taken the oath and so deceived her father in turn. What a horrible joke it all seemed now. "Better not to live, better not to live," she told herself over and over and yet she had no strength to carry out the thought.

The next morning Shilla came upstairs to tell Annabelle that a Mr. Timms, a Union man with a farm west of town, was at the door spouting nonsense about having a load of food for them in his wagon. Shilla had told him they needed no food from Yanks, and he replied that he'd been told the house had taken the oath.

Annabelle nodded to Shilla gravely and took herself downstairs to meet him, and Shilla was at her heels ready for a good fight. When Annabelle reached the door, however, she smiled at Mr. Timms. "By all means, bring the food around back to the kitchen, please," she said. And Shilla stood amazed behind her.

He went back down the steps to unload his goods while Shilla pulled at Annabelle's arm, saying in a singsong of agitation, "What are ye doing, miss? He says we took the oath. It's that spy Yank's doin', I'll be bound."

Annabelle nodded and pulled her arm away. "Yes, but I did, Shilla. I took the oath, and as long as I did, I'll take advantage of the spoils. You know, the war is not going well for the South, and we may as well face it. Those that support the Rebels won't eat until their own harvest if the soldiers don't take it from them first, and I'm not planning to starve. I took the oath, and and when I took it, I meant it. So at least we shall eat."

Shilla's eyes grew watery as she looked into Annabelle's. "You're head of this house, miss, and so we will." And then she slipped past her to help Mr. Timms unload the wagon.

When Annabelle ventured out of the house a full five days from the day the soldiers left, she tried to hold her head high, but still she walked with a tremble to the general store. Shilla didn't feel well enough to go and someone had to. Only a few people were on the street, but already the news had traveled, and already she faced the anger of her neighbors. One man actually spat on the ground as she passed. She almost turned to go back home, but she knew she would have to face this treatment sooner or later and she made herself walk on. At the store, Mrs. Bucknall served her in unusual silence. No one greeted her, not even those who had Union sympathies.

As she walked back from the store, she tried not to cry. A Mrs. Green, whose son was killed in the Battle of the Wilderness, opened her front door as Annabelle passed, and, when she caught Annabelle's eye, she deliberately shook out her skirts. Annabelle winced and put her head down as she heard Mrs. Green's door slam, and it was then she almost ran headlong into Mrs. Casey.

"Annabelle," said Mrs. Casey in her gentle way.

Annabelle looked up and smiled at the hope of hearing something kind.

"I've heard the most ridiculous thing," Mrs. Casey said. "Someone's saying you took the oath, dear."

Annabelle glanced to the side of the road and opened her mouth to speak, but the tears welled up and made the words catch in her throat.

"I told them that was ridiculous, with your father in the army," she went on, "and you as proud of him as could be, that it was the most outrageous lie I'd ever heard."

Annabelle looked up at the sky and then to Mrs. Casey once more. "But I did," she said quietly.

"Hmm, I don't believe I heard you, dear?"

"I said, 'I did,' Mrs. Casey. I took the oath."

Mrs. Casey's hand, which had previously cupped her ear, fell sharply to her side as her mouth dropped open. "You didn't, child. You... Oh, land, how could you do such a thing to your father?"

It was too much and Annabelle turned and ran home.

Once in her bedroom, she fell onto her bed to cry. She cried until her stomach ached and there were no more tears. Then she lay there for an hour and the anger rose up in her heart to overflowing. She knew Shilla didn't understand, she couldn't imagine how Thomas would take the news, she wondered if her father would accept her decision, and most of all she was unwilling to speak of it in prayer. It was then she sat up on the edge of her bed, held tightly to the corner post and decided she would not cry over this again.

Unfortunately, along with the neighbors' knowledge of her oath-taking, many had heard MacBain's wrenching cry for Annabelle and had put their minds together to explain it to themselves. Of course they explained it well past the truth, well past who they knew her to be: in short, well past common decency. After all, this was the girl who thought Brighton's grave had been disturbed, a girl who could shame her Confederate father by taking the oath, and a Union soldier. Well, only think what it could mean for him to have stayed there two nights. What more did they need to know about a woman like that?

And so while the Confederates in town turned away from her because she'd taken the oath, people of both persuasions had decided she was at the least slightly touched, and at the most of questionable character. In fact, the most blatant insult she received was from the hand of Union sympathizers—the only ones who had access to Northern newspapers.

In mid-January Annabelle stepped out on her porch to sweep away a light snow that had fallen the night before. When she turned to go back in she saw that some sort of newspaper was tacked to the door. She removed the folded paper from the nail, then looked up and down the street to see if anyone was watching. If they were, she couldn't see them. Holding the paper in a trembling hand, she stomped the snow from her feet and walked back through the door.

It was a *Harper's Weekly*. She unfolded it carefully, half expecting something horrible to leap at her from the pages. But it was only a copy of the Christmas edition.

She smiled to think it was a sign of peace, and on the page opened was a Thomas Nast cartoon of a Christmas feast. But starving Confederates waited outside the door. She read the description below; it said something about "unconditional surrender demanded for entry." And then Annabelle's eye was caught by a small black scrawl above the picture: "Everyone wants to know just how much Annabelle surrendered to the Union."

She slammed the door behind her as she read the note and let out a cry that brought Shilla running.

Seeing quickly what was the matter, Shilla tried to comfort her, but Annabelle only wiped at her eyes. "It's all right, Shilla. I knew what they were thinking. I knew." More quietly she added, "And I knew what I was doing the day I took the oath, and I'm still glad for it. Isn't that amazing? I'm still glad for it." And she began walking upstairs.

Halfway up she turned and smiled at Shilla. "Hand me that paper, Shilla. I haven't seen a paper in months." Shaking her head, Shilla handed it to her and Annabelle then disappeared up the stairs.

But, as difficult as that portion of January was, January also brought the first letter from Thomas. He had been taken to Pennsylvania. Shilla and Annabelle read the fact with hope, thinking somehow they could manage to visit him there, but the letter told them otherwise. He was not allowed visitors.

But he was alive. And so they were comforted. They replied to his letter and waited for his next.

It became a winter of waiting, but Thomas' letter had unknowingly provided a certain source of inspiration to Annabelle. She had first suggested the idea to herself when she had asked the Union officer if they could keep Thomas' gun. And then it seemed even more possible to her as Annabelle took the gun down for cleaning one day. Shilla became sullen and cross and objected fiercely when Annabelle actually prepared to go out into the cold, but Annabelle calmly assured her Thomas had taught her everything she needed to know.

"Except for what he didn't teach you, because ye know it well enough already. A lady doesn't hunt. It's not in yer station, miss. 'Tisn't proper. Ye know a lady doesn't hunt!"

Annabelle smiled grimly and checked the long bore of the gun with her eye. "Shilla, I am so very tired of people telling me what a lady should do. Thomas isn't here to hunt for us, and so I will hunt for us. It's that simple." She leaned the gun on her shoulder and took the powder horn and bullets from the salt box.

"Ye've taken the oath. We can take rations like the rest has done."

"I don't want to rely on anyone."

"Aye, so I thought! It comes down to pride for ye! Well, it's for certain ye'll kill yourself like poor Samuel Brighton, and where will yer precious pride find ye then!"

Annabelle looked at her intently. "If I wanted to kill myself, Shilla, you know I could have done that easily enough by now."

"Awch!" Shilla replied with horror. "To say such a thing!"

Annabelle softened. "I'm sorry, Shilla, I'm sorry. Please calm yourself. I'll be safe enough. This is a fine gun. Besides, I don't think what I'm doing is very far from the woman described in Proverbs 31. Go and look it up now, you'll feel better! You will!" Annabelle winked, and then she left for the hilly woods behind their home.

As the days passed, Annabelle found she enjoyed being out in the woods alone, coming to know the woods themselves, regardless of actual success in the hunt. The mountain forest ceased to be a forbidden tract of land, a thing to fear. In fact, the terrain soon became as familiar to her as the fences and yards of her city neighbors. More satisfaction came when they cooked her hard-earned work and found it delicious.

So, unlike most of their neighbors, Annabelle and Shilla actually gained weight that winter, a thing her father was delighted to see when he returned for a surprise visit in the early part of February.

He wasn't able to warn them of his coming, and Annabelle thought she would like to burst with joy when he came through their door. She had not seen him since blowing kisses to him in the yard of the house on the hill a full year and a half before.

Ever since she'd taken the oath, she'd worried how she would explain things when he came, but when she saw the twinkle in his eyes, she knew however it came out would be all right. It was the first time she had allowed a little hope to seep into her soul.

After many hugs and tears and shouts of joy, the two women and the doctor finally settled like a flock of contented chickens in the warm kitchen, where he told them how he had come by his visit and how things were going for his boys, as he called them. He sobered as he explained the details of their recent campaigns, and how the war seemed to be coming to an end. Even with some Rebel victories, they were playing a game of cat and mouse now, just to avoid complete annihilation. "There are too many of them now. Just too many," her father explained, and Annabelle agreed and told him how difficult it had become for Mosby in the area.

After a long discussion of recent events, Dr. MacBain looked around him as they sat at the kitchen table and asked how they seemed to have so much when so many around them had nothing.

At his offhand remark, Shilla looked down and Annabelle shifted in her seat.

Dr. MacBain cocked his head and smiled, surely in expectation of some great secret.

"Weem, I have something to tell you you won't like."

"Will I forgive you?" he asked with a wink.

This last was too much, and the strain of the moment overwhelmed her. She brought her head low and willed her tears back, but they kept catching in her throat, keeping her from replying. She gulped and gulped again, and finally she said, "I don't see how you could."

Ludwell MacBain grew serious. He took her hands in his. "Tell me then. You don't need to explain—no flowery descriptions and such. Just tell me, Annie."

"I took the oath of allegiance to the Union."

He took in his breath and let it out slowly.

She made herself look into his eyes, expecting anger but finding only sadness. He looked so very sad she bowed her head once more. This was worse than anger.

"Annabelle," he said quietly. "Say no more about it unless you feel the need."

"You don't want to know how it happened?"

He shook his head slightly. "I can see it's hard for you, child. No need unless you see the need."

She wanted nothing more than to put it all behind her. "No need then."

Another minute passed before Ludwell began again by asking

after Thomas. Annabelle sniffed and looked into his eyes once more. Had he forgiven her? Just like that? He caught her eye and gave her a smile that told her "yes." She smiled back and reached out and squeezed his hand and they sat there for a moment, busily changing their perspectives on each other and being glad for their newfound understanding.

Soon Annabelle read him Thomas' latest letter.

The doctor listened intently, then began to stare out the back window. "Poor Thomas." He looked back at Annabelle and said with tears in his eyes, "I shouldn't have let you stay here, but I thought with all your neighbors you would be safer here than anywhere."

Annabelle ran over and hugged him with a mighty hug.

"You should have told me they took Thomas," he said, his voice cracking. "I would have come right away."

"It's all right, Father." She wiped her tears away. "We've done well enough on our own. It'll be cottontail stew tonight."

He took her by the shoulders then, and held her at arms' length and looked her over. "So, you've learned to cook, eh? Though I'll admit to you after the meals we've been having of late, I wouldn't mind if you had sautéed shoe leather for me, I'd eat it." He laughed with a catch in his voice. "And, by golly, I'd enjoy it, too!"

Her father stayed a full week, and Annabelle was never so glad for anything in her life. Their daily routine didn't change much the first few days. Her father often watched Annabelle do her household duties with Shilla and nodded now and then with admiration, filling Annabelle's heart with good things and fine feelings.

But toward the end of the week, her conscience began to trouble her. She found herself wanting to tell her father exactly what had occurred. Back and forth she fought with herself, but when she began to lose sleep she decided she must tell him.

It was the night before he was due to leave and they were in the kitchen after dinner, just father and daughter. The candles were burning low and a new snow had fallen. All in all, Annabelle thought uncomfortably, it was not unlike the night she'd taken the oath and kissed a Yankee soldier not five feet from where her father now sat so calmly smoking his pipe and reading over his papers.

She blushed uncontrollably as she replayed the moment in her mind.

She grew restless as she sewed but she didn't know her father had noticed until he said, "Annabelle?" And she jumped slightly in her seat. "Annabelle, what exactly is it that's troubling you?"

"Nothing, Weem, nothing of importance," she said unsteadily.

He laid his papers down on the table and looked at her with careful concern. "Annie, I've seen a spirit in you these last few days... It bothers me, to say the least. Are you very bitter that I left?"

"I was once, Father," she replied with honesty, "but I came to accept it, I think. Really."

"Then are you bitter over the soldiers taking our things? They're only things, you know, and they can be replaced, and Thomas will return when the war is over."

She bit her lip as she shook her head and tried to take up her sewing again, but a sob was welling up in her. Finally she laid her sewing down and let the tears come. Her father pulled his chair up beside her and made her lean her head upon his shoulder as she wept.

She was able, after some time, to say in fits and starts and as breath would come, "I... dis... honored you, Father, by taking the oath. I'm so sorry."

He patted her shoulder. "Oh, that." He was quiet for a minute, then asked, "Did you mean it when you took the oath?"

With a tremble, she answered, "Y-yes."

"Have you purchased a slave since taking it?"

She shook her head. "Of course not."

"Have you broken any other laws of the Union since?"

"No." But she half smiled to herself as she thought, *Does it count if you wished you had?*

"Then how have you dishonored me?"

"You know I never wanted to go against your wishes."

"But it's only a taste of my own medicine." He laughed softly and squeezed her shoulder. "I've always told you to follow your conscience, Annie. I've taken an oath, too, but not the one you imagine. The Hippocratic Oath. You know of it? Yes, the doctor's oath. I've never said it to you, really, but it's the only oath I've ever made and the only one I've ever given much credence to, besides the Apostles', of course. Oh, found a pundit."

She looked up at him and sniffed and laughed despite her tears. "But didn't... didn't you have to take an oath to the Cause to become a Confederate doctor?" she asked, her words still laced in hiccups.

He shook his head. "They asked me to, and I said the only one I needed I'd already taken."

Annabelle laughed and hugged him tightly. "You are the most amazing man, Father." But she couldn't help but think about P.D. MacBain when she said it. Suddenly she sat up. "I want to tell you the whole story."

He nodded and she wiped her eyes and then laughed a little. "Where shall I begin?"

"At the beginning, I suppose? There's always a beginning."

She thought back to the day P.D. MacBain first came to the town to visit the cemetery, and so she began there. She told him everything, and she was pleased to find the burden lifting as she spoke.

When she came to the part where she gave MacBain her father's college ring, her father interrupted her. "I went to school with a P.D. MacBain, Jr. He was a distant cousin of mine, so he always said, but we could never figure out exactly how we were related. The description of your soldier sounds a might like him."

She blushed. "Oh, please, don't call him my soldier." And he apologized.

But right away she asked what the fellow at school was like and where he was from.

"Right there, down in Bacon's Castle, Virginia, across the river from the college," he said. "He took me over the James River ferry a couple of times for family meals. Lovely family. Lovely people. I always had the loveliest stomachache when we left. Lost touch with him over the years, and I..." he said it carefully, "I always regretted it. And that's the truth."

She went on to tell him everything she could about P.D. MacBain, and especially his last "visit." She explained why she had felt ready to take the oath, and her father nodded in agreement, which relieved her burden considerably. When she talked about her discussions with MacBain, her father laughed and said he had always enjoyed sparring with P.D., Jr.

There was silence for a time and then she said, "Please take no offense, Weem, but I'd never had someone act as though they cared for my opinion. I guess I was flattered very carried away by it all."

"When I went away you were a girl, yet, Annabelle," her father said kindly, "but I look forward to hearing a woman's point of view from you from now on." And Annabelle grew peaceful and happy with the words.

Finally, she told him about Samuel Brighton and how he was murdered, most likely for harboring slaves on the underground railroad. "Did you really know about it all those years?" she asked in wonder and he nodded solemnly.

"I am a doctor, first, Annie. I care for sick bodies and tell well bodies how to stay well. That's what I like to do. I don't care who they are, where they come from, and too often for our own good I haven't even cared whether they could pay me. Mr. Brighton took a chance having me come the first time. Their own doctor—a Friend of the Meeting, of course—happened to be sick himself that night. After that, Samuel called on me often, as our home was much closer than his own doctor's. And in a way it served his purpose twofold—my working for him—because no one harboring slaves would hire a city doctor, right? All I told Samuel, along the lines of his staying well, was to keep this thing totally quiet and quit having so many visitors at his place."

"Including me."

He smiled and folded his hands over one knee as he nodded. "Most of all you, my very sharp-eyed daughter, who had such a busy tongue at the tender age of eight that I had to fear for Samuel's life because of it." He shook his head.

"Did Mrs. Brighton know?"

"You know," he said thoughtfully, "Samuel Brighton always seemed ready with an excuse for anyone his good wife saw coming out of the barn, and it was always a different person and a different excuse, and in the final analysis, I think she became very confused about it all."

"She was never suspicous?"

"I don't believe she's capable of suspicion, child."

Annabelle managed a slight smile, but then she shook her head. "Mr. Brighton. Poor Mr. Brighton. Do you have any idea who might have murdered him?"

"The Lord only knows, Annabelle. There were certainly enough ruffians around to kill a man if they found cause. I just wouldn't know."

"Could we, uh, unbury him and show everyone how he was shot?"

"Could, yes, but you know it wouldn't tell us who did it, and, I don't mean to impede your curiosity, but don't you think the Widow Brighton has suffered enough?"

Annabelle shivered at the thought of Brighton's bones. "Oh, yes. Yes. I hadn't thought of it. Of course, we couldn't do that. What was I thinking?" They sat quietly for a moment. "Do you know of anyone who had black market connections and could get a hold of a percussion gun?"

He shook his head and laughed. "Your curiosity is a wondrous thing to behold, Annabelle."

Annabelle shook her head and laughed as well. "All right. All right, Weem. I guess we'll never know." And with reluctance she continued the story.

She described briefly what she considered to be an infatuation for this fellow, MacBain, and then she picked her way through the conversation carefully, as if she were walking through a field of nettles.

But her father never even blinked, and so she quickly went on to tell the last horrible thing: Lieutenant Forrest's words and MacBain virtually admitting to the same, that he would have been responsible for destroying Lee's army at the river, with her own father's life perilously included in the count.

Annabelle choked and sobbed to get out the last of it, and she stopped at that description. She didn't tell him how her heart was torn by the knowledge. She also didn't go on to tell him how MacBain had yelled her name for all the world to hear. She couldn't.

Now she and her father sat in a long silence, and Annabelle thought wistfully of all she had lost.

TWENTY-FOUR

Let love and friendship on that day,
Hurrah! Hurrah!
Their choicest treasures then display;
Hurrah! Hurrah!
And let each one perform some part
To fill with joy the warrior's heart,
And we'll all feel gay
When Johnny comes marching home.

From the song
When Johnny Comes Marching Home

Her father tapped out his pipe and refilled it, lit it and began to puff on it once more. Annabelle saw the candle was almost out and got another and brought it back to the table, and although her story was ended, somehow she knew they were not finished.

"Annie," her father finally said, "did you know..." He rested his pipe on his knee. "Now, I'm not saying this to justify what the North does not by any means, but did you know there have been times when my commander has ordered me to leave Federal wounded in worse shape than our own, to tend to our own, and I did it? I did it and I'll do it again because I'll be shot if I disobey, and I figure I'm more good to men alive than dead?"

Annabelle looked over at him sadly and shook her head. "How horrible for you."

"Yes, well, it's a beast, I'll grant you, but war is war. And I'll tell you something else—if your father were a soldier under Lee and not a surgeon, you'd have been more right about P.D. trying to kill me, but we always keep the wounded to the rear or at least out of the line of fire. We were well over the hill there, away from the river most of the time, as I recall. I'm not saying the Union always keeps to it, no, I've seen a ball go right past my nose and then, well, a father doesn't brag about the behavior he exhibits on such occasions. No, ma'am, he does not. He and the rabbits keep such secrets to themselves." He chuckled. "But I'm saying the Yanks don't try to shoot us up. Heavens to Betsy, child, I'd have died a thousand times since I came to camp if that were the way of things, so it's a bit unfair saying he was out to get me killed."

Annabelle couldn't believe what he was saying. "But, Weem, all those men across the river would have died."

"That's true. That's true. A lot of those men would have died, but the war might even have ended right there, and then, you see, then all the ones who have died since might still be alive. Now I'm not saying that's exactly what was on P.D.'s mind at the time, but it'd be likely. Besides, my guess would be Lincoln initiated the whole thing. Now, Annie, how do you think I manage knowing I'm patchin' men up just so they can go out and kill or be killed? I'll tell you, it doesn't feel good. But I've saved a right many, and if his plan could have worked it's certain he would have saved a right many, too."

Annabelle couldn't take it in. She hadn't seen it that way at all. Not at all. She was in shock.

Her father sat back and pulled on his pipe and let a few smoke rings into the air. "Now, what your boy would have done to your father if he hadn't gotten sick, really, is given him some dang hard work, Annie, and now that might truly have killed me." And he puffed away.

Annabelle drew her hands to her mouth. "You're saying you think he did right?"

Her father set his pipe on the table and looked at her. "That, my dear, would be up to you to decide." He winked as he added, "Now that you have—as they say—all the facts of the case."

She stared at the candle and tried to understand. She thought of P.D. standing there at the stove with his thumb in his belt, leisurely stoking the fire on a cold winter night. She blushed as she thought of his kiss and the moments following.

"Now, I don't know this fellow," her father finally said. "I don't know him at all, but I know his father. I remember him well, and I'd have to say you might give his son another look. When this war is over, Annie, and my guess is it'll be over soon, there'll be a lot of trying to forgive and forget, and I'm ready for that, I tell you. I'm ready to put the whole mess behind us and get on with living."

"You wouldn't mind a Yankee?"

She looked at her father in disbelief, and his eyes twinkled. "Well, now, he won't be a Yankee when it's done, girl, will he? He won't be nothin' but a man. I've taken care of Billy Blue and I've taken care of Johnny Reb, and they look downright similar in the basics."

For a moment she began to relent, but then came the image of Forrest's drunken rhyme and MacBain telling her not to take it personally. She thought of how he had humiliated her by calling out her name and how the town had treated her ever since. She remembered the sound of his cry and realized it could be taken for a yell of triumph as much as anything else. She hadn't seen it so clearly before.

She looked back to her father, and she knew she could not tell him everything. The fact was he would never have to consider a Yankee for a son-in-law, for MacBain had been lying all along. Who knows what he would have attempted had they stayed longer? Now a fierce pride welled up and took hold of her with a firm and deadly grip, and her eyes grew cold. "I don't know how you've come to be so forgiving, Father. I don't believe I'm ready to forgive." Waves of anger and humiliation came to her now. "In fact, I don't see why I should forgive. No one's asked me to."

Her father's face was filled with sorrow. "Don't you? Don't you hear anyone asking? I'm sorry to hear that, Annie. Perhaps it'll take more time for you."

"Perhaps it will," she said without emotion and then raised the candle snuffer to the flame and put it out.

The next morning her father returned to his regiment.

Toward the end of February, Federals came through Hillsborough once more and camped outside of town. They were there to look over hill and dale, in house and barn, for Mosby and his men, but putting first things first, they also spent a morning combing the area for food and grain and livestock.

At this time, there came the rumor that a widow in town, Penelope Small, had taken the oath and was receiving food. This was of little surprise to Annabelle, for the woman had been starving before their eyes. Both of her sons had died at the Battle of Shiloh Hill, and ever since she'd relied on neighbors' goods to keep herself alive. But for Annabelle there was a bitter irony. The town embraced the widow for her decision. First, because she had lost her sons, and second, because she was forced to take the oath out of necessity.

One day, when Annabelle was in a particularly foul mood, she stood behind the kitchen table and sulked to Shilla, "I see now if only I had treated the oath like a thing to enable me to steal from the Yankees, I'd be all right in everyone's eyes." Shilla came away from the stove to look at Annabelle, but Annabelle was looking down and running her fingers along the edge of the kitchen table. "Yes, I just went about it the wrong way, didn't I? It's all right for her, starving and half mad, but do a thing because it's morally right, and…"

"Annabelle Shannon MacBain!" Shilla grabbed Annabelle's hands. "Ye always were a strong-headed thing. Ye've done what ye thought was right, and you were right proud of it." She squeezed and shook Annabelle's hands as she spoke. "But listen to me and listen well. Now ye've got to suffer for it. Ye've got to suffer for it, do ye hear? Yer father understands and I understand, but that's 'cause we love ye." Her voice became harsh. "But once you done a thing—and a womanly thing it was, and a hard thing it was—don't be complainin' when people hate ye for it. Don't blame the widow 'cause she's starvin'. Don't blame these people who've lost their sons and husbands. Don't blame these whose menfolk have come back to us in bits 'n pieces. Don't! For I won't listen to it, no, I won't!"

And with that Shilla threw Annabelle's hands out and away from hers, and then Annabelle stood speechless as Shilla turned and in deathly silence resumed her cooking.

March was the hardest month of all.

There was no food, and the farmers were kept from sowing spring crops. The men in blue were everywhere and many of Mosby's Rangers were snared in their traps as the month wore slowly on. The best of the month were the rumors—lovely rumors—of surrender and peace. The worst of the month was to watch the continual destruction. Obvious to all was the fact that even if the war ended, it would take years for Loudoun County to recover. Whatever the outcome, there would be poverty in the land for a long, long while.

But in April, her father's prediction and the rumors came to fruition as the amazing and the unthinkable occurred: Grant and Lee made peace.

The war was over.

Annabelle couldn't quite believe it right away. She'd grown so used to expecting the worst, she simply waited for the bad news to come. But bad news didn't come, at least not to her.

A week after the peace, President Lincoln was assassinated.

Annabelle heard of it and was sorry—sorry to think of the grief of his children and his wife, sorry that his life should end after peace was finally gained—but her last thought was that now P.D. MacBain would have no reason to track down Brighton's murder-er. That was over for good, she told herself; he had no reason to return. She felt nothing as she thought it; not good, not bad, nothing. And, for the first few weeks afterward, nothingness became her state of mind.

And the Widow Small left Hillsborough to follow a man named Mercer from the Capital City to New England to board a ship bound for a place on the other side of the continent called Seattle, Washington, with the promise of a home and employment to wid-ows and orphans of the war. The war had created odd opportuni-ties, indeed.

Sarah and Sally Drum returned a week after the war was ended. Annabelle had written to them all along, but hadn't had the courage to tell them she'd taken the oath. She wanted to see them face-to-face to explain.

She knew Sally would now prepare a home for a husband who had lost a leg. They would live at Drum House, and Annabelle was heartbroken for them both.

In her letters, Sarah had expressed her bitterness at having watched Richmond fall before their eyes, and Annabelle looked forward to commiserating with her over the soldiers' actions. *Won't we have stories to tell each other,* she thought!

But when Annabelle, with Shilla as escort, called on the Drum residence the day after the ladies arrived home, to her shock and amazement, their maid would not accept Annabelle's calling card.

"No one is home for Miss MacBain," the servant said.

She tried once more. "Pardon me. I did not ask to see Captain Drum but his daughters."

"Aye, *Mrs. Lieutenant Alton and Miss Sarah Drum* are not at home for Miss MacBain," she said again in an irritated tone.

Annabelle looked at Shilla and Shilla looked at her, and Annabelle began to tremble where she stood. Her friends' rejection that morning was the one final hurt she allowed herself to feel.

She turned and walked carefully down the steps of Drum House as Shilla put her arm through hers to comfort her. Out of the corner of her eye, Annabelle thought she saw something move and she looked up to the parlor window; Sally stood there, and Annabelle's heart leapt to think it was all a mistake. Sally would listen. But then the small, pale face gave a determined frown and quickly pulled back into the shadows.

It was then Annabelle allowed herself to cry on Shilla's shoulder as she walked home. "If they'd a been true friends to ye, they would na' judge ye so," Shilla said quietly. But it didn't comfort Annabelle. She dried her tears as they entered the town and she pushed Shilla gently away from her side. She would not let anyone see her cry. Annabelle hated to feel the way she did, cast off by the dearest friends she'd ever had, but she was too proud to let it show. Shilla understood and she walked beside Annabelle with her head held high as well.

Once in their home, Annabelle made her way up the stairs to the attic. She stepped up on her desk and carefully pulled down her mother's portrait. Then, when she came back down, she saw her own drawings scattered to the floor. She set the frame down and gathered them slowly and with equal slowness placed them in a drawer. There was nothing for which she cared to raise her pencil. The very thought of it made her tired.

She shut the drawer and took away her mother's portrait to the parlor.

Three days later, Annabelle answered the door to find a tall, thin and pallid stranger standing on the step. His blue eyes watched her from deepened sockets. She looked him sharply up and down, and quickly saw him to be a beggar—a starving beggar at that.

He opened his mouth, but no words came. Soon tears formed in his eyes, and Annabelle was afraid the fellow would break down right there. "Yes, we can feed you, sir," she quickly said. "But we have no work for you."

The look of pain upon his thin face could have made the strongest heart take pause, but Annabelle added, "If you've served the Confederacy, I should warn you this house has taken the oath. There are not many who'll stand to eat with us." She waited for his answer, hoping he would turn and walk away.

But the fellow opened and shut his mouth once, twice, and then finally spoke one little word. "Hulloo."

Annabelle gave a wrenching cry and pulled her hands to her mouth.

It was Thomas.

Her knees began to shake as she realized her mistake. "Oh, Thomas, forgive me!" She threw herself upon the poor fellow and hugged his thin frame.

Thomas O'Brian put his weak arms around her, and hugged her gently in reply. Shilla came to the door then and the three huddled for a long while on the porch, crying and finally laughing and then crying all the more.

In a short time, they had seated him at the kitchen table and offered him a carefully prepared supper—food for a man who'd been served wormy bread, rancid hardtack and fetid water for months on end.

After he ate, Thomas began to speak. He told them he was kept a prisoner in Pennsylvania all that time and was sent out to work almost every day. He didn't want to speak of it much beyond that, and neither woman pressed him, but he did volunteer he had forgiven Hattie Humboldt for turning him in—he was simply grateful to be alive.

Annabelle listened to the words but she couldn't understand the urgency in his forgiveness. She was too well versed in humiliation to feel humbled by Thomas' words and too dependent upon anger to see its own shadow on her soul.

Yet there was one thing in those dark months that pulled her out of herself and into the bright light of day. In the beginning of May, Dr. Ludwell MacBain returned to Hillsborough and to the welcoming arms of home. Annabelle laughed and giggled like a schoolgirl the day he arrived, and for a moment it appeared as though her bitterness was banished and forgiveness had broken through.

As promised, Dr. MacBain brought with him his assistant, Lemuel Walker, and at a glance Annabelle knew he'd heard all about her. Walker was polite but kept his distance, and for her part, Annabelle was too glad to have her father back to care what Lemuel Walker thought of anything. In the coming weeks, Dr. MacBain, Annabelle, Shilla and Thomas tried to settle into normalcy, but when the members of the household began their respective chores they quickly realized it had been years since they had worked together. They had all changed. Dr. MacBain was overly busy, Shilla was overly irritable, Thomas was unusually quiet, and Annabelle, well, her bitterness did not take long to resurface. The change felt odd and disatisfying to everyone concerned, but at least Lemuel Walker fell outside the circle of Annabelle's troubles.

Walker took up residence in one of Mistress Hattie's many rooms and settled into his new life without ever bothering Annabelle again. And so, they mutually ignored all their previous correspondence and moved into a schedule of working about the same office and assisting the same man, while the number of words that passed between them in a day wouldn't make a full sentence.

She found herself feeling relieved, much as she had the day Michael Delaney walked away from her so long ago.

And so when Annabelle heard that Lem Walker was calling on Sarah Drum, she even allowed herself to feel glad for them, but that was all.

Then came the letter from P.D. MacBain. Shilla brought the missive to her, and Annabelle slowly took it up to her room and sat down at her desk to stare at it, now and then nudging it with her finger as if it were going to nip her. *So, he is alive. And well enough to write.* She wasn't sure how she felt about it. Finally she told herself she was being ridiculous. Whatever he had to say would make no difference to her whatsoever, and at that she made herself open the long letter.

April 29, 1865
Miss Annabelle MacBain,
The conflict is over. I am free to discuss the actions and decisions of my past, and with your permission I would like to explain a portion of my history.

As an agent for the United States government, I was trained to garner information from the South and act independently on my knowledge, and, until my illness, I had always enjoyed success.

"Arrogant as always!" Annabelle said aloud as she read, yet her heart pounded as if it would burst.

But it was after the Battle of Gettysburg and while I was scouting out Lee's troop movements for General Meade that I gathered information I believed only President Lincoln would consider useful. On July 7th, I rode to the Capital.

What I had to offer the President he could not read within the army telegrams sent from General Meade's field offices. I had a personal knowledge of General Meade's hesitance to take his tired and bloodied men so soon again into battle, even if to do so might end the entire conflict, and that only the day before Lee's troops had settled on the banks of the Potomac River with no visible means of crossing the flooded waters. And so I had it in my mind to see if there were powers that could be wrested on the southern shore of that river, ones that could trap Lee between our forces and finish the business for good. I had hope from his reply that he put complete trust in my information. This I'm sure I owe to the good opinion he held of my former employer, E.J. Allen."

Here he drew a line through *E.J. Allen,* and wrote in the margin, *You might know him as Mr. Allan Pinkerton, private detective.*

The president told me he knew of no troops south of the river who could be brought up in time to help, but he did know of loyal men and cannons that together might do some damage.

He referred me to Mr. Brighton and his list of the faithful. President Lincoln was famous for his remembrance of detail, and he remembered Hannah Brighton's brother's name, Norris, because it happened to be one of Pinkerton's code names. It was a pleasure to benefit so directly from such an able mind. With Malachi Norris a ready disguise for me, I knew then the Lord was with my effort.

I was sad to discover later that Jedediah Norris died in battle the month before I arrived. I have chosen not to write a letter of apology to the Widow Brighton on my behalf, for I'm aware such an apology might, at this point in time, do more harm than good.

"And you'd only be telling her it was done in the line of duty," said Annabelle angrily, "and that excuse will not buy you much in the way of apologies." She lay the letter down and looked up at the ceiling for a moment to let the tears recede, and then she fell to reading again.

The president informed me there was virtually no communication with the portion of Virginia to which I was headed, due to the restless efficiency of Mosby's men, and that because of same I could have no escort into "Mosby's Confederacy," and so I came alone.

When I then rode to Hillsborough and found Mr. Brighton dead, I thought my duty may end there. But I found the list.

"Found is certainly a gentle way of putting it," she said ruefully.

... and so began the journey to rally men and cannons. I was assured both would be forthcoming, as many Union sympathizers were in the area and one of these sympathizers had in fact removed several cannons from Harper's Ferry at the beginning of the war and was awaiting the proper time to use them, just as President Lincoln had said.

Before I could reach that man, Mr. Bartholomew was dead and the hand of the Lord allowed me to fall ill. Why, I do not know, but entrust it to Him just the same.

So, I tried and failed to do my duty. That is all. I would hope that in this day, with all of this behind us, you too might have reason to see things in this light. You must know I couldn't let my thoughts wander as they do now to the look of worry on your face as you thought of your father across the swollen river. It grieved me then—how much I cannot tell.

Please try to understand, and, if you will, then understand too that I have meant every word and have been true to every feeling outside my first duty.

P.D. MacBain

Postscript:
There will be no further formal inquiry into the death of Samuel Brighton. If you have any information concerning his murder, however, I would be interested in hearing it, with the understanding that my interest in the case will be of a purely personal nature. Please send the information c/o Mr. Pembroke D. MacBain, Jr., General Delivery, Surry, Virginia.

There was no denying it now. He had never meant it when he spoke to her of love, for if this were a love letter, it was the most formal one ever written. The bare thing read as lovingly as a letter written with Lieutenant Forrest standing over one shoulder. No, the true message was quite clear—painfully clear. He was being polite, wishing to smooth things over now that "the conflict is over," as he put it, and his duty was done. This business of "true to every word and feeling outside his duty" meant little to her, since she assumed flirtations were a required portion of those duties. "It grieved me then,…" she reread. "But it does not grieve you now?" she asked aloud. "He's purged his conscience partly by writing me thus, but he'll not have the satisfaction of a reply."

She sat back in her chair to look out the back window. Her eyes rested on the rooftops of their new outbuildings, then on Thomas hammering hard on a portion of fence at the top of the hill.

No, she didn't want to be reasoned with. She was perfectly happy to allow the sins of war to lie entirely upon P.D. MacBain's shoulders, and she was further willing to let him sink under their weight. She folded the letter carefully, then tucked it under the desk blotter and went about her chores.

Her father noticed the dark changes in Annabelle and continually tried to get her to open up to him as she had when he had visited in February. But she continued to tell her father she was fine. "But you don't laugh as you used to, Annie," he would say. "Tell me what's wrong."

"You said yourself I've grown into a woman, Father. Perhaps I simply don't find as much to amuse me as before," she would answer shortly.

And he would look as if he didn't believe her.

The only thing that seemed to pique her interest was hunting and reading the newspapers now and then. The stories of murder always intrigued her, and she began to think on Brighton's murderer. It would be a grand slap in the face to solve Brighton's murder herself and send the information to P.D. MacBain. That would gall him, she was sure.

And so, whenever she hunted for game in the woods alone, she wondered about it. She even went looking for the bloodied tree MacBain had spoken of, but of course all the trees had grown another ring or two since the murder, and the evidence was gone. But once she did happen on a tree whose arms could have held a man propped up, and she allowed herself to imagine the whole of it: The murderer waiting for Brighton to come through the trees, crouching behind a bush, leveling a weapon unfit for anything but assassination at poor Mr. Brighton, firing, watching Brighton crumple to the ground. The murderer dragging the body to a tree such as this, propping him up and shooting him through once more with his own gun. Then dragging the body away and laying him out in the woods with his gun beside him to make it look like a hunting accident. Precise. Methodical. Horrible.

The gray, dry bark. Her mind came back to the tree. The bullet would have to be there in the wood, the bullet that had shown MacBain the truth. She stepped forward and looked at the bark closely just above the spreading branches. There in the center she saw a bump in the bark that made her shiver and shake. She touched it with her fingers and now it was all too real. One shot. One shot was heard. Someone who knew Brighton had done this thing, someone who knew all about him. An execution performed by a neighbor, perhaps even a friend. One who turned from him when he discovered the underground railroad?

Annabelle walked out of the woods that day feeling as if she'd seen it happen with her own eyes, and with no other problems to absorb her time, she thought about it all the time. She thought on Marsden, because he kept Pella from joining Brighton for the hunt that day, and then it struck her: Marsden was a black marketeer for guns. Marsden was most certainly capable of murder. What if he discovered Pella was helping with the Underground Railroad? It had to be he.

And she began to study Marsden, though always at a safe distance.

By summer her life had become intolerably lonesome. Her father was overworked, as were Thomas and Shilla. There was no one to talk to. Although old friends nodded politely on the street, they never invited her to come calling and always politely refused when her father would ask them to come in. They too were unready to forgive.

One day Annabelle and her father were up in the attic looking for something among the boxes there when the doctor found her drawings in the desk. "Why aren't you drawing, Annie?" he asked. "I never see you drawing anymore."

She didn't have a solid answer. "I never quite feel like taking pencil to paper anymore."

He held up a portrait of one of the officers she'd done at an encampment years before. "That's a shame, Annie." He held the page up higher to the light of the window. "You know, this profile has to be the last likeness ever done of Duncan. He died... must have been just two days later, at Sharpsburg." He smiled. "Or Antietam, depending on your point of view, though a man can only die in one place at a time, I reckon."

Annabelle grew flustered as he began to examine the likeness of P.D. MacBain. "Those bring back hard memories for me. Please leave them there, Father."

And she quickly walked to the stairwell and out of his sight.

TWENTY-FIVE

Lou went home this morning. How
lonely I feel, but it is no use to
feel so. I think I will hunt up some
of my quilt pieces, and go to work.

From the diary of Miss Mary E. Lack.

"A young lady hunting! Did you ever hear of such a thing?"

"Well, I never! She hasn't a stable mind."

"It all started when she thought Brighton's grave had been dug up. And then to turn Yankee right at the end."

"Her poor father. She's not quite right in the head."

They would all say it, but they never dared say it to her.

There were times she felt she could stand no more, and then she would rant and rave to her father about her small town existence and how she needed to get away. These explosions her father took rather calmly, but he didn't give in to her whims, and normally these episodes ended with Annabelle's tromping up the hill to the graveyard where she would wander around the old headstones for hours. But she would no longer sit beside her mother's grave. Something kept her from that.

Now and then she would sit by Samuel Brighton's grave, thinking somehow his murderer's name would simply come to her while sitting there. She'd look at Pella's angel, now gray and mottled from the rain and snow, and she'd think back on all those things. It always made her sad, though, and she would have to get up and walk around again.

One gravestone was always an odd comfort to her. It was the grave of a thirty-year-old woman whose name was Virginia Columbus. On her headstone were the bold words, "Sacred to the Memory of Virginia Columbus, consort of William Ricks, Born

July 3, 1818, Died December 1, 1848, Aged 30 years, 5 months, 2 days," and below that in small letters, "These are they which came out of great tribulation and have washed their robes and made them white in the blood."

Annabelle loved to read that headstone.

She felt so akin to it that at times she even laughed out loud, though not without a twinge or two of bitterness. Here the town had forgiven Virginia. "White in the blood," they called her —and the war was over and people were seemingly polite to Annabelle— yet Virginia Columbus would forever have the word "consort" carved in stone above her head for all to see until the granite was itself washed clean by time. When the word "consort" was finally erased, so would be her name.

And so Hillsborough would forever call Annabelle "traitor." *And if they can,* she thought drily, *they will chisel the word upon my headstone.*

But Annabelle was not the only one to spend her days among graves.

When Southern farmers finally began to lay the fields open for sowing once more, they reaped a grim harvest—the bodies of men, the skeletons of men, arms, legs, swords, boots and rifles, all were brought up by the plow.

Two thousand five hundred such bodies were found around the city of Winchester, Virginia, alone, and a Memorial Graveyard was built for them.

But not all of the war's ripe harvest could be consigned to the grave. Its evidence remained in the fatherless homes, the widow's crepe, the crutches, the abject poverty, and the mental anguish that would take years to overcome, if ever.

Yet two things were clear: slavery was abolished, and the Union was preserved. The grand experiment, democracy, so young and inexperienced before the war, had come through its crucible and would be tried in the future by smaller and much slower fires than these, and Annabelle realized her decision to take the oath had been a good one.

She had lost the respect of her friends and neighbors, yet when the count was over, she was glad for what she'd done and pitied those who hadn't moral strength to do likewise. Unfortunately, her pride was evident to everyone but herself.

Every family in town had had at least one close family member killed or maimed in battle, often more than one: a cousin, an uncle, a brother, a husband or a father. Except within the MacBain home. In Hillsborough a woman who did not wear black was most unusual, and so Annabelle was again found to be different, whether she liked it or not. Then there were those who survived battle but never returned home. They settled in states they'd marched through and found more interesting than home, perhaps more prosperous than home, or they chose to go west to seek their fortunes.

But in all this gloom, two cases occurred of soldiers returning who were presumed dead: one was a tailor's son, Michael Burke, and one was John Brighton. John Brighton had lost an arm, but at least he was alive. And Annabelle was glad for Hannah, then; at least one family story would be told with some joy, but what a rarity it was.

With John's return, though, Annabelle had to wrestle with his father's murder once more. Should she tell him? Could he help? Or should she tell the Meeting of Friends and let them handle it themselves? Should she ask her father for advice? No, he seemed so burdened these days, and this was such a trifle, really, compared to his own work. After all, who was really left to care who killed Friend Brighton? It would only cause more pain to the family. She herself was only following the trail as, well, a sort of mental exercise. That was all. She continued to watch Marsden very carefully.

Marsden had kept his Southern head above water by marketeering. He had worked with Mosby's Rangers, and with anyone else who could steal goods for him to sell.

Annabelle decided it was possible he was paid to kill Brighton; she well knew he would do anything for money. The most horrible rumor she had heard about the man was that he had sold his own daughter, Mary, to the soldiers once, when she was no more than fourteen at the time. But the rumors died when she stayed around, for most thought Mary, a strong-headed girl in her own right, would have left if such were the case. And Marsden never addressed the question at all. Like so many private histories, all this would pass away.

As for Hillsborough itself, people had begun to wander back to reclaim and reopen the other stores in town. Only one mill in four remained unburnt, and so Hillsborough's reputation as a prosperous mill town became a portion of its history. The town was now a place of homes and scattered businesses surrounded by the hulls of burned out buildings. Still, the town was lucky, for unlike the vast cities of Richmond and Atlanta, most of the main buildings and virtually all of the homes had remained. But, then, Hillsborough was never so one-sided in its affections as those.

Annabelle's only means of socializing now were occasional dinners out to the homes of Dr. MacBain's most appreciative patients. In payment of one bill, the doctor was given a rather old roan to pull their carriage, and although the horse was far from a race horse or a proper horse to ride, at least they could travel to their invitations in some sort of style. On their first ride, Dr. MacBain complimented the horse, saying it was possible she was even slower than their Birdie. On the spot he christened the roan "Egg." Annabelle saw it coming. "And she's a good egg, wouldn't you say, Annie?"

"Oh, Father." Annabelle shook her head and wished he wouldn't try so hard to make her laugh.

During these meals, a poor mother, often a widow, would stare at pretty, sad-looking Annabelle at the dinner table, and she knew the woman was thinking of Annabelle for her son. And so Annabelle began to ask her father if she might stay home from these dinners.

One hot summer day in August, just after losing an argument with her father over a dinner invitation, Annabelle decided to take her frustration out on some work clothes that needed washing. Her father had asked her to let Shilla do the washing now that the war was ended, and so Annabelle knew it would irritate him if she went to Zilpha's Rock down at the creek. She stomped to the kitchen and took the clothes up from Shilla's basket, grabbed the washboard and tromped out of the house.

She crossed the street, passed next to the tanyard without so much as a nod to the owner and continued her march. But as she crested the hill and looked down, she was disappointed to see someone already at the boiling pot.

As she slowed her charge, she saw that it was Mary Marsden. Mary was tending the fire under the old wash pot. Still watching her, she walked down to the creek, and Mary looked up as she passed. *She must be about fifteen, now,* Annabelle reasoned. Her dark black hair was pulled back under a cotton square like an old woman, and she was wearing what could only have been her mother's dress. Like Annabelle, she'd lost her mother young. The girl's blue eyes held no expression as they stared out from her squarish face, and the head seemed large on her thin frame, a womanly face on a girl's body. *No, it isn't that her head's out of proportion,* thought Annabelle sadly, *it's that her body is pitifully thin.*

Annabelle took herself to the edge of the creek across from Zilpha's Rock and began to scrub Thomas' overalls. The two worked for a while with no words, but now and then Annabelle would turn and catch Mary's eye.

A cart rolled past on the road and the driver began to hail them but his arm dropped when he saw who the "ladies" were.

Annabelle smiled and looked back at Mary. Mary was staring at Annabelle and giving her a hard little smile in return. Annabelle felt an empathy for the girl. She, too, had been ostracized on nothing more than rumor. "Hello," said Annabelle carefully.

"Hello," said Mary.

"And how are you today?" Annabelle went on.

"Grand, miss," she replied, mocking a lady's voice, and yet her voice held the timbre of a child's.

Annabelle laughed a little and nodded. Mary gave a half smile back, watched Annabelle a second more, then grabbed at her stick uncertainly and began stirring the pot again. "My father's looking for a good weapon, Mary. Do you think your father could help him?"

"I wouldn't know, and I didn't give you leave to call me Mary."

Annabelle drew her breath in short, then she let out a long whistle and shook her head. "True enough. I do apologize."

Mary didn't look at her as she kept to her stirring.

Annabelle pressed on, though. "Miss Mary Marsden, do you know anything about your father's guns?"

Mary looked at Annabelle and studied her awhile, gripping and releasing the stick. "I think you're crazy, Miz' MacBain. You don't have to be down here doin' wash like I do, and I wouldn't do it if he didn't make me, so I know you must be crazy. Everybody thinks you're crazy, and I wish you'd go away."

At that Annabelle burst out laughing and sat on the ground, which only made Mary's eyes grow wide as if it all were true.

Annabelle quieted herself. "Let me put it this way, Miss Marsden," she said with a touch of irritation. "If the rumors about you are as true as the rumors about me, I'm exactly as crazy as you are."

Mary's eyes flashed. She lifted the stick from the pot and brought it down beside her. Annabelle lost her smile as the motion played a familiar ring in her mind. It rankled her because she couldn't put her finger on the memory. Saying such a thing to an uncertain girl with a large stick in her hand was probably unwise, but she was relieved and grateful to see Mary stayed where she was. Then, to Annabelle's surprise, all the anger left Mary's face, and she placed the stick back in the pot and began to stir once more as if no words had passed between them at all. But then Mary said very quietly, "Do you really go huntin'?"

Annabelle smiled, nodded calmly and laid down her washboard. "Yes. Does that interest you?" Annabelle stood up and walked toward her.

Mary stopped stirring and cocked her head. "Yea. Sometimes I wish I knew how to use a gun." She stopped and grew icy again. "No."

But Annabelle stood by her still and watched her. She knew Mary wanted to talk because she hadn't started stirring again, and so she waited as Mary stared into the boiling water. "Just... there was a boy we had who used to talk 'bout huntin' all the time," she said, and went back to stirring but more slowly now.

"Pella?"

Mary looked at her with surprise. "You 'member Pella?"

"Of course I do." Now the memory of Mary's stick, Pella's stick, came back to her and it gave her an odd sensation. "Yes, Pella gave me something he'd made to put on Samuel Brighton's grave." The memory of those days poured back into her mind and Annabelle looked out across the creek and smiled grimly, and, as if suddenly weighted down, she sat back down.

"Is that when you saw the grave dug up?" Mary whispered.

"Around that time, yes."

Mary's eyes darted around as if someone might hear them and then she stepped away from the pot toward Annabelle. "Can... can you tell me about it, miss?"

Annabelle smiled and thought of how all the children must have talked about her. "Not if you think I'm crazy."

Mary looked at her in wonder and then turned back to her boiling pot. *Well, I'll grant she's honest,* thought Annabelle and snickered under her breath. Annabelle picked herself up, brushed off her skirts and walked up to the pot. "Mary, I'll tell you what. I'll tell you as much of the story as I can if you'll try to answer some questions for me when I'm done."

Mary thought on it intently, and then nodded.

And so she told her all about P.D. MacBain. She told it quickly and efficiently and without even looking at Mary, and so she was surprised when she had finished to find that Mary had shut her eyes. When she opened them a moment later, she looked at Annabelle blankly, calmly.

What an odd child she is, and Annabelle stared back at her in amazement.

Mary nodded once or twice. "The soldier killed him," she said rather flatly.

Annabelle felt as though she'd been punched in the stomach. "Why do you say that?" she asked with a wheeze and ran her thumb along her waist a little nervously.

"A grave robber? People like that'll do anything for money. Must have killed him and realized later whatever he wanted off him was buried with him." Mary had it all figured out, cut and chiseled, as cold as winter ice and she nodded her head in satisfaction. Case closed.

Annabelle wanted to argue, but she would give too much away. She wanted to tell her, "No, actually, it was your father who killed him," but the theory suddenly sounded too ridiculous for words. Why would Marsden want to kill Brighton? Marsden never lost one slave to the underground railroad, not even Pella.

"You can ask your questions now," said Mary.

"Never mind," answered Annabelle sullenly. "You've... you've solved the case."

Mary nodded and smiled and pulled the clothes out of the pot with her long stick. Then she laid them down and wrung them out one by one, all with that knowing smile on her face.

Annabelle returned to her washboard feeling confused and defeated.

When she heard a loud hiss of water on fire as Mary poured out the wash pot and prepared to leave, Annabelle suddenly decided to ask her about Pella. Perhaps she could at least find out why he didn't go hunting with Brighton that fateful day.

Mary didn't mind stopping to chat about Pella, and she came over and sat down next to Annabelle to talk.

They talked about the day Pella left and wondered what it was like for him as a regimental drummer boy. They talked about how he loved to hunt with Friend Brighton and finally, all within the realm of normal conversation, Annabelle saw her chance. "Why didn't Pella go hunting with Samuel Brighton the day he was shot, do you remember?"

Annabelle thought she'd hit on something when she saw Mary stand up and look over into the woods. "I 'member. Mr. Marsden wanted to sell Pella to a man at Harper's Ferry." Annabelle was surprised at the distance the girl put between herself and her father, calling him "Mister." "He had Pella serve the man all day long."

"The day Mr. Brighton was shot?"

"No. The day before. At the end of that day, the man told Mr. Marsden Pella was too skinny to do the work he wanted and he left. That made Mr. Marsden mad so he beat Pella, and he wasn't even drunk."

Annabelle winced. Mary made it sound as if it were the natural thing to do.

"Pella couldn't move the next day for the bruises," Mary went on, "so he holed up in the quarters and carved on that angel. He told me that angel kept him 'live. He felt better next day, and then we found out about Brighton. Then he thought maybe the angel could make his friend feel better, you know. He didn't understand."

Annabelle nodded and stared at the creek, listening to the water flow around the rocks, hearing the lazy song of summer birds, watching the dappled light dance on the water through the branches overhead, and thinking how very glad she was Pella got away from this place. "You cared for Pella very much, didn't you, Mary?"

Mary laughed aloud, and Annabelle turned to her in wonder.

And Annabelle continued to stare at her, for Mary's laugh had brought a memory to mind, as clear and bright as if she'd just thought on it all day: *She and her father visiting a plantation. Some of the slave children looked so like the members of the household they had just met, Annabelle had tugged on her father's coat to ask a question. "Weem, why are Mr. Duffy's children living in the cabins out back? Is the big house not big enough for all of them?"*

"Hush, child."

"Is it 'cause they like their mammy's more?"

"Lord, give me strength. Annie, please hush. Ask me at home. Don't say another word until we get back home."

But by the time they had arrived at home Annabelle had thought up some childish answer for herself.

She shook her head and felt queasy and so shut her eyes tightly as if it could clear her mind. Then she opened them slowly to look once more at Mary.

Just looking at her brought Pella's face to Annabelle's mind as clearly as if he were sitting there beside her, laughing and then growing deathly quiet as he used to, and suddenly all of it came clear.

She had always known it but never admitted it. Pella was Mary's half brother.

Pella looked like Marsden—the same ears, the same walk—and Mary and Pella laughed alike and shared the same sharp blue eyes—Marsden's eyes.

She hated having the truth jump out in front of her like that, things she'd really known all along. It made her sick to her stomach.

Unbidden, the memory came to her of how Marsden had sold off Pella's mother when Pella was just a baby, and all Annabelle could think was, thank God it won't happen any more. *Thank God it won't happen anymore.* She whispered it before she knew she'd said a word, and then she looked over to Mary to see if she'd heard. She hadn't seemed to.

"Why do you stay in Hillsborough?" Annabelle asked the girl.

Mary didn't answer right away, and finally Annabelle looked over into her face. She was smiling as she looked across the water to the road. "Oh, I got plans," she said.

"Good." Annabelle watched her face and knew God had given this girl a brain for good reason. If anyone could find a way to leave she could.

Mary stood up and quietly gathered her things, then walked back up the hill to town.

Annabelle wanted to cease remembering, cease thinking, but she could no more stop her thoughts than dam Catoctin Creek. Unbidden, the image of a slave woman by the creek came to her— the woman was swaying and moaning; she was wounded to the heart for the loss of her children—and Annabelle shut her eyes tightly, but the vision came stronger in the darkness.

Suddenly she rolled onto her belly as she did when a little girl, pulled herself to the edge of the creek and looked into the stream. There was an eddy whose water was as clear as fancy glass, and below the tide, leaves and rocks were strewn languidly about the soft brown sand. *There is neither Jew nor Greek, there is neither bond nor free, there is neither male nor female; for ye are all one in Christ Jesus.* The water bubbled around her as she looked down, and her eyes became riveted to her reflection.

The brown sand of the creek darkened her image, and it was not hard to imagine what she would have been if she had been born brown.

TWENTY-SIX

Most folks are about as happy as
they make up their minds to be.

Abraham Lincoln

In the fall, the Delaneys heard from Michael, and Hillsborough proceeded to hear from the Delaneys. Michael Delaney was alive! Annabelle felt a rush of relief when she heard the news from Shilla. She hadn't realized until that very moment just how much he had weighed upon her conscience, but then she heard all the news.

He had emigrated west to seek gold, but also—and here Shilla paused and raised her brows—his letter had not failed to mention Annabelle's visit to him in a log cabin. Delaney claimed he was wounded in a skirmish, dragged himself to the cabin and that Miss MacBain had passed through and left him there to die.

Annabelle raised her hands to her mouth in shock. "He said that?" Annabelle cried.

Shilla nodded grimly. "Claims another regiment found him and snatched him from the jaws of death, while his original regiment listed him missing. Said he fought out the rest of the war, but we know him for a liar and no mistake."

"Oh, Shilla, how could he? How could he say it? You see? It's coming back to me full circle. I should've gone back to help him. I'm being punished."

"You would've been punished for sure if ye'd gone back, child. Ye'd be in Californy, now, and I've hurd that's punishment enough for any! Now his family's crying for him as if he were dead again."

"Michael Delaney died long before I met him in the cabin."

Shilla hugged her. "Indeed so, miss. So, I don't suppose yer needin' to take a dead man's words to heart."

"Oh, I'm long past caring what he thinks. Only, think what the Delaneys will say now. They'll…"

"They'll likely want to kill you."

"That's it exactly," said Annabelle.

After that, Annabelle heard bitter rumors the Delaney family were spreading about her, and although she wanted to tell them the truth, and although she was purely miserable with her knowledge, she knew the situation was impossible. They would always believe Michael. That's what a true family would do. So she avoided the family after that and no longer attended church services.

The one bright spot that autumn was the day in October Mary Marsden packed her belongings and left home.

She had found her way out.

She had turned sixteen only the month before, it was said, and she was now old enough to marry. Within that short time, she had found herself a husband, the young son of a couple heading west. And so on the day she married, Marsden, ignoring the people who had come to watch her go, walked behind their wagon drunk as Bacchus and cussed her all the way out of town, but for once the law kept him from doing more.

Annabelle was standing in her front yard when the wagon passed by and she saw Mary leaning out the back of the wagon, her arm draped easily over the boards, staring calmly at her father as he followed from a distance. She had an odd little smile on her face, and as she passed Annabelle's house, she nodded roundly to her and Annabelle smiled. The girl had done what she had had to do to get away, and Annabelle felt her triumph but prayed for her as the wagon trundled out of sight.

On a mild November day, Annabelle took herself to Marsden's Tavern alone. She knew she should take Shilla along, but that would only make the trip more obvious and she did not want to be obvious. She went early, hoping not too many folks would be there yet and was grateful to find the place empty, except for Mr. Marsden at the bar. He stared at her oddly and asked if he could help her. She looked about and said quietly, "I'm hoping you still sell guns, Mr. Marsden."

"Who wants to know?"

"Me. I want to know."

"You tired of your hunting gun?" he sneered.

"No. No, I'm not. It suits me fine. It's that I'd like to start a collection."

He raised his brows.

"A collection of unusual weapons. I've taken quite a fancy to unusual guns."

"Yea." But he turned back to setting up the glasses to show how little interest he had in the subject.

"Mr. Marsden, it's difficult for a woman to collect such things, and…"

"Does your daddy know you want these guns?"

"My father lets me do as I please."

He laughed. "That's for dang sure, letting you hunt…" He spat on the floor for emphasis, and Annabelle pinched her lips together for a spare second.

"If you won't help me, I'll take my business elsewhere." And she turned to leave.

"Now hold on. Hold on." She looked back expectantly. He was holding a hand out to her in truce. "I don't even know what you're asking for. Set down. Set down there." He wagged his hand toward a chair.

"No, thank you. My interest is simple enough. I won't need to stay long." She tried hard not to smile, but she trembled slightly with glee to know she had him hooked. "I'm tired of American guns. I'd like to see some European ones, I think."

He stared at her carefully. "Let me think about it," he said.

Annabelle knew he thought he was circling the bait. "Just let me know when you have something." She smiled and then she walked out of the tavern with a brisk step. As she made her way home, she thought rather smugly that she may figure this thing out by herself after all.

But Marsden didn't contact her for quite a while, and eventually the whole thing slipped from Annabelle's mind.

What she thought about more often in those days was how little she cared for living in her town and how much she wanted to get away. She ran errands only when she had to, because she hated to walk down the streets and see the looks and hear the whispers, and worst of all she hated to see her old friends, especially Sarah and Sally.

It had been hard to avoid the Drum girls, very hard, but Annabelle had done her best, for their sake as well as her own. But on a day when Shilla wasn't feeling well and her father needed cotton, Annabelle stepped into the dry goods store and found to her dismay the only customers in the place were Sarah Drum and the Drums' servant girl. Annabelle knew she should turn around and wait for Sarah to leave, but she stubbornly stayed where she was. Her eyes searched the shelves for the cotton then, and found it just as she heard a voice to her left call her name. Startled, she turned to see Sarah standing before her.

"I am engaged," she said, her eyes slit coldly as she stared hard at Annabelle.

Annabelle had already heard Sarah was engaged to marry Lemuel Walker.

"I know," said Annabelle, alert to Sarah's every movement. "Congratulations." She had no idea why Sarah felt she had to speak to her. They stood and eyed each other another moment.

Sarah turned to her servant. "Dorrie, would you please step outside for a moment?" she said sweetly. "I'll be out directly." Dorrie obeyed.

"I didn't take him from you, Annabelle MacBain," Sarah said in a sudden whisper. "I want you to know that. I didn't take him from you,"

"I know," said Annabelle, afraid to say more and afraid to say less.

Sarah moved her lips to speak again and her body swayed. The movement was familiar to Annabelle. Sarah was incredibly annoyed. *She does not believe me*, thought Annabelle.

"I know, Sarah. He was free. It's all right."

Sarah's eyes grew bright with fury. "Don't you patronize me!" And in a strained voice she added, "He cast you off. He cast you off!" Her eyes darted to the grocer who was out of earshot but watching them. "And don't ever tell anyone differently, do you hear? He simply didn't know you!"

Annabelle began to shake with anger of her own. "Why are you telling me this, Sarah? Are you afraid to take a man who'd look twice at someone like me? That's it, isn't it?" Annabelle knew from Sarah's look that that was exactly what she had meant. "Afraid my poor reputation will haunt you." Her voice rose as she added, "Already such a horror to have had me for a friend 'lo those many years."

"I can't help that you forgot who you were, Annabelle, and all that we meant to you, but I do regret..." She gained some control over her voice before continuing, "I do so regret ever telling you not to marry Michael Delaney. It all started over him. If your bull-headed father had only allowed you to marry."

"Oh, please." Annabelle laughed, then she brought her voice very low. "You know as well as I do, if I'd taken him I'd be west and married to a coward."

"As opposed," Sarah said slowly, "to proving yourself a coward."

Annabelle looked hard at her. "If I were a man I'd knock you down for that, Sarah Drum."

Sarah smiled. "You hunt like a man, don't you? So why ever not knock me down? Why ever not? I do wonder that you can hold your manly self back."

Annabelle was so angry then she couldn't think. She could hardly keep her eyes focused, and the blood beat within her to destroy, but it suddenly brought to mind the time she'd almost killed P.D. MacBain.

She was doing it again, letting her pride get the better of her.

She forced herself to close her eyes, prayed for a moment and let her shoulders slump forward. Then she took a deep breath and looked directly into Sarah's mocking, smiling face. "You have said Lem didn't know me, that much is true. I'll admit I didn't know myself, then, but a true friend—and you were once my good friend—a true friend should have known me better and stood by for an explanation when she heard I took the oath. I thought you and Sally knew me that well. I took the oath because I believed it, because of all that I had seen, because of all that I knew. I could not have done otherwise. And Lem put me aside..."

"Don't call him Lem."

"Mr. Walker."

"Doctor."

"Oh, for pity's sake, Doctor Walker put me aside just as I put him aside. It was mutually understood. I would never tell anyone otherwise." The anger began a slow burn once more. "Besides, if you care to look around this town, you will see there is no one for me to tell." She checked herself before continuing. "But I do thank you for keeping your promise to stay quiet about what you know of Michael Delaney—for his family's sake."

"Oh, but it's been no trouble at all," she said cuttingly, and Annabelle realized Sarah had purposefully kept her mouth shut about the truth of Annabelle's visit to the cabin.

"I see," Annabelle said. "I see there is not a shred left in you of my old friend."

Swaying ever so slightly, Sarah replied, "Well, the Annabelle MacBain I knew didn't make up stories about graves dug up in the middle of the night. She wouldn't have gone romping off by herself with no heed to safety or reputation." Her eyes narrowed. "And she didn't give warm comfort to Yankees." Annabelle's face paled but not for the reasons Sarah imagined. "Yes, let's not forget your soldier in blue."

Annabelle breathed deeply, looked at her shoes and smiled as she spoke, measuring each word to make sure to keep the venom out. "Yes, I do not forget the soldier. I am ever grateful that soldier took the time to help me understand, so that I could take the oath."

Sarah snickered at that and Annabelle blushed.

"If you'll excuse me now, I have some things to purchase."

"By all means," Sarah said with less anger in her voice than before. But still she stood behind Annabelle, apparently waiting for her to make her purchase, and it made Annabelle extremely nervous, for she didn't think she could stand a further conversation.

As she turned to walk past Sarah and leave, Sarah whispered, "Don't tell anyone I spoke to you today, Annabelle MacBain."

Annabelle saw the fear behind that icy look. Her own eyes grew teary although she couldn't know quite why. "No. Of course not."

"And not Lem. You won't tell Lem." Sarah could barely conceal her trembling.

Annabelle shook her head sadly. "Of all the people in the world, Dr. Walker and I have the least to say to each other, Sarah, but I wish you both well. I do," she said gently. For a moment, she thought she saw Sarah soften. "I wish you both well, but I suppose it doesn't matter."

The glare in Sarah's eye came back and she turned from Annabelle to the keeper of the dry goods store and loudly put in her order.

And a dry-eyed but exhausted Annabelle turned and walked home.

The meeting in the store was the last in a series of bitter little gestures and conversations Annabelle wished she could put behind her, and so by December of '65, she thought she could stand it no more. She half wished she had been on board the wagon with Mary Marsden heading out of town or had gone like Widow Small to the great Northwest. And so she began to discuss the problem with her father, mildly at first but then more vehemently telling him he should allow her to get away, to travel.

She got nowhere with him until she said on sudden impulse that he should allow her to go to Europe just as he had been allowed to as a young man. She could finally meet her cousins, aunts and uncles, and see the little cottage in Scotland where her parents met—see the place where Aunt Fiona and her mother were born.

She knew she had struck a nerve.

Suddenly her father wavered in the discussion—the tide of battle had turned—and she pressed relentlessly onward. When he became too tired to argue, he told her slowly if she could find herself a worthy escort, she could go. Annabelle immediately suggested Shilla. After all, Shilla could visit her own relatives in Ireland as they traveled about.

He agreed on one condition, that she wait until spring and take a boat from Alexandria.

"No, I can't wait until spring. That's impossible. I can't stand it here another moment, Father."

"Annabelle, I don't want you caught in a snowstorm on your way there—a storm by land or sea. Wait until Europe has at least a breath of spring and give our relations some time to prepare for your visit, for reason's sake."

Annabelle didn't care about spring and she didn't think her relations needed time. And the need for reason had lost all meaning as well. All she knew was that her own breath was gone, it seemed, for holding it in living such a small life in a small town. Standing over his chair in the parlor and tapping her fingers to her lower lip, she finally asked if March the first wasn't spring enough for his liking.

He sighed. "All right, Annie, March the first."

"Thank you," she said curtly, but then the thought of truly getting away from there and the freedom it would bring welled up within her soul, and she bent down and placed her arms around him. "Thank you, Weem," she whispered. "You don't know what this means to me." And she kissed him on the cheek.

He pulled his arm up around her and gave one shoulder a pat. "You haven't called me that in so long, I'm almost glad to let you go all the way to Europe just to hear it again."

Annabelle brushed back a tear as she stood up. "I'm truly sorry I've been so difficult, Father."

But her father shocked her with his reply. "Well, Annie, if I didn't know better, I would think you were pining away for love."

Her cheeks grew red. "For love!" she cried indignantly. "Father! Nothing like that! It's just I have no friends here, besides the family. You must see I hardly belong here, anymore."

"You'll always belong here, Annie," he said sadly. "Once I thought you and Lemuel Walker, yes, I'll admit it. Once I thought you and he would make a little family for me here, but I see it was a foolish thought. He's not the man for you, Annie. By golly, some days, he's not the man for me, either." He winked, and they both laughed. "Drives me to all distraction sometimes, though he has gotten more reasonable of late."

"I know," she said quietly. "He's engaged to Sarah."

"Do you still have thoughts about that P.D. fella', Annie?" he asked quite suddenly. "You can tell me, you know."

Annabelle looked to the ceiling and let her head fall side to side, but then sat down and pressed her hands against her forehead. "No," she said quietly. "I don't think of him at all." Then she rolled her eyes to heaven and then down into her lap. "Oh, I only think of him all the time." And she said it so pathetically, her father almost laughed.

"Then why don't you write to him, Annie? The war is well over."

"I don't know that I've forgiven. He wrote to me last April, but I couldn't write him."

"Annie! The war is over."

She pulled her head up quickly. "Well, now, that's just what he said. But don't you remember? It was his army that destroyed our things, Mother's things, and caused us such pain. Don't you remember what they did to us here? And remember the boy who died the week after you came home? If you'd had your supplies, you could have helped him, besides the fact P.D.'s work was to have all of you killed."

"Annie, are you going to go on making reason after reason to keep the thing alive? It's only killing you, my dear. It's only hurting you, now. You remember the story of General Lee and the woman who came frantic to him after the surrender and said, *What shall I do? The Yankees broke all the branches in my peach tree. Who will pay for it?* The General told her, *The war is over, madam, chop it down.* General Lee more than anyone has reason for bitterness, and... But you're not listening, are you, girl?"

"I'm listening, Father, if you want me to," she said in a whisper, her eyes cast down.

"Aw, Annie," he said in obvious disappointment.

She was angry with his tone. "Well, why shouldn't I be bitter?" she cried out dramatically. "Nothing ever comes right for me! I lost my mother. I chose a coward for a husband, and now Michael's gone. I always thought I wanted to be a nurse, and I found I hadn't the stomach for it after all. I've lost my best friends. And I can't help how I felt about the war. I took the oath. I can bear that the town hates me. What I can't bear is to be forced to live here day in and day out—no, no, Weem, you know I don't mean you. If it were just us, I wouldn't care, but I may as well be a prisoner in my own home—and this is all providence sees fit to give me. This is all I can expect from life! Why shouldn't I be bitter? And P.D. MacBain can't help me with it, nor can any man. And it can't be that I love him. I hate him too much!" She choked as she said the words, and then she turned to flee up to her room, but as she went her father said softly from behind her, "Now, Annabelle MacBain, I don't see how Michael Delaney may be counted among the losses."

As luck would have it, there was a dinner almost every week in the months before Annabelle left. But with the happy expectation of travel before her, she allowed herself more animation than usual at the meals, even when the suppers took on the undeniable look of a matchmaking interview. And so in the last of those cold winter months she gave real hope to at least two mothers in town, although she was hardly aware of doing so.

On a bitter cold day in early February she was surprised to find one of Marsden's servants at her door asking her to come to the tavern as Mr. Marsden had some news. A bit frightened at first, she soon became excited about the possibilities. Everyone in the house but she had been called away on errands of one sort or another. *Just as well,* she thought, *I'll have to do this on my own.* The servant left and Annabelle bundled up as best she could and finally made her way across and down the street to the tavern.

When she came in the front door, she found the tavern room crowded and warm. Men in thick overcoats were huddled together at tables and bar, and every last one of them turned to stare at her. Seeing them suspended with surprise, full mugs to open lips, she suddenly imagined a flock of turkeys in a rainstorm and thought how the poor birds would die drinking rain water because they couldn't remember to shut their mouths. A smell lay heavy in the air, a poor combination of stale tobacco and rye liquor. But Mr. Marsden had seen her and motioned to a corner table by the window, and the men turned back to their friends with nudges and winks and a light in their eyes due to the new topic of discussion.

Mr. Marsden met her at the table and started talking fast and low, explaining to her he had information on some weapons from Spain and Italy, if she were interested.

She brought her head down low. "Are there any that are quiet as they shoot?"

His eyebrows rose.

"You can imagine as a woman I don't like all the noise of the shot, Mr. Marsden," she said demurely, "and for other more obvious reasons, I like best to keep my hunting quiet."

He grinned with half a smile and nodded.

"I've heard there are guns that don't use powder" she said slowly, watching for his reaction.

He blinked. "Those are illegal."

"I know it'll cost me more," countered Annabelle.

He nodded. "Well, Miss Annabelle, you may be in a heap of luck there. I think I know where I might could find you one of those."

The news brought roses to her cheeks. "Really," she said carefully. This was what she'd come for, the admission that he owned the gun. This was the man who'd killed Brighton.

They were silent for a few moments, but he seemed impatient and finally lowered his head and voice. "You bein' a woman, I s'pose I can't expect you to understand business, so I'll tell you. See, now's when you make me an offer, and I take it to him and like that. Got it?"

"What? I don't know. No. Wait. Who?" *What was he saying? That he didn't own the gun himself?* "You mean you don't have one... on hand?"

"On hand?" He turned his head and spat, making the spittoon ring with the straight shot. "That ain't the way it's done."

She thought hard on the new turn of events. Marsden merely

knew someone who might have this gun? What good would that do her? At the end of this she'd own an illegal gun. No good. "No, thank you," she said quickly.

"If yer impatient, I can get you a Spanish gun with double action and a rear sight by tomorrow," he said with no slight irritation.

"No, no, thank you."

"What, you got to have an air pump gun right away?" Marsden laughed, spat once more and leaned back in his chair. "First off, you didn't tell me you were interested in specialty pieces. Typical woman. Wastin' my time."

"I suppose you're right."

"You sure you don't want to order this thing? This man's got a real good price."

"No."

Now he was angry. As she got up to leave, he said loudly, "Well, you're crazy to want a gun like that, anyway. Plumb out of your mind. Woman's got no business hunting, when she ought to be at home."

"Like Mary?" she shot back.

His eyes grew fierce. "What do you know about it?" He pulled his chair forward.

But Annabelle looked down at him and raised her eyebrows ever so slightly. "With all these women out hunting these days, Mr. Marsden, you had better keep out of the woods, hadn't you?"

At that he jumped up and threw his chair out from behind him with a grunt. The room grew silent and tense. "Get outa here," Marsden said, drawing his hands into fists.

"It's my pleasure," she said bitterly, and quickly made her way out the door. The others laughed uncomfortably as she left. But at the door she turned and said, "You even sound like a flock of turkeys!" And though her lips were trembling she managed to smile as she slammed the door.

As if to goad her in the last mile of the race, the MacBains' social dinners continued throughout the time remaining, and two weeks before she was to leave for Europe she found out from her father there was a dinner at the Brightons' home.

Annabelle wished heartily for a headache that day, but one did not appear by supper time, and so reluctantly she went with her father to the Brightons'. She did not care to go there for the memories it would more than likely bring, and she did not care to see John Brighton, for the poor man was in a deep depression due to the loss of his arm. It would not be a pleasant meal, that much was certain.

But on the ride there, Annabelle thought it was really very polite of the widow to include her in the invitation at all, since she, more than any other, had reason to question Annabelle's sanity. And what evidence had she ever given the widow to think herself sane? Like the visit with Marsden the other day, it seemed that everything she did within the town, from buying pickles to picking up a piece of trash from the street, caused all opinion to point toward but one judgment: Annabelle MacBain—completely mad.

They drove up the driveway, and just as Annabelle had feared, she thought back on the day she rode up to warn Widow Brighton. She saw the stile and thought of his hand on her arm. They walked up the steps and she remembered how she ran from the place in tears. They entered the home and she thought of P.D. staring at her in the hall where he found her. She simply couldn't stop thinking about him. *Perhaps*, she thought drolly, *this is what it means to go insane.*

They were ushered into the parlor then, and she tried to concentrate on the evening at hand.

Just then her father brought the Widow Brighton to her and with a wink to Annabelle he announced, "Of the two ladies standing here, one attended the finest female institute in England, and one is about to visit England on a grand tour. I leave it to you ladies to sort out who may be whom."

Annabelle smiled tentatively at Hannah Brighton, and Hannah gave a formal smile in reply, and under her father's watchful eye Annabelle took a deep breath and dove into a conversation with the woman.

To Annabelle's surprise, the two were soon conversing as easily as old friends.

When they were called into supper, Annabelle decided to ignore all others at the supper table to continue questioning the widow in detail on her knowledge of Great Britain. The Quaker miller and his wife were there, as was the only lawyer in town and his spouse, but Annabelle concentrated all her conversation on the Widow Brighton.

But then, halfway through the meal, Annabelle was at first dumbfounded and soon horrified as Hannah began shamelessly singing her son John's praises to her guests, giving significant glances to Annabelle all the while. Within the nuance of the conversation, she even expressed a desire to join the Methodist church and intimated her John would do the same. It was outrageous. Annabelle nodded politely but said nothing; soon she was desperately trying to catch her father's eye to let him know she wished to leave. But he seemed thoroughly entertained by the display and would not allow his eye to be caught.

Next the sullen John abruptly excused himself from the table, leaving his slightly stunned mother to offer his apologies.

"Though it's taking a while for him to adjust—work around the farm takes a bit longer now—thee should see how he works. Samuel would be so proud."

Annabelle blushed to think of all the memories the father's name brought forth in her. But the widow was saying, "The war was a hard time for everyone, wasn't it, dear? But all is forgiven and forgotten."

Now Annabelle didn't feel like sitting there, either, and her father still would not glance her way. Soon Annabelle couldn't look at the woman, knowing what she knew—knowing everything she knew—yet she had to listen to Hannah Brighton prattle on and on about her John and her husband's pride in him. And then, horror of horrors, Widow Brighton was relating the memory of her husband's passing. "That was the very time Jedediah Malachi... or was it, Malachi Jedediah Norris...." She brightened, saying, "That was the very time Albert's son visited this house—to pay respects to his uncle—and after that," she added theatrically, "he met his own brave end on the battlefield, although," she added worriedly, "there is some confusion about when and where exactly he died."

No, Annabelle could not sit for this.

As delicately as she could, she asked if she might go outside for a short walk around the Brightons' lovely property. Her father politely offered to go with her, but Annabelle declined his invitation, preferring to weep tears of self-pity in solitude.

She walked out-of-doors into an unusually warm and humid evening. A storm was brewing. The wind was kicking up in gusts of warmth and cold, but it wasn't quite ready to rain. The walk would do her good, and it was wonderful to feel able to be out-of-doors once more. She wished she still had Lucy. *I would run her, oh, how we would run. And just up the road where we ran that day...* But then a catch came to her throat and she threw the remembrance from her.

Europe was where she belonged. There would be nothing there to bring up the awful memories.

Warm lightning flashed behind the mountains as she walked around the home and, wherever the lightning danced, bare-branched trees stood out from the shadows, spreading coal gray arms against a velvet sky. A moment of light. Another moment. Then all went black again.

In the darkness she looked about the grounds and saw a light in one of the outbuildings and out of curiosity she headed there. She found a servant working by lantern in a large workroom.

She came near enough to see the man's form silhouetted by the lamp, rearranging things at a table, the left arm of his coat folded into one pocket, and it was then she realized it wasn't a servant at all. It was John Brighton.

She didn't want to disturb him and quickly turned to walk back to the house, but he had heard her and called out, "So, my mother drove you from the house as well, eh?"

Annabelle turned to him and smiled. "Oh, no, I just thought I'd go for a walk."

"Well, I come in here when I've heard enough." He threw a piece of metal into a box as he spoke and then turned to look at her.

They were both a bit awkward as they stared at each other, and Annabelle truly wanted to go back in the house, but then with his one arm, John beckoned her to step in and she came.

"I've heard you like hunting, Miss MacBain. 'Mad Annabelle, the Huntress,' they say."

"I like to hunt, yes," she replied defensively.

He said with a little light in his eyes. "Then you might be interested in these. I keep a little collection in here."

Annabelle nudged her hoop skirt through the opening, stepped all the way into the room and looked around her uncertainly. Like the walls of arms and shields and armor in the castles of Europe she'd read so much about, the walls of the shed were covered with weapons of every variety. She wanted to run right back out, and yet a thought occurred to her that made her stay. She began to pursue the thought and the thought soon drove past her and began to drag her along behind it instead.

"Fascinating. How did you come by all these?" she asked innocently.

"Collected most of them in the war, through my work. I think you're the first person to see them." His lip curled. "Mother doesn't approve."

Annabelle's throat went dry, but she kept on. "Were you a spy, or something?" she asked with forced enthusiasm.

"Something of a spy, yes."

"How exciting," she said, feigning enthusiasm.

"Sometimes. Lots of boring paperwork, mostly, but then I had this collection to keep me interested."

"Oh, then I suppose you didn't do much real spying," she replied coyly.

"I got on well enough," he answered with a bit of irritation. "They put me in charge of rooting out double agents."

"Really?" Her eyes widened to their largest and prettiest. "How very daring…"

"Yes," he said proudly. "But my best work was killing off the underground railroad. I was good at that. Posed as an abolitionist. With my Quaker background and all, it was easy." He stopped as he remembered something. His eyes became suspicious. "But I can't see how that'd be of interest to you, anyway. I heard you turned Yankee."

His words made her go quite pale, and she tried to keep her voice calm and steady. "I did what I could to survive."

He relaxed immediately. He smiled a half-smile. "Well, I can understand that. I suppose if the war had gone on, I might have recruited you, too."

"Yes, I suppose so." She looked around again. "Truly an amazing collection. I suppose I'm thinking so much of Europe these days. Which of these things is European?"

"Ah, European. They are the best, the best. Let's see." His eyes flashed with obvious pride. First, he showed her an English revolver, and then an Italian rifle, and then Annabelle drew him out more, asking what weapons he used when he was a spy. He showed her his revolver, but then she saw a box in the corner of the counter.

"You must keep a very special weapon in there," she said in a whisper.

He looked at her and nodded. "That one is European, too."

"What... what is it?"

He stared at the box. "Do you really want to see it?"

"If you wish me to," she said deferentially.

Hardly believing what was happening, she watched him take a key from under the counter.

He drew the key to the lid very slowly. "It is in a box all to itself. Handcrafted. None of your Richmond rifles here. This was made at the turn of the century in Austria. Used against Napoleon Bonaparte himself. Quite effective." He snickered as the key turned in the lock. "Bonaparte hated the things, hated them, you see, because they don't make any noise." He was grinning foolishly now and opening the lid carefully, and Annabelle found herself shivering with cold. "Highly accurate up to one hundred yards or so." Now the lid was laid completely open.

Annabelle looked at the velvet-lined box, a gun carefully laid out within it like a dueling set, each piece of it lying quietly in its place. The main portion of the gun was about the size of a revolver and graced with a crescent handle, but there seemed to be a rifle attachment, too, and there was something else there she couldn't quite see over his shoulder. He was saying, "But the beauty of the thing is this, this peculiar looking piece right here." He stepped aside and pointed, and Annabelle saw a polished brass globe about five inches in diameter. She couldn't help but think it was a pretty thing, so shiny and bright against the green velvet of the case. "You screw that into the base there and the ball is full of air, you see. This is a percussion gun, the Austrian Spring-Air Rifle, and it discharges the bullet by forced air."

She turned to see his face. His smile was tense and strange, his words forced. She could hardly hear him as he whispered, "You weren't given just one ball. Takes two men to pump them. They gave you four or five to take with you. I have the pump, too. You have to have help. Can't do it alone. I kept it all." His face lost all expression as he finished.

He set the key down just so on the table and wiped his hand on his coat. "You see, the gun makes no sound." But then he simply stopped and continued staring at the thing.

He was pale, even for John Brighton, and so too was Annabelle because she knew exactly what he was remembering just then. She could have let him go on with his explanations. She could have let him skip to the next piece of armament on the wall, and in another time and place, Annabelle would have let him. But instead, she said in a trembling voice, "John Brighton, you killed your own father with that gun!"

TWENTY-SEVEN

And I don't want no pardon
For what I was and am,
I won't be reconstructed
And I don't care a dam.

From the Union Song
O I'm A Good Old Rebel

He took a step back and looked at her and his lids flew open. "Wha-at?" He began shaking, half laughing, still wiping his hand on his coat.

"I said you killed your own father."

His hand slipped to the table to steady himself, and he said with sudden viciousness, "Get out. How dare you! Get out!"

For one horrible moment she feared she'd made a mistake and she stepped back but she did not leave.

"You're mad!" he said even more loudly. "They all say so. An' you don't belong here! Get out! You... GET OUT!"

The truth was too plain.

Who else could know how to find Samuel Brighton in the hunt? Who else could know about his one shot? The one shot that all the servants heard that day, the one that would strike his father in the neck again while he hung dead upon a tree. There could be no doubt. She trembled as the truth of it coursed through her. "And did you think you were justified?"

"Justified?" His eyes opened wide and he began to rub his temple with his one hand. "What do you mean?"

"Did you think you had a good reason, any reason to kill him?" she pressed.

He laughed. "Well, a reason? Well..." He was becoming

unhinged before her eyes. "Well, a reason, yes, justified. Yes."

He began to pace and Annabelle held her breath.

"I had orders to destroy the railroad. Orders. I told you. So I killed a man. I killed an old man who arranged for property to be taken from its rightful owners and shipped to people who had no claim on them. A man who had no respect, no respect. For the law, for a way of life. I killed a man who ran a railroad for slaves," he said in an odd singsong.

She stepped backward to the door as she watched him pace. "You'll be hanged for this, John Brighton!" she blurted out.

He looked over at her and smiled and looked back at his boots as he paced. "No, I won't. No, I won't!" He began to jump a little and then pace some more. "I did it all under orders, don't you see? I did it all under orders and…" His voice went to a smiling whisper, "I even got a commendation for it. I got a commendation for killing him."

Her stomach twisted within her to hear him say it.

She watched his wild eyes as he kept repeating, "I got a commendation."

And then he was touching the lid of the box, then touching his temple and pacing and jumping now and then as he kept repeating the words, but strange as it all appeared to Annabelle, she wasn't afraid of him. *And why should he harm me?* she asked herself. *After all, he was only doing his duty. His duty.*

"Oh, no, no! Not that again!" she said aloud. Now she turned and, still holding her stomach, she tried to breathe, and she rushed toward the house, wanting to get those words out of her mind.

She came to the door and asked the servant to tell her father she had gone home. Hardly knowing what she was doing, she rushed back down the hill toward home as quickly as her legs would carry her. The lightning still played behind the mountains, and the air was growing warmer, but Annabelle Shannon MacBain felt a chill that gripped her bones with pain.

Why, she wondered desperately, couldn't she have let it pass, told her father later and let him manage things? Why couldn't she leave things well enough alone? John Brighton was mad as a march hare. He'd lost his arm as well as his mind. Wasn't that enough punishment? Wasn't it enough?

And was she in danger? Was her father in danger? All those guns. She suddenly wanted to go back to make sure her father was all right. She turned but immediately saw her father's coach coming from the house. A breath of relief escaped from her and she stood there shivering and waited for him in the road.

When he arrived, she breathlessly explained the situation as she climbed into the coach and sat down.

"My child, my child, what have you gotten yourself into?" he said, shaking his head. "I'll take you home right now where you'll sit tight. You hear me? I've got to get some men and go over there." He clicked the horse into a trot. "I'll call on the Friends first."

"Oh, Weem, please be careful. If a man could kill his own father..."

Dr. MacBain nodded grimly.

She thought over her conversation with Brighton. "And is John Brighton right? Would the United States protect him now?"

"Strange circumstance. I'm not so sure. But, remember what you told me about the body, Annie? If there's evidence he was shot from behind..."

"And I know where the tree is, Father. I've seen it, the bump where the second bullet lodged." She was shivering uncontrollably now.

"No, the army won't protect him. We'll just get P.D. up here to testify. P.D. MacBain, I mean."

Her heart froze. "Really?" He couldn't know how the prospect disturbed and thrilled her, but he gave her a sidelong glance, and they said no more for a time.

As they came toward Brandenburg's she said, "Samuel Brighton was such a kind and gentle man. How could he have a son like that?"

"War can drive people to insanity, Annie. The mind is as easily wounded as any other part of the body, but it's a durn sight harder to heal. Well, here we are," he said as they drew up into the stables.

He escorted Annabelle down and she hugged him as he began to unhitch the horse. He asked her to send Thomas up to the Brightons' when she got in the house. She nodded and then watched him as he mounted and rode off.

Annabelle walked numbly into the kitchen and knocked firmly on Thomas' door. He came to the door quickly and as soon as he heard the news, he grabbed his overcoat and gun and ran out the front door. His feverish activity started her shaking again, so she lit a candle and made herself sit at the kitchen table. With trembling hands folded in front of her she sat and watched the flame for a little while.

And then she heard violent knocking at the front door. With a bolt of fear, Annabelle knew exactly who might be there, and she wondered if she should go to the door. She could if she were prepared, she thought, and so she cast about to look for a weapon and found a fireplace poker handy. She came toward the door with the poker at her side while the violent knocking continued. But soon she heard a voice.

It was the Brightons' servant, Jane, and Annabelle rushed to open the door. The girl stood flushed and agitated on the front porch. "It's Master John." she whimpered. "He's shot hisself. Oh, come. Tell the doctor come."

"Oh, my heavens," was all Annabelle could say. She went into her father's office to retrieve his bag, thinking it would be up to her to help John Brighton until her father came and she had no time to fear the thought. As she came back to the door, she asked, "Jane, is it bad then?"

Jane blinked and nodded and brought her hand up to her hair. "In the head, miss. We think he's dead and mistress half-crazy with grief."

Past the door, she saw her father on horseback leading other men, Thomas among them, toward Brighton House.

She rushed out and down the steps. "Weem!" she cried and ran toward him. She yelled out an explanation and then swung his bag up to him.

Off he went in a gallop, the men behind him quickly rallying to follow at a mad pace. Jane ran after them as Annabelle leaned over and tried to catch her breath.

Shaking and teary-eyed, she finally straightened her back and returned to the house. And when she had calmed down, she realized what she'd done. She had grabbed her father's bag, fully prepared to do what she had to do. It felt rather good to know that about herself, that she could be counted on in a crisis, but she smiled to know she still had no desire to be a doctor or a nurse.

Shilla came downstairs and Annabelle told her everything since there was no reason to keep any of it from anyone any longer.

When Annabelle was done explaining, Shilla patted her shoulder, but Annabelle said with bitter disappointment, "And how will we go to Europe, Shilla, with all this hanging over us?"

Shilla cocked her head. "Sounds like a right time to be leaving, it does. Things is all clearing up."

Annabelle hadn't really looked at it that way, but as Shilla said it she realized it was true. A burden had been lifted. She laughed softly. "Leave it to you, Shilla. You're better than a house cat for finding the sunny spot."

"Well, that I am, that I am." And Shilla somewhat cheerfully began to busy herself by making tea, while Annabelle thought of what would happen next—after the town heard that John had shot himself.

"And then they will remember his father's hunting accident, a mortal wound, as well," whispered Annabelle.

"What, dearie?" asked Shilla.

"It's awful, Shilla," she said more loudly. "No one had thought of Samuel Brighton's death as a suicide, but they will now." Strange how they could decide a thing so quickly, but she'd seen it all before, most recently practiced on herself. And the town would say there was an evil eye on the Brighton family, and Hannah Brighton would be shunned, as would John, that is, if he lived.

"But they'll know John murdered him."

"No, they won't. No. They won't. I know what my father will say—that the news would destroy Hannah Brighton. He'll let it go. This time a rumor is better than the truth."

And Annabelle shook her head slowly back and forth with the truth of it. But, although she thought if Brighton had played his hand differently both he and his sons might still be alive. She was remembering the boys when they were younger and thinking perhaps the father had known his sons too well.

Samuel, the oldest, had been a boastful fellow, bragging about his cattle or his prize-winning pigs, completely in love with farming, to the exclusion even of his Quaker duties. He told everyone exactly how he planned to run the farm as he got older. Conversely, John resented his brother's interest and success and kept more to himself. He, too, distanced himself from the Friends' monthly meeting. Brighton sent Samuel to another farm to work and apprenticed John to a blacksmith. She remembered that at the time folks thought Brighton had sent his sons away because he was afraid they'd kill each other one day. Now she realized while that may have been true, it was also true he wanted to keep them away from the railroad.

Perhaps he took on 150 sons and daughters instead. The thought gave her a strange but good feeling; some sort of sense was created from the chaos.

She stared at the candle again as they drank their tea, and then Shilla finally took herself to bed, but Annabelle decided to wait up for her father.

Three long hours later, Dr. MacBain came through the door.

In the parlor Annabelle looked intently at him for a word on John, but he shook his head. "He did a right job of it, Annie. The very weapon... that dimmed air gun. What a sight. Brought back... " But he couldn't go on.

Annabelle gave her father a good, strong hug but soon found her own self weeping as she clung to him. Weeping for his loss and hers, for families like the Brightons, for all she had seen pass before her young eyes, for all her father had seen in his lifetime. "Oh, it's all my fault," she said in anguish. "If I hadn't pressed him, perhaps he would have..."

"Annie! Don't do this to yourself! You didn't pull the blasted trigger!" But she wept as though her heart were breaking, and Dr.

MacBain fell to hugging her more tightly. "I remember when Samuel sent his sons away. The year he sent them off, I decided if he were willing to sacrifice his own family, the least I could do was ask you to stay home, too."

"Yes, you told me before, Weem, but I wish you'd told me then." She looked up at him, and he nodded solemnly. "How terrible to do such a thing to your own family."

"Samuel had a love, Annabelle. He had such a heart for those who needed help. I understand it. You saw me able to leave my only daughter when the war came."

Her face grew red. "Yes, and I didn't take it too well. Perhaps if Samuel Brighton had brought his sons into it, neither would have left the Quaker faith—and they might both be alive. And I thought you should have let me come with you, as well. Perhaps I wouldn't be as bitter."

"Do you really think so, Annie?" He asked it with an honest concern that caused Annabelle a pang of guilt for saying such a harsh thing.

"No, Weem." She gulped. "I don't believe that. No. It's foolishness from a tired, little fool. If I'm saying crazy things, it's because I'm so tired."

Her father nodded. "Then rest well, Annabelle. Things are going to get better."

"Are they?"

"Yes. I know it for a fact." He watched her eyes carefully. "If you'll do just one thing."

She nodded, too tired to argue the point. "Tell me."

"Give up your pride."

"Give up my pride," she repeated softly.

"*Revenge is mine, sayeth the Lord.*"

The words startled her awake. She stared at her father and would have been angry but for his look of deep concern. "You want me to forget everything we've been through?"

"Not forget... forgive."

"But I have a right to be angry!"

"You had a right to be angry."

"It's my life, Father."

"And you can waste it on bitterness or you can waste it on living. You're blaming everyone but yourself for who you are today, and I've seen it all too many times before. Every day I deal with men who've lost themselves in bitterness, and they take every bit of medicine I give them except the one thing that will make them whole."

"Nothing can make them whole. What are you talking about?"

"They need to take responsibility for their decisions in this life before God, blame no one but themselves, and then get on with living."

She looked down as the tears stung her eyes. "But, I can't. I can't."

"You must," her father said, his voice choking with emotion.

"It would take too much of me," she whispered.

His voice grew louder. "It will take all of you, it's true, but you've done nothing God hasn't seen before and forgiven. It's prideful to think He won't forgive you, don't you see? And this, what you're doing now, it's not living, Annie." His voice grew gravelly with effort. "You've consigned yourself to the grave, and I don't think I can bear another loss."

At his words, a well of regret and remorse swept over her the likes of which she'd never felt before. The weeping began from deep in her soul—so deep there were no tears but only a throbbing, racking pain coming up from deep within her. "Oh, I am sorry, Weem. I am so sorry. What have I done?"

And her father came and held her shoulders. "Thank God, thank God," he whispered and pressed his cheek to hers, and Annabelle gave in to it—a full repentance and a cleansing that would bring her back to life. She understood it, then. It had seemed as though it would take all of her—too frightening a thing to consider before now—and so it had taken everything. She'd been through fire and she had survived, and what was left was a creation both beautiful and new.

She had survived the war. The battle was finally won.

A month later, Annabelle and Shilla found themselves in the

MacBain carriage, packed and ready to ride to the docks of Alexandria, the first leg of her grand tour. Annabelle and her father had a tearful parting, but when her father had escorted Annabelle to her seat he took her hand and said, "I have to tell you, Annie, that I wrote P.D. MacBain, my old friend, and told him what occurred at the Brightons'."

"Yes, Weem. Thank you. I just couldn't write."

"I thought as much." And then he smiled and patted her hand. He seemed to have accepted her situation rather well, she decided, and now she wished she could do the same and with equal calm.

And the horses were started up.

During that long trip, she wondered more than once what P.D. MacBain was doing now that the war was over. She wished she could talk to him now; she wished for another chance. But the world didn't really work that way, did it? No, it didn't. She was forgiven, and that would have to be enough.

She did enjoy the travel, despite the rocking carriage. The rolling hills were lovely as they rode along, passing through the small towns and villages that lined the turnpike. They stayed the night at a drovers' rest in Dranesville, Virginia, halfway to the docks of Alexandria, and spent a night listening to a herd of cattle lowing and a flock of turkeys gobbling in the tree outside their window.

The next day, they slept in the carriage for lack of sleep the night before and were awakened by the hollow clopping of horse hooves and the jolting thumps of the carriage wheels on cobblestone as they entered the old town of Alexandria. They rubbed their eyes as the carriage began to sway and thump and they looked out the windows to admire the outer neighborhoods, with their neat rows of fine brick homes, brick walkways and tree-lined streets. Shilla was the first to see the glorious sails of the boats at dock over the housetops. The city had the feeling of prosperity and worth as they entered the business district, with many fine brick buildings and statues and the like. They nodded to each other in admiration.

Soon they arrived at the city hotel, a massive building of brick several stories high graced evenly with tall windows. They had chosen to stay at the hotel because Dr. MacBain had heard the old hostelry had fared well during the war, and she smiled to remember the reason: The proprietor had made his money selling liquor to the Union soldiers quartered in the otherwise Confederate town. A Northern version of Mr. Marsden. Shilla looked at the entrance. "Lore, but it's grand!"

"Yes, it could have been mine!" Annabelle replied impishly. "Only the owner took the oath much earlier than I." But Shilla only clucked her tongue.

The ladies alighted and entered a long foyer where they stopped at the desk to check their reservations. All was in order and when they had signed the register they were asked to follow a porter to their lodgings.

As the young fellow carried their things from landing to landing up the steep stairway, Annabelle grew tired and paused on one of the longer landings. She happened to glance to her right to see a huge and well-appointed room through open double doors. Immediately she knew this must be the place where George Washington's birthnight balls were held. Quickly she nudged Shilla for her to look as well, and Shilla smiled.

On the fourth floor they turned into a wide hallway and the fellow stopped to open the door to their room. He then bowed for them to pass, and Annabelle entered a large room steeped in the colors of red rose and cream. In the room was a canopy bed, a love seat, a tall and slender wardrobe and a pretty vanity table set for a lady. As Annabelle looked about her she truly felt well-loved; her father had secured the very best accommodations. "Shilla, this is like a dream, isn't it?"

"Indeed, miss," Shilla said as she tipped the young man a coin.

Annabelle walked to the window with deliberate slowness, admiring the Brussels carpet underfoot and the intricate mouldings at the rail and ceiling. At the window she pulled aside a curtain of rose damask edged with satin tassels to peer out and take in a bustling city street. *It isn't Hillsborough—it isn't Hillsborough, and I'm on my way to Europe! Thank you, Lord!* She let her thoughts wander along those happy avenues as she stood and stared at the carriages and the hawkers' carts and the well-dressed passersby.

Her stomach grumbled mildly and she realized they hadn't had supper yet. "Shilla, I want you to have a vacation, too. I'm going to call a maid who will help us both to dress!"

"It wouldn't be proper, miss!"

"Hang proper. We're on a grand tour, and it can start right here. Look, you have your own room." Annabelle threw open the double doors to a smaller side room. "Look at this, trimmings as fine as my own room. Now, just you quiet down and enjoy yourself!"

And so Annabelle rang the bell to call a maid and a very young girl appeared to assist them. She introduced herself as Gatey. "G-A-T-E-Y, Gatey like Katie, only my name's prettier," she said matter-of-factly, and Annabelle smiled. Gatey had deep blue-black hair and the kind of dimples that make little boys go daft sooner than they choose. As she smiled a lot and complimented Annabelle on her dress several times, Annabelle encouraged her talkativeness, for the young lady was kind and sweet and appeared starved for conversation, and was more than willing to speak on any and every subject. When they were almost done and Gatey was fluffing the skirts of Annabelle's dress over the hoop and petticoats, she said shyly, "I hope to have a husband who'll buy me such things someday."

Shilla and Annabelle exchanged glances, and then Annabelle politely agreed with her. She gave Gatey one of her lace-edged handkerchiefs in thanks, and the little girl giggled and smiled. She looked up at Annabelle. "And I hope to be a fine lady like you, someday, miss."

Annabelle winked at her. "If kindness makes a lady—and I should think that is the only true test of a lady—your hope is already realized." This statement made the girl smile all the more.

Then they went down for a late dinner. Only one other family was at the table across from them, and they chatted among themselves the whole time. Annabelle and Shilla were finally both too tired to talk.

Annabelle slept hard that night and so she woke up early and enjoyed the sunrise on the quiet street outside her window. It didn't take long before the street began to bustle once more and Shilla woke up, and so Annabelle rang for a maid to help her dress for breakfast. A different maid came this time—an older woman who didn't speak much at all. She seemed in a hurry. *No doubt,* thought Annabelle, *she's used to ladies coming through like this, and mornings must be awful for her.*

Annabelle dressed in a day dress of yellow and white gingham set with lace at the collar and cuffs, what Shilla called her "Daffa-down-dilly dress." She told the servant this, but she was not amused. Nothing amused her, in fact, and the woman practically flew out of the room when she was done.

"She knows I'm a servant, miss," Shilla said nervously. "Please don't ask her up again. Just let me dress ye."

"Nonsense. She's paid the same amount no matter who she works for!" Annabelle tossed her fur tippet around her shoulders while grabbing up her parasol and bonnet with the other hand in an angry sweep. "I've had done with people's opinions, Shilla. I don't give a fig for what anyone thinks."

But Shilla could only shake her head with dismay.

TWENTY-EIGHT

When the mistletoe was green,
Midst the winter's snows,
Sunshine in thy face was seen,
Kissing lips of rose.
Aura Lea, Aura Lea,
Take my golden ring;
Love and light return with thee,
And swallows with the spring.

From the song *Aura Lea*

After breakfast they took themselves outdoors, breathing in the crisp and breezy air of the first week of March. The wind blew down the avenue, taking with it advertising bills and leaves. Annabelle decided to take a short walk and Shilla nodded happily. "Go on with you, Shilla, and I'll meet you at the hotel at noon. Don't you have some people you'd like to visit while you're here?"

"Well, it's true. I wouldn't mind a visit with my cousin, Elna, but I'll not leave you alone."

"Shilla, this is a big, open city with lots of fine people about. You know I'm perfectly safe."

"But is it proper, miss?"

"Look around you. I see several fine looking ladies unescorted. Don't you?" Indeed, women seemed to have a good deal of freedom in this city. And there were many more women than men, thanks to the war, and so the day's etiquette had quietly changed. Shilla watched the pedestrians thoughtfully and finally allowed it was true. And so she agreed to meet Annabelle in a few short hours for the noon meal.

Annabelle walked away quite happy to be alone for a while. Soon she saw a beautiful old brick church and she opened the front gate and entered an ancient cemetery. It was Christ Church. *How interesting*, she thought. *This was Robert E. Lee's spiritual home.* She stood and looked at the gravestones dotting the courtyard. *So, why is it*, she thought drily, *I always find myself in graveyards, while everyone else avoids them until nature insists?*

She smiled. "Don't worry, Father," she whispered. "It's only by accident I came here, but it will serve one purpose. I wish to say good-bye to my old life. A memorial service long overdue."

The sanctuary was cold, with its whitewashed walls and dark wood trim, but the simplicity of the lines were calming to the eye. "General Lee," she whispered to the empty air, "I have chopped the peach tree down, just as you told that old woman to. And I stand here and accept Christ's unconditional love for my soul, refusing the cup of bitterness. Thank you, Lord."

She smiled broadly as she left the church. Down the path once more, she noticed a large square sarcophagus in the middle of the yard, and she read the epitaph carved in the stone lid:

"Beneath this stone are deposited the remains of Mrs. Anne Warren, daughter of John Brunton Esq. of England, and wife of William Warren Esq., one of the managers of the Philadelphia and Baltimore Theaters. By her loss the American stage has been deprived of one of its brightest ornaments. The unrivalled excellence of her theatrical talents was surpassed by the mighty virtues and accomplishments which adorned her private life. In her were contained an affectionate wife and mother and a sincere friend. She died at Alexandria June 28, 1808. Aged 39 years."

Annabelle wondered why she died so young and what sort of bright ornament she was. They were lovely words, really. An English woman, then an actress, coming all the way to America. Was she an actress before or after coming? She must have been homesick at times, like Annabelle's own mother had been. "Unrivalled excellence... mighty virtues." These were not the words typically reserved for actresses—far from them. A good woman she must have been a bright ornament.

At once a great longing welled up in her to make a difference while she lived. Not a legacy of duty. A legacy of love. *An affec-*

tionate wife and mother and sincere friend. And then Annabelle wondered if she would ever be given the chance.

"Lord, show me what I am to do with this wreck of a life I've made for myself." And then she said good-bye to Christ Church and to graveyards, knowing deep in her heart she would never need that sort of comfort again.

She moved along the city streets, and as she walked she had the odd sensation of understanding what she was supposed to do.

How she had avoided such an obvious choice until now she didn't know. Her talent was to draw, and she would draw! Exactly what the Lord wanted her to do with her drawing she didn't know. She only knew she should do so, and the rest would come.

As she finally neared the hotel, another pressing thought occurred. Perhaps now that her heart felt free she could write to P.D. MacBain and ask for his forgiveness.

But what could she possibly say? *"Dear Sir, I'm sorry I almost shot you,"* or, *"It's a good thing Shilla was holding the gun and not me, else you wouldn't be here to receive this."*

It all seemed too ridiculous—and much too late.

It had been so long he had probably forgotten her, she thought morbidly. Likely he had found another, married another, someone more stable. While he was a spy he'd probably met and wooed a hundred girls like herself, and a hundred more beautiful and accomplished than she. He had probably picked one of them, a Northern beauty who didn't brandish guns whenever she was angry. Or maybe a Virginian who'd always sided with the North. A virtuous woman. *A bright ornament.*

No, she had had her chance. She would remember his words for the rest of her life—that he loved her. Then she realized she believed them still, but in a few minutes more she decided it was only her pride at work once more.

Back at the hotel, on her way up the stairs to her room, she heard a surprising sound coming from the ballroom. A single violin, clear and beautiful. She didn't know the piece but it sounded lovely echoing against the pale walls and mirrors and long windows of the huge ballroom. She stepped into the room and looked around her. She caught sight of a small balcony above her head and to her left where a young man sat in a relaxed pose in a musician's balcony, playing an old and mellow sounding violin. His eyes were closed and his mouth set as he swayed with the music. With pale blonde curls about his head, a small pair of glasses hanging from his nose, and clothes of an old cut, he seemed a charming picture lost in time.

Annabelle watched his intense concentration as she listened to the magic of the strings and it was almost as though the instrument were playing him. She knew what that was like, for she lost all track of time in the days she used to draw, and would almost feel someone else move her hand across the page. How strange. All her life she had felt as though the world turned her, and she hated it, yet drawing was the one thing she could lose herself to and never mind the consequences. People asked, but she could never explain how she drew so well; it was as impossible to describe as love.

And so she listened to the music until the piece was over, and as the last note died away, she felt as though she had heard a bit of God's own creation and received His kiss in the hearing. The violinist held his bow across the strings for a moment and looked across into the air as if waking from a pleasant dream. Then he looked down and smiled graciously at Annabelle, and she blushed.

"What a gift you have," she said simply. "What lovely music."

"Thank you." The trance was broken then as he tossed his curly head. "Music for tonight's ball, so you'll only have to hear the piece again, I'm afraid."

"Oh, no. I'm glad I've heard it, for I won't be attending the ball."

"You are a guest here, are you not?"

She nodded.

"Well, then, you are most certainly invited to attend the Birthnight Ball."

"It couldn't be Washington's Birthnight Ball?"

He nodded, still smiling.

"But his birthday remembrance was a little while ago, wasn't it?"

"Well, the management is rather lax on the actual birthday date, but then, that's the way it's always been."

"I think it's wonderful it's still celebrated." She was already wondering what she would wear. She thanked him, and when she left the room, she felt very, very glad she had gone in to listen to the music.

Once in her room, she laid out an appropriate dancing outfit, and then she looked over her silk and accessories. She hadn't been to a dance in ages. It was too difficult to attend anything around Hillsborough after the war. Too, too difficult, with all the looks and the rumors. Now she could go to this dance free from such worries. She knew no one. It felt wonderful.

Oh, no.

It would be entirely inappropriate for her to go alone. Of course, Shilla couldn't be paid money to pretend she was gentry and attend the ball. And Annabelle knew absolutely no one! It was all well and good to say you didn't care for people's opinions, but it was another thing entirely to attend a social occasion without escort. She walked to the vanity and sat in the chair in a slump. She simply couldn't go without an escort. There would have to be introductions. It was impossible. It was then she noticed the note from Shilla, saying she would be late for the noon meal. *So, I have to eat alone, as well!* Annabelle thought sadly.

She dressed and went down to the dining room, fully realizing she would not attend the ball and keenly feeling her sad defeat. The hotel manager came around with an invitation for her to the Hotel's Birthnight Ball and she shook her head and he turned rather red. He saw her predicament, she thought, so she looked up at him and whispered, "I'm afraid I don't know anyone here."

"Nonsense!" he said, and she couldn't tell if he were serious or trying to imply he knew her.

She held the card back up to the manager. "No, thank you!" she said firmly. He took the card from her rather brusquely then and left her alone.

Had she made a mistake? Was it some sort of unwritten rule to never refuse an invitation to the ball? She looked down at her soup and decided she didn't feel at all hungry. Now a tear fell into her soup and she wanted to go upstairs as quickly as she could. To fly up the stairs.

But then an older woman on her left reached over to pat Annabelle's hand. "There, there, dear," she said quietly. "Would you care to attend the ball with us?"

Annabelle looked up to find a kind looking woman with graying hair and a full figure, her little smile sitting happily atop several chins. Her blue eyes sparkled. "Will you permit me to introduce ourselves?" Annabelle nodded. "I am Mrs. Grunwald, and this is my husband, Captain James Grunwald, but I'm certain you know all about us." Annabelle looked past her to see a gentleman with a lovely beard and smiling eyes looking back at her and nodding. Annabelle nodded uncomfortably as she, of course, had never heard their names before, but she believed they must be very important to announce themselves in such a way.

Annabelle perked up considerably. "I am pleased to make your acquaintance. Yes, I truly would like to go, Mrs. Grunwald. Thank you. I am Annabelle MacBain, daughter of Dr. Ludwell MacBain of Hillsborough, Virginia."

"We know, dear, we know." She patted her hand once more.

"Oh, of course," said Annabelle but she couldn't imagine why they would.

Mrs. Grunwald immediately began telling Annabelle all about her husband's work and where they lived in the city, and so on, and how they always attend the Birthnight Ball. Every once in a while Mrs. Grunwald would interject, "But, of course, you must know that, dear," to the point Annabelle believed she was a little batty. Annabelle nodded and nodded and thought it was good she wasn't hungry, as it was fairly impossible to eat under the kind attentions of the talkative Mrs. Grunwald.

Finally she let Annabelle go, and then Annabelle did fly up the stairs. She rang the bell for someone to help her dress and was happy to find Gatey at her door. Gatey helped Annabelle with her bath and toilette and then fitted Annabelle into her blue and black plaid silk, and Annabelle brought out a black velvet waister that made

Gatey let out a happy sigh. An intricate pattern worked in jet beads edged the entire piece and it sparkled in the candlelight. Gatey came to it gingerly and petted it as if it were a brand new kitten, and Annabelle smiled.

"Would you like to try it on first, Gatey?" And before the child could protest, Annabelle brought the wide belt to Gatey's waist and tied it behind her in a firm knot. The velvet tracers fell along the floor behind her. "I believe you look like a princess, dear, even to the train behind your gown." Annabelle turned Gatey to the mirror. Gatey giggled uncontrollably then, and Annabelle thought as she watched her, *If I never make the ship voyage, meeting little Gatey will have made it all worthwhile.* "They say every woman is a princess for one day in her life, you know, even if she's not royalty," she told the girl happily.

Gatey's eyes grew wide. "When is that, miss?"

"On her wedding day, of course," Annabelle said with certainty and turned Gatey back to the mirror. Gatey held a look of awe on her face, while Annabelle at the same moment allowed herself a small bout of melancholy.

Annabelle grew quiet as they began the process of dressing. She had a jet bead and velvet hairpiece set with a proud little ostrich feather plume that Gatey carefully pinned at the top of her coiled braids. When Annabelle stood and gathered her black lace and ebony fan, Gatey clapped her hands and blurted out that she just sparkled all over.

Then she went down the stairs to meet the Grunwalds.

Thankfully Mrs. Grunwald was a tall woman, equal in height to many of the men there, if not to her husband, and so Annabelle found her with little trouble.

When she saw Annabelle, she snapped her fan once in the air, and, like a private called to arms, Annabelle walked quickly to where they stood. Mrs. Grunwald seemed sincerely pleased to see her. "You look quite lovely, dear," she said, and Annabelle smiled and thanked her and then began to look about the room.

The dancing had not yet begun, and Annabelle's eyes wandered up to the musician's balcony where a quartet tuned their instruments. The violinist was busy plucking the strings and readying the music sheets, totally absorbed in his pleasure. She looked around the room, enjoying the dresses of the ladies and the cut of the men's coats. Not all the ladies wore dresses off the shoulder, she was glad to see, as she wanted very much not to stand out with her high neck dress. Mrs. Grunwald chose the moment to compliment Annabelle on her style of dress. Annabelle returned the compliment, mildly wondering if she should be satisfied with the opinion of a slightly insane, although basically kind, old woman.

Soon the music began and the dancing commenced, and Annabelle watched the waltz with growing pleasure. It brought to pleasant memory her first balls, the scent of perfumes and spice, the flickering candlelights and the twirling of so much silk and satin and velvet. She grew dizzy with the happiness. Somehow a ball made everyone look handsome and beautiful.

Annabelle's toes tapped as she watched it all.

Mrs. Grunwald was speaking to her, but she wasn't quite concentrating on the conversation. But then all grew uncomfortably silent, and she blushed to realize that Mrs. Grunwald had asked her some sort of question.

"I'm sorry, Mrs. Grunwald?"

"I said I believe he has stayed away in deference to your feelings, dear."

"Who might you be referring to?"

"Why, your husband, dear," Mrs. Grunwald said with not a little surprise.

"My hus... No, no, Mrs. Grunwald, please. Pardon me, but I have no husband." Annabelle blushed uncontrollably and wondered if any sense could be made of Mrs. Grunwald's statement. Then she suddenly realized she hadn't introduced herself to them as a "miss." But Mrs. Grunwald was pulling her chin into her chins and "tsking" with her head which made Annabelle think she didn't believe her.

How rude. Annabelle's face was now red with indignation as she looked about the room once more.

Soon, a gentleman presented himself to the Grunwalds and was in turn presented to Annabelle. To Annabelle's great dismay, Mrs. Grunwald introduced her to the fellow, a rather handsome man named Mr. Portnoy Tunhill, as Mrs. MacBain. Annabelle looked at Mrs. Grunwald with controlled anger and found it was impossible to correct the situation at that moment.

They began to dance and the fellow engaged her in polite conversation at the first opportunity but constantly referred to her as Mrs. MacBain. He exasperated her further by referring to her fictitious husband as a "lucky man in the extreme." Finally she could take no more.

"I'm sorry, Mr. Tunhill, but Mrs. Grunwald is under the mistaken impression I am married."

"Oh, my." And the fellow didn't speak another word to her the rest of the dance.

It was as if Annabelle had stepped into a strange dream world where the usual conventions were thrown out for no apparent reason—like the goings on in that odd little book, *Through the Looking-Glass*. She must have done something to indicate she was married but she couldn't imagine what.

When that dance was over, another fellow came and was again introduced to "Mrs. MacBain," and the ritual was repeated. Annabelle decided she would have it out with the Grunwalds or retire to her room at the end of this particular waltz for the situation was ridiculous and fast becoming quite embarrassing. When the music ended this time, Annabelle returned to the Grunwalds with a determined look on her face.

As she approached, Mrs. Grunwald turned her head from the door of the ballroom and shook her gray locks slightly. "Mrs. Grunwald," Annabelle began with a tolerant smile, "I must insist to you I am not a married woman. If you could simply introduce me as Miss MacBain, I would appreciate the favor immensely."

Mrs. Grunwald shook her head again. "I would be glad to honor your strange request, my dear, but your husband is here, and he would make that quite impossible for me, I'm sure..."

"Wh-h-h-a-a-at?" Annabelle asked, pulling the word from her mouth like hot tar from a fire.

TWENTY-NINE

I think my song has lasted,
Almost long enough,
The subject's interesting,
But the rhymes are mighty rough.
I wish this war were over,
When free from rags and fleas,
We'd kiss our wives and sweethearts,
And gobble Goober Peas.
From the Southern song *Goober Peas*

"I'm afraid so, dear, but see for yourself." Mrs. Grunwald snapped her fan shut and neatly waved it toward the door.

Annabelle looked over to see P.D. MacBain chatting with two gentlemen in uniform.

Annabelle's face grew hot then cold. Feeling light-headed, she pulled one hand to her cheek and moaned within herself. She was glad and then frightened, squeamish and then thrilled, and she found herself in a muddle of such odd emotions she couldn't speak.

"I... I... uh..."

Mrs. Grunwald took her gently by the hand and drew her to a ballroom chair by the wall where Annabelle sat down and immediately wondered if he had seen her, and what she would say to him, and how she might approach him, and...

Mrs. Grunwald interrupted her thoughts. "Whatever your troubles are, my dear, I'm sure young love will win out."

Annabelle looked at her with concern. "Do you know him?"

"Know him!" Mrs. Grunwald smiled. "Why, didn't he tell you? He works in the office right next to my husband at the new department."

"Department?"

"Oh, my, yes, it's all new. Of course there wasn't a Secret Service at all before the war, you know." And then she proudly added, "The President himself asked P.D. and Captain to work with him on a case just last week."

She wanted to laugh. *Secret Service. The new department. Of course!* All this time, he was only a few hours ride away. And he had not come looking for her. The truth was all too clear. "But Mrs. Grunwald, P.D. is not my husband," Annabelle said with a blush. "He is not even a friend."

"Now, now," Mrs. Grunwald said in a motherly voice. "Captain and I have been married thirty-two years this June, and I have to tell you, child, honesty has been the mainstay of our union. You don't know where such talk can lead, and I'm certain whatever he's done does not deserve the vanquishing of your vows from all memory." Mrs. Grunwald's eyes grew large with disapproval as she expressed her quite solid opinion of the situation.

Annabelle was shaking her head at the woman's words when a shadow fell across her lap. She looked up to see P.D. MacBain smiling down on her.

"Good evening, Annabelle." His eyes twinkled and his brows were raised in expectation as he looked at her.

He was beautiful. Beautiful. Her mouth dropped open, but then she looked back down to her lap, snapping her fan shut as she did and simply staring at its ebony bones. She couldn't think what else to do. Finally, when she realized no one was going to say anything until she gave him a reply, she steeled herself to look up at him. "Good evening, Mr. MacBain," she said.

She tingled head to foot.

He smiled broadly.

"Mr. MacBain, would you be so kind as to inform Mrs. Grunwald that there has been a mistake?" she said unsteadily.

"What sort of mistake, my dear?" he asked with a crooked grin.

She rolled her eyes at his impudence. "She's been misinformed, I couldn't imagine by whom, that I am related to you."

"My wife?"

"Why, yes!" she said in a flame of embarrassment.

His face grew serious as he looked at her and cleared his throat. "But, Annabelle, how can I?"

"Whatever do you mean?" she asked suddenly and stood up.

He stepped back. "But how could I want her to say otherwise?" he said with feigned hurt in his voice.

"Sir!? I am not your wife!" she said indignantly.

"What have I done to deserve this?" he asked, arms raised in dire supplication.

She looked at him intently. "Nothing, you've done absolutely nothing to deserve my ire, until this unimaginable insult!" Her face grew pink as he looked at her, and she thought for one moment he would take her in his arms, and in another moment that she would help him to it, so she added, "This unpardonable insult to my person!" And she drew back from him.

He smiled. "Do you deny then that you gave me this ring in pledge?" He raised his left hand to her amazed eyes to show her a ring that looked to be her father's.

"That cannot be my father's college ring?" she whispered.

"Can't it?" He removed it quickly and brought it close to her eye. It was her father's ring; his initials were on the inner circle, and she couldn't think for the life of her how P.D. had come to have it again.

"What?" Her head was spinning as fluidly as the silk skirts of the ladies dancing just behind him. This was a dream, a bad dream, a nightmare.

"Perhaps if you dance together," Mrs. Grunwald said quickly, "your vows will come back to you, my dear. Captain and I always say a good Schottische clears the head of cobwebs." She nudged Annabelle toward P.D. with a doting smile.

But Annabelle's eyes stung with hot tears as she looked into his smiling face. Right then she felt only the humiliation of his words. Why would he do this to her? And why in Heaven did he have her father's ring? She shook her head and pushed past the both of them and ran from the room.

She stumbled up the stairs, rushed down the hall, unlocked her door quickly and pushed her way in, chased all the while by a tangle of chaotic thoughts.

When she closed the door she leaned against it, gasping.

He was here. Downstairs. Her fan dropped to the floor with a thump. He was alive, but somehow he had only taken their meeting as a means to humiliate her once again. She walked forward and fell onto her bed and began to cry, not caring that her hoops were crushed beneath her, not caring that her tears would stain her fine silk sleeve or whether her feather was crushed. Let it be crushed. How could he do such a thing?

And then it all came back. The night at the bridge.

She looked up and blinked. Despite her tears she let out a little laugh and then a moan. He had gotten her back for that night, horribly and decisively taken his revenge, and now they were even. She laughed again as she thought back on the last few minutes, her blushing face, her mad rush from the grand ballroom in all her finery. She laughed aloud at the silliness of it.

Yet what was the purpose? That certainly was her father's ring on his finger.

She heard a knock at the door and her heart rose in her throat. She got up quietly and went to answer it. She opened it slowly and peered out to find that no one was there.

But as she shut the door, she heard a more persistent knock.

With a little thrill she realized it wasn't coming from the hallway at all but from the door of the adjoining room.

Annabelle walked over to it slowly, fearfully, and cocked her head. "Who is there?" she whispered.

"P.D. MacBain."

She shut her eyes and smiled despite herself. "Oh, it's you, is it? My long-suffering husband." She couldn't breathe.

"Long-suffering, yes. Husband? No."

"So soon the honeymoon is over?"

"Open the door and see." he said cheerfully.

"I'll not open the door to you, sir, and you can keep such rudeness to yourself!"

"Annabelle. Dear Annabelle, please open this door." He rattled the knob.

With mock cruelty she replied, "You were in uniform when you last seduced me, sir. I flatter less easily now."

"So I've heard."

She blushed. "What do you mean? How have you heard about me at all?"

"You may have guessed your father sent me this ring, Annabelle."

She had not guessed that. And so she stood with her mouth open, quite unable to understand him. He tapped the ring on the door then and waited for her reply. She stepped away from the door. "Why ever would he do such a thing?" she asked.

"Because I asked him to." This made equal sense to her—which is to say, no sense at all. Then he laughed a little. "I thought it might break the strain between us at our meeting. I suppose it wasn't such a brilliant idea after all, although your father thought it wasn't half bad."

Annabelle stepped back further and sat on the chair at the vanity. "My father? Did he send it to you when he wrote your father about John Brighton?" Still incredulous, she pulled her hands to her warm cheeks.

"No."

"No?"

"No, actually he sent this to me a while back. I think it was around the time you made the boat reservations. Your father and I, we've written to each other quite a bit in the last year. He... he's told me how things are with you. How people have treated you unfairly."

"Not so unfairly," she said sharply. "Despite whatever my father wrote to you, I was never sorry to have taken the oath."

"That's exactly what he told me. I'm afraid my training had me asking him quite a lot about you." He hesitated. "No, that sounds foolish. I want to put it plainly to you." And then there was a long pause. "But can't you open the door for me, Annabelle?"

She straightened her back. "No! It wouldn't be proper."

All was quiet for a moment. "Well. Well, then can we go downstairs and speak together like civilized people?"

"You have a terrible habit of asking too many questions, Mr. MacBain, and besides which I'm afraid to be seen with you, I think. Afraid of what you've told people!" Her tone was serious, although she was still smiling.

She heard a thump and realized he had let his shoulder fall against the door. "Still playing games then," he said with disgust. "But wait. What did you say about Brighton?"

"You didn't get my father's letter?"

"About Brighton? No."

And so she told him what had happened, and he was quiet on the other side of the door for a long while. "Annabelle, you could have been killed," he finally said.

She couldn't answer.

"You were crazy, you know, to accuse him like that, to his face." The doorknob rattled. "Open this door, Annabelle."

"No. Oh, ask me about crazy, sir, the town feels I'm an expert on it."

He laughed. "Do you really care what they think?"

"No."

"Then open this door." And he rattled the knob once more.

"I'll not."

"Annabelle," he said firmly. "Open this door, because I have something of great importance to tell you."

"Words come quite easily through wood, sir, or isn't that obvious?"

"What I have to say, I have to say…" But he stopped. Annabelle held her breath. For all the world she was afraid to open the door. "All right. All right, Annabelle, then just…" He sighed loud enough for her to hear, "… just come nearer the door."

She had to laugh under her breath as she came closer. "All right," she said quietly.

"Annabelle MacBain, I love you."

Her heart began to pound. "Well, I *hate* you. I said so, didn't I?"

"Tell me why," he asked simply.

She tried to think why. Something about doing his duty.

Something about the war. But suddenly it seemed so unimportant, she wearied of trying to remember. "Well, writing to my father without my knowledge, flashing his ring in my face and claiming to be my husband."

"But I want to be your husband," he said carefully.

She stepped back from the door and drew her hands together pensively.

"Besides, Annabelle, in all honesty my father wrote to your father first, on behalf of his son. He explained to him—I think you know they attended college together—that his poor son was pining away for Ludwell's daughter, and what was the girl thinking of him, he wanted to know." Annabelle smiled to think how charmed her father must have been by such a letter. "Your father... gave him—gave me—some hope. It was then I began writing him myself."

All this and no brilliant response came to mind. "Oh," was all she said.

"And I'll accept the fact you hate me," he said gently. "I will, if you can open this door and say the words to my face."

She shook her head while blushing and was relieved to know he couldn't see her. "I'll see you in the hall in the morning and tell you then," she said, pressing her hand to her heart.

"Tell me now." He rattled the knob loudly. "Tell me now or I'll come to the front door and wake the whole hotel, begging my cruel wife to let me in!"

She laughed to herself and then stopped short. "If you'll be a perfect gentleman, sir, I will open the door."

"I promise to be a perfect gentleman," he said quietly.

"No more rudeness."

"No more."

Fully intending to make him suffer until she could stand it no longer, she turned her face to the mirror, put on the most stern look she could muster and then rose and smoothed out her dress. Finally she walked over and unlocked the door.

He stood before her and she looked at his face briefly, his eyes, his hair, the way he stood. He took a deep breath even as she did.

At that moment she hurt from the joy of seeing him and wondered just how long she could hold her icy stare, and then her eyes were suddenly caught by the buttons on his shirt; the top buttons of his formal shirt were undone and so she turned her face away. "A perfect gentleman, you promised."

He looked down to see the problem and Annabelle gave him a sidelong glance as he fumbled with the buttons, and she did her level best to keep from smiling.

Finally he said, "There. Now tell me."

And Annabelle looked up in stony silence to his slightly worried face.

Her eyes caught on his buttons once more. He'd buttoned his top button to the second one down. She looked up at him and then looked down at the buttons. "I... I hate..." But a giggle came from deep within her. "I hate a man who can't dress himself."

He looked to see what she was staring at. "Drat," he said and took on a look of irritated concern and then laughed outright.

"Forget your blasted buttons. I simply don't believe I can lie to you anymore." And she pulled him in close to her.

Their embrace was long and followed by a longer kiss. And as he held her there, he asked her again, in plain English and with a decided lack of etiquette, if she would become his wife.

She smiled and touched his face. "I wonder if you'll be able to scare up my father's consent as easily as you did a provost marshal's signature?"

"As a matter of fact," P.D. drew his head back from her, "I have asked Dr. Ludwell MacBain for his daughter's hand, and he shocked me with his answer."

Remembering Michael Delaney, her heart skipped a beat as she pulled away from him. "What do you mean?" she asked worriedly.

"I mean, you must be used to getting your way, because he told me you're quite capable of making up your own mind on the subject of marriage."

"Really? He said that?"

"That surprises you?"

"Indeed it does. If I'd had my way on the subject, I'd be long married and have gone west by now."

P.D. laughed even as Annabelle grew uncomfortable with the thought. But her father's opinion had made her very glad. All became quiet again and then P.D. cleared his throat. "I don't know everything about you, Annabelle, but I was bold enough to hope for an answer tonight."

She looked up at him and smiled as broadly as heaven would allow. "You couldn't doubt my answer, could you?" They kissed and held each other and the world could have stopped revolving then and there with no difference to their joy.

They stayed up talking long into the night and made their happy plans. Annabelle asked when he wished to marry, because she had the small problem of a ticket to Europe on a boat due to leave the next day. They discussed her going and returning for the wedding. But only a second of a look told them both that was impossible.

It was P.D. who suggested they marry in the morning and he would buy a ticket on her boat. That sounded perfectly wonderful, until Annabelle remembered her father.

"But, P.D., I'm not sure I could stand his not being here."

"Well, let me give you this. Perhaps it will make a difference." He pulled a yellow envelope from his vest, and she immediately recognized her father's stationery.

"It's sealed? You haven't read it?"

He shook his head. "That may be because it's addressed to you. Your father simply said to give it to you if we were able to patch things up." She smiled and opened it with shaking hands.

Dearest Annie,

You know my only concern over the last year has been whether you would take General Lee's advice and chop the old tree down. I thought I saw you go to the shed for an axe now and then, but you always stopped yourself. How I prayed that tree would fall, Annie, and then a month ago my prayers for a cruel end to that old gnarled tree were realized.

And so your future should hold only the expectation of the warmth of old logs in the fireplace while sitting beside your love. Forgive an old man his sentimentality, my dear, but I will admit the idea pleases me no end.

I'm certain P.D. has explained our own correspondence over the last year or so. I am guilty. I had told you of the high respect I held for his father in school. He convinced me the same respect was due his son. Then his son convinced me all over again by his own hand. However, as he may have told you, I consider my own approval of this fellow to be beside the point, and the effect of my approval to have been merely a certain amount of enthusiasm for our correspondence, the sending of a certain ring, and the putting off of my daughter's trip to Europe until March for the clandestine purpose of warning a certain young man of your arrival in the port city.

The decision is entirely yours, my dear, but from personal experience I feel I should remind you Europe makes an absolutely splendid place for a honeymoon.

With love and glad affection,
Ever your Weem

Annabelle blinked tears away as she looked at P.D. "I suppose my father is used to my flying in the face of convention. And you! You two already had the honeymoon planned!"

P.D. just smiled. "We could marry right here in town. Christ Church. It's not far from here."

"Christ Church? Of course." Annabelle smiled at that but without explaining how exactly perfect the suggestion sounded.

"It is not Methodist, though. I confess that I am not a Methodist."

"Is your church a Christian church?"

"Of course."

"Well, I am a Christian, and I simply must be married in a Christian church," she chided.

"I see," he said, all smiles then. "All right, Christ Church. It's settled. But now I have another confession to make." Annabelle raised her brows. "Would it bother you very much if I did some work while we were in England? The department hasn't given me leave for a honeymoon. It's that they have a project for me there, but, and here is my confession—one reason I told my office mates I was married was to make it more, uh, palatable when I took my wife with me on business in London. Tell the truth, I was afraid they'd think I wouldn't get any work done if I were on my honeymoon."

"You shock me, sir. Am I to be a mercenary bride, then?"

"As much as I'm a mercenary husband, I think," he said laughing.

"More spying?" she said and clucked her tongue.

He grinned. "More spying."

She pulled a finger to her cheek. "It could be difficult separating business from the honeymoon. Would they mind very much if your wife helped you in your work?"

"Well, I do feel a might safer having you on my side of the fence this time around, so to speak."

"Do you, sir?"

He put his hands at her waist and pulled her in to him. "Yes, ma'am, I do. Why do you think I asked you to marry me?"

"Oh, I thought perhaps you'd grown too fond of my father's ring."

"Ah, the ring. That reminds me. I have a rather amazing story to tell you."

"I love a story."

"Oh, and I know you'll like this one." He winked at her.

"Go on with you then!"

"Well, actually it's an interesting case."

"A case? By the Lake of Kinchyle, not another case just yet, please," she said, becoming half-serious.

He laughed. "No, no, it's solved. A solved case, like, well, you know, and actually it's a loose end to that one."

Annabelle's eyes rolled in her head as she laughed. "I'm only barely keeping up with your logic, my dear. Could you please start at the beginning?"

"All right then. The beginning. There once was a slave boy named Pella. He was a kindhearted boy who suffered much. He used to help a Quaker man named Brighton."

"Don't I know this history, love?"

"But you asked me to begin at the begin..."

"Yes, yes, go on," she said with impatience.

"It's easily shortened. After he was with our camp, he served the Union with distinction as a drummer and in one particular battle he picked up and carried the regimental colors when he saw the color-bearer go down. It was there he was shot in the left wrist and lost his hand."

"Oh, Pella," Annabelle said quietly.

"It's all right, Annabelle. I never saw a man so proud."

"A man?"

"I saw Pella only last month, but then I'm not keeping to the story. Pella came to a hospital here in Alexandria. After he got well, he took a job at the hospital and watched as some of the soldiers during their convalescence began to teach freed blacks to read and write. Pella began a class with one fellow that lasted about ten months, he told me. Samuel Brighton had already taught him to read and write, and so the fellow taught him everything he knew, which turned out to be a smattering of Latin and a lot of law."

"Union soldiers did that?"

"As a matter of fact they did."

Half smiling, Annabelle said, "You have my full permission to be smug about it."

P.D. let out a laughing grunt. "He stayed in Alexandria and kept working in the hospital..."

"Pardon me for interrupting, but does all this have anything to do with Samuel Brighton's Bible?"

"You're quick—very quick—but you're ruining my story, child."

"My apologies." And she reached out and squeezed his hand.

He wrapped his hands around hers then. "Anyway, he worked and kept studying, and after the war a Freedman's Court was established in Alexandria City. Pella had kept studying up on Latin and had gone on to study law all on his own—just like Mr. Lincoln, he told me—and he came out best qualified among his peers to be a counselor in the new court."

"That's wonderful!"

"He thinks so, although I told him going from a slave to a lawyer looked like two sides of a sad life. He didn't appreciate the humor."

"I should think not, after all he's been through."

He cleared his throat again and gave a sidelong glance to his future bride. "Yes, well, all poor jokes aside, I met up with him only last month right here in Alexandria, as I said, and he told me all this about his past, and I'd been calling him Pella all during the conversation, and suddenly he up and says, 'I have to tell you, Mr. MacBain, I don't go by Pella anymore. No, sir. Out of respect for Samuel Brighton, I've taken his name and have joined the Society of Friends.' That sobered me up quite a bit, and right away I thought about the little Bible I'd been carrying around with me all that time. I said, 'Well, then, uh, *Friend* Brighton, I reckon I have something for you,' and I took out that little Bible and gave it to him. I'm not ashamed to say we were both choked up. He loved the man like a father."

"Yes, he did," said Annabelle.

He smiled. "I'll admit I felt a twinge when I gave him the book. It was the only thing I had that linked the two of us. But I had an odd feeling that if I didn't give it away, you wouldn't come. Isn't that strange?"

"Not so strange," Annabelle replied with a kind smile. "There was something I had to give up before I could see you again."

He smoothed her hair with one hand. "I know," he whispered.

They kissed again lightly and Annabelle felt a flood of contentment as they hugged each other. "Thank you for telling me about Pella," Annabelle whispered. "It's a lovely story. Really lovely."

"I knew you'd like it. One to tell our children and our children's children, I would think." Annabelle blushed to hear him say it.

"P.D., do you have time to visit Scotland before your work begins?"

"Absolutely, if the ship is quick about it."

"Good. I want you to meet my relatives, and I want us both to see a certain cottage there," she said smiling, "now that it seems I've finally grown up."

"Indeed you have."